THE SHADOWS OF REGIA

BOOK THREE

BY

TENAYA JAYNE

COLD FIRE PUBLISHING, LLC

Cover design by Thander Lin

Edited by Dora Furlong and Ally Robertson

Cold Fire Publishing, LLC

ISBN-13: 978-0-9986741-7-9

ISBN-10: 0-9986741-7-6

For Judy

Characters from the Legends of Regia

Forest

Half-elf, half shapeshifter. Skilled warrior, now the highest judge in Regia. Has the elven ability to become invisible at will. Can shapeshift her full appearance, except her eyes. Caries a sword of obsidian glass infused with lightning. Mated to Syrus. Daughter of Rahaxeris. Mother of Tesla and Maddox.

Syrus

The vampire prince. Mage and master of the Blood Kata. Has the power of lightning. Can heal almost all wounds and illnesses. Gave up the throne, in favor of making Regia a republic. He works in the Obsidian Mountain, training other masters in the Kata. Mated to Forest.

Shi

Dryad princess. Died when her race was poisoned and existed for thousands of years as a ghost in the Wolf's Wood. Close friend and adopted mother to Forest. Mated to the late vampire king, Leramiun.

Netriet

Vampire. Thief. Murderess. Sacrificial messenger. Tortured by the leader of the werewolves, resulting in the loss of her arm. Possessed by a dark entity. Used as a pawn by Baal, a priest of the *Rune-dy*. Given an illegal, alien robotic arm. Finally finds redemption in the love of her mate Merick. Mother of Melina.

Rahaxeris

Elf. Father of Forest. Former high priest of the *Rune-dy*. World jumper. Strong magical abilities, some unnatural. Loves his family but nothing else. Deadly. No scruples. No morality. On a constant quest for more knowledge and power.

Journey

Alien. Storyteller from the world of Illumistice. Has the power to look inside your heart and spin a *story* from your deepest desires. Can hypnotize you with just her voice. Gentle, and healing nature. Mated to Redge. Childless.

Shreve

Clone. Shapeshifter. Created by the wizards. Has Rahaxeris' DNA. Considered Forest's brother. Deadly fighter and weapons master. Lived as an outlaw. Redeemed through family love. His blood was the key ingredient in the blood lock that kept out the wizards before the war. Mated to Sabra. Father of Sophie.

Sabra

She-wolf. Became the leader of the pack through combat. Lost her sister to the insurgents. Mated to Shreve. Vicious in battle. Loves without restraint. Mother to her people, and Sophie.

Tesla

Daughter of Forest and Syrus. Half vampire. World jumper. Has the power of lightning in her hands. Can manipulate natural laws. Created her own mix of magic, science, and technology. Revered as a legend and the savior of Regia. Killed the wizard king. Mated to X.

X

Human. Necromancer. Cursed by a witch. Has the power to always know the truth. Helped Tesla save Regia from the wizards. The only human able to survive in Regia. Tesla's soul mate. Granted unnatural long life by the heart of the world. Works in Regia's government as an interrogator.

The Heart

Deity. Lives under the ground in the Wolf's Wood. No one had ever seen the Heart. All that can be seen is the manifestation. The manifestation is an immortal flame that burns in a circle of crystal trees. Speaks to few. Protected and served by the Dryads.

Prologue

You shouldn't be here...but you don't know where you are or even how you got here. More than anything, you hope you're asleep. *It's just a nightmare*, you try to console yourself. You don't belong here. The air is bitter. The smoky light is bitter. The landscape before you is bitter. Bitterness is imbued inside everything in this place.

Look to the sky, but you won't see it. There is no sky. You are underground. The faint light shifting over you coats your skin in muddy color. You never knew light could feel so tainted, and you cannot tell its source. Grey flecks float in the pungent air. Reach up and touch one. Ashes. Ash falls like a lazy snowfall.

Before you are the ruins of a great cathedral. The stone pillars and foundation are brown and grey. It's not beautiful. No vines grow on the walls. Compelled, you know you must go inside. You turn your head from side to side, but you see no one and nothing. You hear it though, the raspy, wet, snarling of a beast. It's a warning.

The entrance of the courtyard is flanked by statues of crouched hyena-like monsters. They too are ruined, places of the carved stone are missing, leaving them deformed. You pass slowly, and your heart clenches. The growling is coming from them. Their eyes are set with onyx, and they glint at you. The stone grinds. The statue to your right opens its mouth, baring broken, stained fangs.

Mustering your courage, you continue forward into the cathedral. A tree stands in the center, its roots snake over and through the brick floor. Pity and revulsion in equal measures enter your heart as you gaze up at its bare, twisted branches. The black trunk is covered with mouths. Each one is different. Some hang slack. A few smile predatorily, the teeth broken and stained brown. And a few are babbling, the words crossing over one another in conflicting subjects, making it all unintelligible. Every mouth quiets and smiles.

"Visitor," the tree purrs with every mouth simultaneously.

A wet tongue drags along the lips of the largest mouth. "Sweet blood in your veins."

"Sweet blood," all the other mouths whisper excitedly.

You take a step back.

"You must give me a taste if you wish to pass. One bite, that's all. Give me that, and I'll let you see her. That's why you've come after all. No one ever comes to see me... But still, I must exact a price."

"Just one bite?" you ask.

"One bite, one bite, one bite..." all the mouths say.

Stepping forward, shaking with fear, your heart beating painfully hard under your ribs. "Okay." You tell yourself it *is* okay because you know you're dreaming. You have to know who is beyond.

Your shaking grows stronger as you move closer and press your forearm against a mouth. The lips part, soft as flesh, moist as a passionate kiss. The teeth break through the membrane of your skin. You step back as the mouth swallows. It wasn't so bad.

"Sweeter than I thought," it says.

Branches whip out and down, wrapping around your arms and ankles, jerking you into the air like the legs of a spider. It laughs at your screams and tears your clothes to shreds. Tongues, lips, and teeth, assault your bare skin. Powerless against the branches, it moves you up and down all over itself, each mouth taking a turn.

"Stop! You said one bite!"

"Silly, sweet thing." It laughs with cruel pleasure. "One. Bite. Each."

The statues outside howl, the sound mixing gleefully with your screams. The harder you strain to get free, the deeper it bites. Blood runs from each mouth in bright red lines, sliding into the bark's crevices. Knowledge bites into you harder than the teeth. You aren't getting out of this.

The tree is eating you alive.

Moans of pleasure vibrate deep inside the tree as it swallows your flesh. Your vision darkens, cold penetrates your empty veins.

"That's enough," a woman's voice chides.

The tree drops you to the ground, your blood soaking its roots. Nothing left to pump, your heart slows.

An angel with no face leans down and picks you up. She is the night sky. Her hair is moonlight, and her skin swirls with galaxies and sparkles with stars. She gazes down at you. You know she's looking at you even though she has no face.

She turns to the tree. "Just couldn't help yourself… So spiteful, Darksong. You could have at least let me talk to her before you killed her."

The largest mouth heaves an exasperated sigh. "I'll leave the next one alive for you. Promise. Although I don't see the point. None of them make it out alive whether I bite them or not."

The sky angel says something else to the tree in harsh tones, but you cannot make out the words. All you can hear is your heart. Count the beats in your head. One...two...three...four...

ONE

A current of gold shot from Maddox's hand. Syrus swung his sword up, the current hitting the side of the blade. The power bent and ricocheted around the sparring arena of the Obsidian Mountain.

"Watch it," Syrus ground out through his teeth.

"What's the matter, old man? Reflexes a little slow?"

"Perhaps they are. I'm not the mage I used to be. My ability is slipping." Syrus shook his head and sheathed his sword. The next second he became *almost* invisible, using his shadowing technique, and darted to the side.

Maddox blinked, his eyes straining to see his father, then it was too late. Syrus was behind him and crushed Maddox's arms down to his sides, lifting him a few inches off the ground and choking the breath from him in a bear hug.

"Or maybe not." Syrus chuckled as he dropped Maddox back on his feet.

He turned to his father and straightened his shirt. "All right, all right. You're still the big dog."

"Don't forget it either, puppy."

"I find the term 'puppy' somewhat offensive. I'm a mage, too."

Syrus smiled. "Care to test your current against my lightning?"

"Let's go." Maddox cracked his knuckles.

Walking to opposite sides of the arena, they faced each other. Syrus lifted his right hand. "Ready?"

Maddox lifted his hand as well and nodded. "On three?"

"One. Two. Three." They counted together.

An earsplitting, electrical crack echoed off the obsidian as Maddox's current hit Syrus' lightning. Their power streamed from their hands in snaking, horizontal lines. Sparks shot into the air where it collided. Maddox shifted his feet for better balance. The red lightning and the gold current pushed and pulled against one another like a magical arm-wrestling match.

Maddox's watch pinged. "Time out, Dad," he yelled over the snapping and rushing.

They both eased their power back and dropped their hands. Maddox looked at his watch, his eyebrows pulling down. Melina never called this early in the morning. He tapped the watch face.

"Hey, what's up?" he asked casually.

She didn't respond. Scuffling, odd crying or muttering filled his ears. "Hello? Mel?" His voice rose.

"Maddox, it's Sophie."

He blinked and rechecked the number on his watch. "Sophie? Are you okay? Your call came up as Melina's number. What am I hearing?"

"Nothing is okay. There's been a battle. Something happened to Melina."

His heart clenched. "What do you mean? Is she hurt?"

"I don't know. She's in shock. She won't let anyone near her. She let me take her watch, but that was all. I thought—" a strangled cry came from the background, interrupting Sophie. "I thought if anyone could get near her, it would be you. You have to come now."

"Where are you?"

"Just outside the boundary of the Wood, the east side."

He ended the call and turned to his dad. "I have to go."

Touching the medallion on his wrist, he opened a portal. Stepping through, Maddox landed in a mess of carnage. Bodies, body parts, weapons, and blood covered the ground around him. The fighting was over, but he still pulled his sword, the power in the glass connecting to the power in his hands. His eyes cut through the scene and landed on Sophie. She turned, desperation heavy in her eyes. He moved forward, dryads shifting out of his way. What the hell was happening here?

He spotted Melina and froze in his tracks. He pinched his eyes shut. *No. I didn't just see that. When I open my eyes again there will be something different...I didn't just see that.* Opening his eyes again, his breath jerked in and out, shallow and fast. He sheathed his sword as he ran forward. Sophie grabbed him by the arm.

"She killed him and then...she...The things she's said. The sounds she's made. It's like she's lost her mind. She won't let go of his sword."

Maddox exhaled and nodded. He focused on his breathing. He didn't feel calm, but he had to at least appear calm. "Okay. You were right to call me." He turned to all the bystanders. "Let's give her some space. Back off."

Everyone muttered but did as he asked.

He waited until the forest around them was empty before approaching Melina. Outwardly collected, inwardly however, Maddox was a jumble of confusion and denial as he drew close to her. On the ground, Mel cuddled up to a corpse like a lover. The dead guy's chest was open and hollowed out. His ribcage drying out in the open air. Gloves of dried blood blackened Mel's palms and fingers. She caressed the guy's face with one hand, a sword gripped in the other. She whispered to him.

This had to be a nightmare. He wouldn't accept this horror as reality.

"Mel?"

She blinked and lifted her head. Her eyes were distant and wrong. It was as if he looked at a stranger and not his best friend.

"Maddox?" She blinked a few more times and looked back at the corpse. "This is Tristan."

"Come here, Mel. Let me take you home."

She shook her head and wailed. "No. I can't leave him. I belong with him."

He took another step closer. "Why is that?"

Sobbing, she pulled closer to the body. "I love him. He's my future. My life mate." She sat up and dropped the sword, gazing at her blood-covered hands. She clutched at her chest as if she searched for something lost. "I killed him. I killed myself."

He opened his arms to her. "Come here. I'll take care of you. We'll sort this out together, okay?"

Melina trembled, her gaze darting back and forth between Maddox and Tristan. Then she shook her head. "I can't leave. I have to protect him."

"He's dead, sweetheart. He doesn't need protection. Come on."

His hands touched her shoulders. She jerked away from him and clung to the body.

"What did I do? What did I do?" she sobbed. "Why him? How could this happen to me? What did I do to deserve this? I can't bring him back..." A stillness settled over her. "I have to die, too. Then we can be together. I can be with him without shame…oh…I'm ashamed. So ashamed. I'm so bad."

Grabbing the sword again, she turned it on herself. Maddox surged forward and pulled the weapon from her hands. Her eyes spun and she screamed, coming at him like a wild cat. He dropped the sword and grabbed her, his power sliding from his hands over her skin. Gold light snaked up her forearms and bound like a rope around her ankles, knees, and wrists. She cried out and thrashed, but she couldn't shake the restrains he'd put on her.

He tapped his watch, calling his life mate, Erin.

"What's wrong?" she asked when she answered, catching his feelings through their spiritual connection.

"Get Journey. Take her to our house. I'm bringing Mel. I don't know what's wrong with her, but it's bad. She's covered in blood…it's not hers, so don't panic when you see her."

"I'll meet you there." Erin hung up.

Turning, he searched for Sophie. She came forward from a clutch of trees, a dryad close behind her, and Maddox immediately recognized the guy's protective and possessive body language in regards to Sophie. They were together. Interesting, but he didn't have time to ask his cousin personal questions about her taste in men. Sophie handed him Melina's watch. He slid it into his pocket.

"Please let me know how she is tomorrow."

"I will." He opened a portal, leaned down, and picked Mel up. "You did the right thing, Sophie. I'll take care of her. Don't worry."

Melina sobbed out curses mixed with sentiments of gratitude. The portal kicked them out in his garden. He tightened his grip on her as she shouted and jerked again to get free.

"It's okay, Mel. I promise. We'll figure it out. Whatever's happened to you, I'm here. Erin, too. We love you. It's okay."

Her gaze locked on his and seemed to clear a little. "I'm sorry, M," she whimpered. He was about to tell her he would do anything for her but then her eyes widened. Terror swirled her pupils as they expanded. It was like looking into the face of someone falling to their death. "Tristan's calling to me. I feel him pulling. He wants me to join him."

"Tough shit. I've got you and I'm not letting go. You're not going anywhere."

Melina went limp in his arms. The terror in her eyes vanished and all the light went out of them, the warm brown turning cold and lifeless like a doll's.

"You're wrong, M," she whispered, her voice as flat as her eyes. "You don't have me. No one ever will. I will always be alone. You can't keep me here. I'm already gone."

With his emotions choked up in his throat, he headed into the house and laid her on the living room couch. His throat tightened around the lump bolted there. Keeping her in restraints drove a knife between his ribs. But there was no other choice. She was broken. Broken so far that his oldest friend had vanished. She lay there like a corpse.

He ran a hand through his hair and paced the length of the room. Once. Twice.

A portal ripped open. He whirled to see Erin and Journey emerge, their expressions tight.

Erin immediately ran to Mel's side asking her what was wrong and what had happened to her in a frantic voice. Mel didn't respond. Maddox put his hands on Erin's shoulders and gently pulled her away. She turned in his arms asking him the same questions she just asked Mel.

"I don't know," he said.

Journey stepped forward, her eyes set on Mel's chest, reading her heart. Her gaze shifted to Maddox and Erin. "Leave me alone with her. This could take a while. We need total privacy... Take these binds off her. I'll keep her sedate. I won't let her harm herself or me, I promise."

Touching Mel on the wrist, Maddox pulled his power back. She didn't respond. He gathered Erin against him, and they left the room. He closed the bedroom door behind them. The worry they both felt for their friend transferred back and forth between them in their connection. Erin pulled tight into his chest.

"What happened?" she asked quietly.

He closed his eyes, steeling himself against the memory. Trying to make sense of it. But there was no sense to be made. He opened his eyes and sighed. The words tumbled out as he filled Erin in.

Erin's eyes turned to saucers, a hand flew to her mouth. "Oh, poor Mel... Are you sure she killed her life mate? It wasn't someone else?"

He shook his head. "She said she killed him and when I first got there, Sophie said it, too."

Trembling, Erin hugged herself as though cold. Tear built in her warm hazel eyes. "I...I can't imagine what that must feel like. I don't *want* to imagine it."

His arms locked around her as he imagined losing her. He'd come close to it once before. The memory of Kendrick holding a knife to her throat surged up, unwanted. His consciousness barely touched the edge of it and pulled back as though burned. He put his face in her hair and inhaled. *I won't let go of you. Not ever, Erin.* "If you died I don't know how I'd go on without you...but if I killed you... I think I would commit suicide, too."

Her tears touched his face as her lips pressed against his with bittersweet pressure. Her heart spoke to his, beyond words. Breaking their kiss, she nestled against his chest.

17

"We're going to have to watch Mel closely for a while. She'll be a danger to herself. I almost feel bad about that..."

"What?"

"Stopping her from killing herself. It might be kinder to just let her...I can't believe I just said that..."

Maddox shook his head. "I understand. I feel that way, too. But she can move on. She's so strong. I know she can. Many have lost their life mates and continued living, found love and happiness again as well. Just like her father, Merick. I know she can."

The soul bridge between Maddox and Erin burned and twisted like cords of rope. The situation thrusting them into overwhelming gratitude to have one another and a determination to never lose their connection.

The shreds of Melina's heart hemorrhaged anguish gilded with poison. The pain lacerating her psyche, unraveling the shape of her identity. Unfortunately, that wasn't the worst of it. Her mate had imprinted some of himself on her, threading her with strands of grisly malice.

Steeling herself for what would come next, Journey began to sing, the hypnotic power of her voice taking hold of Melina. Melina blinked and turned her lifeless eyes to Journey. Looking straight into Melina's mind, she focused on her childhood first, the notes she sang changed, reaching into her consciousness, grabbing the cords of her memories and using them to spin a transparent tapestry. Images of her past laughed and danced on the air, the fabric of Melina's memories projected like a movie in the room.

Journey didn't have to work hard on this part, Melina had a happy childhood. In truth, she was stalling. The problem wasn't the past.

Melina's eyes dilated, and her pulse slowed as Journey changed her tone and opened the vault of horrors of her splintered soul, searching. How did she give the young woman a reason to live through this? There was only one thing in the darkness Journey could find to use, and she didn't like it. In truth, it terrified her, went against her better judgment, and her nurturing nature. But she could find nothing else.

The notes of the song dug deep and hooked Melina's desire for revenge against Destiny and pulled it out of her, weaving it into the tapestry. At least, it was a purpose. A reason to keep living. Maybe it would be enough to carry her through the worst of her grief and perhaps when she surfaced from it, she would be strong enough to go on. Journey frowned as she sang. Revenge came from darkness. Weaving with darkness pained her, especially now she felt Melina respond to it.

Hypnotized by the song and transfixed on the moving tapestry of the story, Melina stood, walked slowly up to the image, and touched it with one blood-covered fingertip. Her finger slid through the images, disrupting their shape for a moment. Melina smiled, watching herself chasing down Destiny.

"NO!" a voice roared from the story.

Journey jumped back, gasping. The ghost of a man invaded the images she'd built. His chest was an open hole. He glared at Journey and then began to grab at the story, breaking it with translucent fingers until it fell to pieces. The malevolent spirit reached for Melina and cupped her face, pressing his forehead to hers. The edges of him slid into her skin.

"Forget all that, Melina," he said. "Destiny didn't curse you. You must come to me."

"How?" Melina whispered.

"You have my heart. It will lead you."

He pressed his lips to hers and then vanished. She cried out and grabbed at the air as if she could catch him and make him stay.

"Tristan," she sobbed, turning in a circle.

Journey moved forward and gripped Melina's shoulders, her eyes still darting around the room. "Look at me," Journey commanded.

Melina's third eye opened and snapped its gaze on the Storyteller. Those eyes were the darkest tunnels she'd ever seen, open and pulling Journey down a straight highway into her broken heart, but the pain was only indulged for a few seconds. She saw the rage ignite and climb from the depths of Melina's pupils. She bared her fangs at Journey and grabbed her wrists.

Journey sang again. Quickly. In self-defense. Melina's grip slackened as the notes slid into her. Journey took a step back, raising a new story in the space between them. This time she didn't alter the memory, she left it in its honest, pure form, directly from Melina's mind.

"Daddy?" Melina's eyes went opaque as she gazed at the new transparent tapestry.

TWO

"It's time, Melina."

"Time for what, Dad?"

"Time I really began your training."

Fourteen-year-old Melina scoffed at her father and rolled her eyes. "You've been training me my whole life. I can kick Maddox's ass. I think I'm good."

Grabbing her by the arm, Merick jerked her to her feet.

"Oww! Dad!"

"Maddox is just a boy. Well trained, yes, but still just a boy, hardly stronger than you at this age." His fingers dug into her arm, making her wince. Her father had never hurt her like that. Her young heart smarted at the pain and that he would inflict it.

"You're hurting me."

"Better me than someone else. Someone who won't stop. Someone who will take everything from you." He let go. "Now get your mind and attitude in the right place and come outside."

Her sullen teen attitude didn't want to let go just yet. "I don't want to get all dirty and sweaty right now. I just fixed my hair. Can't we do this later?"

"Put your boots on and get your spoiled ass outside. You've got three minutes." His tone made it clear she wasn't getting out of this.

He left, slamming the door behind him. She scowled at the door. What had gotten into him? He'd never acted like that before. Lacing her boots up and pulling her freshly styled hair into a ponytail, all the while lamenting all the time she'd put into curling it. She came out of her room and spotted her mom sitting on the couch, reading a book.

"Mom," she whined. "Do you know what Dad is trying to make me do?"

Netriet didn't glance up. "Yes." Her voice was flat.

"Can't you talk to him?"

"I do. Every day."

"No, I mean can't you just—"

"Nope." Her mom cut her off. "I agree with him. Now do as he says and be respectful. He'll explain."

Stomping outside, she made her way around the side of the house to the clearing in the woods where she knew her dad would be waiting. Her attitude proved stubborn as she tried to adjust it. Resentment pulled inside. She liked training and fighting, but she was supposed to meet Maddox soon for a date, and now he'd never see the pains she'd taken to make her hair look good for him.

"All right, I'm here. Can we get this over with quickly?" Her bitchy tone made her cringe.

He sighed and sat on a fallen tree.

She sat next to him.

"I'm sorry, Dad."

"Listen to me. I'm only going to tell you this once. I don't want to recount it again."

Oh crap. She swallowed and nodded. His words and demeanor were so grave.

"I never wanted you."

His words shocked and grabbed her by the throat. He reached around her, pulling her against his side as tears burned and spilled from her eyes.

"Past tense, sweetheart. Listen carefully." He wiped her tears. "It's time I told you about your siblings."

"My what?" Her muscles locked, and her hands clenched. "I'm an only child!"

He handed her a tarnished throwing star embossed with a symbol and the letters CB. "I was a royal soldier. Climbing the ranks in the Crimson Brotherhood as a young man. I found my destined life mate at the age of twenty. Life was happy and normal for years. I provided well for her, and we had two kids one right after the other."

Mouth gaping, her mind tripped over his words. Indignation flashed hot. Why didn't she know this? He turned his face away, his breathing ragged.

"Where are they?"

"Dead. All of them murdered by my best friend, right in front of me, while I was powerless to stop it. I was left for dead...I wasn't supposed to survive. I wouldn't have had I not been saved by a passing stranger. I changed my name and lived on the thirst for revenge until I had it. For many years, I just existed. My circle of friends was all I had. Then your mother came into my life and resurrected my heart." A small smile lifted his mouth. "We saved each other."

He shook his head and sighed. The smile vanished. "But then our friends, everyone that mattered to me for fifty years, all died in an attack... Most of me died again on that day. Nothing good. No light remained in my heart. I wouldn't have gone on living had it not been for your mom. And then you."

She squeezed his rough hand. He kissed the top of her head.

"I didn't want you," he said again. "A child...after losing the others. I know the pain, pain beyond description, beyond words. I couldn't risk it again. But your mom wanted you so much. She started dropping hints but then she grew serious and impatient. We fought over it a long time. I didn't know if our relationship would survive. We'd never fought like that before or ever again for that matter. I caved to her so I wouldn't lose her, all the while hoping she wouldn't get pregnant. When she did, I was terrified, because I loved you from the moment I knew you were growing inside her."

He went quiet and gazed into the distance. The sun shifted in the sky, then shifted again and again and again. She waited. When would he speak again?

Maybe she shouldn't interrupt him, but she needed answers. "Dad?" She drew it out, her voice low.

"Hmm?"

"My siblings? What were their names? How old were they?"

"Michael and Marah. He was six. She was four. Don't press me, please. I'm sorry. Some other time I'll tell you more about them."

He stood and faced her. She got to her feet, and he grabbed her by the shoulders, his dark eyes bearing down on hers.

"Do you love me?"

"Yes, Daddy." Her voice was adamant.

His grip tightened. "Then survive. If you love me, you'll survive because what's left of me would fade away completely if you died. No matter what you have to face. No matter the pain. You survive."

Conviction immersed her. She nodded.

"Now you're going to learn how. Prepare yourself. This will hurt. No training I've given you in the past has been like what today will be and all the days after until you are a survivor through and through. Until you can fight faster, meaner, dirtier."

He held his hand out, and she placed the throwing star in his palm.

"When you earn it, it will be yours." He pointed to a pile of leather armor, folded at the edge of the clearing. "Put that on. You're going to need it."

Adrenaline ricocheted under her ribs. Her dad was going to fight her for real!

The memory faded, Merick's words echoing faintly. "If you love me, you'll survive."

Melina blinked, lucidity returning to her as Journey stopped singing. She stepped forward into Journey's open arms, clinging to her, desperate for some shred of comfort.

"Thank you, Journey."

The Storyteller ran her hand over and over down the back of Melina's hair. "Just get through today. This is the worst day of your life. The pain of it will echo through you for a long time, but each day you survive puts more distance between you and this moment. So whether you're driven to track down Destiny or by your father's plea years ago, just stay driven until today is just distant memory that has no say in the purpose or direction of your life."

Tears streaming down her face, Melina nodded in silent agreement. She stepped back and held her hands up, gazing at the dried blood. "I killed my life mate...How could I do that?"

"It's not how, but why?"

Why? Why had she done it? She took a deep breath. "Because when we connected, I saw everything about him. Rejecting him wasn't enough. I had to end him, and I was perfectly positioned to do so." Revulsion rolled up her body. "I wanted to touch him. I wanted to kiss him. I did, so I would know what it felt like. But he had to die. I couldn't live tied to a psychotic rapist murderer." Her hands shook. "Oh... His soul touched mine. His disease infected me. I feel traces of it deep inside my heart like crawling bugs and slinking shadows."

Melina's expression crumpled, and she hit herself in the head with the heel of her hand over and over in a quick staccato. Journey grabbed her wrist.

"No choice. No choice. No choice." She wailed. "Part of me loves him. Part of me wants to die and be with him. The rest of me wants to vomit at the thought."

"Pull away from the part of you that wants him. Dismiss those thoughts as insanity when you have them. Learn how to cope. Remember what your father said."

"I'll try. I swear I will try my best. I can't let this destroy me."

"That's right." Journey pulled her close again. "If you need me, you know where to find me. Day or night. It doesn't matter."

"Thank you."

"You're welcome. Remember my words. Any time you need me. Now let your friends and family take care of you for a while."

Journey walked to the closed bedroom door and knocked. Maddox and Erin came out. Melina looked away from their worried gazes.

"I'll help you get cleaned up. You can borrow some of my clothes." Erin hugged her.

A spark of panic ignited in her chest at the offer. She had to keep her secret. "I'd rather go home. Please just open a portal for me to my apartment. I know I'm a mess. I...I just want to be alone."

"No way." Erin's voice had never been so hard. "You can go, but I'm coming with you, and I'm staying with you."

Maddox came up behind Erin and put his hands on her shoulders, looking Mel in the eyes. "You're just going to have to put up with us for a while."

"So, I'm on suicide watch?"

"Bet your ass you are," Erin answered.

She hung her head. "Okay. I understand. I just want to go home."

Erin touched the medallion on her wrist and opened a portal. Melina's hands covered her chest as she went through it after Erin. They landed in her Paradigm apartment.

"I'm going to shower."

"Not alone."

"Oh, come on, Erin. I get it, but please..."

"Nope. Sorry."

Melina's fingers tightened on her blood-covered collar. "I promise I won't hurt myself...I just..." she sighed, "This is going to sound sick, but this is Tristan's blood. It's all I have of him. I want to wash it away, but I want to be alone. I'm going to cry over it. Please, Erin. I promise. Just a little privacy."

The hard line of Erin's lips softened. "Okay, Mel. I'll give you some space, but just keep the door cracked. I'll ask you how are while you shower."

She swallowed hard. "Thank you."

Pulse hammering, Melina went to the bathroom and left the door open a sliver before turning on the tap. She kept her eyes trained on the tiny crack as she pulled off her pants and shirt. Carefully she unhooked her bra and bit down on her lips to keep from crying out in pain.

His heart peeled away from between her breasts. Sinking to her knees, she cradled Tristan's heart in both of her hands. Why had she kept it? Why had she hidden it in her bra? Why had she cut it out of his chest? What madness had overtaken her? What did she plan to do with it?

Grimacing at her own line of thinking, she acknowledged the whys. She intended to keep it. But how? How to preserve it? The dead flesh would soon rot.

Her fangs throbbed. There was still blood in his heart. She wanted to drink it. Lifting it up next to her lips, cold terror stopped her a second before it was too late. What was she doing? Drinking the blood of the dead was dangerous. Vampires who dared sank into madness.

"Do it, Melina." Tristan's voice came faintly through the steam behind her. "I will always be inside you if you drink."

Shaking her head hard, she gently wrapped his heart up in her bloody clothes, hiding them in the bottom of her hamper under her dirty laundry. She turned to the shower. His grey form blended into the steam, and the water sliced through him.

Steeling herself, she stepped in beside him and pulled the curtain. He gazed at her as the water hit her skin. Blood ran down her body and swirled the drain.

"Why are you still here?" she breathed.

"I wouldn't be here if you didn't want me with you. You kept my heart. I marked your soul with my own. Until you come to me, until you are mine, fragments are all we will have. Do you really want to live like that? I know I don't. I might be dead, but I want you. I long for you."

"You're disgusting. Why would Destiny match me with you?"

His unsubstantial hand caressed her cheek. "You know why. You're not as nice as you pretend to be. We're perfect for each other. You like the dark. You *are* dark... I thought Sophie was all I would ever want, but the second our eyes met I learned how wrong I was. Sophie is too sweet, too passive. Not like you." He leaned closer. "That kiss...before dying." His smile was devious, knowing. "Only you would kiss me and then kill me." His hands roamed over her body intimately. It felt like a cold, biting breeze on her skin. "My bad girl. My beautiful vampire."

Turning away from him, she scrubbed her hands, trying to erase the last traces of his blood. "Leave me alone. I know what you did. I know about the people you killed. You raped Sophie. You killed a child. I might be dark, but I'm not dark like you."

"Lies," his whisper echoed in her ear. "You're a killer, too. You killed me, didn't you? It doesn't matter, Melina. Destiny paired us, like it or not. You'll never have love. No one will want you, except me. I know you're ashamed. You should be. You're nothing like your friend out there. She is light...you must come to me. It's the only way..."

His voice faded away along with his presence.

Come to me. It's the only way.

How could she come to him? The only way for them to be together was for her to die. Pinching her eyes shut, she leaned her head against the tile. Her life began to flash behind her closed eyes. Did she truly have no future anymore? She didn't want to die. She didn't want to be with him...and yet she did. Was he right about her? She knew his nature, did he know hers? Their souls mixed. Was there a choice for her at all?

We're perfect for each other... You are dark... no one will want you.

She groaned and hit her forehead against the tile as hard as she could. Erin knocked on the door.

"Are you okay?"

"I'm fine." Melina managed to keep her voice steady. "I'll be out in a minute."

Leaving the shower on, she stepped out of the tub and opened her medicine cabinet, grabbing the scissors. The light glinted off the metal through the haze of steam. She didn't question what she was doing. Heart torn, she faced her reflection, staring deep into her own grief-hollowed eyes. She bunched a handful of her long blonde hair in her fist. The scissors severed her hair in a jagged line. Her vanity was as dead as her life mate.

Muscles jerking in quick spasms, she continued to stare into her own eyes as she cut all her hair close to the scalp in random, uneven lengths.

Cutting her hair marked death. Not just Tristan's. She had died, too. Who she was yesterday was not who she was now. Her desires had died. Her ideals. Her future. She wasn't a beautiful young woman anymore. She was only a smear of agony disguised as a person. Her skin held the same shape, but underneath, her structure was twisted and scorched as if screaming came from her blood in a resonance of piercing rage. The pain racing through her veins left no room for denial.

The door opened. Erin gaped at her for a second, her expression betraying horror and pity. Her features smoothed, and she moved forward, taking the scissors from her hand.

"Here, let me help you even that out." Erin's voice was warm and patient.

"No!" Melina snatched the scissors back. "I don't care what it looks like."

"Why did you cut it?"

"I don't know. I just had to."

She nodded and picked up a towel, draping it over Melina's shoulders. Erin's arms wound around her in a tight grip.

"You're going to be okay, Mel. I know it. I'm so sorry I can't take this pain away from you."

Slumping, she pulled the towel tighter around her body and turned away from Erin. "I'm going to get dressed and lay down for a while."

"Okay, hon. I'll be here."

Paradigm's night lights winked through the curtains. On the other side of her window, the city woke up for its dark revelry. She'd loved that sound since she moved there but now twisted in her ears like screeching metal. The blood pulsing through her temples beat like bass drums. What was wrong with her? She was sick and she'd had a nightmare. Groaning, Melina rolled to her back, both hands clenched over her heart. Her fingernails dug into the skin over her sternum as if her hands desired to tear her heart out.

I'm done, that's all. I'm done, her heart whispered in a voice bludgeoned into hopelessness.

It was the worst nightmare. It was the worst reality. And it still was only the first day. At dawn, she had faced Tristan, connected with him, touched him, loved him, and killed him. A new day had not even started yet, she was still stuck in the very first day.

"Melina..."

Tristan's ghostly arms wound around her. She pinched her eyes shut tight.

"Why haven't you come to me yet? I'm in such pain, such torment without you, Melina... You're in pain, too. Only when we're together will the pain stop."

Sighing, she rolled over and faced him. It was so unfair, why was it him? Her heart clenched as she gazed into his face. How could such malice live in such a beautiful body? It had only been a moment, that was all, just one fragment of time that she had looked on him alive, but that was all it took. Every finite detail of his face was imprinted in her mind.

An angry growl vibrated from his chest. "Why are you making me wait? There's no escaping this."

His hand moved to her chest, and she could almost feel the pressure of his touch. A small shiver of peace moved through her from where his fingertips brushed her skin as if she was water and his caress had caused a ripple. He hovered there, just on the surface of her. She rolled to her back, and he moved over her as if he wasn't a ghost, as if he was real, as if he was her lover. Melina was lost inside the fantasy of it for only a second. For a second the pain eased around the edges, and she rushed toward the source of relief, faint as it was. But that was only a second.

Objection and rage snapped through her like small explosions. His eyes flashed in response and the hand that had so gently teased the surface of her plunged inside. She strangled on her own breath as his ghostly hand sank into her heart.

"It's mine. By rights, I hold total ownership. There's nothing you can do to change that."

His grip burned and tore, but her scream froze silent in her throat. His fingers bit deeper but instead of causing more pain, the farther in she felt him, the better it was. After a whole day of unspeakable pain, at this moment, she felt good. She could breathe again. He held her heart his hand, his fingers sliding through her flesh and the streams of her blood. She looked up at him amazed. He smiled.

"Mine," he whispered. "Come to me."

"How?"

"You know how. Deep inside, you understand. That's why you kept my heart. Follow it."

Before she could ask him anything else, he faded away, and she was alone again. Her pulse raced, her breathing uneven as her body tried to right itself. She placed both of her hands over her heart, trying to hold the sensation there. It felt good. And it felt dirty, so, so dirty.

Sliding out of bed, she crept to the bedroom door and peeked out. Erin was still there, fast asleep on the small couch. Perfect. This was her chance. She slunk to the bathroom, retrieved Tristan's heart from her hamper, moved out past her friend, and slipped into the night.

In the pitch black of his personal chambers, Rahaxeris' ruby eyes slit open, and he scowled in annoyance. He wasn't used to intruders breaking in in the middle of the night, in fact, he couldn't remember a time anyone had ever attempted it before. So who in the hell had the guts to come into his space in the dead of night and wake him up? He got up and left his room.

Holding still in the hallway, listening, it only took him a second to realize the intruder was in the library. He listened for another few moments. Even though the person's movements were quite stealthy, he detected desperation. He came around the corner and stopped in the doorway, just observing for a moment. The light that naturally emanated from the Bellis stone walls was faint but adequate at night, but still, she held a candle up to the spines of the books as she moved around the room. *Melina*. He recognized her after a few seconds, even though she had her back to him, and her hair was oddly butchered.

He wasn't totally surprised she was there. He'd been expecting her to come back after the last time she'd showed up seeking answers since a new psychic ability had woken inside her and was showing her future memories. Despite knowing she would come back, he certainly hadn't expected her to come back in this manner.

Not wanting to startle her, he sent a wave of calming energy into the room before speaking. "What are you looking for, Melina?"

Gasping, she turned to face him. He narrowed his eyes and frowned. Whatever had happened had broken her. Grief-induced madness undulated around the edges of her eyes. Her gaze darted fearfully to a bloody, fabric-wrapped lump on the table in the center of the room. She set the candle down, quickly snatched up the thing, and held it protectively against her chest.

He regarded her, holding his hands out in a show of peaceful passivity. He could see it all over her, she was swamped in fear and disjointed with shame.

"What are you looking for?"

"I'm sorry for coming here like this. It's crazy. I shouldn't have barged in..."

"What are you looking for?" he repeated.

Hands trembling, she laid the thing she held back on the table and unwrapped the clinging, bloody fabric. His sharp eyebrows rose ever so slightly in surprise.

"Who did that belong to?"

"My destined life mate... I have to preserve it, but I don't know how. It seems his spirit is tied to his heart, either that or it's tied to me, but his ghost keeps coming back to me, and he keeps talking about the fact that I kept his heart as if he thinks it's important... I'm sorry." She shook her head, her shoulders slumping. "I know this is disgusting. I don't know what I'm doing. I thought your library might give me some answers, but I don't know what I'm looking for. It wasn't my intention to involve you."

"Not your intention to involve me?" He didn't hide his irritation. "This is not a public library. The knowledge that can be found here is dangerous, and it's my job to guard it. If there's something here you seek, you must get my permission first. And moreover, even if I let you acquire the information, you would have no idea how to wield it. Perhaps you have lied it to yourself as much as you have to me, but you came here for my help, so ask for it."

"I'm sorry. You're right. Please help me."

Intrigued, he moved forward and looked closely at the heart on the table. "I don't understand what it is you want."

"I don't know what I want exactly. I need more time. I need to keep his heart, but it will start to rot soon. The flesh will not remain, and it will not give me the time I desire to figure things out. I need more time. I don't want to destroy the bridge he has to me… Not yet. How can I preserve the connection?"

He knew what to do to achieve what she requested, but still, in all the years of his life, no one had ever asked such a thing of him before. Perhaps it would be in her best interest to refuse, but he was curious to see the outcome.

"What's your favorite color?"

"Huh?"

A smirk lifted his mouth. "I'll help you. What's your favorite color?"

"Red."

His smirk broadened into a smile. "Fitting, and ironic. All right, let's get to work."

Picking up the candle from the table, he scanned the spines until the light fell across the one he needed. Pulling the heavy tome from its place, he nodded at the heart on the table. "Bring it."

She picked up the heart and followed him down a hall and into a lab.

"Lay it on the table."

The book opened with a groan, the pages sticking together. His elegant fingers picked through chapters, hunting. "Okay...we're going to turn this heart into a piece of jewelry."

"What? Are you serious?"

"Completely. Don't worry. When I'm done, it will look like a stylish necklace that no one will suspect has magical ties to the dead. I'm quite good at making jewelry. You've seen Forest's Hailemarris necklace I assume?"

"You made that?"

"Yes."

"Well, I won't worry about your sense of style then. I've always thought that necklace was gorgeous. It has power, too, doesn't it?"

"Subtle powers, yes." He didn't take his eyes off the book and stopped flipping pages. "Here we go. I'm going to pull the essence still inside this heart, not that much is left, but it must be enough since you keep seeing a ghost. Another day or two and all traces of him would be gone. Then I'm going to pour the essence into a new stone and trap it inside."

She trembled again, and fear filled her eyes.

"Have you changed your mind?" he asked.

"No. I trust you."

The heart fell to dust under the light and power that came from his long, sharp hands. He ignored the strong, tainted vibe the heart gave off. It wasn't his business, he told himself. This was what she wanted because the heart belonged to her life mate. Malicious or not, she wanted the tie to him, it wasn't for him to tell her she should move on and forget keeping this bond alive. So he used his power and crafted a red stone, burning the dust of the heart inside it, sealing it. A flickering pulse thumped inside the stone, letting him know he'd been successful in crafting it.

"Silver or gold for the chain?" he asked.

She moved closer and gazed at the small, heart-shaped stone. "Gold, please... Wow. I see it beating." She touched it with her fingertip. "I can feel it."

"I doubt anyone else will be able to see or feel it. Just you."

"That's a good thing. I don't want anyone to know what it truly is."

He finished it with a long chain so the heart hung directly next to hers. She thanked him repeatedly and burst into tears. He patted her stiffly on the shoulder, opened a portal for her back to her apartment, and sent her on her way. When she was gone, he cleaned up the lab and returned the book back to the library. He wasn't fussed at all about what he'd done.

The only thing that would have stopped him from making the necklace would have been if he knew the heart had belonged to the blackguard that had threatened his grandson and raped his granddaughter. Had he known, he would have destroyed the heart completely, regardless of how Melina felt, or what she wanted. But he didn't know.

THREE

Back in her bedroom, she held her breath and listened as the portal closed behind her. Through the cracked open door, she could hear Erin's peaceful breathing from the Livingroom. She was still asleep. Melina closed her eyes and heaved a sigh of relief. She'd made it there and back and achieved her goal of preserving Tristan's heart with no one the wiser. No one would know this piece of jewelry was anything but a piece of jewelry.

"Good work, Melina," Tristan whispered from behind her.

Turning, she faced him, a whimper lodged in her throat. A jerk lurched in her core, instinct flooding her with the desire to go to him. She held still in spite of the pull. He sauntered toward her instead. It didn't matter he was a ghost, and that all his color was gone, he was the most gorgeous man she'd ever seen. She shook herself. It was just the connection that made her feel like that. The damn connection twisting her thoughts to believe she'd never been so attracted to anyone. But trying to force herself to out-think it didn't work. He *was* gorgeous. His beauty brought an acid etched regret inside her. Too bad he was a psycho who had to die. Too bad she'd never know what it was like to screw him. He was her mate. Sex would have been perfect with him.

He came close and wrapped one arm around her back. "I can see the heat signatures in your body, Melina. You want me."

Her cheeks burned hot. "So? It's impossible."

"Maybe. Maybe not. It won't be if you come to me. When your body matches mine, we can make love."

"Matches?"

"You have to die, too." His voice was soft, coaxing. "It's nothing to fear. I know. I've crossed the divide. It doesn't hurt. And if you cross over, too, it will be even better than being alive together. You'll see. I've never felt better. You'll feel better, too. And I'll make you feel so many things. More than I ever could have confined by flesh and blood... Please, Melina. Don't make me wait any longer. We will be together in the end anyway."

"What do you mean?"

"When you die. Our souls are bound together eternally. Death cannot sever it. As you can see, it hasn't. I'm here. We're still tied. So there's no need to struggle and prolong it. The rest of your life will be terrible if you do."

"What does it matter? If the end will be the same, why do you want me to come to you now? What is time for the dead? If you love me, why wouldn't you want me to live and have a full life?"

Sorrow laced his smile, and he leaned in, pressing his lips to hers. "If you could have a full life, I would want that for you, and I would happily and patiently wait. But you can't have happiness at all. You don't realize it yet. You think you've felt pain, but you're wrong, my sweet vampire. It's only because I'm still here that you don't really feel it yet. I've been shielding you from it."

"What are you talking about?"

"If I'm not near you, you will begin to feel a pain no one in Regia has ever endured. You murdered your own soul. It's only because of the part of you I touched... If my soul hadn't mixed with yours before you killed me, you wouldn't be able to even breathe for the pain. I'm holding you together because I love you and I don't want you hurting, but I can't hold on for much longer."

His words swirled cold under her skin. "I didn't realize."

"If that wasn't enough, consider the shame."

"The shame?" she breathed.

"Soon all of Regia will know of my crimes. I shall become notorious as word spreads. Many people saw you kill me, and the story will come out. Everyone will know Destiny tied us together. No one questions Destiny. You will be an outcast. Shunned because they will all know what type of person you are...Evil."

"But I'm not evil," she argued.

"Who will believe you?"

"The people who matter most."

"Perhaps, but remember, even if they believe there to be some good in you, they will always look on you with suspicion. Are you on the edge, about to snap and begin to act as I did? Or even if they don't go that far, the pity will never leave their eyes. Never, not for one moment will they stop feeling sorry for you. You will forever be shunned or treated as a charity case." His cold wisp of a thumb ran over her lips. "I know you. You don't want that. Just come to me now and you won't have to suffer anymore."

"Come to you how? Where?"

"The realm of the dead. Either come to me like that or kill yourself now. Of course, if you kill yourself, your loved ones will have the mess to deal with, and that's inconsiderate on your part, it will just make it more painful on your family and friends. If you come to me here you can leave them with your soft feelings and the knowledge you are happy and peaceful."

She closed her eyes. "I need to say goodbye. Do I have time? If I come to you tomorrow night will you be able to keep the pain at bay that long?"

He pursed his lips, seeming to mull it over. "I will do my best. I think I can manage it, though my strength is wearing thin already."

"I don't see much choice." Her voice was so lifeless. "But I have to say goodbye."

Leaning to her again, fading away as he slid through her. She touched the stone of her necklace. It had seemed like such a good idea, but now it just felt in vain. If tomorrow was her last day to live, whether Tristan's heart rotted to nothing or not didn't matter. She lay down on her bed, pulling her pillows around her for comfort. She hurt so much. How could it be worse than this? Fear froze a coating over the pain under her skin. More pain was coming. Pain she hadn't really felt yet. Soul murder.

Shuddering, she touched her chest, feeling the pulse under the flesh. Was her soul gone? Was it truly dead? How could she know? She centered the red stone necklace to rest on her sternum where she could feel the flicker of it next to her own heartbeat. The connection was still there. It reached down into her heart and hooked it with barbs. Of everything she'd lost since she made eye contact with Tristan, her freedom was the biggest loss. She was caged. There was no key. There was no door.

Melina closed her eyes, begging sleep to wash back over her again. At least asleep she didn't have to bow under the weight of her shame. She drifted off, but the eye inside her eye never closed.

Blood flooded her lungs as she tried to breathe. Strange lights hovered over her. No, not lights, eyes. The strange little floating creature stared into her eyes and then focused its attention on her hand. Melina pulled her hand to her chest, it was the only part of her body she could still feel. She couldn't move or think clearly as though she was drugged.

"No."

The little thing ignored her, its hands lengthening into sharp points before stabbing her through the wrist. It dragged its knifelike fingers up her the back of her arm. Splitting her open in a perfectly straight line.

The dark silhouette of a man stood nearby. "Good," he purred. "It's a good start, but there is still so much more to do. I wonder if she'll survive."

The vision vanished as she woke with a jolt. Groggy, she squinted at her bedroom curtains. The light looked wrong to her. It should be morning. She glanced at the clock. Damn, it was already afternoon.   She wiped the sweat from her forehead, her stomach twisting as she sat up in bed and looked around. It had been her fourth vision. Rage flared in her as she thought about each vision she'd had. The desire to gouge out her eye clenched in her hand. What good was this psychic ability? Rahaxeris said she was having future memories, but there was no way that could be right. The only vision she'd had that affected reality was the one that led her to Tristan.

Her hand closed around the red stone. It didn't matter.

Maddox was slumped on her couch, scrolling through his watch. He sat up, staring at her. She stared back. His gaze was intense and steady, she didn't flinch or look away. Her whole life, he'd been there. They knew each other better than they knew themselves. He got to his feet and pulled her into his arms. It all broke loose inside her then, and she wept against his chest. Words were unnecessary, and he didn't offer her any. He just held her. She knew how he felt. It was how she would have felt if he was in her situation. He was her oldest and best friend. How did she tell him goodbye?

When her eyes dried out, she pulled away from him. "I need a favor."

"Anything."

"I need something to take the edge off this pain."

"Like what?"

"Human blood."

He frowned. "No."

"You said anything."

"Well, I didn't mean it."

She raised one eyebrow at him. "Of all the using you've done, are you really—"

"All right, all right, I know." He narrowed his eyes and then sighed. "Fine, one hit, but don't ask me to get it for you again."

She nodded. "Okay."

Grabbing his jacket hanging by the front door, he put the hood up to shadow his face and headed out. One second after the door shut, it opened again. "Will you be okay by yourself?"

"Yes."

"You swear to me on our friendship you won't harm yourself while I'm out?"

"I swear, M."

"Don't go anywhere. I'll be back in a few." He shook his head and muttered, "I can't believe I'm doing this." The door closed behind him.

She stood still, staring at the door to see if he was gone or going to stick his head back in. He didn't. She exhaled a sigh of relief. She was alone. It wouldn't last long. He'd be back in a matter of minutes. She was thankful it was Maddox with her now and not Erin. Erin wouldn't have left her alone for a second, and she wouldn't have dreamed of asking Erin to get her illegal substances.

Her mind shifted to her parents, and she winced. Just their faces coming into her mind's eye slammed a pain through her like bones breaking. Her folks didn't know what happened to her yet. She didn't have to ask if someone had talked to them or not. If they had known, they would be there.

Ashamed, but at that moment shame mutated into something stronger, heavier, and she sank to the floor under its weight. On her knees, she pressed her forehead to the floor. How could she? How could she do what she planned? How could she leave the mortal realm without saying goodbye to her parents? Burning hot tears slid out from her closed lids and dropped on the floor. She didn't have a choice. Or she didn't want to recognize she had a choice. She already knew their faces the moment she told them everything. Her shame would become theirs. Their only child was so broken and messed up, Destiny had paired her with a murderer.

Damn it! She wouldn't look at their faces like that.

Taking a deep breath, she found the strength to stand through a flash of determination. She was alone. This was her only chance. She found a piece of paper and a pen and sat down at her tiny kitchen table. She hesitated, the tip of the pen hovering over the paper. What did she say? It wasn't a suicide note. She wouldn't think of it in that way. It was just an, *I love you* and *farewell*. The words poured from her on the page. She just let them go. When she finished and signed her name, she realized this goodbye was also an apology.

Coward. Pathetic, worthless, coward.

She folded it, wrote her parents' names on the outside, and took it to her room, setting it on her vanity. As she went back to the living room, Maddox opened the front door and came in, annoyance twisting his mouth.

"Thank you," she blurted out before he could complain.

His features softened, and he nodded. "It's lucky I'm better at shifting my appearance since I became a mage. If I was recognized and that nasty headline ended up somewhere, I'd be in the doghouse with Erin. It was still a risk, so I hope you appreciate it."

"I do, M! I swear."

Pulling a small, corked bottle from his pocket, he handed it to her. "I paid out the nose to get the pure stuff. Not that you can trust drug dealers, but it should be clean."

"Thanks. And I couldn't care less if it's diseased right now."

His eyebrows rose. "You've never had it before, have you?"

"No."

"Drink slowly."

The smell made her head spin, and she took a greedy gulp. Her eyes rolled back in her head as she took a second drink. Maddox caught her as the floor under her feet went missing. He laid her down on the couch, taking the bottle from her hand.

"Giv'm bac," she slurred.

"Nope. I doubt you could bring the bottle to your mouth again anyway and end up sloshing the blood up your nose." He looked down at her and chuckled, shaking his head. "Such a lightweight."

"M'not."

He laughed harder. "Yeah, you are. Feels good though, right?"

Her eyes rolled in their sockets again. "Yes. Good. Ss...so good."

"Well, enjoy it cause like I said before, I'm not getting it for you again."

Breathing slowed, she drifted in a soft euphoria as though thousands of flower petals skimmed over her naked skin. All the pain and darkness silenced, and her thoughts danced away like ribbons in the wind. She couldn't catch them so she just watched them go. It was too short. Long before she even wanted to think about coming down, she began to sink like a stone in the water.

Melina blinked, coming back to herself, and gazed at the ceiling. It was night outside the windows. She rolled to the side. Maddox was sitting on the floor, his back propped against the couch she was laying on. His fingers were typing at top speed on his watch and then he chuckled. She didn't mean to, but she caught a glimpse of one of his messages.

"Geez, M," she complained. "Don't sext with Erin while you're sitting right next to me."

He looked at her over his shoulder, completely unembarrassed. "She started it, and you were totally out of your head. Speaking of which, how's your comedown?"

"I don't know. I'm a little shaky, but otherwise, I feel normal." It was a lie. Her skin itched under the surface, and she was desperate to know where the bottle was so she could drink what was left.

"That's good." His voice was serious. "A good sign you're not the intsa-fiend type."

"Why don't you go home? You don't have to babysit me."

He frowned. "I don't mind."

"Sure you do. Obviously, you're missing Erin and she's missing you if she's sending you naughty messages. I swear I'll be okay."

"You seem okay right now, but—"

"I *am* okay. I swore to you earlier, remember? I'll swear to you again. I swear on our friendship, I won't harm myself."

He pursed his lips and looked away from her. His features smoothed out, and then his face hardened in anger. "You're lying."

"I'm not. I promise—"

He turned and touched the tips of her jagged hair. "This tells me the truth, Mel. You can get pissed at me if you want, but I will not leave you alone. I'll forgive you for just about anything right now. I don't even want to imagine what you're going through. You're not stable yet. I can't trust what you say."

She sat up and covered her face with her hands. Why did she think she could lie to him and get away with it?

"I want to tell you something...can you not judge me?"

He reached for her hand and squeezed it. "I think so. I'll try my hardest anyway."

Her throat dried up and clenched as she tried to form the words. He waited for her to speak. "I want to see Tristan. I just have some questions."

"That seems natural enough."

"I thought maybe X could help me. I could ask him about the dead, at least. I want to do what I have to, to heal and move on, but I feel like I need some kind of closure first. Maybe I'll never get it, but I want to try. Do you think X will help me find Tristan?"

"I don't know. I think he has the ability, but what you ask might go against his moral code." Maddox shrugged and shook his head. "I really don't know, but it doesn't hurt to ask. I think he would be willing to talk to you about it if nothing else."

She twisted her hands in her lap. "I was just thinking, *Well, my mate is dead but I know a necromancer.* It seemed like what I should do."

"It makes sense, Mel."

"Will you open a portal for me to their house?"

"Right now?"

"Yeah. Um...I don't know how late it is..."

"It's not late. Barely dinner time. I guess there's no harm in it."

They both stood.

"I want to go alone."

"Why?"

Her cheeks heated. "It was hard enough to say what I already have. Please. And you don't have to worry about me because I won't be alone. Just open a portal to their house and when I'm done, I'll ask Tesla to send me back here. Okay?"

"I don't know. I'll just come with you."

His watch pinged. She was pretty sure it was Erin, and she jumped at the opportunity.

"Ask Erin to come here. You two can be together for a little while alone and when I get back we can all eat junk food and watch a movie or something like that." She smiled as best she could. "I would really like that."

Her smile and the message on his watch seemed to distract him perfectly and he nodded. "Okay. I guess that will be safe enough."

He opened a portal for her. Her gaze lingered on him. The realization that she would never see him again lurched hot and sharp in her chest. Not able to say goodbye. Not able to hug him. If she did anything but walk into the portal, it would alarm him. Flashes of memories of the two of them slapped her viciously over and over. *Maddox*, her first and best friend. Her first kiss, first childhood infatuation, first partner in teenage rebellion. *Hold still. Stay frozen. Just think what you would say... I love you. Thank you. Goodbye.*

The portal kicked her out in front of Tesla and X's house. As soon as her feet hit the ground she went down on her hands and knees, pinching her eyes shut to hold in the tears blurring her vision. She'd told him the truth, except the part of her coming back. She wasn't coming back. The walls of her heart crumbled, dry clay falling, breaking, turning to dust. Her life was over. Her identity wrecked to the ground. Time to move on... *If you remember me, please remember only the good things.*

Getting to her feet, she dusted off her knees, walked up to the front door and knocked. Her hand closed over the red stone. No one answered. The house seemed quiet. She knocked again, louder, a small jolt of panic lurching under her ribs.

It's all right. Calm down. They're here.

Desperation grabbed her by the throat. She beat on the door with both fists.

"Please! Please! Tesla! X! I need help! Please!"

The door opened abruptly. Panting, she swallowed hard, trying to calm down. It wasn't Tesla or X that stood in the open doorway, but the demon, Fluffy. He looked down at her, confusion in his red eyes.

"Oh... Hey, Fluffy."

She pushed past him into the house. He could have stopped her with his pinky finger, but he moved aside and let her in.

"Melissa, right?" His shadowy voice rumbled like gravel.

"Melina," she corrected.

"Sorry. Melina. Tesla and X are not home. It's their anniversary."

She averted her eyes from his. "Oh...I'll just wait for them to get home. Don't mind me. Sorry I disturbed you. Just pretend I'm not here."

"Whatever... Your issue is none of my concern, but they won't be back tonight. I don't think they'll be back for a few days. They went off-world, not sure where."

She looked back up at him, the blood draining from her face. "Oh, no. No, that's not good."

He shrugged his massive shoulders, his smoky edges undefined. "Stay or don't. I'm sure they won't care since you're a friend of theirs. Excuse me." He turned his back and began to walk away.

Scowling at his retreating form, she didn't know what to do. This ruined her plans. "Where are you going?" She didn't even know why she asked. She'd never had an actual conversation with the demon. He was always so aloof and unapproachable. He was more of a stranger to her than anything.

He stopped and glanced at her over his shoulder. "I'm going home. Good evening."

"You don't live here?"

Annoyance filled his gaze as he faced her. "I live on the grounds, but not here in their house."

She looked down. "Oh...I'm sorry I disturbed you," she repeated.

"Forget it."

He didn't leave as she assumed he would. She chanced to look up at him, an awkward silence began in the midst of awkward eye contact. He crossed his massive arms and scowled. She'd never really looked at him this closely before. It made sense why he was feared and shunned. It was hard to look at him directly as if he was more of a trick of the light. He moved constantly, even when he was perfectly still. The black edges of him danced like heatwaves. She searched for his face in the haze. His eyes stood out because of their blood-red glow, aside from that, you *almost* couldn't see anything of his face or his body for that matter. The moving haze hid a defined form underneath. A solid shadow hid behind a screen of dark smoke. His gaze settled on her necklace, and something flashed in his eyes. She wrapped her hand around the stone protectively.

"What's wrong with you?" he demanded. "Why are you desperate to see Tesla and X?"

"Umm...well...it's nothing really...I just—"

"*Nothing* had you beating down the door, begging? The hell are you thinking to bring that thing around X?" He pointed at her necklace. "Do you think he wouldn't immediately detect the spirit shard trapped inside?"

"That's why I'm here. I hoped X would take me to the realm of the dead so I can be reunited with my life mate."

He laughed. The sound, so deep and dark, raised heat and shivers under her skin.

"No way. X would never do that."

"How do you know?" she shouted. "X would want to help me!"

"Exactly. Taking you to such a place would violate his ethics, he would never agree. X is my best friend and has been for over twenty years. I'm confident he would refuse, for your own good, because he cares about you."

Defeat clawed down her body and bent her over. She pinched her eyes shut and rubbed her temples. She didn't want to have to commit suicide in the natural way. She just wanted to fade away.

"How did you manage to hang on to a part of your mate like that?" he asked. "Trapped in a stone?"

"I killed him. Cut out his heart and used it. Rahaxeris helped me with the alchemy," she said it as if none of that made her feel anything.

Silence again. Heavy silence. His gaze pressed down on her like a new atmosphere. She looked up again into his face and even though he was on the other side of the room, she took a step back. What was that look? Curiosity? Sincere interest? Hunger?

"You killed your life mate. On purpose?"

"Yes." Her voice was little more than a whisper.

He laughed again, the sound bouncing off the hard surfaces in the room. "You're so petite, like a cute little bunny. Who would think you'd be capable of murder? And murder of your life mate, no less. There's some serious intent inside that little package."

"Are you making fun of me?"

"A little," he chortled. "The pain in your eyes tells me you're pretty broken, but if you want to go the realm of the dead, I'll take you there."

Her eyes rounded. "You will?"

"Sure." He shrugged.

"Why? After you told me why X wouldn't—"

"Because I don't care what happens to you. You want to die? I'm not going to tell you why you should make another choice."

Her mouth parted, her eyes rounding wider. He was in earnest. She blinked and looked down. "Umm...thank you. Can we go now?"

He laughed again. "Well, I've got nothing else to do. So, yes."

He moved toward her then. She kept her eyes down, and her heart began racing. He stopped two paces from her. She swallowed hard and looked up again into his face.

"I meant it. I don't care if you die. When we get there, whatever happens, is up to you. I'm not going to interfere. I won't rescue you."

She didn't know how she looked to him, but she felt the shift in her expression at his words. The look in his eyes shifted too, confused or incredulous. She wasn't sure.

"Honestly?"

"I won't rescue you," he repeated.

A smile slid over her lips. "Thank you."

He blinked. "You're weird... Are you ready?"

"Yes."

"Follow me."

Clear moonlight cast long shadows along the ground as he led her outside and around the back of the house. Tesla and X had a large plot of land, she'd been there many times, too many to count, how was it possible she'd never noticed the building in the distance, hiding in a thick of trees? Sleek like the main house, it peeked out through the growth. That must be where the demon lived. Was he taking her there?

He stopped and faced her.

"Keep your eyes open," he ordered. "This isn't a portal like you're used to. Keep close behind me, but don't touch me."

"Why?"

"I don't like being touched."

"Oh...okay."

He turned away from her again and walked up to a towering boulder. "We'll enter here. Keep your eyes open," he repeated.

His hand plunged into the shadow of the boulder. It clung to him as he pulled his hand back. What had just been a defined, flat shadow now opened and filled. It rippled around his hand like water and continued to open up. The shape of the shadow lengthened and widened, bleeding out vertically on the air before her like a mortal wound.

"You won't be able to see the reality of this realm because you are still alive."

"What will I see, then?"

"Hmm... Something like a metaphor, or a dream. It will be like art, honest, but a distorted representation of what is really there. Nothing there will be safe for you. You can still change your mind."

She lifted her chin and met his gaze, gesturing for him to lead on. He turned and walked into the shadow, and she rushed after him.

Crossing the shadow barrier wasn't easy. The darkness held solid against her skin like a sheet of ice. Digging her heels into the ground, she pushed. It bowed, vibrating. Slowly it began to give, and she slid through, her body passing into a place it didn't belong. The barrier sliced...burned...tore...stabbed.

Melina gasped as her lungs filled with toxic smoke. Her senses cringed. This place was poisonous. Natural warnings jerked spasms all through her. Her mindless survival instinct screamed for her to get out now. She ignored her gut. She came here to die. It didn't matter.

Strange light and colors ran down all around her like waterfalls. Her eyes strained to grasp colors she'd never seen, and the shades of light deviant to her mortal sight. Oddly beautiful but instead of beauty she only perceived nightmares, though there was nothing obviously scary. She didn't belong...yet. She didn't know the physical rules. Were there any boundaries?

She pinched her eyes shut for a second, her pupils constricting, her third eye pushed hard from deep inside as if it was trying to rise to the surface. A million voices breathed in her ears. Laughter, screams, words of love, murmurs of escape, an endless, shapeless ocean of desires whispered to her. Melina covered her ears, but that did nothing to block it out.

"Hey!" His voice jolted her.

Opening her eyes, she locked her gaze on him. The demon was the only thing she knew to be real in this place.

"I told you to keep your eyes open."

"Oh, right. Sorry."

"If you do that again you'll be lost. You won't reach your life mate before your sanity is absorbed into the horde."

"You didn't warn me of that!" Freaked out anger shrilled her voice.

"I told you to keep your eyes open," he repeated.

"You didn't say why."

He sighed. "You're tiresome. What direction do you feel your mate pulling from?"

Pulling? She almost closed her eyes again just so she could focus on the sensation. Melina turned in a slow circle. The necklace flickered, its pulse thumping. She turned in another circle. The pull wasn't in her heart as she'd assumed it would have been, but in her feet. She stopped turning and looked down, crying out in alarm. The ground under her feet was invisible, more of a force field, a chasm of shadow and space filled with stars and galaxies.

She pointed down. "The pull is coming from there."

Fluffy huffed. "Of course. No good deed goes unpunished. I should have known better than to get involved."

"What's your problem?"

"Never mind. We have to go through the museum to go down a level."

"Museum?"

"Well, that's what I call it, just stay close behind me. Don't touch me, and don't—"

"I know," she snapped. "Don't close my eyes."

He smirked, "Shall we take a walk on the sky, little bunny?"

Her stomach swooped as she walked. The nothingness was solid as rock under her feet. She kept her eyes glued to his back and resolved to not look around. Coldness surrounded her on all sides, a cold so mature it caressed with skilled intent. The only heat was flaring out from the demon. She drew closer to him to feel the warmth in his wake. A quiet slammed down, heavy and absolute, and she was filled with somber respect. This must be the museum, and she couldn't help but glance at the lives on display as she followed him.

"Only the greatest are here," he said over his shoulder in answer to her unspoken question. "The best lives manifest like this in this realm. But, of course, I've no idea what it looks like to your mortal eyes."

She swallowed, unsure if she should try to speak at all. "It is as you said...I see a metaphor. I understand why you call it the museum."

Life histories played out beautifully before her as she passed, like walking down endless rows of movie screens, vast, yet flat. Of course, Tristan wouldn't be here. This was a place of honor and reverence. He was below in the shadows where he belonged. The thought gave her a painful tug under her ribs, where she belonged, too. Her destination was wherever he was. Her stomach turned. What was she doing? Was this a mistake?

Voices she didn't know but somehow recognized at the same time called to her. Distracted from her path, she stopped and turned to the side. A house on fire. Children screaming from inside. *Oh gosh*. Melina covered her mouth as tears instantly sprang to her eyes. Her father was there, in this memory, on his stomach on the ground, two swords through his back, reaching up toward the flames. The screaming of the children coated her soul in a bitter ache. Her siblings. She didn't want to see this.

Melina turned away.

"Melina! Wait!"

Halting, she stopped and looked back, gasping as she beheld her brother and sister for the first time. So beautiful. So adorable, they smiled as they ran at her. Their sweet faces held a resemblance to hers. They both had Merick's warm brown eyes, just as she did. Holding hands, they slowed as they came close to her. She reached out, but an invisible barrier prevented her from touching them.

"Remember what dad asked of you, Melina," Michael said.

"What?"

"She remembers," Marah assured him. "Girls remember things better than boys."

"We want you with us...but not yet. Remember what Dad asked of you," he repeated.

"Wait," Melina called as they turned and ran away, hand in hand.

They didn't stop and after a few paces, they vanished. What did they mean? What was she supposed to remember? Her necklace flared hot, bringing her thoughts back to Tristan. Her siblings were long dead. Echoes of lost children couldn't understand what she was going through and what she had to do.

Fluffy came up to her side, his heat warming the surface of her skin. "If you linger here, you'll die before you reach your life mate. You don't have much time left."

You don't have much time left. His words brought her focus back where it needed to be. Tristan. She had to find Tristan. She'd given up her other choices. It was too late for anything except to see it through. She nodded at the demon and gestured for him to lead on. He turned and continued. She kept her eyes glued to his back. She couldn't be distracted again.

"We're close to the gate," he grumbled. "Don't scream when we cross through. Screaming is so annoying."

Insulted retorts rose up her throat, but then she gasped as they indeed crossed through into a new depth of dark and cold. He didn't stop or slow his stride. The floor began to slope downwards, and the darkness around her spiked up in layers of varying complexity. Pressure bowed the air on either side of her. It was like following him down a narrow hallway made of black glass. Whispers tickled her ears again.

"Ignore the voices." He turned to face her. "Is the pull getting stronger?"

The pulse in her necklace turned into a hum. "Yes. It's..."

He stepped to the side. "You lead."

"But...but..."

He snickered. "Nothing to fear. Well, nothing because you came here to die. I'll see you to your destination. The walls won't keep you from going the direction your sweetheart is, you can just walk through them."

She sneered at his use of the word, *sweetheart*, but didn't see the point in setting him straight. She walked in front of him and held still for a moment. *Deeper, still deeper into the darkness*, his soul whispered, the necklace hot against her sternum.

The darkness ahead of her opened like a tunnel. Metaphor, she reminded herself. This place of shadow was her future. Darkness would hide her shame. It was the only comfort she could draw from this.

"Well?" the impatient demon asked behind her.

She moved forward into the tunnel. Tristan was close.

The ground under her feet continued to slope downward until she reached a shore. Melina stepped into the waters of a swamp. Cold and thick, the water clung to her legs like mud. She glanced back. The demon had stopped at the edge and not entered the swamp, not that she blamed him. Her necklace throbbed.

"Melina..." Tristan's voice rippled the water's surface.

She stopped as he materialized right in front of her. Her soul jolted as their eyes met. Shimmering light illumined his blue eyes like a clear sky. The nightmare flashed into a dream. The cursed darkness vanished into soft, water colored landscape. Her numb heart awoke. Nothing mattered anymore. They were together and always would be. The chords of their soul connection ghosted through her body, a faint whisper of what had been when he was alive.

"Come to me. Bring me back the pieces you cut out. Make me whole again."

Instinct shivered on the shadows. *This is a mistake.*

Tristan smiled and reached for her. His physical beauty distracted her from the gut warning, and she moved to him, shaking off everything she felt. Together. That was what mattered. He gathered her in, and she sighed in relief. Instinct shivered again. He felt so cold against her, like an empty shell.

His lips pressed to her earlobe. "Thank you, Melina," he purred. "Such a wonderful gift."

Thunder rumbled overhead, and rain began pouring, washing away the illusion. The peaceful watercolor ran down the walls, exposing the truth again. He chuckled softly. His hands moved up her back and gripped her shoulders. Black snakes slithered around his wrists, their grey tongues flicking out, tickling her shoulders. She tried to pull away.

"Don't mind them." Tristan's voice was calm. "They won't hurt you. They're a part of me after all. You'll like how they feel once you get used to them."

Bile rose up her throat. *This is a mistake.*

"Let me go."

His lips lifted with a cruel slant, and dark light flashed in his eyes. "There's no going anywhere." He chuckled again, his voice growing louder and louder until it escalated into a mad cackle. "You believed me! You came here as I asked."

He leaned forward and licked her cheek. "Even in death, I get the joy of killing. You've given me such an amazing gift. I love you so much. Now scream for me, be my victim. Prepare to be a sacrifice to my wrath and my love. You killed me, now I'll kill you. It's perfect."

This is a mistake. I'll take the pain and the shame. I don't care.

She jerked back from him. He wasn't beautiful anymore. He looked the way he had when Maddox had pulled her away from his corpse. His torso open, his ribcage exposed. More snakes twisted around his ribs and up his legs from the black water.

"No." Her voice trembled as she backed away from him. "I don't want this. I don't want you."

"Bitch," he spat. "You think you have a choice? You're here now. You're not getting out of here alive. And you're mine, *forever*. Now bring me my heart."

"I'm not yours."

"Ah...you want to play. That's so good!" He moved forward. "The fear in your eyes really turns me on. We only get one shot at this. Do you long for your death to be as perfect as I do? Beg and scream for me while I tear you to pieces. Maybe then I'll forgive you."

"No. I don't want to play your sick game. I'm not yours. I've changed my mind."

He raised one eyebrow. "You can say anything you like. It won't change this. We are forever. Nothing can come between us. There's no one else for you but me. Nowhere for you but here."

Maybe he was right. Maybe there was no way to back out. She'd come here to die. But still...she had changed her mind. Her father's voice came back to her. Oh, yes. This was what her siblings wanted her to remember. *If you love me, you'll survive.* She had to try at least to go back on this mistake. Her spine hardened, and she wondered why it had gone so soft to begin with.

"Maybe that's the truth, but I need more time, Tristan. I'm not ready for this."

Melina turned, the sludge around her legs clinging. He grabbed her from behind, wrapping one arm around her waist. His other hand stabbed under her ribs and grabbed her heart, only it wasn't like before in her room, when it felt good. This was ice and metal. It was death.

Fluffy watched Melina march to her fate with mild interest. No way was he going to touch that water. He'd come far enough. He'd brought her where she wanted to be so he could leave now. Witnessing her death didn't appeal to him. It was a stupid waste of life, but whatever...his opinion didn't matter. He didn't care about her or feel anything other than this was a break in the monotony of his usual routine, until...the kids that ran at her, spoke to her...a small thorn pierced his heart. Annoyed at the sensation, he tried to ignore it.

Then the bunny's life mate materialized. He sneered. What a disgusting soul. Malice slithered all over him.

What could Melina see? To his eyes, words branded the guy with his worst sins. Murderer, rapist, deviant, pervert, power-lust, liar, thief, stalker...no wonder she killed him. But why was this her mate? She didn't strike him as an angel, but she wasn't like this guy.

This seemed so wrong to him, all of it, and now he felt a sting of guilt for bringing her here. Now he really didn't want to watch her die. He turned and began to walk away, anxious to forget this night as quickly as possible.

"Maybe that's the truth, but I need more time, Tristan. I'm not ready for this." Her voice echoed.

Then she screamed. He glanced back. He hesitated a second until his pissed off took over and he charged into the water, grabbing the guy by the throat and lifting him off his feet. His fingers dug deep. He could kill his soul easy and quick if he wanted to. His grip eased. It wasn't his place to bring him a second death.

"She said she needs more time. You should honor what a lady says, slimy bastard."

He dropped him and turned to find her. She was unmoving, face down in the water. Grimacing, he scooped her up and carried her out of there. Dripping, unconscious, and her cheek rested against his chest. He bristled at the sensation. He hated being touched. He hated water even more.

"Hey, asshole! That's mine!"

Fluffy didn't even pause his stride. "Yeah? Do something."

Tristan didn't follow.

The sound of her shallow, disjointed breathing was louder to him than all the whispers of the dead as he walked up through the lower level to the museum. They all looked at him. He knew most of them personally. Cringing awareness of being a spectacle clung to him as he continued to take the living girl out of the realm of the dead. What was he doing? He said he wouldn't interfere. He thought taking her where she wanted to go would be a nice way to kill some time, since he was bored.

She was so fragile in his hands. He couldn't remember ever touching someone like this before. His hands were made for killing, not that he'd done any of that since the war of the wizards, but still...

She didn't wake as they crossed through the barrier and back out into the garden. What was he supposed to do with her? Her mate had damaged her heart. Another few seconds and she would have been dead. What did she need to heal? She was a vampire, she needed blood. He didn't have any to give her. A frown pulled hard into his brow. The hell? He would have given her his blood. Was that really what he'd been thinking? He shook himself. He didn't have any blood, so it didn't matter what he was thinking in any case.

He debated, looking at the main house and then at his own. There was no reason to take her to his house. He shifted her in his arms and took her back into Tesla and X's house. She slid limp from his hands to the living room couch. Shivers rose on her skin and she moaned. He frowned again. She was cold. He stalked to the guest room and grabbed the cover off the bed. His evening certainly had been a break in his routine, he mused as he draped the cover over her.

Gazing down at her, he took a few steps back, wondering what he should do now. The front door creaked on the hinges, startling him. Who? The next moment Maddox strode around the corner, mild surprise in his eyes as he took in the scene.

"Um...what's going on?" Maddox moved to Melina's side and touched her forehead. "Mel?" He looked up at Fluffy. "Why is she unconscious? Why is she wet?"

Seriously uncomfortable, he turned and began walking away. "I'll let her tell you all that. She's probably going to be sick for a while. I'd get her some blood if I were you."

"Where's my sister?"

It was rude of him to walk away. He kept walking. "Off-world. Date night."

The night breeze slid through his hazy exterior as he strode out of the main house toward his own. Why was he embarrassed?

FOUR

Crisp moonlight played on Sophie's shoulders and the soft, cool ground under her bare feet sent a wave of pleasant shivers over her skin. She was nervous and simultaneously peaceful as she thought about what was about to transpire between her and Eli. She hadn't seen him since the battle. Over a week had passed since then. She had no way to contact him, except to just show up, as she was about to do. But still...something inside her let her know he was waiting, expecting her. They weren't destined life mates but there was something connecting them beyond feelings. Sophie smiled to herself as she considered *them*. What she shared with the historian was unique.

The haunting light of the wood ahead made her smile wider and her cheeks warm.

He was there, just a little ways ahead, leaning casually against a large trunk and twisting something in his hands. His lips curved as he glanced at her from the side of his eye. She held back the urge to run to him and continued forward at a slow pace. Her eyes settled on what he was messing with, and she half scowled.

He stood straight and sauntered toward her.

"I'm afraid to ask what you plan to do with that." She pointed at the thin strip of fabric in his hand.

He chuckled and reached for her. She melded to him as he took her mouth. "I've been missing you so much and that's the greeting I get?"

"Well?"

"It's just a blindfold, coward." He tapped her on the nose with his index finger. "I have a surprise for you. Turn around."

"Not yet. I need more." She stretched up on her toes and kissed him again.

He smiled against her passionate lips. "Hold up, hotness. You have all night to work me up. Let me keep my head long enough to show you what I made for you, well, for us."

She heaved a great sigh and turned around so he could blindfold her. He tied the blindfold gently before leaning down and kissing the side of her neck.

"I love you, Eli."

He put his mouth next to her ear. "And I love you," he whispered. "I've been crazy without you the last few days. I hope you like what I did...I'm really nervous about tonight. I want it to be perfect for you."

"Show me your fantasies, and I'll show you mine."

He chuckled and took her by the hand. "You talk a good game, but you just freaked out over a blindfold. Not sure you're as brave as you try to seem."

"I just want to be everything you want me to be," she confessed seriously.

He squeezed her hand. "I'll address that, but not right now. We're almost there. I hope this makes you happy." He stopped and moved behind her, placing his hands on her shoulders. "Be kind to me," he said, untying the blindfold.

Sophie blinked and gasped. "Wow..."

She knew where they were, but the area around Eli's tree was completely changed. Huge trees that hadn't been there last week now rose up to the night sky. The new trees formed a circle around Eli's tree. Vines laced the gaps between the trunks, blocking out all visibility of what was behind them. The two trees in the front bowed out enough to form an arched doorway. Roots perfectly spaced made a short staircase to the door. The door itself was a solid piece of wood carved with beautiful designs.

Sophie hadn't expected anything like this. She assumed she'd just spend the night in Eli's branches, as she had once before. But in the week they'd spent apart, he'd grown her a house.

She faced him, and he wiped the single tear off her cheek with his index finger. "This is amazing. It's so beautiful. Like the best dream ever... Can I go in?"

He smiled and handed her a long, thin key. It felt strange in her palm. "What kind of metal is this?"

"It's not. I can only make things of wood. It's petrified, essentially stone."

She looked up at the door and shivered. "I'm so excited."

"Me too, now you have my wood in your hand."

She snorted and rolled her eyes. "Are you ever going to stop with the wood jokes?"

"The odds are not good."

She huffed and narrowed her eyes at him.

"You're so cute when you're exasperated," He said. "Are you going inside or not?"

She rushed up the root steps to the door and slid the key into the lock. The door swung inward and again she gasped. Eli's tree was in the center, illuminating the space with the beautiful peacock colors glowing from deep in his leaves. Moonlight cast down through the branches of the roof. Soft moss carpeted the ground under her feet. Branches grew up and along one side in a staircase to Eli's canopy. The other side was blank space where she envisioned furnishing to suit her tastes.

Eli came in and latched the door behind him. He gathered her against his chest. His heart was pounding so hard she felt it. "Do you like it?"

"It's wonderful."

He exhaled, and she caught the edge of his nervousness as his heart pounded faster. "Will you call it home?"

She framed his face with her hands. "I'm moving in, with or without an invitation from you. This place is mine."

He exhaled and smiled. "We don't fit into any typical Regian coupling."

"So? It doesn't bother me."

He held out his hands, palms up, words appearing on his skin like carvings. "I've learned about many different mating customs throughout Regia's history, looking for something that might fit us, but nothing really seems right. I'll do whatever you want."

"Oh, no. I hadn't really thought about it, well...okay, I've thought about it but there's nothing I'm settled on. I didn't realize you'd want anything like that."

"Come closer." One hand held the back of her head and the other banded around her lower back. Her eyes slid shut, and she moaned as her heart quivered. Pleasure blossomed in her brain. He didn't need to say anything, all emotion, intention, determination, and possession pulsed through the way he held her. Her heart and soul swayed into him.

"You said you want to be everything I want you to be, as if somehow you're not already." His voice, so quiet and serious, trembled over the words. "It was so fast, Sophie. I fell so fast. I was terrified you'd vanish. You're free to go anywhere, while I'm confined to such a small piece of the world. I'll try to not cling too hard. If you need to travel, I'll understand. If your presence is required in the mountain, I won't complain. Whatever you need to do...I just want...I *hope* you will be willing to do something as a show of what we are to the rest of the world. You're everything I want. I swear it."

She pulled back enough to look in his eyes. "I fell fast, too. You see my true face, Eli, something only my destined life mate should be able to see. Yet you can see it because I decided you were for me when I died. I've thought of what we can have as a symbol of our love and commitment."

"What is it?"

"I'll show you later." She let all the desire she felt for him fill her eyes.

His lips lifted in a knowing, sexy, half smile. "Much, much later, Sophie. I feel as if I've waited an eternity for this night, and I'm going to take an eternity to make love to you."

The man was as good as his word...

Sophie woke in Eli's branches right before the dawn. She yawned and nestled tighter in his arms, splendidly sore and still weak from the onslaught of pleasure he'd given her. He roused the second she tried to get loose from him, pinning her with an intense look.

She groaned and smiled. "Monster."

"Is that a compliment?"

"Hmm..." She gripped his wrists and kissed his mouth as hard as she could. "You're all mine. Only mine. Forever. Your body, and what you did with it last night...I'm possessive, Eli. You ever give it to anyone else, and I'll cut you down." He swelled with such a burst of ego, Sophie laughed. "There's your compliment and a serious threat."

He stretched and jumped down from his branches, landing on his feet. She looked down at him. He smirked and gestured for her to jump too.

"No way. Maybe if I wasn't so sore. I'll take the stairs."

He scooped her up when she reached the bottom and held her tight to his chest. "Will you tell me what you've thought of for us as a show of commitment now?"

"This might hurt a little," she warned.

"Bring on the pain."

Stretching out her fingers, Sophie grabbed the color off the closest tree trunk and pulled it into a small, sharp edge. Without flinching, she cut a line on the top of her forearm, her blood rising up and spilling out. Before she could ask, he held his arm out to her, and she cut him in the same way. Sophie rubbed her finger around in a small circle a few times in the red until her finger was covered. She mixed the red into his golden, dryad blood.

Closing her eyes, she exhaled and began to paint on the air with her unique gift. It only took her a moment to complete, and she opened her eyes and looked at what she made.

It was small and simple. A red wolf beside a gold tree. The art hovered in the space between them.

"Now what?" he asked.

"We absorb it, together."

"How?"

She held her hand up next to the art, her palm facing him. "Take my hand."

The art sandwiched between their hands and broke in two. One half going into her, the other absorbing into him. They both shivered as the art slid on their skin, moving up their bodies. Eli laughed as though it tickled. When the gold wolf slid up his sleeve, he stood and pulled his shirt over his head.

"I knew this was just a ruse to get me out of my clothes again."

"Please." She rolled her eyes. "I'll give you direct orders to strip if I want you to."

He chuckled as the art moved over his chest and up over one shoulder. "Well, well, one night with me, and you've turned into a total minx."

She stood, too, feeling the gold tree move to her back and settle between her shoulder blades. "Turn around," she said.

He obeyed, and she smiled broadly. The red wolf settled between his shoulder blades as well.

"It's done."

He turned back around. "Let me see yours."

He unzipped the back of her dress, gently running his fingers over the tree, before leaning down and kissing her back. "It's beautiful, Sophie...I love you. You make me so happy."

She shivered as his lips continued to move over her back. "I love you, too. So much...I...have to get back to the lair soon."

"Hmm..." He acted as though he hadn't heard and continued to work on her with his lips.

"I shouldn't keep my mom waiting too long...I promised her I'd be back for...oh never mind," she conceded as he did something wicked. "I'm too punctual anyway."

He laughed darkly and caught her up against him, kissing her mouth. "I see I'm going to have to remind you your first loyalty is to me, always."

She gave him an impish little smile. "You'll have to remind me often. I can be forgetful."

Melina kept her head down, the hood shadowing her face. She rubbed her hands together, attempting to ease the ache in her knuckles. It had only been a few days of consistently drinking human blood, but she acknowledged she was a junkie now, and the ache in her joints was the first sign she was coming down. Her shame that Tristan was her life mate, dead or not, was so heavy, she barely felt twinges of guilt that she'd embraced addiction. Confessing her connection to Tristan to her parents had been the worst. Their faces had been exactly as she knew they would. The flashes of that memory made her reach for blood and drink it with reckless abandon.

She wasn't clear. She knew it. Her parents hadn't just been shocked and disappointed, they were heartbroken and suffocating her with love and concern. Their love was unbreakable, but she didn't want to be around them until she sorted her shit out, reinvented herself, and could hold her head up again. Maddox and Erin still took turns babysitting her at night. She didn't know if they knew she was drinking blood the way she was. Maddox kept looking at her from the corner of his eye, scrutinizing, but he didn't say anything.

People walked past her on the stone stairway that circled the inside of the Lair. She pulled her hood down more and leaned back against the boarded-up door of Tristan's apartment. Her stomach shuddered as she thought about what she was there for. It was disgusting, but she couldn't help herself. She'd tried. The guards who let her into the mountain accepted her half-truths.

How could she do this? Tears threatened, and she pinched her eyelids shut. Maybe one day Sophie could forgive her.

"Melina?"

Sighing, she lifted her head and met Sophie's guarded gaze.

"Hey, Sophie...I hope this isn't a bad time."

Sophie snorted derisively, but then she pulled Melina into a tight hug. "Poor thing," she murmured. "Anything connected to Tristan is a bad time. I was told you were waiting for me. Why are you here?"

"Answers. Clarity. I'm sorry. This is so gross. I just want to see where he lived. I keep trying to understand why this happened to me. I can't help wanting to know all I can about him, even though knowing hurts me."

Sophie grimaced and nodded. "Okay. I see."

She touched the stone of the wall next to the door, pulling the color off, shaping it into a small crowbar. Melina's eyebrows shot up.

"Whoa! How long have you been able to do that?"

"Forever. I just never let anyone see." She jammed the tool in the board nailed to the door and pushed down. The nails creaked as they came loose, and the door swung open. The tool lost shape and absorbed into Sophie's skin as she gestured for Melina to enter the dark apartment.

Her necklace, hidden under her shirt, pulsed hot next to her sternum. Shivers raced up her spine as she inhaled the stale air. Sophie flicked on the lights and closed the door behind her. Melina turned in a slow circle, frowning.

"Not what you'd expect, is it?" Sophie asked.

"No. Not really."

"I was shocked by it the first time as well, but once he explained, the old lady décor made sense. This was his childhood home. He killed his parents when he was a kid, but he kept everything as it was. This was how the place looked when they died. Despite the fact that he murdered them, he held onto their memories and honored them in a twisted way..." Sophie shrugged. "I guess it made sense to him."

Questions she couldn't bring herself to ask mixed with nausea in her stomach.

"Do you mind if I look around?" Melina asked.

"A little..." Sophie shook her head and sighed. "What I mean is, well, I should show you the bedroom, then I think I'm going to leave you here. I can't stand this much longer."

The two young women, both victims of this madness, looked long and deep into each other's eyes, but instead of there being a bridge of support and understanding, a feeling of animosity arose between them. Melina understood what she asked for was disgusting and offensive.

"I'm sorry. I know I shouldn't have come here. I tried to stop myself, so many times. I don't want to hurt you, Sophie. I don't want to be enemies."

Sophie shook her head again. "I'm sorry, too. What happened to you isn't your fault. This is just...odd and embarrassing."

"I'm embarrassed, too! Beyond embarrassed."

Sophie exhaled, her shoulders sagging. "Please don't ever tell anyone what I'm about to show you."

"I swear it if you promise never to tell anyone why I was here and what I asked."

"Okay. We agree this is a one and only time kind of thing. We never revisit this place or speak of these things ever again. Agreed?"

Melina nodded. "Agreed."

Sophie opened the bedroom door and flicked on the lights. Melina's breath clogged in her lungs as she walked into the room. *Oh gosh, I'm going to vomit.* She turned in a slow circle, her face hanging limp. Her gaze settled on the life-size carving of Sophie at the foot of the bed. Her whole body went cold except for the pulsing heat of her necklace against her sternum. All the muscles in the back of her neck tensed up, and her hands clenched. This was the spider's lair. His trophy case. Where he let his darkness out to play. It was worse than she imagined. If only she could surgically cut out the part of her that loved him. That part was a tumor, cancer. She wanted it out.

Sophie put her hand on Melina's shoulder. "You did the right thing."

"What? Killing him?"

Sophie nodded.

Melina's eyes wandered to the wall of sex drawings. "Was it like that with him?" Oh shit, she didn't mean to ask that. It was terrible, but it was too late to take it back.

Sophie's cheeks flushed. Melina felt like running away. How could she have asked such a thing? The next moment, Sophie snickered.

"No. Not at all. For all his charm, the man was pathetic in the sack. The only thing good about being raped by him was it was over so fast." Sophie faced her and put her hands on Melina's cheeks. "You're lucky he's gone and you're not stuck mated to such a minute man for the rest of your life."

Shame burned Mel. "That was awful of me. I'm so messed up. It just slipped out. Please forgive me for asking you that."

"Sure, forget it. Let's get out of here. There's no point wallowing in the past."

She turned to leave the room, and Mel caught her by the hand. "Wait...let's burn it. The pictures, the statue, all of it. Let's do it together."

Sophie raised one eyebrow. "I can get behind this idea."

She walked over to a dresser with candles on the top, grabbed the matches, and brought them back to Melina.

Sophie's eyes glazed. "This was my prison... He always knew what to say to make me hold still."

"Even in death, it seems he knows what to say to me as well." She put her hand over the heat of the necklace and shivered, remembering how it felt as he crushed her heart in his hand, killing her.

"This never really happened," Sophie said. "When the smoke clears I will only remember this place as a nightmare... Just a dream. I will let it fade from my mind. I will forget."

Melina admired Sophie's resolve and, maybe through force of will, could make herself believe it. She envied her. No amount of determination or brainwashing could erase Tristan from Melina's mind and heart.

Sophie struck a match and held it up between them. "Together."

Mel wrapped her fingers around Sophie's hand and together they threw the match on the bed. Side by side, they watched the fire destroy everything in the room. Neither of them budged until the fire ate everything.

Sophie shut the door and faced Melina as the fire died out. "This is over for me. I refuse to revisit anything that has to do with Tristan. Don't come back here. Don't ask me anything about him ever again. As far as I'm concerned, this never happened. I don't mean to be harsh, Mel. I just can't."

Melina shook her head. "You've done more than enough for me. I understand. Thank you. I won't seek you out again unless it's for something totally different. I hope we can still be friends in the future. I'm going to track down Destiny and make her answer for tying me to Tristan."

Sophie blinked a few times. "You're going to...That's crazy, Mel. You can't do that. It's impossible. Just move on. Do what you need to do to get over this shit and live your life."

Mel put her hood back up and stalked away. "Thanks again, Sophie." Her voice was as dejected as her heart.

Five

You can't do that. It's impossible. Just move on.
Sophie's words played on a loop in Melina's mind as she closed her apartment door and locked it. Sighing, she slumped against the door for a minute.

"She's right, you know," Tristan said from the corner. "Give up this crazy idea you could find Destiny."

Melina glanced at him and then away. "I thought you weren't speaking to me."

He shrugged. "I'm still mad at you, but I don't see—"

"I'm gonna get high now," she cut him off. "So drink a tall glass of shut the hell up and don't ruin my buzz. And don't even think about touching me if I pass out, pervert."

He chuckled and moved closer, his ghostly form sliding through the furniture in his way.

"I mean it, Tristan! Back off."

"I'd believe you more if you stopped wearing that necklace."

She scowled and took it off, clasping the stone tight in her palm. "You have a point."

He stopped, fear in his eyes. "What are you going to do?"

His reaction jolted her. Why hadn't she thought of this before? Ever since he died, she had his heart in one form or another. Was that his link to her in this world? If she destroyed it, would he be blocked from haunting her? She smiled. "If you shut up and vanish, I won't smash it. Keep bothering me, and I'll grind it to dust."

"I love you..." His whisper echoed around her as he faded into nothing.

She pinched her eyes shut and exhaled. Her hand shook around the pulsing stone. *Let go*, she ordered her hand. *Let it fall to the floor so I can break it under my foot.* Her grip tightened. She sighed again. That wasn't going to work. Well, even if she couldn't bring herself to destroy it, she didn't have to wear it anymore.

Wrapping the chain around the stone, she took it to her bedroom and tucked it in the back of her vanity drawer behind her cosmetics. She sat down and looked at herself. She'd been avoiding mirrors and anything reflective. Melina grimaced but after a second, she relaxed again. What did it matter? There was a morbid pleasure in looking this bad. Her fingers combed through her short, uneven hair. Bitter laughter rose up her throat as she realized she resembled a dust mop. The dark circles under her eyes and shaky hands added to her overall *I'm seriously messed up, don't talk to me*, look.

Her fangs began to throb and she got up, heading to her hidden stash of human blood, more than ready to go numb to the pain. Flopping down she pulled the bottle out from under her bed, uncorked it, and brought it to her lips. Sliding down her throat, the illegal human blood instantly began to make her thoughts float and her nerves exhale in ecstasy. She wasn't quite there yet. She could go higher before she passed out. Taking a deeper drink, pushing the limit of consumption to a dangerous edge, at the last second something pulled her back from breaking free.

Pain stabbed deep in her eye, sobering her a bit. *No. Not again.* The here and now broke to pieces as she was plunged into another vision. Another future memory.

Blood ran hot down from the gash on her forearm to her wrist. The sword was too heavy. Exhausted, she swung it again, connecting with nothing. Not here. Not yet. She'd never find him if she died here. It couldn't end like this. She wouldn't let it. Why was she fighting? Who was she fighting?

Her opponent jumped to the side, light glinted off their blade, burning her eyes. This was it. Death breathed down the back of her neck... Nope. Not today, you son of a bitch. Come back tomorrow. *Tired and injured, between one heartbeat and the next she remembered everything her father taught her. Her grip tightened on the sword handle, and her muscles rushed with her last shred of strength.*

Swinging her sword up, she deflected a killing strike, the blades clanging right next to her ear. Growling, she shoved their sword back with hers. She couldn't see who she was fighting, the sun burned behind them. The blades clashed again and broke. Three inches and the hilt was all she had left. Heart-rending screaming filled her ears as she plunged the broken sword into her opponent's stomach, pushing deep until half the hilt buried into the flesh. Blood gushed over her hand as she pulled it back. The woman in front of her fell into her arms.

She couldn't show her feelings. She was the victor. Still alive for one purpose, and yet she was dead inside to everything and everyone. Driven to see it through. That was all she lived for. She had to find him... Who? Who was she looking for?

A quick succession of flashes shoved her through the same thing over and over... of her killing someone. Bodies fell against whatever weapon she held, swords, axes, knives...she couldn't see the faces of the dead, but she felt the give of their flesh as her blades slid inside. So many. She killed so many. Each death marked by the deafening roar of applause.

Melina jolted awake choking on a gasp. She panted and her shirt clung to her sweat. She rubbed her eyes with the heels of her hands and swore aloud, coming down from her high and her vision at the same time. She swallowed hard, attempting to regulate her breathing, and stop the shaking of her hands. She held her hands up, almost expecting them to be gloved in blood. The pain of killing a friend rushed on her like the tide. It was real, and she curled into a ball, the pulsing, clawing agony hovered over her heart. She killed a friend. Someone she loved. It hadn't happened yet, but it would.

Taking a deep breath, she forced herself to sit up and wipe her tears away. She had to pull away from anyone she cared about, anyone she could hurt. She wasn't safe anymore. She didn't know who she was or what she was capable of. She couldn't trust herself. The future memory...the monster she would become. There was no context to what she saw herself doing but what realistic reason could there be for killing so many people? She shuddered, her stomach twisting. A beast hid beneath her skin. When would it break free?

A knock sounded on her front door. She glanced at her watch. Damn it. Dinner with her folks. That must be them. The afternoon had slid past her as she tripped and lived visions of her screwed up future. So much for things improving for her if she kept her head up and soldiered on. Melina got up and headed to the door.

The second the door swung inward and she looked at her parents a flood of sorrow swelled within her. She wasn't strong or proud or anything they had brought her up to be. Tears spilling over, she rushed at them, clinging as if she was a small, frightened child again. They didn't ask her what was wrong, they just held her between them and let her cry. She was so grateful they never wasted time or breath on things most other people blathered about.

Finding a shred of composure, she let go and wiped her nose. "Come in."

They came in, hanging their coats by the door and put the food they brought on her tiny kitchen table. She sat across from them and averted her gaze. This was one of those times she wished she had a sibling so they couldn't focus on her quite so much.

"Thanks for bringing dinner," she mumbled.

"Here, before I forget, I wanted to give you this." Netriet pulled a ring from her pocket and set it on the table in front of Melina.

Mel blinked a few times and then glanced up at her mother. "Is that what I think it is?"

Her mom smiled. "If you think it's Forest's portal ring then, yes. She gave it to me a few years ago. Said she doesn't have a use for it now Tesla's made personal portals for all their family. It still has some sentimental value to her, but she insisted. I've only used it a few times. I want you to have it. Especially since you're in a bad way right now. I want you to be able to go where you need and want to."

Melina picked it up with her thumb and index finger, a giddy excitement akin to getting the keys to your first car sparked behind the backdrop of her depression. The simple metallic ball set in a plain metal band offered freedom. With this ring, she could open portals, as many as she wanted, anywhere in Regia. The glimmer was short lived. She knew why her mom was giving her this and unfair and ungrateful as it was a rage lit by the fires a fear began to burn in her heart. The flashes of her vision washed over her again. They needed to get away from her. She would hurt them. Her thoughts didn't hold water, but she didn't take time to think before speaking.

"I see. This is so I can run home if I ever feel like killing myself again, right?"

"Watch your tone," Merick threatened.

Netriet stared her down. "You can find fault in my motivations to give you that? You're one hundred percent correct. I want you to have the ability to get to help in a moment, no matter where you are. I'll not apologize for that."

"Why are you so selfish?" Melina got to her feet.

Netriet and Merick stared open-mouthed at her.

"The hell has gotten into you?" he demanded.

Netriet grabbed his arm as he stood as well. He looked down at her, and she shook her head. "Why don't you go home ahead of me? I'll just be a few minutes."

He brushed past Melina, slamming the front door as he went out. *I'm sorry, Dad. It's better this way.*

Her mom crossed her arms and raised one eyebrow, perfectly composed. "Selfish, huh? How so?"

"I wish I'd never been born. You just *had* to have a child. You forced Dad into it, too. I know about that. He told me he didn't want me. I bet you never even thought about what kind of a freak your kid would be, or maybe you just didn't care."

"I did want you, more than I've ever wanted anything, Melina. What freakishness are you talking about?"

Melina pointed aggressively to her eye. "Polyhedron! Where your arm came from. A part of me is android. You have no idea the shit this is causing me. The things I can see." Her heart slammed fast under her ribs. She regretted every word she was saying. "I'm a murderer, Mom. It's my destiny. I can't escape it, just as I couldn't escape Tristan." Her resolve broke apart, and her voice lost its conviction. "I'm sorry. Please get away from me. I won't kill myself. Love me from far away. All I'll do is hurt you, Mom."

Netriet stood and pulled Melina against her. "Say whatever. I'll stop listening."

Tears broke loose again, and her arms shook as she held her mom. "Please. I'm begging you. Leave me."

"Never."

She pulled away, walked to the door, and opened it. "Get out." When her mom didn't budge, her heart broke harder. *"Go! Leave!"* she shouted. "There's something dangerous inside me. Don't you get that?"

Something shifted in Netriet's eyes and demeanor. "Yes. That is something I understand very well. My circumstances were different, but I pulled away from those I cared about, too, for their safety. You don't have to hurt my feelings to make me leave. I understand, and I'll give you space, so long as I know you aren't going to hurt yourself."

"I won't."

Netriet walked slowly toward her and stopped, placing her cold, robotic hand gently on Melina's cheek. "You are and always have been the light of my life. Freak or not. Murderer or not. You're my daughter. Remember where you came from. Remember what we taught you." She dropped her hand and walked out the door.

Mel closed it behind her, falling to the floor, her face in her hands, tears streaming through her fingers. Well, she was alone now... No, that wasn't right. She wasn't alone. Tristan was here. Ugh. Even if he was silent and invisible, he was here. Anxious again, she went back to her room and drank the rest of the human blood in the bottle, capturing another hour of oblivion.

The vibrating of her watch woke her.

I'm fine, M. Don't come over. She responded to his message.

I'll check on you in a few hours then. If you don't answer my messages immediately I'll come in person.

She sighed and typed, Understood.

Her throat was dry as she swallowed. The portal ring was clutched in her sweaty palm. She'd been holding it the whole time she was high. Gazing up at the ceiling, rolling the ring between her fingers she contemplated what she'd done and wondered what she should do?

Was there anything she could do to regain a sense of herself? She couldn't go back, but she couldn't continue on as she was either. It was disgusting.

Tristan stood perfectly still in the shadows of the corner, watching her. She met his gaze. Sorrow and longing pooled in his ghostly eyes.

"Why?" he whispered.

She didn't have to ask him to clarify. "I changed my mind."

"You could have just rejected me while I was alive. By killing me and now refusing to let me kill you, you've trapped both of us in a loop of despair. You know the end will be the same no matter what you do."

She pursed her lips. What had happened that night she went to the realm of the dead? She changed her mind and then what? Only blackness and pain came after that. Melina got to her feet. There was only one person who could tell her the rest of the story. She checked the time. It wasn't too late, but did the demon sleep? It seemed unlikely.

A small smirk lifted one side of her mouth as she thought about her interaction with Fluffy. Was he zero bullshit or nothing but bullshit? The thought of seeing him again made her feel almost...hopeful? He wasn't someone she could hurt, physically or emotionally.

Melina threw on a hoodie, put the portal ring on her finger, and turned it so the metal ball was in her palm before thinking where she wanted to go. She spared

Tristan a backward glance as she stepped into the black rushing hole in the atmosphere behind her.

She landed outside the boundary of Tesla and X's property. The protective magic shimmered and opened as it recognized her. She passed through, but for the first time, she didn't go up to the front door. Instead, she stalked past the main house and headed for his. *Cool place*, she thought vaguely as she came close to the small, sleek house. Clean lines, only glass, and metal. She pushed her hood off her head, took a deep breath, and knocked on the door.

Nothing. She counted to thirty and knocked again. Faint music drifted under the door. She knocked louder, then she pounded on the door with her fist. The music stopped and in a moment, the door swung inward, and she looked up into his shadowed face.

Mild surprise filled his eyes. He recovered and chuckled. "It's the killer bunny... Are you lost?"

"No. Can I come in?"

"Come in?" he repeated, incredulous.

"I want to talk to you. Do you mind?"

"Talk, huh?" He chuckled again. "Whatever." He moved aside and let her in. "You're not planning to beg me to take you back to your dead boyfriend, are you? Because if that's the case, you can save your breath."

"No. That's not it," she assured him.

A pang of jealousy twisted in her chest as she glanced around the room. The space was dark except for light coming from a hallway at the far end. Everything was obviously expensive, minimalist, and modern. Lines of water ran down the wall of glass behind the low-profile couch, making the window a water feature. Moonlight filtered through the water lines, the light bending and dancing on the glossy grey floor.

She faced him as he closed the front door. "Nice place. Mind if I sit down?"

"Are you planning to be here a while?" He was still incredulous.

"I dunno. Am I interrupting something?"

"No. Not really."

It was all the encouragement she needed, and she sat on the couch. "What was that music you were listening to?"

"None of your business." His voice was firm. He stood rigid while she stared at him. "What's with you?" he demanded.

"What do you mean?"

"You're looking right at me. No one does that. You didn't use to. I remember seeing you before, you never looked directly at me, like you are now."

She did look away then. "I'm sorry. I didn't realize eye contact made you uncomfortable."

"That's not what I meant... So, why are you here exactly?"

She focused on a spot on the floor and rubbed her hands together nervously. "Umm... You said you wouldn't rescue me, but you did. I don't remember anything after Tristan grabbed my heart. Everything was so cold and dark. I changed my mind. I made a terrible mistake... When I woke up, I was back at my apartment. Maddox said you were watching over me, but you left and wouldn't tell him anything."

"You didn't need to come here to tell me what I already know."

She looked back at him. "You saved me... Thank you."

The demon flinched and looked away. "Well...I...you're welcome. Is that what you came here to say?"

"Part of it. Why did you rescue me?"

"It pissed me off he didn't listen to you when you said you needed more time to decide... I, um, sorta felt bad that I took you there. It didn't seem right to me. You and that guy. Why would he be your life mate?"

"Oh, my gosh! Thank you!" she exclaimed emphatically, throwing her hands up. "Thank you for saying that! You see it, too! I'm so full of rage! I mean how could Destiny do this to me? What did I do to deserve being paired with that?! I can't accept it! I want to find Destiny and make her answer for this, but everyone says I'm crazy and should let it go and move on."

"Screw that. Don't listen to them. If finding Destiny is what you need to do, then do it."

Her eyes bugged. It was hard to breathe. "You...you really think I could?"

He shrugged. "Why not?"

Melina stood, her gaze locked on his. He tilted his head and blinked a few times.

"What?"

She didn't answer but took another step toward him and held out her hand. "I know you said you don't like to be touched, but would you let me touch you? Just for a moment?"

"Why would you want to?"

"Just to know. Curiosity, I guess. Does it hurt when someone touches you?"

"No, that's not it." He turned his back to her.

"What is it, then?"

"Damn it!" he shouted. "It's none of your business. Nothing here is your business. You wanted to thank me. Fine, you have. There's no reason for us to have anything else to say. Goodbye."

"All right. Be like that, jerk." She walked to the door.

"Did you seriously just called me a jerk?" he demanded.

She glared at him over her shoulder. "Yeah, so?"

He laughed, the deep gravel of his voice, full and honest, lifted the hair on the back of her neck. "I swear I've never met anyone like you, Bunny."

She turned, facing him, hopeful. "So, can I touch you?"

"No." He kept laughing. "Get out."

Dejected and confused, she opened the door but found she couldn't move to actually leave. Standing in the open doorway, she hung her head and put her hood back up. He stopped laughing. She blinked, staring at her feet. The moment dragged. She could feel his gaze on her back.

"I thought...maybe we could be friends. That's why I really came here," she whispered.

He was quiet a beat. "You're smarter than that."

She nodded and walked away, leaving the door open. "I like the sound of your voice...I guess I'm just stupid."

Hands jammed in her pockets, she stalked to the magic barrier. It shimmered for her. Unable to stop herself, she glanced back. He was standing in the doorway, looking at her. *Shit*. She cringed, covering her eye with her hand. Pain stabbed her third eye as if it was trying to push forward.

"You all right?" he asked loudly.

Holding one hand over her eye, she opened a portal behind her. She flipped him off before stepping into the rushing pull. The portal dumped her back in her bedroom. Tristan was still standing in the shadows.

"I missed you."

She rolled her eyes and huffed. Everything she felt mixed together into a poison, and it broke loose. Her gaze filled with malice, and she stared at him contemplatively. "Okay. I've had enough of this shit. Nothing is going to stay the same."

"What do you mean?"

She didn't elaborate. Sitting at her vanity, Melina sectioned off the longest of her hair on the top of her head and began to shave the rest into a short fuzz on the back and sides up to her temples. When it was even, she let down the top and trimmed it to a good length for spiking.

Tristan watched, captivated. "Not that many women are beautiful enough to pull that off. It's really sexy. I like it."

She shook off the clippings and headed to the shower. "I didn't do it for you."

Once she was clean, she dressed to go out. Tristan still hadn't moved. She sat back down at her vanity and applied her makeup and put on jewelry.

"Where are you going?"

"Out. Anywhere you aren't."

He scowled. "Dressed like that...that's dangerous."

She laughed. "Don't wait up for me, love. And don't ask me what I did when I get back. Trust me, you won't like the answer."

"Slut! Don't even think about being with someone else. You're mine! Body and soul."

She laughed again and shook her head. He continued to shout at her. She ignored him, checked the balance in her bank account, and then headed out of the apartment.

Her stride ate up the sidewalks of downtown. Paradigm didn't sleep. She was thankful for that. Self-destruction couldn't wait for morning. Her pulse rushed with excitement and a freedom she didn't know existed. She honestly didn't give one damn. Not one. Her heart raged against her life and licked at the taste of her hatred of the hand she was dealt. As if she was falling headlong from a terrible height, the ground coming up to meet her. She would smash. She welcomed it.

She turned down a dark alley. The entrance she sought was tucked discreetly in the shadows. A place she'd never been, but it was *the* one. The one everyone whispered about and warned the unwary away from going anywhere close to it. Stone steps led her down like teeth into the mouth of a monster. Adrenaline swallowed her along with the darkness, and she realized a truth...only those on the edge of death and danger knew what it felt like to be alive.

Her eyes adjusted to the dimness of the basement. Everyone there glanced at her. Ninety percent men, all looking the part, dangerous, hard asses, criminals, and dregs, probably wishing someone would come along and love them enough to save them. She met their stares with indifference. The smell was stale but not the disgusting stench she'd expected. One round table sat in the center, covered with different substances. She recognized a few, but most of them were so illegal she didn't even know their names.

A big guy came up behind her. "I'll give you three seconds to run."

"I'm not lost, buddy."

He spun her around, leaning down, putting his face three inches from hers. His gaze probed into her, searching and demanding the truth. His brows rose, and he leaned back from her. "I guess not. How hard do you want to fall, angel?"

A couple of others came up behind her until she was surrounded on all sides. One grabbed her wrist and pulled her close. "Do you have money? Or are you planning to pay us with your body?"

"Please say body," another guy said. "Not that we won't take what we want anyway."

She glanced around, amused. They were all high. If she wanted to drop them all, it wouldn't be too hard. Then one of them, a dark-haired, muscled wolf, pulled a syringe out and waved it at her back and forth like a metronome. He leered at her like prey, clearly meaning to cause terror. "Aren't' you going to scream?"

"Give me that, dog." She grabbed the syringe from his hand, stabbed the needle in her forearm, and pushed the plunger all the way down.

"Holy shit!" he exclaimed, then he laughed and pulled her away from the others. "You are one reckless broad!" It hit her head fast, and the room spun. He caught her and carried her away from the group. "Those were my drugs, so she's mine tonight, gentlemen."

SIX

Maybe we could be friends... I like the sound of your voice... can I touch you?

The demon sat on his couch and stared at the water as it slid down the window, her voice on replay in his head. Damn it. Why did he panic and send her away like that? Why didn't he tell her why he didn't like being touched and why it was important he didn't touch her again since he'd been forced to touch her once already to save her? He didn't have to think of it as personal, he could have just explained the effect touch had on him.

Maybe we could be friends...

He didn't have friends outside of X. He didn't even really consider Tesla his friend, or the rest of her family, even though they were always polite and friendly to him. It wasn't something he needed, or even if it was, it wasn't for him. He couldn't have what other people had. He lived in Regia but he wasn't Regian. There wasn't a place for him to fit, he'd stopped looking long ago. So, he was content with his job, his income, and his music.

It was enough... it had to be.

But she *looked* at him. She wasn't scared, not even a little. Was it a trick? She didn't ask for a favor or offer him some bodyguard type job. She didn't ask him to kill

113

someone for her. *Friendship.* No one had ever offered him friendship. His friendship with X came after what had started as an impersonal alliance. Friendship just happened. It wasn't offered. Was that normal? He honestly didn't know. Did people single out those they wanted to associate with and just say, 'hey, let's be friends'? It seemed odd, but not nearly as odd as a beautiful woman saying it to *him.*

Sighing, he wished he would've behaved better. She offered something freely. Something he didn't know he wanted. Something he didn't think about. But now, if he was honest with himself, her offer made him want. He looked at her in his mind and cursed her. She'd messed up his carefully balanced contentment with only a few words.

What if... He shook his head. No, friendship had to be a give and take, right? He didn't have anything to offer her in return. He wasn't good company. He didn't know how. She was a desirable woman. Regardless of what she was going through, many men would be hungry to pursue her. She didn't have any business or reason to spend time with the likes of him.

But I could help her find Destiny. That's what she wants. I could offer her that. The little voice in his head argued. He got to his feet. Sure, what the hell? He could try. He'd have to apologize first. That wasn't so hard. Not that he'd ever apologized before, but how hard could it be? *I'm sorry.* Simple enough to say. She might not accept his apology.

He strode outside and looked up at the night sky. When he touched her, the tenor of her soul imprinted on him, just faintly, but it was enough he could find her wherever she was in Regia. He closed his eyes and listened to her song. It told him what direction to go.

He couldn't open portals, but he could travel through shadow almost as quickly. The darkness of night made getting to her easy and swift.

He didn't have any expectations as to what he'd see when he did find her, nonetheless, he was shocked.

This place was... He frowned, taking stock of his surroundings. A seedy night club? No, it was worse than that. He knew she was here, but he didn't see her. None of the patrons noticed him. In the dark, they probably couldn't see him very well, and they were all intoxicated or high anyway. A small ruckus broke out in the back. He followed the noise.

"I told you she's mine for tonight."

"Stop being greedy. You've had more than enough time to do her. She's not putting up a fight. The rest of us want a turn."

"I haven't done anything to her yet, and I don't feel like sharing. The angel is so clean. Her first dirt will be mine. After I've used her good and proper, I'll hand her off to you."

The handful of men began pushing and fists started flying. Then he saw her, laid out on the nasty floor, totally incoherent, and about to be gang banged. It wasn't any wonder either, the way she was dressed in this place. Growling, he moved around the brawl, scooped her up, and swept her out of there through the shadows in the corner before the morons fighting even noticed. Damnit he was touching her again, but it couldn't be helped.

Back at his house, she moaned, her head lolling over his forearm. He didn't know that much about drug use, but he knew one of the only ways to sober someone was cold water. Bracing himself for her to scream, he propped her up in the shower, fully clothed, if you could call her outfit fully clothed, and turned on the tap. Melina didn't scream, she whimpered. Her eyes slit open, and she fell forward. He caught her under the arms, holding her away from him. The water splashing over her pelted the backs of his hands. Dangerously touching her again, the sound and feel of her soul growing stronger inside him. This was what he was trying to avoid. Touch built awareness and knowledge of her like intense memories.

Spirit and water mixed. The hell? He almost dropped her as he tried to yank his hands back, but he managed to hold on and drag her forward out of the fall of water. The undulating haze of his body clung to the water on her skin. Where he touched her painted a mark. His black smoke mixed into the water, turning it dark like ink and spread lines over her body. Twisting, intersecting vines and patterns. He needed to break contact with her, but he didn't want to drop her, so he lowered her to the shower floor in a sitting position instead so the water could continue to help sober her.

"Rain..." She moaned the word out in such a way a jolt went through him. Melina arched her back and said it again. "Rain."

"It's not raining. You're in the shower."

Her eyes snapped open and even though she looked at him, it was obvious she wasn't really seeing him. Her eyes had changed. He knew for sure they were different than before. Her eyes were chiseled into his mind down to the smallest detail because she was the only person to stare at him the way she had. Now her right eye was more grey than brown and both of her pupils were tiny, sharp, star shapes.

She sighed and reached for him. "Don't leave me alone, Rain."

He moved back. "Wake up!"

She didn't. Her eyes stayed the same creepy way. She held her hands up, gazing at the designs on her skin and smiled. "Pretty. How far does it go?" Her voice took on a dreamy quality as she stood and began to pull her clothes off, searching her body for more designs. He turned his back to give her some privacy, but he'd still seen a lot. The next minute she turned off the tap and sauntered past him. Grabbing the towel on the hook, she wrapped it around herself and went straight for his room.

"Hey," he protested, following her.

She threw the towel at him and slid sinuously into his bed. All he could think was, *that escalated quickly*.

"What are you doing?"

"Hmm?" She closed her eyes. "I'm tired."

He just stood there in shocked disbelief, staring at her as she rolled to her side, pulling the sheet with her, and fell asleep. There was a naked woman in his bed. He laughed and had to cover his mouth. If only he was mortal, it would make this so much better. Hmm...how long had it been since he'd had such a thought? He wasn't a sexual being, but still, staring at the outline of her body...he couldn't look away. The marks on her skin faded and then vanished completely.

The song of her soul quieted to a faint hum as she dropped into a deeper sleep. He'd touched her too much. He was stuck with the awareness of her, probably forever. At least the tenor of her didn't annoy him. He rather liked the sound.

He smiled to himself as he continued to stare at her. She had given him another break in his routine. So what was he supposed to do now? Just let her sleep it off? What about when she woke up? This was awkward. She'd probably be embarrassed. She might be angry at his interference, but he couldn't stomach the idea of just leaving her to the guys fighting over her. Why was she in a place like that anyway? He thought about her dead life mate and it made more sense. She was trying to go numb. Hmm...he could help with that, too.

Her hair was different, he noticed. Better than before, but he thought back to the long platinum blonde mane she used to have. Frowning, he realized he knew more about her than he thought, or rather, that he'd noticed her before. His frown deepened. He'd always been aware of her. No matter what she did when she woke up, he would remember this night forever.

She grimaced and moaned. He came closer. Her eyes moved quickly back and forth behind her closed eyelids. She was dreaming. Melina curled in on herself, her hands gripping the sheet. Then she cried out. Nightmare, he thought. Touching her pulse and listening closely to her breathing, he gauged how stoned she was. She was beyond being shaken awake. The resonance of her soul grew louder as her heart raced. He couldn't wake her, but he could chase her nightmare away.

Heading down the short hall, he opened the door to his sanctuary. His music room. Instruments from Earth, Regia, Mordian, and many other worlds lined the walls. He contemplated the sound of her soul, chose his favorite acoustic guitar, and took it back to the bedroom. With nowhere else to sit, he climbed on the bed next to her and leaned against the headboard.

He turned the knobs to reach notes only he knew and began to play. The tune mixed with the resonance of her soul, but that alone wasn't enough to really change her nightmare, he had to sing.

His voice grabbed the atmosphere in the room and reshaped it to suit him. Time slowed, the clock's second hand halted, and instead of ticking, it hovered back and forth between six and seven, not going far enough to either side to engage the gears. He sang through the song once, not paying attention to the words, he mostly hummed. He couldn't see into her head. He didn't know what she was dreaming, only her spiritual response to it. His voice held her captive in the moment. The world didn't change, the night didn't mature, nothing moved ahead in this place only his voice could reach. There was no rush. He could keep her here until he was ready to let her move forward.

Time was halted, but he moved when everything else was frozen. He sang a lullaby to the woman beside him. The sound of her soul vibrated one long endless note through his head. Mixing the sound with his music until the agitation in her sound eased. It was enough. Her muscles relaxed again. He put the guitar on the floor and lay down next to her. Time restarted and marched on as usual.

Bemused at his actions, he stared into her face, close but careful not to touch her. He'd never made time echo for anyone, not even X. No one knew he could do that. It was intimate knowledge he held close to his chest. Melina wouldn't be aware of it when she woke, so his secret was safe.

His body hurt. Why? Why had he shared his gift with her? It didn't matter that she slept. Shit. He was scared. His ability to affect time was the only clue he had to his real identity. Forget it. Forget it. She doesn't know. She won't remember. It doesn't matter.

He continued to gaze into her sleeping face. Damn, she was beautiful... If only he was mortal.

Oh, hell, what had she done? Her memory of last night was as shaky as her hands. She was coming down hard. Whatever she'd injected wasn't her type of high, and she had no desire to have it again. Fully awake, she'd yet to open her eyes. She knew she wasn't in her own bed, and she wasn't quite ready to face the consequences and see who'd she'd ended up with out of that pack of low lives.

The sheet was soft and slippery against her skin and it smelled good. That was unexpected. Steeling herself, she dragged her eyes open and stared at a light grey ceiling. Blowing out a breath, she turned her head to the side and looked at her one-night stand.

She blinked her eyes at super speed, her mouth hanging open. The next moment her laughter was so loud it echoed around the room.

"What's funny?" he asked.

She continued to laugh as she lifted up the top of the sheet just to confirm she was naked.

"There are no words," she chortled. "Oh, my gosh!"

"Melina?"

"Okay, okay, I'm sorry if my laughing hurt your feelings."

"Umm...that's not...I mean..." He stumbled over his words.

"I knew when I went out last night, ending up in a strange bed with a strange person was a possibility, if not damn near guaranteed...I just never, and I mean *never*, thought for one second it would be you!" She broke out laughing again. "You have to tell me what you did to me."

"I don't think that's a good idea. Wouldn't want to embarrass you."

"What? I need to know."

To her surprise, he smirked or seemed to. "If you can't remember, that's not my problem."

The humor faded, and her cheeks burned. She put her hands on her face as she remembered her interaction with him before she went to get high, when he kicked her out.

"You more or less said you didn't want to be my friend. You should have clarified you were more interested in being lovers."

He sighed, a purely irritated sound, and got up off the bed. "We didn't do anything, Melina. I can't. I'm not capable of sexual acts. You were passed out before I found you."

"Why am I naked then?"

"You were about to be gang-raped in that basement. Aside from wanting to wash off the filth you picked up from the floor, you were not lucid. I thought cold water would sober you. You're the one who decided to take off your clothes."

Her cheeks had never been so hot. "Oh...umm...why were you looking for me anyway?"

"I want to be friends. I wanted to apologize and tell you that. I think I can help you find Destiny."

"I see." She rolled away from him so he couldn't see her smile. "I should warn you, I'm a train wreck. I'm probably not good friend material."

He chuckled. Then he laughed harder. "I should shun you, then?"

"I don't want you to, but yes. Probably."

"Yeah. I'm scared." Heavy sarcasm.

She rolled back to face him. "I'm possessive, I have visions, I get violent, and..." She sighed and closed her eyes. "I'm a blood addict."

"I actually knew all that except the possessive bit. In return, I'm ugly, I'm a social outcast, I have no idea how to have friends, and I think I stared at you way too much last night."

"How could you know about my visions?"

"When you were stoned last night, your eyes went strange, and you spoke nonsense."

"Damn. I don't remember it. I always remember them, not that I've ever had one that excites me about my future. It must have been the drugs, why I can't remember."

"You sounded sorta *excited* when it was happening."

Raising her eyebrows, she smirked at his inference. "Really? It sounded hot?"

He shrugged and looked away. "Yeah."

"Are you blushing?" she teased.

"No. I don't think so. No."

"You are! You totally are!"

He cleared his throat over the sound of her laughter. "Since I offended you when you asked if you could touch me, I wanted to explain my response...and I'm trying to derail our conversation from its current direction."

She snorted. "You're kind of a blurter aren't you?"

"Blurter?"

"It's cool. I think that might be something I could come to like about you. It will make it easier for me to trust you. Most people wouldn't admit they were trying to derail a conversation."

"Why not? It's the truth. How can we be friends if we aren't honest? I thought that was a major part of being friends. I can deceive if I want to, but it seems like a waste of time."

She sat up, pulling the sheet around her body. "So what's your deal with touch?"

"It forms a connection. My appearance scares most people so they keep their distance, but that works for me so it's not that hard to avoid touching others. I touched you when I saved you from your mate. That was how I was able to find you last night. I can hear you. Before I touched you, I couldn't hear."

"Hear what?" she asked.

"Your soul...like your fingerprint, is unique. You are the only one who sounds the way you do. The more I touch you, the deeper the connection I will have to you. I know things about you no one else could ever know because they cannot hear what I do."

"Wow. That's amazing, and a little frightening at the same time. I guess I wouldn't touch many others either if it was like that for me. It sounds really intimate."

"It is."

She shifted, thinking about what he said. "Well..." She knew what she should say but the words felt stuck in her mouth. "I'm sorry my *sound* was forced on you."

To her surprise, he laughed. "I was, too. At first, anyway. Now I'm attached to the sound of you. I like it. And if we can maintain a friendship, it will remain a sound I enjoy hearing."

She smiled. "What do I sound like?"

He shook his head. "I can't...you wouldn't be able to comprehend it. Your ears are deaf to the notes and music I speak of."

"Do you think you hear it because you're dead?"

"I'm not dead!" he snapped, his eyes flashing.

Okay. She mouthed the word silently. "Obviously I touched a nerve."

He huffed and crossed his arms. "I'm not dead," he repeated in a calmer tone. "I don't know what I am, but I'm not dead. X tested it and confirmed it many years ago. The only thing I do know for sure is I'm damned."

"Surely you know more about yourself than that, Fluffy."

"Okay, that's something else. Don't call me that. It's not my name."

"But, I've always..."

"It was a joke. X thought he was funny when he called me that the day we met and I swore myself to him. I didn't fight it because..." He looked away and sighed. "I don't know my name."

"So pick one. Since being called Fluffy pisses you off. I can understand that, by the way. I wouldn't want my name to be a joke."

He shook his head. "It's too late. It's the name people know me by. I don't want another fake name. I'll remain like this until I know my real name."

"Is there a way to learn your real name?"

He was quiet for a minute. She waited.

"Can we talk about something else?" His voice was barely more than a whisper.

"Sure. Where are my clothes?" She scooted to the edge of the bed and stood up, totally unashamed, and faced him.

"Geez," he said under his breath.

Melina put her hands on her hips as his gaze roamed over her.

"I thought you weren't like that. You said you couldn't—"

"I can appreciate…nice looking things," he retorted, still leering at her.

"*Nice looking things?*" Her voice oozed sarcasm. "Wow. What a compliment."

"You're stacked like a stripper, if you'd prefer me to be frank."

She laughed. "That's better."

"Your clothes are hanging up in the shower. They should be dry."

She walked down the middle of the hall as though she owned it. His gaze was hot on her ass. A smile played at the edges of her mouth. He didn't understand friendship… It must just be the traces of his lost mortality that made him even the least bit interested in looking at her like that.

The size of the house made it easy to find the bathroom. She didn't remember being in there last night, and she was jealous. The space was so nice and sleek. She really loved his posh little house.

Her clothes were still a little damp but she put them on anyway.

"Sheesh!" She jumped as she turned around and found him watching from the doorway. "Don't do that!"

He smirked. "Do what? You can't possibly mean give you privacy after the way you just behaved in my bedroom."

She huffed trying to hang on to her annoyance, but it proved impossible. "Don't sneak up on me… I'll get out of your hair now. I'm going home."

"When will you be back?"

"When do you want me to come back?"

"Um… Dusk, I guess. Does that work for you?"

She nodded and smiled. "That works."

He walked behind her as she made her way to the front door. "Wear normal clothes when you come back, please. We might go hunting."

"Hunting?" she giggled.

"Hunting Destiny, yes. Wear shoes you can run in if the need arises."

Excitement flashed in her heart. "Okay. I'll remember. See you later… Um, is it okay if I call you F, for the time being?"

"That's tolerable," he conceded.

She glanced back after she crossed outside the barrier, just as she had the last time, only now she waved instead of flipping him off. The ring opened a portal for her back to her apartment. The lightness in her heart crashed when she landed back in her living room and immediately spotted Tristan skulking in the corner.

"Thank goodness you're back. I've been so worried." He sounded sincere.

"Get lost," she snapped. "Unless you want me to crush the necklace right now?"

"Melina, please… Just be with me for a minute. I won't talk if that's how you want it." He moved toward her. "Please just let me touch you."

"No. Not today."

"When?"

The ghost thread that tied her to him gave a little tug. She hated there was even a glimmer of longing. The longing existed there against her will. But she wasn't going to live with it. She smiled to herself as she thought about what F said. They were going hunting tonight. She would take her first step toward freedom with the help of her new friend. Dusk couldn't come fast enough.

As soon as Melina left, the demon walked over to Tesla and X's house and let himself in the side door, as was his habit. Neither of them were in the main areas of the house. Music thumped through the walls from Tesla's workshop. He knew not to disturb her when the music was blasting like that.

"X?" he said loudly.

"In the study."

He walked down the hall to the end and into the study. X's white-blonde head was bent down as he made notes on an evidence form for Fortress. "What's up? I don't think there's anything happening at work today," he said, not looking up from the paper.

"Yeah. About work, I'm going to be taking some time off."

X did look up then. "Oh?"

"I've got a little project that might take some time to finish. It's not a problem, right?"

"No. No problem. Take as much time as you need, but you've got me curious what you're up to since you never take vacations."

"It's personal."

"Ha!" X leaned back in his chair, smiling broadly. "Now I'm *really* curious."

"Don't go sticking your nose in my business just because your life is so boring."

"Oh, those are fighting words. Don't force me to trap you in one of my palm stones."

They both chuckled and Fluffy sat down. "Actually, I was hoping you could help me. I want to find Destiny."

X frowned and tapped his index finger against his lips. "Hmm...that's sketchy."

"I know. I have an idea where to start, but I was wondering what you knew if anything. I'm interested in even the most outlandish and unreliable information."

"What is this about? Are you finally ready to learn your identity?"

"Huh? Oh, no that's not what I'm after." Fluffy assured him. "I've not changed my mind about that."

"You know I'll help you when you're ready."

"I know, but I still feel the same way I used to. Tracking down Destiny is for a friend."

X grinned. "Made a new friend? I didn't realize you were being more social these days."

"You heard what happened to Melina?"

X nodded gravely. "Yeah. Sucks big time...oh, I see." A mischievous light lit X's eyes. "Pretty girl in trouble and you're going to swoop in and save her?"

"Exactly that, prick." His teasing tone died out as he thought about her. "She's different. She looks at me... It was her idea, to be friends, I mean. She's the one who asked if I would."

"Congratulations." There was nothing false or mocking in X's voice when he said it.

Fluffy cleared his throat. "I want to be able to do this for her. Do you know anything or not?"

"The only thing I can think of is to ask Jin."

Fluffy sighed. "Yeah, that was what I was thinking as well. The problem is taking Melina to him... Jin will exact a price for his help. You know how he is."

"You've dealt with him more than I have. When Tesla stops blasting that music, I'll talk to her. She might have a few ideas for you."

"You really can't think of anything else? With all the world jumping you've done?"

"Not off the top of my head. You've traveled as much or more than I have. I'll keep thinking about it, but that's all I've got at the moment."

"Okay. Thanks...oh and could we just keep this to ourselves for now?" he asked.

"Just you, me, and Tesla. Is there someone, in particular, you don't want to know about this?"

"Yeah, Maddox. He's protective and possessive of Melina. I've seen it. If she's going to tell him, that's her decision, and I'm sure he'll find out eventually. I'd just rather that was later and not sooner."

"You got a problem with Maddox?"

"No. But I will if he interferes in my friendship with Melina."

Seven

Nerves and excitement bounced around inside Melina's stomach along with a pang of embarrassment as she strode up to his door. She was a little early, but she was so anxious to see him again that she found it too hard to wait any longer. Dressed casually in jeans, a black tee-shirt, and combat boots, she decided to forgo putting on any jewelry, but she couldn't stop herself from applying a little makeup.

It felt so good to be doing something proactive about her Tristan problem. She had to acknowledge that some of her excitement and nerves had nothing to do with the prospect of hunting down destiny. Hand raised to knock on his front door, she hesitated as yet again she heard music. The sound was muffled. She stopped breathing and stood perfectly still, trying to hear better. The notes grabbed a hold of her mind, and her consciousness drifted lazily to another place.

Her eye twinged, like a warning. The pain jolted her mind back to the present, and she knocked loudly on the door. The music stopped immediately and, in a moment, he opened the door. She could feel her smile was a little too broad, too eager, but she couldn't control it.

"Hey, F. I'm a little early, but I didn't have anything else to do." She lifted up the bag she carried. "I brought food. Probably stupid of me. I don't know if you eat. I just thought I'd bring enough for both of us, just in case."

He stepped aside. "Come in."

He shut the door behind her and took the bag from her hand, taking it to the kitchen and setting it on the counter.

"I don't need to eat, but I do sometimes just to try to feel normal. Just as I don't need a bed for sleeping. It's pathetic, but sometimes I pretend I'm just like everyone else, so I do the things they do... The food smells good, I think I'll have some. Thanks for bringing it."

Melina knew everything about where she was and what she was doing was odd as she sat at the counter and he got plates out, but she didn't care. Odd or not to sit and have dinner with the demon, she was enjoying herself.

"So, what did you do today?" she asked.

"Prepared for tonight mostly. What about you?"

"Not much of anything. I talked to Maddox for a while, just to set his mind at ease, and let him know I wouldn't be answering his messages tonight, but not to freak out and come looking for me."

"Did he accept that?"

"Yeah. He's still worried about me. Both he and Erin tend to helicopter. It will probably take some time before they will accept that it's safe for me to be on my own, and they don't have to check on me constantly."

"Did you tell them anything else?" he asked. "Do they know what you're trying to do?"

She frowned and looked away. "I didn't mention it. They know what I want, but they've said what everyone else has said, that it's impossible and I should just move on. I don't want to hear that anymore." She stabbed at her food and chewed with more force than was necessary.

"We're going somewhere very dangerous tonight, unless you change your mind."

His words created a rush of excitement up her body. "Sounds good to me. Dangerous how?"

He didn't answer but tilted his head a little to the side and looked long and intently at her. She squirmed and looked down. His gaze felt like a thorough investigation.

"Why are you looking at me like that?"

"Just trying to understand you better... To answer your other question, the danger will be in you agreeing to more than you can afford to pay, and me getting you out in one piece."

"Pay?" She lifted her eyebrows. "For what?"

"Information." He set a small vial of blood in front of her. "That's Tesla's blood. If you drink it, I will be able to take you to the Everpath. We have to jump to another world and reach a dark place."

"I'm not afraid of the dark."

"I know that, Bunny. But are you afraid of dragons?"

She snickered. "You're joking right?"

"Not at all."

She blinked at him a few times. "Dragons really exist?"

"Yep."

Her excitement grew another layer. "Awesome. Do you think this dragon will want to eat us for dinner?"

"Not likely. Jin is...particular in every way. Ancient, but his age only makes him stronger. The origins of things are his specialty."

"How do you know him?" she asked.

"We used to play poker."

"Seriously?"

He nodded. "Seriously. He likes games. Just watch your mouth with him. If you agree to something he'll bind it on you."

"Okay. Anything else?"

"Stay beside me at all times. He might try to separate us."

She stared at him. It was his turn to squirm.

"What?" he asked.

"As you said... Just trying to understand you better. You're really different, F."

He held his hands out as if to give a theatrical bow. "Obviously. I'm the only one of my kind in Regia."

"I don't mean the way you look or what you are. You say and do things that confuse me. I don't have a handle on you. I'm used to men treating me either as a friend or a love interest. I get comradery or chivalry... You give me neither...and both. I'm not complaining. I like it. I just don't understand yet. You're willing to put me in danger."

He pushed the vial of Tesla's blood closer to her. "Ride or die."

She reached for the vial and uncorked it. Her gaze met his, steady and defiant. She held his gaze as she brought it close to her lips and smiled. "If only you were..." She didn't finish the thought but drank the blood.

Lightning ran all through her veins as the blood slid down her throat. Ecstasy mixed with adrenaline, and she braced her hands on the counter, pinched her eyes shut, and bit down on her lips to keep from moaning. Tesla's blood turned her inside out and upside down leaving her with a sense she could do anything.

"That was incredible to watch." His voice broke through her reverie.

Opening her eyes, Melina gasped. Is this how Tesla saw the world? She turned in a circle. Invisible curtains and doors were everywhere, but she could see the shape of them as one sees the wind in its effect on its surroundings. Light rays from cracks in the atmosphere broke her heart with their odd beauty and colors. Then she looked at him and staggered back a step, covering her right eye with her hand. The eye inside her eye was pushing to the surface again. Her pulse sped up, and her throat grew tight. She forced herself to swallow before dropping her hand and looking at him again.

"Wow," she breathed.

He shifted as though self-conscious. "What?"

"You look different. I can almost see the shape and features of a man behind all that smoke. I mean I could sorta see a solid core to you before now but...it looks like I could blow all that away and then I could really see you."

"Maybe some other time."

"Why not now?" She took a step closer.

"The effect of Tesla's blood will wear off. We need to go and get back before that happens."

She chuckled. "You're shy."

"No. That's not it...I don't think that's it."

She chuckled again. "Okay, let's go see the dragon."

He set a small box on the counter and opened it. She watched his hands closely, intrigued at the change she could see in his body. He truly had two layers. The smoke on the outside, always moving, and a solid shape underneath. She could see through the smoke better than ever. She could make out the definition of his arms and his height. He wasn't as tall as his exterior, not even typical ogre height. Tall, really tall, but not so much that she would feel like a small child in his embrace.

Okay, that was a weird thought. She shook herself and focused back on the orb swelling out of the top of the box like a huge soap bubble. It rose up into the air and floated past her. A spark ignited in the center. F came up beside her and moved toward the orb.

"Come on." He reached out and touched it. It broke open into a portal. She followed him through, her heart striking hard and fast like the blacksmith's hammer on a glowing new blade.

Het boots hit a sleek, light grey floor, and she straightened up. "So this is the Everpath?"

"This is it."

Melina's stomach swooped as she stared down the hallway. She couldn't see the end. Perfectly straight, the hall stretched out before her, lined on both sides with plain, identical doors, all perfectly spaced. She turned and looked down the other way. It was the same. Fear tickled the back of her neck. Was there an end at all?

"Relax," F said.

"It's creepy as hell."

"True enough. And there are many dangers. But you're safe with me. I've spent a lot of time here. Don't

worry. We won't get lost. This door is the one we want."
He opened the door to her right and walked into the
shadows within. She followed. The door closed behind
them.

The smell of old books and incense filled her lungs.
The air was dry and warm. Firelight danced in the four
corners of the immense room. The light winked off a
mountain of treasure piled against the far wall.
Bookshelves from floor to the 300-foot ceiling lined all
the other walls. She looked up, craning her neck back as
far as it would go, getting her first glimpse of the
dragon.

The magnificent beast hung from the ceiling, upside
down like a bat. Her pulse sped again as she gaped in
awe. His wings fanned out from his body, lazily moving
like a lounging cat absentmindedly flicking its tail. The
dragon was everything she could have imagined and
hoped for and yet she still found herself surprised by
him. He was the color of midnight. A deep metallic blue
tipped the ends of every scale. He held the book up
close to his face, carefully turning the pages with the
end of one long claw.

She was certain he was aware of their presence, but
he was ignoring them. His nostrils flared, and tiny sparks
danced playfully from his nose as he exhaled. His eyes
settled on her, and her heart gave a hiccup. She gulped
as he closed the book and turned his gaze to F.

"It's been a while, demon. I've missed our little games.
But you didn't come to play, did you? You've brought
someone with you. That's out of character."

The dragon's voice rolled so deep she felt the vibration in her bones. She took a few steps back as the dragon dropped from the ceiling, his wings slowing his descent to the floor. The talons on his feet dug into the stone floor as if it was made of soft sand. His long neck curved with serpentine grace, bringing his head down until he looked her in the eye. Melina swallowed but returned his gaze. His eyes were like diamonds, a strange fire behind them. Just facing something of such size and power made her adrenaline rush harder than it ever had. So much danger looking her right in the eyes.

"Who's this?" The dragon flashed his perfect teeth in a wide smile as he spoke. His teeth, like his eyes, looked as if they were cut from diamonds, and his breath was so hot it dried out the surface membrane of her eyes. "A gift? A sacrifice? A bride?"

"None of those. She has a question, Jin," F said.

"Ah, yes," the dragon purred. "A question only I can answer? I'm glad you brought her. Beautiful, and she smells amazing. I can hear her heart in her chest." His eyes reflected light into hers. "Unique creature. Her origins are singular. Her ability has a flavor I've not encountered before." He inhaled, sniffing at her. "Seer."

"Why don't you just tell her you fancy her in a normal way?" F asked, crossing his arms over his chest.

"Where's the fun in that?" The dragon shifted to the side, moving all the way around her and F only to slide back to where he'd been before, his strange eyes burning as they settled on hers again. "It's been a long time since I met someone new. How can I live up to the hype if I act normal?" Jin heaved a great sigh, sparks floating out of his mouth. "What do you want to ask me that you cannot learn on your own, Seer?"

Her tongue was stuck for a second. "I...How can I find Destiny? Where do I need to go?"

"Hmm..." His voice rumbled, sending a tremor through her chest. "Destiny. So sad. So bitter, not that I blame her. I will answer half of what you want to know and then we will discuss my fee for the rest."

She held her breath. She must not miss a single word he said.

"The answer to *where* lies in your own world."

"What?"

"My turn...if you want the rest of your answer, down the last detail of exactly where to go, how, and even what to say when you get there, along with whatever history you might like of why Destiny exists and what drives her, you must give me your shiny third eye."

"My ey—" she clamped her mouth shut as she remembered F's warning. She had to guard her words. He would try to trip her up. "Why that?" she asked.

"Obsessive love for treasure is in my blood. You have something interesting. I want it."

She glanced at F. He held himself rigid. Melina tried to weigh her words, but she needed to know the answer to her question more than she needed anything.

143

"If I agree, you have to also tell me his name." She inclined her head toward F.

"Leave me out of this," F snapped. "This is about you."

"You already know his name," Jin hissed.

"No, I don't."

He lifted one long spiked claw and pointed it directly at her right eye. The tip was so close, her eyelash skimmed it when she blinked. "Right there. You've seen his name." The dragon pulled back, chuckling. "You know it, but I can remind you, since you've forgotten. Now, will you pay me what I ask?"

She thought about for a second. Losing her visions would be a blessing. "I don't have any great love for it. I can live with one eye… How would you remove it?"

He flicked his knife-like claws at her. "These are sharp enough. Now, say it. Say I can have your eye."

She exhaled. "You can have my eye."

The dragon's tail whipped out, wrapping around her legs like a snake. It dragged her closer, coiling her up, pinning her arms to her sides. He brought his face so close to hers, the heat of his breath left her feeling sunburned.

"Now you're mine, and you shall stay here with me forever. If I plucked out your eye it would be nothing but dead flesh. So, I will have your eye as you've promised me, and the rest of you as well. Now see something for me, Seer."

She strained pointlessly against his hold, barely able to fill her lungs. "It doesn't work like that. I can't see your future, only glimpses of my own."

The dragon laughed a throaty chuckle. "Soon you will. I'm going to keep you, so our futures are now tied together. Soon you will see my future."

"Hey, Bunny?" F asked loudly. "You cool with this arrangement?"

"No. Can't say that I am."

"A contract with a liar is no contract, Jin. You always cheat and deceive. Let her go." Authority and warning laced F's tone.

Jin reared up on his hind legs, opened his terrible mouth, and blasted F with a line of fire.

F laughed. "Did you really think that would work?"

"No, but I've wanted to test it since the last time you beat me at cards."

Melina's eyes widened as F rushed at the beast and punched him in the chest. A ripple went out over the dragon, and he coughed, fire flashing from his mouth in strangled bursts. He coughed a few more times and cleared his throat.

"Ow... I think you cracked my sternum."

"Let her go."

The tail coiled around her again, pulling her closer to the dragon's body. "I never let go of anything after I've claimed it. She's now a part of my collection. I will kill her before I let go."

"You and I are about to have a real problem."

"Why? What is she to you?"

F looked at her, and a jolt clenched her heart. He didn't take his eyes off her as he answered the dragon. "She's my friend."

"If that is true, why did you bring her here? I suppose you didn't realize the way she would appeal to me. Is it perhaps because you don't fear bodily harm? The fact that you can't die has blinded you... That's too bad. I'm keeping her. She's so soft. Fragile. You should have taken better care of her. But you need not worry. I won't harm her... You can come to visit her, but she's mine."

"I'm not property, beast." Her voice echoed around the great room. "Turn me loose, or kill me."

"You think I fear your temper?" Jin asked her.

"You should fear mine," F interjected.

The dragon straightened up, his eyes and teeth flashing. "Bring it on. Show me."

"Killing you would be a shame...are you sure you want to force the issue?"

The dragon laughed, his wings opening. Wind blasted through the space as he launched into the air, flying back to the ceiling. Wrapped in his tail, Melina was jerked sideways and up as he went. F remained where he stood, looking up at them.

"Is that all, Jin? You're just going to run?"

"Hardly." The dragon grabbed a huge book off the shelf, threw it into his mouth, and swallowed. "Let me see what you can do with this, demon."

He opened his mouth, fire falling from his throat like a waterfall. Twisted figures rushed in the fire toward F. He rose up to his full height as the mob of creatures landed on the floor, surrounding him. They all sort of looked like him, black and smoky with burning red eyes. But where F was broad, they were skinny, their long, sword-like hands dragged on the ground behind them.

"Bastard," F snarled up at Jin.

Melina froze inside as the creatures crashed into F all at once.

"What did you do?" she shouted at the dragon.

He laughed, watching the brawl below. "I can't do any damage to him, but those are scathers. Bottom-feeders of the dead. They'll mess him up but he'll probably be okay."

"Probably?"

"Should be a good show. If they get a good hold on him, they'll drag him back to the hell he came from."

Her eyes were glued to the fight below. F tried to fight off the scathers, but there were too many. He knocked one back and six more grabbed him from behind.

"He can't win. Please stop them!" she pleaded.

Jin turned his full attention to her, bringing his face close to hers. "You have nothing left to bargain with. You belong to me completely."

"Okay, fine. I'm yours, but if you don't call those things off him, I'll never speak to you. Not ever. I'll make myself completely worthless."

The dragon laughed again and turned his face back to the fight. "Pout as much as you like and for however long. I'm not fussed."

There was nothing for her to do. She couldn't move at all. She tried to clear her head but it was flooded with panic. The panic pissed her off. Her throat clogged as F vanished under the pile of scathers. Had they won? Would they take him back where he came from? Would she ever see him again? Everything seemed to stop...almost. All movement of the monsters swarming below slowed. A ripple moved through the air. Her heart beat and strained to beat again, stuck in between.

The pile of scathers exploded backward as time accelerated. F looked up at her, and she swore he smiled.

"Stimulating as this has been, I'm ready to end it. I'm taking her back now."

Jin's tail constricted tighter. One second, that was all she had left. She couldn't fill her lungs again, not even to gasp. Her bones and internal organs compressed in on themselves. *It's over. This is it.* Her ribs boke first. Unconsciousness began to rub her down. Before she could blink, F was rushing toward her, monsters like a black wave rising up behind him. Fire and darkness. Showered in sparks, glinting diamonds, and a dragon's furious growl. She closed her eyes.

Blood rushed through her veins again as the coils dropped away. No, that wasn't it. Warmth rushed up from her feet and slid over and through her like silk in a breeze. She was still surrounded but now there was no pain. Arms held her from behind. She looked down, bringing one hand up, and running it along the muscled forearm that held her. They were engulfed in grey smoke. F had her. All her worry vanished. She leaned her head back against his chest, her third eye expanding. Rhain. She remembered now. His name is Rhain.

His body was vibrating. She tried to feel her heart to confirm she was alive or dead. It beat, then held again. Time went hazy.

She looked up sideways at him and gaped. That's what he looks like under all the smoke? Damn. I'm moving him out of the friend zone. She wanted to turn in his embrace and face him so she could get a better look but she couldn't move. The vibration coming from him turned into violent shaking. His hold on her turned into a death grip, even so, it was gentle. It didn't hurt at all.

Dropping, breaking, gasping, they fell together through floors and barriers but all she could see was the dancing smoke. She closed her eyes again and rested against him, enveloped in complete trust.

The peace she felt broke apart as time raced forward and the ground jolted under her feet, making her ankles burn. Her equilibrium swooped in a sideways flip. The air shredded her lungs as she coughed. She blinked, seeing her hands braced on the grey floor of his living room. For a moment she just needed to stare at the floor, feeling the relief that they were back in Regia.

His hands ran over her back. "Melina? Are you all right?"

She turned around, sitting on her butt, and looked up at him. She didn't feel all right. Her ribs were broken. Her whole body felt rubbery. But he was more interesting than anything at the moment.

"Your name is Rhain."

He recoiled from her. "Don't do that."

"What?"

"Don't make shit up."

Melina shrugged but she was far from letting it go. "What did you just do to me?"

"I had to...sort of...absorb you. I'm sorry that didn't work out the way you hoped and you didn't get your answer. I'm sorry you got hurt."

Grimacing, she got to her feet, as her ribs ground together. "Well, that was quite the experience. I thought you were going to be torn apart by those monsters, and I was going to be stuck forever as a dragon's pet. But I can say I'm not sorry for any of it. It was a total rush! I got some of my answer, and I learned your name."

"Jin didn't tell you my name," he argued.

"No, he didn't. And I had no memory of knowing it, but just now, whatever it was you did to get me out. Being that close to you...I remembered it. Rhain."

"Stop it!"

Unperturbed she took a step closer to him and then another. His heatwaves feathered on her skin. "I saw your face. I felt your arms. The part of you that's hidden. I want to see it again. Can I just walk through the smoke?"

He didn't answer. He just gazed down at her. He looked impervious, but she knew better. He was afraid. He could face a dragon with no hesitation, but not her. She smiled and moved closer. The smoke tickled and teased her skin. She walked into him.

The room vanished. All she could see were waves of smoke and him in the center. Not a monster, but a man. He was all monochrome, but she didn't need or care to know what his coloring had been in life. Nothing about his appearance was smooth. He looked like a barbarian warlord. His hair hung past his shoulders in coiled dreadlocks and his jaw was shadowed with stubble. His strong brow pulled in a frown, as his lips set in a tight line. His eyes were the same hellfire red she'd seen before through his exterior. She wondered that they didn't bother her. They *affected* her with their sharpness, cutting straight through her, but she wasn't repelled. Her brain twisted a bit over the backward feeling she was experiencing. To know and care for someone, like and value them, all the while not knowing what they really looked like. Then to learn afterward a serious hottie was hidden underneath.

He wore only a plain pair of pants but his clothes were the same color as the rest of him, like a ghost always wearing what they died in. His huge muscled arms crossed over his bare chest. She moved closer. There was a mark on his chest under his crossed arms. She could see the edges of it. Something about it drew her in, like a memory. She needed to see it.

"Rhain..."

A visible shiver rolled over his skin. "Why are you sure that's my name?"

"Why are you sure it's not? I think I had a vision about you when I was stoned. That's why I don't remember. That's why the dragon said I already knew your name."

He looked away, his cheek tightening. "You said it, but I thought you were talking about rain from the sky." There was no change in his skin tone, but she could swear he was blushing. "You said it in such a way..." His voice trailed off, and he shook his head. "Impossible."

She reached out and touched his wrist. He felt strange. Pleasantly warm but insubstantial as if she could break him with enough force. No, he wasn't fragile, she thought. He could punch through dragon skin and bones. His eyes snapped back to hers as she moved into his personal space. He was so tall, the top of her head came to his shoulder.

"Let me see." She pulled lightly on his crossed arms.

He sighed and let his arms fall. It was a black circle. Incomplete. A tiny place was missing so the circle didn't connect. She'd seen a circle like this before in a vision. Reaching up, she skimmed her fingertip along the edge of the mark. It was raised and felt cold and solid compared to the rest of him.

"Broken clock..." she whispered.

He grabbed both her wrists in his hands. Black designs blossomed on her skin from where he touched her. Her lips parted, her breath trembling as she exhaled. The designs continued to move, more sliding up her arms. She shivered and licked her lips, her eyes dilating with desire. The marks on her skin felt like a warm sweep of lips.

Abruptly he let go. "This is weird. I've never felt..."

She swallowed as the marks began to fade. "That was incredible. You can do it again if you want."

"This is too intimate."

"What are you afraid of?" she whispered.

He closed his eyes and exhaled. "Longing... I'm afraid of wanting something for myself."

"What do you mean?"

"There's not much to my life. I've learned to be content. You've disrupted my peace. I sent you away when you said you wanted to be friends because it made me want. I'm afraid to want."

She reached up and touched his cheek. He was so honest, just admitting he was afraid. The mild surprise in his eyes made her smile. "I'm spoiled. I've always been spoiled so I don't understand. It makes sense, but I can't say I've ever felt that way. Since we seem to be having a vulnerable moment, I'll tell you I feel greedy about you. Especially now."

"Especially now?"

"You're so beautiful."

"That's not funny," he growled.

Ignoring his anger, she pushed on. "I like you. Something in the way you talk to me. Being with you makes me feel different than when I'm with anyone else. I like how I feel with you. I trust you in a way I don't trust anyone. And that's odd. We haven't spent enough time together for me to feel the level of trust I have in you. It's selfish and greedy, but I'm glad almost everyone else is scared of you. I don't want to share."

He blinked, a look of disbelief on his face.

"There's no one else like you in Regia," she continued. "And now I know your name and what you really look like. *I* found you. I want to keep you to myself."

"Your words are only making me afraid again...because it sounds like you're saying something you couldn't possibly mean."

She smirked and raised one eyebrow. "How can you be so sure I'm not?"

The next second he grabbed her by both shoulders and almost lifted her off her feet. Only her toes touched the floor.

"Listen to me. Every word, because I'm not going to repeat this. Are you listening?"

She nodded, eyes wide.

"If you offer something, I will take it. I won't talk you off something you say you want or warn you the dangers of it. If you say something to me, you better mean it. If you make a mistake, that's on you. I won't ever apologize for taking you at your word. That's who I am. Got it?"

Heat and excitement flashed through her whole body as he spoke. Not for the first time did his words and actions touch something inside her, an appetite that no one before had tapped. He eased her back down to the floor.

"I got it," she answered. "So, I'm in charge of what happens or doesn't between us?"

His hand wrapped around her throat. She could breathe easily, his grasp gentle. "I could kill you so easily. I could make you do anything I wanted. It's best if you call the shots. I won't take anything you don't offer." He let go. "You're safe."

She shook her head. "No. I don't like this one-sided arrangement. I understand what you've said and why, but it can't be like that. I trust you. I know you won't hurt me. If you give me the time, I'll show you."

He frowned. "I don't understand at all."

"Everyone has boundaries. If you push one of mine, I'll tell you, and I expect you to back off and respect that. I'll do the same for you. I don't want to have all the control."

"I see... Okay, but what I said still goes. You better mean what you say to me."

"I heard you, and I won't forget it. If I do slip up, the blame is mine."

His gaze grew so hot and searching. Her heart raced. A question hung in the space between them and dragged the moment out. Neither of them moved closer or away. She didn't know what was possible or not with him. Her eyes stayed locked on his, unflinching. She could feel the strain under his surface. He was holding himself still. Right there, so close, but not touching. *Come on. Come on.* She urged over and over in her mind, trying to will him to hear her silent invitation. Anticipation twisted her nerves tight. He lifted one hand to her face and stopped a breath from her skin. She wanted it, whatever it was.

He exhaled. "I doubt you."

"Don't force me to make the first move. Please."

He cupped her cheek and leaned down, kissing her mouth. She'd been waiting for this. Longing for it without realizing it. But she knew she wanted it desperately because as soon as he touched her, she was triggered. He moved away, a frown pulling on his brow. "That crosses a friendship line, right?"

She chuckled. "Yes. But we've never been friends."

"We haven't?" He sounded hurt.

"No. All our interactions have been bringing us to this. You've never treated me as though you weren't interested in me as a woman, even though you've said you're not capable of sex. All of it has been a flirtation."

"Oh...I didn't realize. Why didn't you say something? Correct my behavior?"

"Well, I was flirting, too. Not that I realized it before now."

He turned his face away. "I'm confused. I need some time to think about this."

"Okay. I'll step out." She smiled up at him. "Nothing could make me regret this night. Now I know your name and your face. Thank you, Rhain."

"You got to meet a dragon, too."

"Meh. Pales in comparison."

He smirked. "You're so odd, Bunny."

She backed up until she was back in the living room, facing his smoky exterior again.

"Well, I guess I should go home now...Thanks for the crazy, life-threatening experience."

"Shall we have another one tomorrow night?"

Her smile was broad. "Duh."

He opened the door for her like a perfect gentleman. "Goodnight."

"See ya."

Crossing the property to the shimmering barrier, she glanced back before she crossed through.

He was still watching her.

EIGHT

What just happened? If they weren't friends, what were they? What would she be willing to try with him? How far could he stretch her comfort zone? What was possible for them? Could he give her physical pleasure even if he could have none?

Rhain's thoughts went around and around after Melina left. The direction their interaction had taken took him by total surprise. His fear of hope was choking him, but it was outweighed by the excitement of the possibility of winning her heart. Somehow they had shifted from trying to be friends to way more. However faint the possibility was, could he gain her love? How did he go about that? Was it different than his approach to being her friend? She said she liked him. He must have done something right so far.

He'd kissed her lips! Not that he could really feel it, but still. And she wasn't repulsed. She didn't seem bothered or even surprised. Thinking about her lips sent a whisper through him like phantom pain, as if somewhere buried deep within him was the memory of physical touch and sexual desire. Things he knew but couldn't experience anymore. The memory of her stoned and in his shower stung his inability to feel her. The way she said his name that night... What was he doing to her in that vision? Did that mean he would be able to...?

Thanks to her, he knew his real name. What kind of name was Rhain? He shut off his interest in it hard and fast. He wouldn't probe into his identity. He'd made up his mind on that a long time ago. His name was enough and on her lips...a shiver rolled over him...on her lips, his name was the best thing ever.

He shook himself and scowled. He couldn't let his imagination get carried away. She was probably regretting everything that happened between them right now. She wouldn't fall in love with him. It was impossible. Her actions had just been the aftermath of almost being killed by Jin and maybe some effect of his absorption of her to save her. Had that amount of touch made her feel closer to him? It should wear off. When he saw her again, he would be reserved and not let her know the direction his thoughts had taken when she left.

If tonight was only a spark that died out as quickly as it ignited, it was still enough to fuel fantasies of her and what he would do to her if he was mortal...if he could feel touch the way she could. Damn, his thoughts went dark and hot. How had he managed to get so lucky to have her look at him? Of all the women he'd seen in Regia, she was the most beautiful, in your face sexy, and she was his kind of crazy.

Listening to her song over the distance between them, he groaned, realizing his mistake too late. Her sound had changed and now it wasn't just a pleasant resonance, but a siren's song, as if she was daring him. His fantasies tangled with her sound. How could he want these things?

Going back to her apartment had been borderline painful for Melina. She locked the door, took off her boots, and flopped on her bed. She was more than relieved Tristan wasn't lurking, especially since she was all bound up inside with lust. She sighed, pressing the back of her hand to her fevered lips. A few guys she'd dated had turned her on, but this was nothing like that. All that before felt like such a mild and polite desire. This was wild, and her thoughts were so filled with abandon, she blushed even though she was alone. The feel of those designs skimming over her arms unmade her. She wanted to strip down and feel them everywhere on her body.

It wasn't fair he could affect her to such an extent with barely a kiss and a moment of touch, while it seemed she couldn't return the favor no matter how hard she tried. Why did she have to want someone she couldn't have?

I'm not capable of sexual acts. That's what he told her. Remembering that almost brought her to tears. She wanted to be his. She closed her eyes and groaned, seeing him in her mind, the face and body he hid under the smoke. He was incredible and even if he had been mortal, he still would have been way different than anyone she'd ever been attracted to. She liked smooth, pretty guys. Rhain was neither and again she thought he looked like a barbarian warlord.

He was as alone and as broken as she was. He was afraid of wanting. She thought about that for a while, staring at the ceiling and absentmindedly twisting the ends of her hair between her fingers. He was afraid of wanting her...because he assumed he couldn't have her? So used to rejection and being shunned... He thought he was unlovable. Her lips curved into a smile. She'd show him he was wrong. Maybe she was the only woman in Regia who could see past his exterior, that was fine by her. She didn't want competition and if anyone else could see that hunk, she'd have more competition than she could handle.

He fought his fear to be her friend. That meant something. She was happy to have him as her friend, until a little while ago. After feeling desire this intense, no way did she want to stay *just* friends. She just hoped that he could overcome his fear again, and they could try to be more. But how exactly? She didn't care, she'd made up her mind.

There were too many hours between now and when she saw him again. She needed to help herself get through the time and she really needed to cool down, otherwise, she might give in to temptation and run back to him now. The thought to take a hit of blood crossed her mind, but the desire wasn't there.

Melina headed to the shower. She'd let the water cool her down, and then she'd go to bed and sleep it off. She kept looking around, waiting for Tristan to show up and ruin her night. When she dried off, she slipped into a thin shirt and a pair of boyshort underwear. Rhain kept breaking into her thoughts as she lay down and closed her eyes. *Think of something else, think of something else*, she kept telling herself. She fell asleep with him in her mind.

Melina woke abruptly from her fevered dreams where Rhain was doing all kinds of wicked things to her. She groaned and rolled over, looking at the time on her watch. It was two hours before dawn. She rubbed her eyes, wondering what woke her when she heard knocking. Swearing, she got out of bed. Who in the hell was at her door now? Had Maddox gotten paranoid about her again? She'd kill him. She opened the door. It wasn't Maddox or Erin, or her parents.

In the shadows, Rhain was almost invisible except for his eyes.

Caught off guard, she tried to pull herself together and come up with something casual and snarky to say instead of *get in here and give it to me*, like she was thinking. "Um...hi. I thought you could move through shadows, why knock?"

"Respect. I wasn't invited. You might not want me here."

She stepped back and gestured for him to enter. He strode past her, and she locked the door behind him.

The city lights filtered through the curtains, aside from that, the living room was dark.

"What's up?"

"I'm sorry. I woke you, didn't I?"

She shrugged. "It's okay. What do you want?"

"I have a proposition for you."

She thought her smile would break her face. "Is that right?"

"I can't talk to you like this." He grabbed her by the wrists and pulled her forward into his interior. "You seem to like this face better."

He let go as soon as she had crossed through the smoke. Face to face with him, all the desire hit her again. She had to keep her cool.

"Whatever this is, it couldn't wait till tomorrow night?"

"No, it couldn't. I want to play with you." His voice was totally serious.

"Huh?"

"I want to defy logic and experiment. I want to see if I can take you. The thought might disgust you, the reality might injure you. But I want to be your man. Let me try, Melina. Don't look to anyone else to heal your heart. I'll probably screw up since I'm clueless how I'm supposed to treat you, but stay with me anyway. When I mess up, forgive me, and keep your eyes on me, just me."

She gaped at him.

"It's reckless and stupid," he continued.

She held still and silent, staring at him, studying him. "Is this a joke?" she asked in a whisper.

He shook his head and smiled. Oh, hell, he was gorgeous. This was the first time she'd seen his smile, and it was so devilish she almost had to catch her breath.

He held his hand out to her, still smiling. "I dare you."

Damn, he understood her too well. She took his hand. "I accept."

He pulled her to his chest and wrapped her in his arms. Her heartbeat kicked up fast and hit hard. Designs began sliding over her skin again.

"What are we doing?" she asked, already somewhat breathless.

"You can feel me… So, I can give, even if I can't feel. Your pleasure will be enough for me. I want to hear you say my name again the way you did in your vision."

She shook her head. "No. You have to let me try to give you pleasure, too. I don't want to use you like that. If you're my man then you'll be my lover, Rhain, not my tool."

He picked her up, and she wrapped her legs around his waist, kissing him hard on the lips. His tongue filled her mouth, surprising her how normal it felt. No, it was better than normal kissing, and he was actually *really* good at it.

"How's that?" he asked, worry creasing his brow.

"Excellent. How is it for you? Can you feel it at all?"

"Sort of. A little more than I thought."

"Well, let's keep at it and see if you feel more over time."

She fused her mouth back to his. He walked forward until her butt hit the kitchen counter. He set her on the counter, his hands gripped her hips as he continued to take her mouth. Am I still dreaming? She wondered. Wrapped in smoke, she felt like they were in their own little world where nothing could touch them. A place no one else could see or understand.

Making out like that was incredible, and he was winding her up so tight she thought she might break if she didn't have more soon, but behind that was a nagging worry this was more one-sided than he was letting on. Something about this felt so off. His hand slipped into her shirt, designs spreading over her breasts.

"Stop." She pushed his arm down until he pulled it back out of her shirt. She jumped down from the counter. "We need to talk more."

"Did I do something wrong? You seemed like you were turned—"

"I am," she cut him off. "Really am. I just need to understand what this is like for you. Where are we headed, physically?"

"I told you I want to take you."

"And I told you I don't want you to be my tool. Explain what this feels like."

"I can't feel any more than I do with anything else. My body isn't like yours. Touching you, kissing you, makes me happy, but there's nothing building in me. Not like I see happening with you. I can hear it, too. Your sound is changing the more I touch you. I want to hear what it does if I push you over that edge."

Tears began layering her eyes. She wasn't hot now, she was very, very cold. He wiped the tear sliding down her cheek.

"Why this?" His voice was quiet.

She sniffed. "Think of something else. I want to find something we both feel, together."

"Why should that matter? I'm happy to just give to you."

Why should it matter? She rested her head against him and put her hand flat on his chest. She closed her eyes and exhaled. "Because...because it has to be equal if you're mine and I'm yours... I really want to be yours."

Everything about him, his eyes, his expression, his physical stance, all shifted into rage. He slammed his hands on the counter behind her, boxing her in. "What did I tell you?"

She didn't cower, she just quirked her eyebrow. What was he talking about? Oh, yeah, she thought she knew. "What? *You better mean what you say to me?*"

"Yes," he snarled. "How could you be so heartless?"

She crossed her arms, unperturbed that he still had her pinned. *"If you offer something, I will take it... I won't ever apologize for taking you at your word..."* she repeated what he'd told her before. "You're right, you know. You are clueless. Don't you realize what you even said just now about being my man, and looking to you to heal my heart? I accepted, dumbass. Or was it a lie?"

"No."

"It was simply the answer to your question of why it mattered. I won't toy with you. Have some faith in me."

He let his arms fall to his sides, and he looked away from her, his eyes going flat. "I...I have to go."

"Okay," she said lightly. "See you later?"

"Yeah." His voice was empty as though he wasn't sure what he was saying, and he strode toward the door. She followed. He stopped and turned back to her, looking dazed, like he'd just been hit over the head. It spurred her on.

Stepping back into the smoke, she reached for his hand with both of hers. He stared at her, a look of total disbelief on his face as she brought his hand up to her lips. "I want to be yours," she whispered. "Whatever that means, however it looks, I'll be yours."

He just stood there, still looking dazed. "Is it the truth?"

"Yes. It will get annoying if you keep asking. It's sudden, I guess. Do you want to give me time to mull it over?"

"No! I don't want you to change your mind." He seemed to wake up from his stupor.

She smiled. "I didn't want to leave when I did earlier. I wasn't able to think of anything but you, even in my sleep, I dreamed of you, before you knocked and woke me up."

He picked her up by the waist, and she wrapped her arms around his neck. "I have what I came here for, I just never imagined I'd be successful. I thought it would take a lot longer, if you ever consented."

She tightened her grip, thinking of what he said to her when he turned down her friendship and used the same words on him. "You're smarter than that."

He laughed. "I'm not at all...and I'm terrified by this. I was sure you'd reject me." He kissed her again. Her heart ached at the touch of his lips. It wasn't just a kiss. It was pain and a promise.

"It's a risk, for me as well. I know it was hard for you to come here and ask, I don't know how hard. I'm impressed."

"What does it mean to you? What does this *you and me* look like? What do you expect and want?"

She chuckled. "I like these questions, but I don't have any answers yet. I'll have to think about it. I want to know how you answer these questions, too."

Stinging cold pricked at the skin on her back. Shit. Tristan was close by. She needed to get Rhain out of here. The three of them in the same space was a bad idea.

"Hey, how about I'll come to your place a little later, after I take care of some stuff and we can talk more then?"

"You want me to leave." He said. It wasn't a question.

"Can I bring some stuff when I come, so I can spend the night?"

Her attempt at misdirection didn't work and hurt filled his eyes, making her panic.

"I have to take care of something unpleasant now. Please. It's really embarrassing. Don't take this as a rejection of any kind. I'll see you later. I can't wait until I can show up at your place later."

Doubt filled his expression.

"Look, if I didn't want to be with you, I'd just say so."

"Is this one of your boundaries? Whatever you have to deal with?"

She smiled. "Yes. Exactly."

"I see. Okay. I'll wait for you to come to me." He set her back on her feet. "Can I kiss you goodbye?"

"Don't ask again. Kiss me whenever you want."

He leaned down, and she tipped her head up to meet his lips. Sweet as it was, she couldn't enjoy it, afraid Tristan was about to appear.

Melina groaned, resting her forehead against the door after he left. The cold continued to sting. She didn't have to look up to know the exact moment he was there.

"You just have a thing for dead guys, don't you?"

"He's not dead." She turned and faced him.

"He's not alive, either... What are you doing, Melina? You're mine. Anything you can try to have with someone else will only ever be fake." He put his ghostly hand over his open chest. "I've never felt anything that hurt as much as seeing you in his arms."

"Good! I'm glad it hurt."

He smiled and moved toward her. "You're not as cold-hearted as you pretend to be. You still love me."

"That's not love. It's a shackle. A disease I contracted against my will."

His smile slanted a wicked angle. "Such a nasty mouth. I want to suck on your sharp tongue."

"Go away."

"No. Not when I'm all turned on by the challenge of this other guy circling around you."

"Stop talking, Tristan. You gross me out." She turned her back to him. That was a mistake.

His hands slid through her back and grabbed her heart. Damnit, it felt good, she couldn't deny it. "He can't do this for you...I know you hate me," he whispered in her ear. "I know you're not going to come back to me, no matter how I ask...I have to wait, but we can be together like this, half-life. It can still be sweet, Melina. Hold still. Let me show you."

She moved away from him. He came after her. "Get off, rapist." She rushed to her bedroom, to her vanity. Pulling the drawer open she dug into the back until her hand wrapped around the necklace. She held it up for him to see. He stopped advancing, but his smile didn't fade.

"You're bluffing."

She wasn't, not at all, but yet... Straining with all her might to break it, she sank to her knees, tears building behind her eyes. She couldn't do it. Her hand shook, her palm slicking with sweat around the stone. He got down on the floor as well, his face close to hers.

"You want to, I see you do. But you can't. You're not capable. The ghost of our bond is enough to stop you. I know you're sad. I don't mind. Just stop fighting it."

Closing her eyes, she sighed before getting back to her feet. She put the necklace back in the drawer. "I'll never stop fighting this tie I have to you."

Frustrated and dejected she pulled her suitcase out from under her bed and began to pack her clothes.

"What are you doing?" Tristan demanded.

"Getting ready to leave. I'll be staying with Rhain."

"For how long?"

She shrugged. "Until he gets sick of me."

"That shouldn't take too long." He sneered. "I'll comfort you when he breaks your heart and sends you back here to me. He's just getting my leftovers anyway. There's nothing to salvage of you."

"Yeah, yeah. I suck." She put her earbuds in to shut him out and kept packing.

Since Rhain didn't remember anything of his life before becoming what he was now, he couldn't remember ever feeling this excited or alive. He also couldn't remember feeling this scared. In his mind, Melina stood before him, seemingly within reach, but how could he actually take hold of her? It felt impossible she'd really said any of that just now. Words were only one part of the impossibility. He'd turned her on. *Him.*

An embarrassingly wide smile spread his lips. It was far from perfect. They couldn't have a normal romantic relationship, but she was willing to try other things...he closed his eyes and shook his head. He couldn't get his hopes up, regardless of what she said...No... Even if it only lasted one day, he'd wring it dry. Every smile or kind word she gave him. No one could take that away.

He had to give her everything he could. He'd never have a chance like this again. He knew it wouldn't last. He had no doubts about that. She was flesh and blood, no matter how she felt right now, flesh and blood was what she needed. She might be okay with pretend for a while, but it wouldn't last.

He thought back to the night she broke into his life, wild-eyed, banging on Tesla and X's door, wanting to go to the underworld. She didn't look like that now. She was better. Her eyes were clear. She didn't look on the verge of total mental breakdown. That was something to celebrate.

He got an idea.

NINE

Melina spent most of the day aimlessly wandering around Paradigm, pulling her suitcase behind her. She couldn't stand staying in her apartment with Tristan one second longer than she had to. By the afternoon she didn't see the point in wandering anymore and used her portal ring to take her where she really wanted to be.

Nervous how he might respond to her suitcase, she knocked on Rhain's door. He didn't answer. She listened. No music drifted under the door. She knocked again. She tried the knob when he still didn't respond. The door swung inward.

"Rhain?"

No response. All the pain bound up inside her sighed and let go. This was a safe place. Nothing could touch her here. How would things be between them when he came back? Would their time together last night just feel like a fit of lunacy? Brought on by the night?

She pulled her suitcase into the living room and sat on the couch. Where was he anyway? What was he doing? Would it bother him, she let herself in? It wasn't like she was going to snoop...much. She stood again and paced around the room a few times before going down the hall. There were only three doors. The bathroom, bedroom, and the last one was shut. She didn't go in there. He'd show her when he was ready. She'd spent the night in his bed before so it seemed okay for her to be in there, she rationalized as she walked into the room. The bedroom was like the rest of the house. Modern, minimalist, and posh. She stopped in her tracks, surprised. A simple, black satin dress was laid out on the bed, a small box, and a card with her name, on the top of it.

Melina snatched up the card and tore it open.

Bunny,

I feel awkward writing this. The dress is a gift from me. I thought tonight we could have a little dinner party in celebration of you. Just an intimate thing. Dinner at Tesla and X's house. Them, you, me, Maddox and Erin. What do you say? Last night, I was thinking how far you've come. How well you're doing. How strong you are...I believe all that is something to celebrate. It's not a problem to cancel it, if you're uncomfortable with the idea. There's no pressure at all. I haven't told anyone about us, and that's not my purpose here. I'll be back soon.

Because of you, I can sign my name. Thank you.

Rhain

She read the note three times before wiping her tears with the back of her hand and laughing lightly. Her heart was pounding so hard and fluttering filled her chest.

"I think that demon just stole my heart," she said to herself as she hooked her fingers through the spaghetti straps and lifted up the dress. It was plain but she could almost smell the money on the fabric. It wasn't cheap, that was for sure. She laid it back down and opened the little box, a gasp escaping her lips. The burned gold chain was long, a round sunset stone hung at the bottom. She took the necklace into the bathroom to see how it looked in the mirror. Melina had always wanted a sunset stone but never had enough money for one. Few people did. Considered Regia's most precious stone, the deep autumn hues appeared to flow or burn, like fire and wine, depending on the way it caught the light.

She took it off and put it back in the box, setting it back on the bed, before going into the living room. She sat on the couch, twisting her hands in her lap for a minute. Then she got up and got the necklace again and brought it back to the couch with her. She put it on, holding the stone between her thumb and index finger, turning it side to side, watching the colors change with the light.

They were just things. The necklace, the dress. And yet she didn't feel the same way as she had when any other man had given her a gift. It wasn't a down payment for sex. He was thinking of her and not what he could get out of it. And he didn't care if she wanted to cancel dinner. Not even that had some kind of payout for him. How often did anyone receive gifts that didn't give something back to the giver?

I'll find a way to give him something, too.
Somehow...someday... I'll show him the same amount of
care as he's shown me.

The front door opened, only it wasn't Rhain, it was Tesla. She strode in, a box tucked under one arm.

"So, you are here. He said you might be. I hoped to sneak this in before you got here." Tesla smiled and held the box out. "I forgot them before."

Melina stood, feeling a little awkward as she took the box and lifted the lid.

"The look would be ruined without the right shoes," Tesla said as Melina gaped at the strappy black stilettoes in the box.

"Whoa! These are..."

"Yeah, they are. I've never bought such an expensive pair of shoes before, I can tell you. Not that it was my money."

"You picked the dress and the necklace, too?"

Tesla nodded. "Don't get the wrong idea, though. This is totally from Rhain. It's funny to call him that. I'm trying to get used to it. He only told us his real name this morning. Anyway, all this is from him. He told me exactly what to buy and he paid for all of it. I tried to talk him out of the sunset stone, but he wouldn't listen to me... How do you feel about dinner? Are we going to go through with it?"

Her cheeks were burning, imagining what Tesla must be thinking. "I...I didn't expect...he..." the words just wouldn't come out.

A bemused look, almost amused settled on Tesla's face, and she crossed her arms. "It's not my business, but I'm curious."

Tesla had always been like an older sister to her, and all this must look odd from the outside. She cleared her throat. "He's been helping me. We've been hanging out...We care for each other... He's really amazing once he lets his guard down."

"He's never let his guard down with anyone except X, not even me. Not really. He said he knew his name because of you. How did that happen? X was a little peeved he let someone else help regain some of his identity. X has been offering to help him with that for a long time."

Melina looked down, realizing that Tesla didn't know about her eye. Maybe it was time. "I've been having visions of my future. That's how I learned his name. He didn't want to know... There's an eye in my eye."

"May I look?" Tesla moved forward.

Melina nodded and met her intense gaze. Tesla didn't stare long, just a few seconds before she smiled and backed up. "Polyhedron. I can't believe I didn't notice before. Are your visions fragmented?"

"Yeah. They make no sense at all. Some of them are terrifying. I have to think about how to avoid some of them. Change the future."

"You can't. It's not about choice."

Melina scowled. "Because they're future memories?"

"Yes. Polyhedrons access their memories out of order, but they *are* memories. When you have a vision, what you see is a truth of your life. Some manifest more through emotional response, so the memory might be slightly different than reality, once it comes to pass. But you cannot change it. "

"That's your opinion."

Tesla shrugged and then smiled warmly. "So, do you feel up for dinner at our house tonight, or not?"

"He bought me a *sunset stone*." Her voice was emphatic. "This is my first chance to show it off. I'm not missing that."

"You are more like yourself again. I'm glad. I'll send the invitation to Maddox and Erin, since you've decided." She turned and headed to the door, typing a message on her watch. "See ya later," she said over her shoulder before closing the door.

She put the box of shoes in the bedroom with the dress and sat back down in the living room. In a minute, the door opened again. Rhain came in carrying an armload of ancient looking books. She gave him her sexiest smile.

"Hello, gorgeous."

He snorted and set the books on the kitchen counter. "That's my line."

She got up and came over to him. "What's with the books?"

"Research on Destiny. I thought we could start going through them after dinner. Unless..." His voice trailed away.

She walked into the smoke and reached for his hand. He gave it, threading his fingers through hers. "Thank you. I'm really looking forward to tonight."

"You like what I bought you?"

"Very much."

He blew out a breath. "Whew. I was afraid you might be mad. That I overstepped or something." His gaze fell on the necklace. "You're wearing it."

"I've always wanted one, since I was a little girl... The cost though...why would you choose this?"

"Don't you understand?" His voice went quiet.

"No. I don't."

"You will."

Moving closer, she put her hands on either side of his face, as he gazed down at her. A bittersweet pain beat inside her heart. It wasn't fair. Why was he trapped like this? Somewhere between life and death, denied so much. He was denied and now so was she. There were so many things she never would have thought of except now they were removed. Her hands slid down to the broken circle on his chest.

"Why don't you want to know who you are? Why are you afraid to learn the truth? Learning might free you."

He grabbed both of her wrists and held her hands away from his chest. "I don't have many boundaries, but this is one of them. Don't push this issue."

"But I want to help you...the way you're helping me. What if—"

"No, Melina. Let it go. I don't want to fight with you. I hope the time comes when I can tell you why...until then..."

She backed a step away and looked down. "Okay, Rhain."

He chuckled. "Are you pouting? That's so cute."

"I'm not pouting."

"Are, too. You should see your face."

She sighed, realizing he was right. "I like getting my way."

He tipped her face up and kissed her lips. "Is there anything else I can do for you?"

"I'm already spoiled. I should learn to be content."

He smiled. "I don't think I'll be a positive influence on your endeavor to become content. I'll give you anything you want, if it's within my power."

He was trying to lighten the mood, but his words had the opposite effect on her. She swallowed and touched his face again. "You really are gorgeous, you know. I love the way you look. The way it feels to be close to you wrapped in this warm smoke. The sound of your voice puts me on an edge of feeling totally safe and completely in danger simultaneously."

"Does it really affect you that much?" He got a faraway look in his eyes.

She nodded. "Your voice is such a turn on."

She gasped as he abruptly spun her around. He grabbed both of her hands and forced her to brace them on the counter. He pressed against her, his mouth on her ear, biting down on her lobe. "Oh, hell..." she breathed. "What are you doing?"

"I have a really bad idea. Wanna try it?"

"I..." She couldn't answer. Her heart began to race so hard.

"You can say stop any time." The stubble on his jaw scraped her skin as he kissed her neck, raising shivers all over her body. "I'd never hurt you, Melina. I just want to try something. If it doesn't work or you don't like it, I'll back off. I just...I want to try to be close to you."

"How?" she whispered. "I don't want to feel when you can't."

"This isn't about feeling with your body, it's feeling with your mind."

"That sounds great, except I can tell you I'm feeling a lot with my body right now, and it's getting frustrated."

He backed up, still behind her, but not touching. She blinked a few times and turned to face him. He was frowning and looking away from her.

"What?"

"I know that… Sorry, there seems to be some buried desire in me. The pull to touch you even though I can't feel you…it's there. I did have an idea for something else though, I was just enjoying the change in your breathing and your pulse. To know I was the one that brought that change…"

Her heart warmed for him, and she gave him a small smile. "Whatever you've lost, your male ego isn't missing."

"Ah, is that where that comes from?"

"At least some of it," she smirked. "So what was this other thing you wanted to try?"

"Give me your hands."

She did.

"Now close your eyes."

Melina exhaled, letting go of any worry she had, and closed her eyes.

"Think about me. About what you wish we could do together. Whatever your desires are... Imagine it in as much detail as you can."

A deep blush heated her cheeks. The images she experienced in her dreams last night came back to her, and she was wrapped in heat. She remembered it all so clearly and it replayed without variation. Her body was overwhelmed as the images slowed, and he pressed down on the pulse in both wrists, his hands vibrating. The sound of her heartbeat filled her ears, but where it had been fast a second ago, now it was labored. She fought the temptation to open her eyes. He made love to her in her memories of her dreams. Almost... It was so real, but out of reach. Like an amazing aroma, filling your lungs, teasing you into almost believing you can taste it...almost. So good and yet torment. Her pulse slowed more just as she began to break in pleasure. In that moment of imagined ecstasy, her heart held still, all the hormones of a real climax sliding through her brain in a slow flood.

She was trapped. He held her immobile in that moment and didn't let time move forward. In reality she felt his lips on hers as time restarted and she gasped, opening her eyes. She clung around his neck, aftershocks sparking through her.

"Thank you," he whispered.

She couldn't answer. Her pulse rushed, and her lungs jerked around the air as if she'd just been running for her life, as if he'd stopped time, and now she was desperately trying to catch up.

"Wh...what...did...you...do?" she panted.

"I waited for the right moment then I made time echo."

Violent chills rolled up her whole body. "You what?"

"It's hard to explain."

"Were you in my head? Did you see?"

"No. I wish. I listened to your song. When it began to change and escalate, I kept you there, in that moment."

"Whoa. I feel..." She shivered again. "I feel like you hijacked my brain and tricked it into thinking what I was imagining was real."

He smiled. "That's good, right? It was satisfying?"

Her cheeks heated again. "Um...yeah."

"You said that with hesitation. You didn't like it?"

She gazed up at him, her heart beginning to riot. She hadn't known what was coming, she hadn't been prepared, and now regret poured through her. In a way, it had been what she wanted. In a way, they were in the same place at the same time. She'd felt his presence when time had *echoed*. And yet sorrow cut deep with its dull edge. It was still pseudo. He hadn't meant to hurt her, and he was fragile emotionally. She needed time to sort out what she felt, to understand it herself before she could try to make him understand. She had to weigh her words *very* carefully. "I've never felt anything like that before. I've never heard of what you're talking about either. I'm not sure what I think about it right now." She placed her hand flat against his chest. "I need to process it. Can we talk about it later?"

"Of course." He smiled and kissed her.

Her heart fractured painfully around its contours. She didn't want to dwell on the pain. She was tired, so very, very tired.

"Do you mind if I lay down for a while in your room? I want to be my best for dinner tonight."

"Make yourself at home."

She covered her mouth with her hand when she lay down on his bed to keep him from hearing her cry. What was wrong with her? Why was she crying? Was it too fast? Too casual? What had he actually done to her? Time echo? What the hell was that? Why did it make her so sad? Maybe they really couldn't be together. No. She rejected that thought as she touched the stone on her necklace. He was desperate to give to her. She recognized it. What he didn't understand was she was just as desperate as he was. She had to calm down and just let whatever happen. She had to be patient and accept the limitations of their relationship.

Rolling to her side, she looked out the window. He came into the room and shut the door. She didn't say anything as he closed the drapes, throwing the room into darkness. He lay down behind her, enveloping her in smoke as he wrapped one arm over her.

"Are you upset? Was that a mistake?" he asked quietly.

"I don't know. I haven't figured it out yet."

"Is this okay? Holding you like this?"

"Yes. I love this...I wish we were the same physically, you know?"

"Yeah. Will you try something for me?" he asked.

She smiled and turned to face him. "What?"

"Will you bite me? I really want to know what that feels like... It's one of my fantasies." He closed his eyes and grimaced. "Never mind. I mean, there's no blood in this body. I would probably taste terrible."

All the negative feelings inside her vanished. He asked for something. Something she wouldn't have thought he would want. Maybe it would be futile, but she had no desire to deny him. Quite the contrary. She nestled closer, brushing her lips lightly against the side of his neck. His hand braced on her shoulder, light pressure pushing her back.

"No, Melina. Thank you, but—"

"Don't tell me no." Her voice was forceful.

He stopped pushing her away. Closing her eyes, she sank her fangs into him and pulled with her lips. No, it wasn't blood. She didn't know what she was drawing into herself, as if she swallowed light, sound, and spirit.

Clasping her against him, his body jolted and he cried out. She didn't stop. It wasn't a cry of pain. Something was happening. The waves of smoke around her moved faster, buffeting her like a warm wind. Designs rushed over her skin from his hands and unbearably beautiful music filled her head.

Her third eye opened wide, seeing beyond sight, perceiving past flesh, that which is intangible. She drew him into herself, down deep inside where she was color and sound. His color and his sound wrapping around hers. They twisted and tied, the music escalating to pain. The knot they made broke apart into a million sparks of light.

Gasping, Melina opened her eyes. His lips were parted, and he looked astonished. She recovered first, still breathing hard, and laughed. "Oh, hell yes...*That* was..."

He kissed her lips, slow and hard. "You've never looked more beautiful."

"Please tell me you felt that, too. We were in the same place?"

"Yes," he whispered. "I can't believe it, but yes."

She closed her eyes and sighed contentedly. Before she could realize she was going to, Melina dropped into sleep, overwhelmed with a level of exhaustion she'd never experienced.

Maddox buttoned his shirt and watched Erin from the side of his eye while she got dressed. He tried not to grin. She knew he was watching her, but she acted oblivious even as her movements became exaggeratedly sexy. Her dress was laid out on the bed, and she flounced around in her lingerie, muttering to herself about what shoes to choose. He wondered how hard she would try if he ignored her? Smoothing his expression to blank, he went into the closet and took his time picking a tie. She began to sigh theatrically.

"No. Not these," she said. "Maybe the black. I don't know...Oh, dear, I don't know what to wear. The dress I picked is wrong."

He was finding it harder and harder to not laugh. He continued to pretend to ignore her.

"Maddox, do these shoes work?" she demanded.

He looked around the closet door at her. It took great effort to not really respond. She was looking at him over her shoulder, still in nothing but her lingerie, and a pair of stilettoes, holding a seductive pose, her hip popped to one side. As if he could notice her shoes, all he saw was black lace on her sweet ass.

"Nope. They're definitely the wrong shoes," he said in a bored tone.

Her cheeks colored a little. He laughed and swooped down on her, picking her up.

"You want me to check you out? There's no need for the charade, baby. I'm always checking you out."

She pushed out of his arms and walked away, flipping her hair over her shoulder, her hips swaying in exaggerated invitation. "I don't know what you're talking about."

He laughed again and put on his suit jacket. "Sure. You're innocent. You just wanted me to know exactly what you're wearing under your dress tonight so it winds me up while we have to socialize."

She slipped her dress over her head. "I don't know what kind of a girl you think I am."

He strode up behind her and zipped the back of her dress up before kissing her shoulder. "I know *exactly* what kind of girl you are," he whispered in her ear, "my redheaded vixen."

She turned and wrapped her arms around his neck. He held her tightly and she sighed, all the playfulness fading away. "I hope this dinner thing is a good idea. Mel's been really distant. She answers my messages as soon as I send them, but her responses are vague."

"Same here. The invitation Tesla sent said we're celebrating Mel doing better, but she also put an emphasis on making a show of support...I mean, we've been supporting her, so I'm not sure what that means, but she really made a point of it."

"Hmm...well, better or not, Mel is still fragile."

"She's a junkie."

"What?"

He nodded. "I didn't want to tell you, but she's hit the blood hard. I was giving her some time to go through it and not try to stop her, but I think that time is about up, depending on how she looks and acts tonight."

"How bad is it? Blood addiction?"

"I don't know. Human blood is a nice high, but I'm only half vampire. She's a pure blood. It's the strongest addiction from what I've heard from my father. He was on it for years."

"Is there anything we can do for her?" Erin asked.

"I don't know. Let's just see how she is tonight."

Maddox opened a portal for them to Tesla and X's property. He looked up momentarily at the clear night sky before knocking on the front door. His sister opened the door with a warm smile on her face.

"Come in."

They followed her into the living room where she abruptly turned on them.

"I'm glad you're here before they are, but they will be here any second, so please listen to me." Tesla's voice was urgent.

"Okay," Maddox said slowly. "Who exactly are you talking about?"

"Mel and Rhain."

"Who's Rhain?" Erin asked.

"Fluffy... That's his name. His *real* name. He's only just discovered this but it's important to him that we call him by his real name from now on."

Maddox shrugged. "No big deal. We can remember that."

Erin nodded in agreement.

"This dinner party was his idea. He and Mel have been spending time together. He's convinced that he can help her with her plan to find Destiny, and he wants us all to be more supportive of her. He wants us to at least voice our support if nothing else."

Irritation flared inside Maddox and he scowled. "The hell?"

Tesla held her hands up. "Don't get upset with *me*... They've become friends. I guess he feels protective of her, and he truly is convinced that she can find Destiny."

"Do you think she can?" Maddox demanded.

"I don't know. She's chasing the wind, but maybe she needs to. All I know is this is what was asked of me, and Mel really is better. It seems as if this new friendship is what she needs right now. We all love Mel, and regardless of our opinions of what she can and cannot do, we need to support her."

"I'm glad she seems better. I want to see it for myself. But don't tell me how to treat my oldest friend. No one knows her as well as I do."

"Relax, Maddie," Tesla said.

He gave her a dirty look at her use of his nickname. Erin squeezed his arm. He looked down into her intent gaze and nodded. "All right." He sighed, not sure why all this made him so agitated.

They all turned as the front door opened behind them. Mel breezed into the room, Rhain behind her. Maddox blinked a few times. Mel looked way better than the last time he'd seen her, her eyes were clear, and the dark telltale under-eye shadows of a blood junkie were faded. Warm glowing energy emanated from her as she came up and gave him a hug.

"Hey, M."

"You look great, Mel."

"Thanks." She kissed his cheek and flounced away.

His gaze followed her, and he narrowed his eyes. He wasn't lusting after her, he wasn't capable of lust for anyone except Erin, but it was impossible to not notice Mel looked like a full-fledged sex kitten at the moment, and she was glowing. He hadn't been Regia's most notorious playboy the last few years for nothing. He knew exactly what made a woman shimmer like that. Who had she finally given it up to?

The three women grouped together.

"Maddox." The demon came up beside him.

"Hey...Rhain. I get that right?"

It was awkward, as if Maddox suddenly didn't know the person beside him.

"Yes. I appreciate you showing up. This means a lot to Melina."

Maddox scowled and turned his face to glance at Rhain. Was the demon trying to take *his* place as Mel's best friend? Is that what was going on here? Is that why he was so irritated? He took a deep breath and schooled his feelings. Mel could have as many friends as she wanted, it wouldn't change their connection. He was being a jerk.

Still...there were some odd vibes going around the room. Wait a minute...he looked closer at the smoke monster beside him and then almost burst out laughing where his mind had gone. He looked away, covering his smile. That monster and Mel? No way.

Eli was restless. Even though Sophie slept peacefully beside him, her breathing soothing, her warmth the best comfort, he still couldn't sleep. The moon gave him enough light to read and something Sophie said a few days earlier about her friend wanting to confront Destiny stuck in his head. Holding his hands close to his face, the words surfaced on his palms as though carved there. The place in history he wanted came up with just a thought.

The history read plainly but after a few minutes, it became disjointed. Words missing. Information scrubbed. That's right. He remembered now. The Heart blacked this out. He pushed on it with his mind but the story of Destiny wouldn't come clear. It pissed him off. Nothing else was hidden from him. He was the Historian, damnit. How was he to keep the history if it was partial? How could he trust what he knew? Were there other things hidden from him and he just hadn't realized it yet?

Frustrated, and even less tired than before, he slid into his trunk where he wouldn't disturb Sophie and prodded at the Heart with his mind. It answered immediately.

Can't sleep?

"I'm troubled," Eli said. "I want you to give me the history. *All* of it."

The Heart sighed. *All right. I wanted to put it off longer, but I can feel your agitation. This is going to be unpleasant for me, but I don't want to lose your trust.*

A rush of information and sensations filled him. The hidden history burned its words along the spiral of the rings of his trunk. Flashes of images filled his mind. His heart jolted and he gasped. Now he understood why the Heart had kept it hidden and he wished he hadn't pressed for this. His nightmares would be saturated with the blood of the slaughter of those children.

"I'm…I'm sorry I… asked for this…" Eli's voice broke over the words.

Darksong wasn't only the first dryad, he was the first Regian. The Heart's first child. Destiny was the second. For a while, it was just the three of them. Darksong was pure and guileless. Destiny was shrewd and short tempered. When the Heart explained to her what her purpose was, she was proud and excited. She was to read the souls of all Regians and match them in perfect harmony, so the world would flourish in secure love and commitment.

New life began. Many new dryads sprang up from the ground in the forest around Darksong.

"Why did she do it?" Eli asked.

I wanted to leave them alone for a while and see how they managed. I became silent and went into a deep sleep. I should have explained better. It would have turned out differently if I had. The Heart paused and sighed again. *Destiny thought I had left her out. That she was cursed to be alone, as the only one of her kind, forced to find love for everyone else while she was denied that same happiness. That had never been my intention. By the time I told her that, it was too late.*

She convinced Darksong that I planned to kill him. The new children meant that I no longer loved him. He was simpleminded. He believed her. She used her own jealousy to poison his pure heart. He was easily led. She cultivated deep hatred and confusion in him. She couldn't see past her own feelings.

I woke to screams and the blood of the little ones running down into me.

I was awash in death. I couldn't bring myself to kill Destiny and Darksong. So, I grounded him inside his trunk and made him drink the blood he spilled through his roots. It twisted his body and his mind further. When he realized Destiny had lied and used him to murder the children, he went crazy.

When Destiny learned that I intended to make more of her kind as well, that she wasn't cursed to live alone, her guilt and regret were so heavy she begged me to kill her.

"What will become of them?" Eli asked.

They were my first children. I built them strong with long lifespans. When they die, I will absorb them and we shall reach a place of forgetting. Neither they, nor I will remember it anymore. I am looking forward to that day.

I love you very much, Eli, my chosen historian. Take care of this dark piece of the past, as I know you can.

"I will. I promise."

He felt the presence of the Heart leave him. His chest hurt and it was hard to breathe for a few minutes. It was a terrible story. So what did he do with what he knew? Did he tell Sophie where the entrance was to the prison that held Destiny and Darksong? So she could tell her friend how to get there?

TEN

Melina came awake in a wash of aquamarine moonlight. After dinner she was so tired she crashed into Rhain's bed almost as soon as they got back to his house. She rubbed her eyes and rolled over. He wasn't beside her. Melina slid out of bed and padded out of the bedroom. The rest of the small house was dark, except for the moonlight. She would have called out for him, but there was something special about the quiet at that moment.

It felt so right she realized, as if this was her home. As if she found the one little corner of the world perfectly shaped for her. It wasn't the house, she loved the house, but it was him. She accepted him as he was even as she wished both of them were different. She shut off the wishful desires with a flash of anger. Wishing was useless, and it didn't suit her. If it was something she could change, she would. If not, she would take it as it was and be thankful. She was mated to a dead psychopath and Rhain was trapped in a half-life. So what? No one needed to understand, so long as they understood. Screw normal.

The door to the other room she hadn't been in yet was ajar. She walked into the center of the room and turned in a circle. Instruments hung on the walls and lined the floors around the edges. Some she recognized, some she didn't, but each one, regardless of the size or type was beautiful. She smiled. It was like him, he valued the quality of things. So that music she'd heard before...he made it. Rhain was a musician...and it was personal. He hadn't told her yet...but he left the door open.

The cool night breeze whispered into the room from the open glass door in the back. She looked at her reflection on the glass. Who she had been before was gone forever. Before she learned about her third eye...before Tristan. Melina wasn't lamenting, she didn't waste the time to care. Realizing that hit her sideways. She didn't miss who she was. She wouldn't go back if she could... *Really?* She argued with herself. No, it was the honest, odd truth. She wouldn't go back, because going back would mean Rhain wasn't in her life.

She'd fallen at his feet, completely broken. He'd picked her up and was trying to put her back together. Chance had placed her in his way and she finally looked at him. He'd always been there, in the background. She'd never been unkind, or so she thought. Ignoring someone was its own unkindness. When her life shattered, the blinders on her eyes fell off as well. She'd never put them back on.

She stepped outside on to a porch. He was standing still, looking up at the crisp night sky. She came up beside him and rested her hand over his, braced on the railing. The smoke curled pleasantly around her hand and up her wrist. Serenity flowed through her as she gazed up at the sky, too.

"I must have done something to deserve my damnation. I must have been a monster, so now I'm cursed to live as a monster, if I'm actually living."

"That's why you don't want to know your identity?"

"Yes. I could have learned it long ago. Many times I came up to the edge of knowing, but I'd always back off of it with a sense of dread. X never understood. I hid my fear from him so he didn't think me a coward. It frustrated him, but it was always my choice. Finally, I just made a firm decision to never know. That would be better. I already know anyway. I know I was something horrible. I'd rather not face the details. I can live honorably. I've managed that as best I can."

She squeezed his hand. "I understand now. Thank you for telling me."

"I love you." His voice was quiet and steady.

She hadn't expected it but she didn't gasp or object. He looked down at her. She exhaled and smiled, letting his words sink into her. It was new, this feeling. She'd been told those words many times by friends and family, the occasional boyfriend, but hearing it from him...it was something new.

"Are you sure?" she whispered.

"Yes. No one understands time, Melina. But I do. It's a part of me. Who I am. All that I hear, everything you can't... It's all connected to time and the way it moves. That's how I can make time echo, with music... No one knows that about me, except you. Not even X. It's not an impressive or dramatic power. I can't travel through time or turn it back. I can only hold it still if I want to prolong a moment." He faced her and drew her into his interior, touching her cheek, gazing into her eyes. "Time is like a stream flowing before you, sometimes something lovely floats by. If you hesitate too long it will move past you. Then you will only see it in the distance and in a moment it's gone and your chance to have it has vanished."

She leaned into him as he wrapped his arms around her. "Chance...Vanished..." she breathed. "Give yourself to me." Her voice came back forcefully. "Give me everything, Rhain."

His eyes widened. "How?"

She licked her lips as they trembled. "Will you marry me?"

He blinked once. "You got it."

"I'm serious."

"You think I'm not?"

She gasped on a rush of excited nerves. Was this for real? Oh gosh, was it right? Did she mean it? Did he? Could they really get married?

"I can feel your heart racing in your chest," he said. "If you regret saying it, I won't hold it against you if you want to take it back."

"I don't want to take it back...unless you want me to take it back."

"Come here, Bunny." His deep voice whispered over her as he picked her up.

She closed her eyes and sighed in pleasure. Nothing else was required. He held her and she held him. Just like that, she knew for sure he was all she needed. No one else had ever made her feel half as much as he did. Beyond her feelings for him, and her desire to be with him, was a deep certainty that his embrace was her place. It was hers if she chose to claim it.

"When?" she asked.

"You tell me. Whenever you choose. Whatever you want, we'll do that."

"Really?"

"The cost is no issue. It can be as big and extravagant as you like," he assured her.

She nestled closer to him and considered a big, social event. Smiling, she shook her head. The old her would have wanted that and some, but now... she thought about his needs.

"I don't think that will suit us. I'm not ashamed of what I feel for you, this request doesn't come from anything like that."

"Request?"

"I want it to be private. I don't want us to be a source of gossip or scandal from people who could never understand. Not many will ever really accept us as legitimate and...real. I don't care at all what anyone else thinks. We can't fit into society's mold. I don't want to waste my life trying. We will always be unconventional. I'm starting to like that about us...I'm not ashamed," she said again fervently. "But I also don't want anyone to know, so they don't try to stop us."

"Shall we do it now, then?" He set her back on her feet.

Looking up at the moon, Melina breathed in the beauty and serenity of the night. She smiled again. She knew there was something special about this night. "I think so," she whispered.

He wrapped his hand gently around her wrist. His grip connecting like a cuff. "All that I am is now yours. The power and the weakness. When you cannot stand I will hold you up. When danger comes I will be your shield."

That was all he said. Until then she would have thought so few words couldn't be enough. But it wasn't just enough, it overwhelmed her. He offered complete commitment. Now it was her turn. She would try to be as clear and concise as he had.

His hand was still wrapped around her wrist. Her cheeks were burning, and her heart was in her throat, but she didn't flinch away from his gaze. Melina swallowed hard.

"I will freeze my heart in this moment. It belongs to you and I will keep it right here. There is no longer you and me, my identity is now merged with yours. I will follow you, lead you, and walk beside you. No matter what...I will stay. That is my promise... I will stay."

His hand around her wrist began to vibrate, and a jolt shot through her arm. He let go. A simple black band circled her wrist. It looked like a burn but there was no pain. She smiled up at him but then she narrowed her eyes and pointed sharply at his face.

"If you betray me or break my heart, I will destroy you slowly and painfully."

He returned her threat with the warmest smile she'd ever seen from him. Rhain caressed her cheek. "Killer Bunny...I absolutely adore you."

"I mean it."

He chuckled and scooped her back up in his arms. "I've known from the start you were a yandere. Of course, you mean it."

He carried her back inside and they consummated their marriage in the unusual way they experienced intimacy. Not as a physical act, but a spiritual one.

Melina couldn't sleep anymore that night. She closed her eyes and tried, but despite her newfound joy and excitement, a cold metal sliced in the background of her thoughts. There was something she had to do. Something she'd been unable to do. But now...she was strong enough.

Rhain lay still beside her, incapable of sleep, but offering her his warmth and the comfort of his presence. She rolled away from him, got up, and began to dress.

"What is it?" he asked.

"There's something I have to do right now. It can't wait. I'm going back to my apartment."

"I'll come with you."

"No." Her voice was sharp. "This is the last thing I have that I will do alone. That's why it can't wait. It's bugging me."

"Does this have something to do with Tristan?"

"Yes."

They gazed at each other in a power struggle.

"I promised to be your shield."

"I'm not in danger. I want to show you I can do this on my own. I feel strong enough because of you, but I don't want you to be there. Will you trust me?"

"I trust you."

"Okay then. When I finish my task, I'll start to pack. Will you come in the afternoon and help me move?"

"Whoa! I didn't say you could move in. That was never discussed. I believe the key to a happy marriage is separate residences."

She laughed and put her hand on her hips. "I guess we're going to be unhappy then because I'm moving in and nothing you say will stop me."

He tsked. "Buyer's remorse is setting in already. I want an annulment."

"Too bad. You've had your way with me."

"That was pseudo," he grumbled.

She used the portal ring to open a way back to her apartment.

"See you later," she said loudly over the rushing of the portal and stepped into it.

The portal kicked her out in her living room and closed as she landed on her feet.

The dawn was close to breaking, the sky outside the windows swirled grey and deep blue. Tristan stood in the shadows in the corner of the room. She didn't wait for him to speak or make a move toward her. She rushed to her bedroom, opened her vanity drawer, and pulled out the necklace. Holding the accursed stone clasped in her palm, she came back into the living room and faced him.

"This is goodbye, Tristan."

He looked at her hand and smirked. "We've been here before. You don't have the guts or the strength."

"I didn't before. That's true, but I'm the woman who killed you, remember? My lack of strength and will was temporary."

His gaze settled on the band around her wrist, and rage burned in his eyes. "Love has made you full of yourself, bitch."

"You cannot understand love. It *has* made me stronger. His faith has fortified me."

"It doesn't matter what you do or who you do," he fired back. "You're mortal and that is temporary. When you die you will come to me. There is no choice. Destiny has revoked your right to choose."

"I'm taking it back." Her heart burned as she said it, the simple statement was a declaration of war.

She dropped the necklace to the floor. "This is the end, Tristan. We will never see each other again in this life or the next."

He laughed. "I will make you cry and scream and beg when you come back to me."

"Time will tell which of us is right." She gazed intently at him. His beautiful eyes...his gorgeous face...his malignant soul. "Goodbye."

She brought her heel down on the necklace. He cried out as his ghostly image broke into three sections. Gritting her teeth she brought her foot down on it again, this time twisting her sole as she did, grinding the stone. He fractured more and more and began to blow away like dust even though there was no wind.

"Melina..." His voice faded with the rest of him.

She exhaled when he was gone. The single tear sliding down her cheek was an amalgamation of all her feelings surrounding Tristan. Offense, rage, love, disgust, shame, regret, and hate. She wiped it away and relief rushed in the aftermath. A terrible weight lifted off her heart as the sun broke the horizon. New strength. New life. New love. It was a beautiful new day.

Around lunchtime, Rhain knocked on the front door.

"You don't need to knock any more, you know?" She smiled as she let him in.

He reached for her, enveloping her in smoke. "Did you complete your task?"

"I did. Now I'm just packing. And I must say I've never enjoyed mundane work quite so much."

He looked around at all the packing she'd accomplished. "Busy little bunny. I think you're due for a break."

"Is that right?"

He leaned down and kissed her mouth. "Your new husband wants to play with you."

She giggled as he picked her up and carried her to the bedroom.

Worry mixed with annoyance inside Maddox. Melina
was taking too long answering his message. Regardless
if she was better or not, they still had an agreement
that she would answer him quickly so he wouldn't be
concerned. It had been hours since he last messaged
her and still no response. Scowling he messaged Erin
instead.

What's up, babe?

Have you talked to Mel at all today? **He wrote.**

No. Why?

She hasn't answered my messages at all. I'm going to
check on her.

Let me know when you find her. I'm worried now, too.

I'll let you know.

   He hung his sword on the rock wall of the arena in the
Obsidian Mountain and grabbed his jacket before
touching the medallion on his wrist and opening a

portal just outside Melina's front door. He knocked loudly.

"Mel? Are you here?"

He pounded again.

"Mel?"

"Hold on!" Her voice came muffled through the door. "Why are you here?"

He scowled. "You didn't answer my message. We agreed. Now open up."

She swore and opened the door. His eyebrows shot up, and he was instantly almost as embarrassed as she looked. Her cheeks were bright red, and she was averting her eyes. He didn't see anyone behind her, but she obviously wasn't alone and he'd just interrupted some afternoon love. That much was obvious by the look on her face and the fact she was only wearing a short satin robe.

"Um...I'm sorry. But you didn't answer my message. I was worried." He couldn't help the smirk that lifted the sides of his lips. "Who you got in there?"

"Nunya. As you can see, I'm fine. Now go away."

Maddox almost swallowed his tongue as Rhain appeared in the bedroom doorway behind her. The demon crossed his arms and glared at Maddox.

"You have impeccable timing." Rhain's hellish voice ground with sarcasm.

He walked up behind Mel and wrapped his smoky arms possessively around her waist. She looked perfectly comfortable in his embrace.

"I forgot my watch at your house last night," she said to Rhain. "I never saw his message."

The demon leaned down and kissed her temple. "I should go anyway. X needs me in the office for a little while. I'll see you this evening."

"Okay."

He walked past Maddox and left.

"Well, you might as well come in since you already ruined my lunch date."

Discombobulated, Maddox came in and shut the door behind him. "I can't even...I mean...this is a joke, right? It's not even possible."

"Shut up before I throat punch you."

"What? Seriously? Can he even?" The blood drained from his face as his thoughts spun. "Are you all right? Did he hurt you?"

Mel snorted and rolled her eyes. "No, he didn't hurt me. And it's not your business."

"Well, yeah, but why would you even want to try something so risky...and demented?"

Her eyes flashed at him. "Watch your mouth."

"I will not. I love you, Mel. You're my best friend. I'm seriously worried about you. Before I was afraid you were going to hurt yourself, now it's like you've lost your mind...and he's taken advantage of you."

Her hand whipped out and cracked a slap to his face. Stunned, he touched his burning cheek. He gauged the look in her eyes. He'd seen that look once before, many years ago, right before she beat the shit out of him. He took a deep breath. He wasn't trying to fight with her, just the opposite.

"I'm sorry. I'm not trying to upset you. I'm really just shocked and worried. Honest. You helped me when I hit bottom. I'm just trying to be there for you, too."

Sighing, she dropped her attack stance. "All right. Just don't insult my husband."

"Husband?!"

She held her wrist out to him. There was an odd black mark, the same color as Rhain's smoke, circling it like a bangle.

"For obvious reasons, we're not advertising it. Sheesh. If I can't even trust you to not lose your head over the truth, I'm not in the mood to deal with everyone else. Please keep it to yourself... Just know that he has not hurt me in any way ever. What we do in the bedroom, unconventional or not, is our business. This is what I wanted. And he didn't take advantage of me, if anything, I took advantage of him."

"You could have someone else, you know? Someone *alive.* You're giving up a lot and you don't even realize it."

She shook her head. "If this situation was reversed I might say the same type of thing to you, so I won't lash out again. But you don't understand. No one can understand me and Rhain. Don't worry so much. I'm happy. I've never been happy like this. Let that be enough for you and let it go."

"Hmm..." He sighed and nodded, but he wasn't even close to letting this go. "I need to get back to work. I just had a few minutes to check on you anyway."

He turned and walked out the door.

"M?" she called.

He looked back.

"I'm okay...I promise. I need you to believe me."

"I believe you." He did, too. He could see she was okay, but he wasn't done protecting her. There were a few things he needed to know before he could even think about accepting this. He headed to Fortress instead of back to work.

Maddox walked down the halls of the castle to where X did his interrogations and leaned against the wall. Voices drifted through the door. He wouldn't have to wait long. No one could lie to X and if they tried to just keep silent, Rhain would scare the hell out of them until they talked. He'd never been afraid of the demon, but he'd never contemplated confronting him, either.

The door next to him opened, and X stepped out with a relieved looking man beside him.

"You're free to go. Thank you for cooperating."

The guy muttered his thanks and took off like his feet were on fire. X crossed his arms as he looked at Maddox.

"What are you doing here?"

"I need a few words with Fluf—I mean Rhain."

X gave him an amused look and stepped up to him. "Is this about Melina?"

"It is."

The amusement vanished from his face, and he leaned close to Maddox. "If you weren't a mage, I'd fear for your safety…" He jerked his head toward the open door. "Don't be an asshole."

"I'm afraid that might be unavoidable at the moment."

X smirked and shrugged. "Maybe I'll need to start planning your funeral after all. Don't get your blood all over. I just cleaned in there."

Maddox scowled and headed toward the door. "I appreciate the familial support," he said sarcastically before closing the door behind him.

He turned and faced Rhain.

Rhain blinked at him and sighed as though bored. "I figured you were going to be a pain in my ass. Say what you came here to say."

"You're tainting her so she can't have a real future. All you can see is what you want."

"Huh... Anything else?"

"You're an opportunist and you've taken advantage of her."

"I don't have to answer your accusation, but I will." Rhain crossed his massive, hazy arms over his chest. "From the moment I knew it was possible for her to love me...when I decided to jump into this game, I was in it to win. I have no shame over that. I'm not afraid of my feelings, or hers. I'll admit it openly to anyone and to myself. I know you love her but she's not your woman, nor could she be and you wouldn't want her like that anyway. She's your dearest friend?"

"Yes," Maddox said. "She is."

"Don't you want her happiness then?"

"That's exactly why I'm here. I want her to have everything she could ever want. You can't give her everything."

Rhain appeared to grow a little taller and the temperature in the room seemed to drop. "Ah...yes. This is where you tell me if I love her I'll let her go?"

"Well, yeah."

"Screw you, Maddox. It's *because* I love her that I won't let her go."

"Selfishly," he accused.

"Love is selfish to the core!" Rhain growled. "Obsessive, possessive, consuming and ultimately greedy. I will take this opportunity, but I would die for her without a second hesitation. There's nothing I wouldn't give her or give up for her. I am selfish and greedy..." His eyes turned a darker red and he looked down at Maddox with devious calculation. "Greedy for her soft words, her smile, her lips..." he dropped his voice an octave. "Her cries of pleasure. They are *mine*. You might think you know me. You don't."

"It can't last."

"I know that!" Rhain shouted. "I know she'll leave one day. Sooner or later. I won't try to stop her. When she's ready to leave...I'll let her and be thankful for the time she gave me."

They stared at each other for a moment, then Maddox sighed and lifted his hands in a show of surrender. "I'm sorry for prodding at you. I just had to know for sure...You're right, I don't know you, not on a real personal level. I know Mel, though. After seeing this side of you, I think I can see why she's drawn to you. I *do* want her to have everything, but maybe you two are a good match...I trust you'll honor your word and let her go when the time comes. You won't catch any more shit from me."

"Good, because this time was free. Stick your nose in our business again, and I'll make you swiftly regret it."

Maddox headed for the door. "I believe you."

X grinned at him as he came back into the hall, looking totally unashamed that he'd been listening to everything. "*Whew*, did you get off light. It's rather miraculous, actually. His temper is not one to be tried, I can tell you."

"Again, thank you for the familial support," Maddox said dryly.

X shrugged. "I wouldn't have let him kill you, only because Tesla would be sad."

Maddox socked his brother-in-law in the shoulder and turned to leave, a small smirk on his lips. X never had any respect for Maddox, but since his life had taken a sharp turn for the better, his relationship with X was getting better, too. They might never be friends, but they were family and they had each other's backs.

He shook his head as he left Fortress, thinking on the conversation he'd just had. Mel had strange taste...not bad he guessed, just strange. Whatever. Rhain wasn't going to hurt her and that was really all he needed to know.

Eleven

Moving boxes were stacked here and there, a few open and spewing their contents out. Melina's stuff was all over the place. Rhain's careful order hid in fear under the chaos. Laying on her stomach on the floor, propped on her elbows, Melina turned the pages of the book in front of her. She made cute little sighs as she read. He was trying to read, too, but she was making it impossible. His gaze kept darting off the words and on to her. The way she scowled at the pages or licked her lips, the little circles she made absentmindedly with her pink, fuzzy sock-covered feet as she crossed and uncrossed her ankles...just that she was there. All the details of her made his heart clench.

Wife.

His mind tripped over the word.

"Huh?" She glanced up. "Did you say something?"

"No. I was staring at you like a stalker, though."

She flashed him a sideways smile. "You're just attentive."

"Interesting way to look at it. You've got a monster staring at you, contemplating all the ways he can devour you and you smile and flirt."

"Devour, huh? Sounds like good times to me."

He chuckled. "Thank you."

"For?"

"Being here."

She turned her face back to her book. "I'm not doing you a favor."

He looked back at the open book in his lap and found the spot he'd left off, trying to focus. Her breathing changed, drawing his attention again. Her skin flushed, and she was trembling, her breathing quiet but unsteady. Fear swam in her eyes as she met his gaze. Not terror, but what was that? Determination? Distress? Her bottom lip shuddered.

"I love you," she whispered.

Physical pain, not the phantom of pain, but real pain slammed into him. Time held still even though he didn't make it echo. *I love you*. Those words...no one had ever said those words to him. It was true power.

The exterior of his heart tore open and he bled out. His strength broke. He couldn't even move. She hadn't said that before, not even when she'd said her vows to become his wife. He said it to her, but she hadn't said back. She handed him the elements. Had he ever breathed before now? He wasn't waiting for it, he never expected it. Truly, had he ever breathed before? No. He hadn't.

"Rhain? What's wrong?" She got to her feet and walked to him.

Laying the book in his lap aside, she sank through the smoke, straddling him. Haze danced around her as she brought her face close to his.

"Don't be scared." Her voice was barely a whisper.

How did she know? What did she see?

Melina set her hand on his chest in the center of the broken circle. "I love you," she said again, this time without a trace of fear or hesitation. "Feel it. It's okay."

Nothing was okay about this feeling. She leveled him. Rendered him totally powerless.

"I can't...It's not...how do I..." He exhaled. Such a terrible weight on his lungs. "I don't know what to do."

Her smile was slow and warm. "Yes, you do. You always know with me...and even when you don't, it's okay." She leaned her forehead against his and closed her eyes. "Us. Just us."

Greed exploded through him. *Mine, all mine.* Lifting her up, he carried her to the bedroom. They had to merge right then. He had to touch her spirit as he had when she bit him. He had to strip her down and see his darkness slide all over her skin. They had to exist in the same place at the same time, beyond the barriers that held them apart. He had to find new ways to claim her. He *would* find new ways.

Any moment now, I'll wake from this beautiful dream... Any moment.

Melina slept deeply, her head on his chest. He held her against him with one arm, but he resisted the urge to touch her more than that. He wanted to run his fingertips over the black marks covering her skin, but he didn't want to disturb her rest. So beautiful. So warm and generous. Wife.

Mine.

It was really true. He had someone who was his. He pinched his eyes shut and groaned. What was he doing? Had Maddox been right? Had he taken advantage of her? Was he tainting her? Had he messed up her chances at a real future?

Of course, he had. He'd done all those things.

I love you. Her voice echoed through his mind. *Us. Just us.*

He smiled down at her. No one would understand them, he wouldn't be one of those people. He understood his own relationship. Screw everything else.

She gave a little jolt and whimpered once. Her eyes moved back and forth behind her eyelids for a moment. She settled again. All the dark lines and designs covering her body slid back from her hands and feet. Running like ink up her arms and legs, over her stomach and shoulders, pooling between her breasts. She gave another little jolt as the shapeless black mark stretched into a circle.

A broken circle.

Oh no. He watched intently, but it didn't fade or vanish. The smell of burning flesh filled the air as the mark seared into her skin. She didn't wake. Everything he'd just been feeling disappeared behind a wave of panic. What had he done to her?

The glyph, the brand of the curse, now marred her.

He listened for a moment to the steady rhythm of her heart. Pulling away from her, he covered her with a blanket. He gave himself one second to stand next to the bed and gaze at her before turning and leaving.

Help me. Help me. Help me.

Too many years of living with Tesla and X did away with any thoughts he might have had to knock and wait for them to let him in. He cast his eyes around the darkened Livingroom as Tesla strode up to him.

"Help me!" he pleaded.

"How?"

"There's a curse on me and now it's transferred to Melina." Panic bore down on him. "I can't let her suffer the way I have. Please. I have to know who I am. Maybe if I know who and what I am, I can break it."

"Okay." She held her lightning covered hands up. "We'll help you. Breathe. And we'll help Melina." She turned her head to the side. "X!" she called.

She was too calm! This was urgent!

"Look!" Grabbing her by the arm, he pulled her into his interior.

He'd never had anyone this close to his real body beside Melina. She looked like she wanted to say something but decided against it. Her gaze settled on the broken circle on his chest.

"Yes," she breathed. "I see. I...I've never seen anything like it."

That was the last thing he wanted to hear from her. She moved closer. Her eyes narrowed as she looked intently at the circle, as though she was dissecting it on a molecular level with just her gaze.

"I don't recognize any of the magic embedded inside it."

She reached up and touched the circle with her fingertip. The electric current from her finger jumped on the broken edge, raced around the circle to the other end, connecting the broken ends in a complete circuit.

Sand. Millions of fine grains of sand rained through his body. The sand sparked in his eyes like bright lights, blinding him. Rhain was pulled backward into an abyss too strong to fight where all his senses were smothered into darkness. The darkness breathed him in. He was reset. The completed circle burning on his chest was all he knew.

TWELVE

Blood ran down Melina's arm into her hand. It collected at her fingertips, growing into swollen blubs. Drip, drip, drip, drip... She spread her blood across the broken circle. "Wake up! Rhain, wake up!" Her voice cracked with desperation. He didn't wake. "Please...please...I've come so far. I can't lose you now."

She sobbed against him. It couldn't end like this.

"WAKE UP!"

Her lungs struggled to fill as her eyes returned to normal, the vision fading, leaving her covered in a cold sweat and her heart thrashing. Her limbs shook and tears welled up and spilled over. She worked to calm herself. It was just one of those damn visions. Relax. She put her hand over her racing heart and winced. Melina blinked as she looked at her chest and gently touched the burn. It matched Rhain's broken circle. Chills rushed up her spine. What did this mean? It couldn't be good. Was it as bad a sign as her gut was telling her it was? She hadn't fallen asleep alone, but she was alone now.

"Rhain?" Her voice was a plea.

She held her breath, listening, but some part of her knew he wouldn't answer. She felt alone as she never had. Alone in the absolute.

Was this one of those moments? The ones that break your world and force your feet on a new path…one you would never choose? Instinct whispered it just might be.

Getting out of bed, she began to dress. Not quickly, not haphazardly. She dressed with the unknown in mind as if she was on the start square of a journey. Why did she feel like this? Shit. She wanted to dismiss her gut, but she refused to be foolish just to entertain the seduction of denial. Something was very wrong.

Fully dressed, boots laced, she hesitated only for a second holding her sunset stone necklace before setting it down on the nightstand. She might lose it if she wore it now. The stone burned bright against the dark wood it lay on. She swallowed the lump in her throat. Leaving it was a goodbye.

Last, she put Forest's portal ring on her finger. It wouldn't work outside of Regia. She hesitated, then took it off and set it on the nightstand also. She might lose it and it would be useless once she left.

Striding to the main house, Melina knocked loudly.

"Come in," X's voice sounded through the door.

She came in, her mind on a forced stoic setting. Tesla was crying in X's arms. The sorrow in her eyes sank deep as she looked up at Melina.

"I'm so sorry!" Tesla wailed. "It was an accident!"

"What happened?" Melina's voice was so flat she didn't even recognize the sound of it herself. Under that, she was hysterical. Hysteria had to be kept in the background.

"He was scared. He said he was cursed, and it was transferring to you, that he couldn't let you suffer the way he had," Tesla sobbed the words out. "He said he needed to know who he was. He showed me the circle. I...I touched it. I'm sorry. I shouldn't have touched it with my bare hands. My electric current closed the circle. The next second he was gone. Just vanished. I'm sorry, Melina. I'm so sorry."

"We'll find him," X said firmly.

"No. I'll find him."

X lifted one eyebrow. "You're not a world jumper."

"So, help me. Give me what I need to travel, but *I* will find him. *I'm* his wife."

Tesla shook her head. "Too risky. Rhain was trying to protect you from—"

X gave her a severe look, full of meaning Melina couldn't read, but Tesla seemed to understand.

"But..." Tesla said to X.

"We'll look for him, too, but she's his best hope," X argued. "Her limitations don't factor. Just as mine didn't when I rescued you from Lachlan... Love is the strongest magic. You know this. Let her have your blood."

Tesla bit down on her lip and nodded. "Okay, but we don't even know where he originally came from, if he's even there now. Where do we even start?" They both looked at Melina. "Did he tell you anything? Give you any information about his origins?"

"He has power over time. He can make a moment echo. He told me time is tied to music, but he didn't know where he came from. He was afraid to learn who he was."

X frowned. "Music...time echo...no worlds I've been to..." He looked pointedly at Tesla. "What about you?"

She shook her head. "No. Never."

"Look, I don't need to know that. I've already seen that I find him." Melina argued. "I will be able to find him after I get my sight enhanced."

"Huh?" X said.

Melina pointed at her eye. "I just need to get to Polyhedron. If I can fully access my future memories—"

"Oh, yes," Tesla said. "That might work. Polyhedron isn't so far. You'll need to be careful. I haven't been there in a long time. Be sure to—"

The clock was ticking. She didn't have time for anything else. Melina stepped forward and sank her fangs into Tesla's neck. It was out of line to grab her like that. It was a seriously bitchy thing to do. At the moment, she didn't have the reserve to care. Her mind was trapped on her task. Tesla could have blasted her into ashes, but she held still and let Mel take her blood. Tesla's lightning snaked through her veins and the eye in her eye contracted and expanded.

Polyhedron was in Melina's blood. She could get there. With this borrowed power, she could get there.

X's firm hand clamped like a vice on her forearm and pulled her back. "That's enough."

"I'm sorry." Melina wiped her mouth.

Tesla shook her head. "I'm the one who's sorry."

Lightning raced through Melina's muscles and wrapped around her bones. With her bare hands, she did something beyond her capabilities and tore the atmosphere open directly where she needed to go.

Darkness then blinding light as her feet hit solid ground. Her senses cringed inward, disoriented as they all tried to catch up. It was all there, the fear, the confusion, and curiosity, all the normal things she would have felt were buried under the suffocating storm of desperation. She had to find Rhain. There was no time to lose. Recklessly, she plunged ahead into the unknown without a second thought to her own safety.

The air was so clean it stung her nose. The lack of scent almost hurt. The eye inside her eye jolted and rushed to the front. Pushing out like a baby struggling to be born. The warm brown of her iris split apart as the grey overtook it. Blood ran from the corner of her eyelid and down her cheek as the android eye settled and locked into place like a deadbolt. Pain spiked in her temple as her eyes tried to sync.

She was in a courtyard of sorts, a wall encased the space with a building at the end jutting straight up like an obelisk, dazzled by the novelty of it at first, thinking she found it beautiful. Perfect order, perfect balance, perfect temperature, perfection on every level. She glanced at the sky, but the word didn't really apply. The flat periwinkle expanse overhead looked more like a ceiling than a sky. Was there a real sky beyond? She didn't know why, but she doubted it.

A line of white light moved over the ground under her feet from one side of the courtyard to the next like a lazy wave rolling up the shore. Her grey eye saw the truth of the light, the fabric of this space was refreshing itself... code, numbers, language, information updating. Tingles ran up her body from the bottoms of her feet to her scalp. The light wave didn't just update the space around her, it updated *her*. At that moment, Melina realized it wasn't just her eye that was android, traces of their genetic code lightly dusted her blood and bones. The light wave seemed to be trying to re-order her thoughts. She would have been pissed about it, but it actually felt good, almost as good as a blood high.

People moved around her, sleek androids, walking at a perfect pace. She didn't even attempt to not stare. They were all different, she hadn't expected that, but they all looked perfect, too. Rahaxeris told her they were alive. Not robots, but machines that lived and died. Light pulsed from their chests like a heartbeat. There were men, women, and yes, even children. The children took her surprise more than anything else. The light was blue on the men, red on the woman, and green on the children regardless of their gender. She wished she read more than the introduction of that book Rahaxeris gave her on this world. She knew next to nothing about this place and these people.

No one noticed her. They walked into the courtyard and straight for the building at the other end, looking ahead, not talking. The children didn't play, scamper, or cause any trouble. They walked stoically beside their parents.

She backed up until she pressed into a cold wall. Light jumped to life on the wall in response to her touch, sparking around her like bright confetti. The confetti swept away with the next wave of white light. The light wave hit the building and everything changed.

They all stopped. Every eye turned on her. Her thundering heart and shallow breathing were the only movements in the entire courtyard. What did she do now? What were they going to do to her?

"O.A.," they all said in unison. The androids faced the building again and continued walking forward.

All except one woman. She walked briskly toward Melina. Melina planted her feet, prepared to fight but another light swept under her feet, forcing a calm over her. The woman's appearance changed the closer she came. The dark charcoal of her glossy skin lightened steadily until she was a dull beige and the cables of her hair changed from blood red to brown. The red light on her chest and in her eyes also lightened into pink.

"Welcome," she said in a soothing voice.

"Uh… thank you," Melina muttered.

"Try to not be afraid. I understand fear is the typical response of newcomers, but I assure you, there is nothing to worry about. No harm will befall you. This world is welcoming and interested in outsiders."

"Please help me. I need to access my future memories as quickly as I can. It's urgent. "

"Of course I can help you. Please follow me."

The woman walked in the opposite direction. Hesitating a second, Melina glanced back at the building. It looked like an official place, maybe she should go there instead. Torn, she looked at the woman again. Should she go with her? Maybe in this world, her request was trivial and easy, nothing to bother official people with. The woman stopped.

"Forgive me," the woman said, walking back to Melina. "I don't believe I gave you the information you need to feel at ease."

Could this android read her mind or was she that transparent?

"My name is Sally and I'm a member of the P.O.P. or Polyhedron's Outreach Program." Sally smiled, flashing a perfect row of metallic teeth. "Most call us Poppers because of the acronym. Isn't that cute? It's my job to welcome in people like you, those who are new here and need a guide. What is your name?"

"Melina."

"What a nice name. Please follow me."

Melina exhaled and followed Sally. They stepped out of the walled courtyard, they were on a path, 30 feet wide, and barely a shade darker than the sky. Melina's boots squeaked on the smooth surface. A city of light grey spires lay ahead like a landscape of icicles, each one topped with a bright light.

"It's beautiful," Melina said.

"Yes. All the cities of Polyhedron are beautiful. This is Marx. We are smaller than the capital, but we are growing."

The androids they passed on the road glanced at her, some of them whispered, "O.A."

"Um...Sally?"

"Yes?"

"What does O.A. stand for?"

"Hmm? Let's turn here."

The road split to the side and sloped down a hill. Glass walls rose up on either side of the path, and they continued to walk downward into the lower level of a building. Sally opened a clear door and gestured for Melina to follow.

"Please come in."

A light wave rolled over the seamless walls and floors just like the one in the courtyard. As it had before, her thoughts and emotions re-ordered, calm washing over her. The whole space was sterile white when they came in, but just as Sally had changed colors, the walls turned a warm peach color. There was no furniture but various frames like door-less doorways here and there around the room. Melina avoided walking through any of them.

Sally faced her and smiled again. "Accessing all your future memories is your desire?"

"Yes."

"No problem." Sally gestured to the largest frame. "Step under here. It will only take a moment and there will be no pain."

Unafraid, desperate to get the knowledge and get out of there, Melina moved under the frame. She had to find Rhain. She didn't care if there was pain or not.

"Very good. Place your hands on the frame and the knowledge will come," Sally instructed.

Melina put her hands flat against the smooth material. Threads shot out from the frame and wrapped around her wrists, ankles, waist, and neck.

"Hold still now, or the strings will slice through your flesh."

"Is this how I get my memories?"

Sally smiled again. "Yes. It will only take a few minutes. Close your eyes and tell me what you see."

Threads came out of the top of the frame and connected to the ends of her hair. A rush of thoughts, voices, and color rolled through her. Her eyelids clamped shut. Where was Rhain? How long would it take for her to see the memories she needed the most to find him?

The threads connecting to her hair lit up, pouring heat and light into her head. She floated in an expanse of creamy clouds. Peace, so much peace it made her sleepy. All thoughts evaporated.

Why was she here?

"Catch the bird," a voice instructed.

A small creature with pink wings fluttered past her.

"Catch the bird."

It flew barely beyond her grasp. She lunged forward, following it as it soared through the clouds. Was she flying, too?

"If you can catch the bird, all your desires will be yours. Are you worthy? Catch the bird."

Melina surged forward faster, hands outstretched. The bird flew in a straight line in front of her. She was so close, almost...she could almost touch the very tip of its feathers. Her hand closed around the tail just as the bird disintegrated into tiles and bits of code. The rest of the world around her shattered into pieces, a sound like glass breaking filling her ears.

Melina opened her eyes and blinked, face to face with a stranger wearing a smug expression. "I swear, didn't your mother tell you never to talk to strangers?"

"What?" The threads around her neck sliced through her skin.

"Stop moving!" the woman shouted. "The frame will cut your head off. We only have a minute before they come for us. I'm not going to get caught by them. Chose now, come with me, or take your chances with them." She gestured to Sally, lying lifeless on the floor.

Melina took one second to measure the person standing before her. She wasn't an android, or not completely anyway. Both of her arms were robotic from the elbows down and a metallic port with a blinking blue light stuck out of her cheek in front of her ear. Aside from this, she looked like a normal person. She could have been Regian or human. Sunglasses hid her eyes, but the way she held herself and the smirk on her lips convinced Melina. This woman was a badass. Maybe she meant her harm as well, just a different type, but if she freed her, that's all that mattered at the moment.

"You."

"Good choice, O.A."

Extending her index finger and pushing down on the hinge of her knuckle, a line of blue light shot out of her fingertip like a laser. Melina gritted her teeth as the woman cut the threads with the line of light. Her hair singed on the tips as the light went over her head. The woman caught her as Melina fell out of the frame.

"I won't slow down for you, so keep up."

With the same laser she used to cut the threads, the woman drew a circle on the wall. Code fragmented and scattered away from the blue light leaving an opening. She raced through the hole, Melina followed as an alarm began screeching, and the walls and floor turned red. Instead of continuing to run the woman turned back to the hole. She tapped the wall with her fingertips quickly as if she was typing, and the hole in the wall closed as if it had never been there, the red vanishing and the alarm quieted.

"Let's go."

The woman was fast, but Melina stayed right behind her. The tunnel changed as they ran deeper. The same sleek material she'd seen everywhere flashed and shifted into a dark, mottled brown. The floor sloped down, and two inches of tepid water rushed around their feet, spraying from hoses on the walls. Her savior didn't slow down. She charged into the water as it became deeper. Up to their waists, the woman turned and shoved a small device at Melina.

"Put that in your mouth, unless you can breathe underwater. I hope you can swim, if not I'm sorry I couldn't save you."

Melina took the thing. It was long and thin like a writing stylus, lights and small buttons on the top. "How do I—"

The woman grabbed the device back, tapped one of the buttons and pressed it against Melina's mouth. It shuddered, tiny tubes snaking out and going up her nose and into her mouth, feeding her air. Putting an identical device on her face, the woman dove into the water.

Plunging in the dark water, she stroked hard, following the little blue lights on the woman leading her. *This has taken a bad turn* she thought as her heart raced. *I'm not going to drown. I will not die here. I'm going to find my husband. If the task kills me, so be it, but I won't die until I see him again.*

Growing colder, and darker, a strong current began pulling them faster down. Pinpricks of light broke through the darkness. The current swooped in a down rush. She was falling. Melina slammed into a rock-hard surface on her hands and knees as the tunnel spit them out. Water splashed over them like a waterfall.

The woman grabbed the breathing device and pulled it off Melina's face. Her nostrils burned as the tubes came out, and she coughed, blinking and looking around. They were in a vast open space, tunnels leading off in all directions. Huge places of broken code like rust holes spreading cancer covered the ceiling and walls. Graffiti marred some of the space in a language she couldn't read and other places had scrolling information in illuminated words, but it too was broken.

"Welcome to level 3, or as we few renegades fondly refer to it as, *the basement*."

"What's your name?" Melina stood and stepped out of the water.

"Cope."

"What would have happened to me back there?"

"Sally would have put you through a number of tests, each one extracting more and more of your identity until you were a drone. Then she would have delivered you to the popper's main building where you would have been studied until you died. O.A.'s like you have it the worst if they catch you. You look like you're 98% organic." Cope tsked and shook her head. "Sally got you fast. I didn't have a chance to beat her to you once she knew you were there."

"Why would they study me? And what does O.A. mean?"

"Organic Android. There aren't many like you, at least not in this world. The fact you were born with any level of their biological makeup without it being implanted fascinates them no end. Some of them get a bit excited by the notion of procreation with organics. Creating a new race. It divides their society. Some believe it to be immoral."

"I need my future memories. That's why I came here. Can you help me?"

Cope snickered. "Is that how Sally lured you? Told you she could give them to you?"

"Yes. She said it would be quick and easy."

Tilting her head to the side, Cope smiled slowly. "Just how stupid are you?"

Melina huffed. "Pretty stupid obviously. I *need* my memories. I'm desperate."

Cope shook her head, chuckling. "Come on. Follow me, newbie."

"My name's Melina."

"Whatever," Cope waved her hand over her shoulder as she led Melina down a shadowed, snaking tunnel. "If you're going to survive you need to keep your eyes open, learn fast, and humor Salem."

"Salem?"

"You'll meet him soon, and Inesia. There's just the three of us on this level. You make four. We haven't been able to save any new O.A.s in a while. You look a little tougher than the usual, so maybe you won't be a wasted effort."

"Thanks," Mel said with false sweetness.

Cope snorted and nodded approvingly.

"Actually, I'll offer you real appreciation for saving my neck back there. I'm not a wasted effort. I swear."

"I guess we'll see."

Broken code illuminated the dingy walls on either side of them, and the air was dry and heavy. Melina observed and analyzed Cope as she led her farther down into the unknown darkness. Despite her obvious strength, her frame was feminine and willowy as if she'd been a dancer in another life. She was a few inches taller than Melina and the way she moved gave her away. She wasn't trained in any fighting style, but she could handle herself. Street scrapper, that was her style. Anything and everything, unless Melina was mistaken.

"What are the most immediate dangers?"

"Lucky for us, the poppers don't come down here, and the other surface dwellers are too scared to come this low. It probably wouldn't even occur to the average android to go below the surface. It's level 2 scum we have to look out for. They live above us. Low-class janitors and brain-bleached O.A.s who've been turned loose after the poppers have used them up as much as they can. As best we can tell, we're regarded as rats that need exterminating. Until I tell you you're ready, don't try to leave this level."

"Fair enough," Melina said. *I'll leave when I've got what I need and nothing is going to stop me.*

Blinking lights and faint whirring noises drifted down the tunnel from an open hatch at the end.

"Home sweet home," Cope said sarcastically. "Think fast."

Inside the hatch, a knife came flying straight at her head. On any regular day, she would have dodged, but with Tesla's blood inside her and her android eye dominant, the blade seemed to move comically slow. She snatched it out of the air.

"Oh, nice!" Cope said. "This one's fast. Should we keep her?"

"Hmm…I doubt it," the knife thrower said lazily.

Melina eyed the person across the room and considered throwing the knife back at her. The only thing that stopped her was the beauty of the young woman and her age. She looked about seventeen, a different race from Cope, but she was similarly altered with cybernetics. She had one false hand, the sleek light grey material looked like a glove against her dark skin. Her hair hung in a dense riot over her corded, muscled shoulders, fine filaments of blue and green light snaked through the curly strands as though they grew from her scalp as well. Lighted ports peppered her body, unlike Cope who only had the one on her cheek. She glared at Melina and got up from the makeshift bed she was lounging on.

"I swear, why can't you find a hot, *male* O.A.? I'm sick of Salem being my only choice."

Cope chuckled. "Liar. You love him, you just don't like sharing." She gestured from Melina to the other woman. "Melina, this is Inesia."

Melina tossed the knife back at her. She caught it and slid it into her belt before walking toward the hatch, bumping Melina hard in the shoulder on her way out. "I'm going shopping, Cope." Inesia narrowed her eyes and pointed at Melina. "Stay away from my stuff, stray."

"No problem."

Inesia slammed the hatch door after her.

"She likes you." Cope smirked. "The last O.A. I brought didn't even get one word from her for the first week they were here."

"Where are they now?"

"Dead. Where do you think? She couldn't handle living underground. Lost her grip pretty fast and went to the surface. Well, make yourself at home."

Home was bleak. They were in some kind of abandoned control room. Old, busted, dusty machines lay in piles against the walls. Cables hung here and there from the ceiling or snaked down the walls. Everything was ugly and antiquated compared to the beauty of the surface. Two tunnels connected to this room, snaking off in different directions. The bed Inesia had been lounging on was nothing but a narrow metal frame jutting from the wall with a torn, thin mattress on top. Her heart hurt for these people. Forced to live like this to survive. Was there something she could do to help them?

Cope sat in the only chair in the room.

"How long have you been here?" Mel sat on the edge of the bunk.

"I stopped counting the days when we hit a year. Inesia, Salem, and me...we arrived here together, the property of the same slaver. He sold us to the poppers for a fortune. Us and a bunch more organics he'd collected from other worlds. The three of us..." she paused, biting down on her bottom lip. "A few others, too. We were the only ones to escape with our *moderate upgrades*. The rest...well some of them are still alive, sort of. A few are the brain-bleached that hunt us. Someday, we'll get out of here. I hope."

"Maybe I can help. I'll try. But I really need to access my future memories. How do I do that?"

Cope gave a snort of derision. "Ask Salem when he gets here... Why are you so desperate for your memories anyway?"

"I have to find my husband. He vanished. I have to learn where he is."

"Maybe he ran off with another woman."

Melina snorted. "Yeah, no. He's cursed, but the curse was dormant. It was activated, and he vanished."

Cope's eyebrows rose, and she took off her sunglasses, giving Melina her first look at her strange marbled blue eyes. "Sounds like a real catch."

"He's incredible, but no one else will look closely enough to see it, and that's fine with me. He's mine and I love him."

The snark vanished from Cope's face and she nodded. "I see. We'll try to help you. If Salem balks, I'll put the hurt on him. Love is...worth sacrifice. I understand your desperation now."

"Thank you! Really, thank you so much!"

Putting her sunglasses back, Cope waved her hand dismissively. "Your odds are shit, just so you know."

"My odds are fantastic, actually. I've already seen that I find him. I just need to know where he is."

The hatch swung open.

"Well, now, what have you brought me, Cope? Plaything? Dinner? Or just a stray?" the man in the doorway asked.

He swaggered into the room, throwing the huge, makeshift sword in his hand into the corner. Shrugging off a beat-up leather jacket, he tossed it on the bed next to Mel, grabbed Cope's hand, kissed it, and yanked her out of the chair. He slapped her ass as she moved away and left the room. He plunked down in the chair, pinning Mel with his gaze. She blinked a few times. This guy was incomprehensible.

Leaning back casually, he put one gloved finger in his mouth, biting the fingertip as he pulled his hand out of the leather. He tossed first one glove, then the other on her lap. She ignored the gloves, refusing to break his gaze. His brown hair hung in a stylish mess around his face and framed his deep copper eyes. They were unlike any eyes she'd ever seen, and the light behind them was sharp and wild. This man was an animal. He'd survive in hell.

He looked her over. Assessment of ability. Then he looked her over again. Sexual appreciation. His lips curved to one side. He spread his legs wide and unzipped his pants.

"I'll let you stay here... Get on your knees and show me your gratitude, stray."

Mel smiled broadly, flashing her fangs at him. "Sure thing."

To his credit, he didn't show any panic. He laughed and zipped his pants again. "Oh... Vampire. Lucky find. Your kind is fast if my information is correct. I could use that. I'm Salem. What's your name?"

"Melina."

"Spoiled princess name. So, *Melina*, why are you in this world?"

"I need all my future memories." She pointed at her grey eye. "I was born a partial android, but I've never been to this world before. I made a mistake when I arrived. Cope saved me. Will you help me?"

He sighed and made the chair spin in a circle once. "Wow. You really don't know anything. Oracle is corrupted code. I could hack it and patch you in, but the information you'll get is worthless...It's all a lie. It always was. If you have any future memories, trust the ones in your head. Anything beyond that is a game. Fantasy. RPG. Get it?"

Mel jumped to her feet. "You're lying."

"Perhaps. Either way, you're asking for a lot. Connecting to any main information engines is a real risk for us. All of us. You're not worth it to me...*yet.* Provide some value and I'll consider it."

"Provide value how?"

He tsked. "Sit down. You're making me hard, standing there like you wanna fight."

She sneered and sat back down. "You're ninety percent sexual harassment, Salem."

"You think that because you've only known me for a minute. You'll soon realize you've underestimated me... Hell," he slapped one of his knees and got to his feet, looking down at her. "It's been a while since we've had a new stray. There's something important I forgot to do."

"What?"

"Stand up," he ordered.

"You just told me to sit down."

"So?"

She stood. He gave her no room, and his aura was so strong she could almost feel it teasing her skin.

"I need to check you. I'd use my hands but as much fun as that would be, it wouldn't be as thorough as MUGi."

Salem took a step back and before she could ask, a ball rolled into the room, circled her feet in a figure eight and lifted into the air. The baseball-sized android shot a light over her, running up her body from her feet to her neck. It hovered close to her face, focused on her grey eye, and then zipped back, circling Salem's head once before landing on his shoulder like a pet bird. He grabbed it, tapping the back with his fingers. His eyes moved back and forth, reading something she couldn't see.

"You didn't scream or cower. I thought for sure I'd have to coax and calm you into holding still… Too bad. I wanted to hear you scream, but I'll just have to get it another…" His face fell, and he looked up from his reading, his eyes slicing hard into her. "No way. MUGi must be broken."

"What?"

His gaze sharpened. "You're Regian?"

"Yeah, so? Where the hell else do vampires come from?"

"Lots of places, princess." He tossed MUGi over his shoulder. The droid plummeted toward the floor, slowing in the air and rising back into a smooth hover before gliding into the other room. Salem crossed his arms over his chest, an unsettling satisfaction on his face.

"Well, it doesn't matter where you're from. You're here now." He sat down and spun the chair in a circle again.

She wasn't fooled. She saw the goosebumps rise on his forearms before he threw the droid. She sat back down, too.

"I guess I've just added value."

"How do you figure?" he demanded.

"Don't bother. I saw you. I won't forget just because you've recovered your bravado. The fact I'm Regian means a lot to you. Why? Will I fetch a good price?"

His eyes flashed appreciatively. "You would, for sure. Unfortunately, I've got no buyer at the moment."

"Will you help me get my memories?"

He pursed his lips. "Hmm..."

"What do I have to do?"

"I'll think about it, but until I know what you're good for, being friendly with that *erogenous* body of yours will get you a little way with me."

Mel shook her head. "I'm married."

He lifted one sharp eyebrow. "I don't give a damn about your commitments. You're in my domain now. Don't forget that."

She gave him a malevolent glare.

He pretended to shiver. "Stonewall. That look in your eyes gave me a chill."

"I'll do anything I can for you, but not that."

Smirking, he turned the chair around so she faced his back. "I'm messing with you more than anything. I'm not suffering for affection."

Mel smiled even though she tried not to. "I'm sure you're not."

He chuckled as code projected in front of his face. "Flattery will get you nowhere, but thanks."

"I'm in a hurry."

"So am I!" he shouted, spinning back around. "I've been stuck here for three years! Seven of us escaped the poppers after they filled us with ports and chips and wires. It's just been the three of us for a very long time. The others weren't strong enough, no matter what I did. There wasn't enough food for them. They needed more. If your kind needs to eat too much, you'll die down here, too. You're not trying to survive, I could respect *that.* You're just hunting information, running from heartbreak probably. So, forgive me, if I don't give a shit."

"Fine, you win!" she shouted back. "You're tougher than me, you've lived through the fire. You're fighting for your life, and I'm only fighting for my heart. You're right! You win!"

The armrests groaned as his fingers dug in. Leaning forward, eyes burning, breathing ragged, Salem was an animal ready to pounce on his prey. "You know what I want to do to you?" The question, on the edge of attack, whispered through his lips as a seduction.

She swallowed. "I don't want to know."

He eased back, letting go of the armrests. "You raise your voice to me again and I'll show you."

Try it, asshole...it was in her mouth before she clamped her lips shut. Bad idea. Salem as a person was the embodiment of a bad idea. But he was right. She did have tunnel vision, and she wanted help from people who had next to nothing. She had to calm down. She knew she would find Rhain. She'd seen it, what her vision failed to show her was if she was able to save him or not.

Sighing, Salem turned his back to her again. "So, tell me. Will there be a rescue coming for you?"

She thought about Tesla and X. They knew where she was. She considered how Maddox would react when he found out what she'd done... What her parents would do.

"It depends on how long I'm gone."

"Hmm…"

It wasn't an idle sound in his throat. She couldn't tell if the news of rescue pleased him or not, but he was calculating either way. He'd use her if he could, of that she was certain.

"Cope? Where are you, sexy?"

Cope came back into the room. "What? I was about to start running scans."

"Where's Inesia?"

"Shopping."

He nodded and rubbed his chin. "I need to go to level 2. Show this stray the ropes, will you? And let's try to keep her undamaged. She's valuable."

"Fine. Anything else?"

"I love you. You're my favorite."

"Shut up." She rolled her eyes.

He put his jacket and gloves back on, grabbed his sword, and headed through the hatch without a glance at Mel. She couldn't deny the relief she felt once he was gone.

"So, you're with him?" Mel asked.

"I'm with him all the way, in any way he wants or needs. I owe him my life."

"I meant…"

"Romantically?" Cope scoffed. "Does he strike you as the type to ever be *with* someone?"

"No."

"Salem is an equal opportunity lover. You can have him if you want him, but there's no cage that can hold that beast. He belongs to no one but himself."

"I don't want him."

The light in Cope's eyes seemed to say *liar*. "Follow me."

She led Mel into one of the other rooms. Cables hung like vines along the walls, lights running down each one like patterns on a snake. Multiple screen projections floated in the air, code, images, and words cascaded down each one. Cope walked through the projections and grabbed a cable, shoving the connection at the end into the port on her face. She closed her eyes, tremors twitching her eyelids.

"I'm scanning for news of you," Cope explained.

"But Salem just said connecting to information engines was dangerous."

"I'm not actually connected, just looking. This is different than what you're looking to do, getting your memories, I mean. I'm accessing the public feed so it's unlikely you'll show up, but this is where I have to start. Hopefully, your arrival went mostly unnoticed. I've been doing this for a while...I've learned there are secret codes sometimes...flags for the right people embedded in the wording of the basic news...ah, there you are."

Mel was alarmed. "What?"

Cope's eyelids continued to twitch. "Well, not you directly. There's a report about Sally. It's vague, the public will gloss over it...more of a heads up to the poppers that one of their own has died during an acquisition. Sally was low on the totem pole so perhaps they won't take direct action. We can only hope, but all of us have to be extra careful for a while. They might amp up the brain-bleached in their endeavors to wipe us out."

"I'm sorry."

"This is typical. Don't worry about it. It's the risk we take saving O.A.'s from what they did to us."

"Is there anything I can to do to show my appreciation?"

"The most you can do for now is not be stupid. Don't go anywhere by yourself."

"I promise," Mel said seriously.

"Scanning is my job. I do it every day, on and off. Inesia is more restless and stealthier than I am, so she scours the upper levels for food. She's like a mouse in that regard."

"Androids eat?"

Cope chuckled. "Well, that's the problem. They don't. Food is reserved for ambassadors from other worlds and O.A.s. Needless to say, Inesia is in the most danger on a daily basis because of where she has to go to find food. She's been altered extensively, much more than either me or Salem, so she can access information faster and easier. She usually knows if she's got a tail or not."

"What about Salem? What does he do?"

"Beats me. I mean I know some of what he does, but there's plenty he keeps to himself. He makes weapons some of the time, from scraps he harvests from level 2. He kills the brain-bleached when he encounters them. It puts him in a foul mood, though. It's hard to face those we once traveled with and cut them down, but their personalities are gone and they've been programmed to kill us... Salem knows the pulse of Polyhedron better than I do, even with my daily scanning. If we ever do get out of here, it will be his doing. It's what drives him."

Over the next few hours, Mel hardly moved. She stayed quiet, so as not to disturb Cope. She didn't know what else to do. She kept her ears pricked for the telltale signs one of the others had returned. Restless, she wished she had a job instead of just not being stupid. Closing her eyes, went through all her visions, one by one, observing the details, not dismissing the ones that didn't seem related to her finding Rhain. She looked for patterns and clues, finding none. Was she in the right place? Had she done the wrong thing?

There was no sky to see through the windows, no way for her to count the passing of time. Her stomach began to growl. It wasn't a big deal, only now, knowing there was very little to eat in this place, her light hunger already felt acute. She'd have to learn to ignore it...but then there was the issue of blood. She could go a while without it, but too long and she'd begin to die.

The pulse in Cope's neck caught her attention. She didn't want to take anything from these people, but if she had to remain there, the time would come when she would have to ask for blood. She turned her head and looked at the floor.

"Okay, I'm done, for now." Cope pulled the cable out of her cheek and rolled her neck. "Sorry, that took me a while. I'll show you around more now, before the others get back for the night."

"How do you know it's night?" Mel asked, following Cope.

"I've been here too long. Actually, we just call it night because it's when we sleep. It's night on the surface already. The androids are asleep, or *recharging*, not that it makes it safe for us to go roaming about, quite the opposite."

Tunnels, tunnels, and more tunnels. Her shoulders began to hunch as she cringed inwardly against the oppressive environment.

"It's like a dark cage. How do you stay sane?"

Cope laughed darkly. "What makes you think I'm sane?" She took off her sunglasses and looked Mel in the eyes. "We're all a bit off down here. You will need to be, too. Just lose it in fun ways, okay? Make shit up, wander, start a nasty, sweaty fling with Salem, hallucinate, sleep, cut yourself, start fights with the rest of us...all that's good and fine. Just don't go to the surface, don't connect to the information engines. Crazy is all good, psychotic won't be tolerated. Understand?"

Mel nodded. "I understand. You said to wander, but what if I accidentally go to level 2?"

"Can't you tell which way is up?" she snickered. "Relax. You'll be fine. I can tell. There's not much else to see right now. I'm hungry. I bet Inesia is back. Let's go home. I'll show you more tomorrow."

Mel paid close attention as she followed Cope back. The cables running down the walls of the tunnels were slightly different in size. She'd learn her way around by the cables.

The smell of blood jolted Melina as they walked through the hatch. Inesia was there, blood covered her clothes and hands.

"What happened?" Cope asked.

"I'm fine. Ran into Salem on my way back. He's in a mood. He took out a few brain-bleached."

"Is he hurt?"

Inesia shook her head. "No. He killed them. Walls was...among them."

"Shit." Cope turned to Mel. "When you see Salem again, tread lightly for a while. He just killed an old friend." She looked back at Inesia. "So why are you covered in blood?"

"Salem needed a little comfort. The jerk got blood on me." Inesia pinned Mel with a harsh glare. "Don't eat too much, stray. If you know what's good for you, you'll keep your head down and do what you're told until you grow a brain." She looked back at Cope. "I already ate. I gave Salem food when I ran into him. He said he won't be back till late and the stray can have his room. I'm going to shower."

"Stop being so pleasant. It's going to ruin your carefully constructed sour disposition." Cope teased. "The newbie isn't bad. I'm going to get her to spill some of her personal history after we eat. I know you don't want to miss that."

The scowl on Inesia's face smoothed out, and she looked almost interested. "I won't be long."

Melina refused to eat any of the strange food, regardless of how hungry she was. Instead, she told the two other women about Regia. Neither one interrupted her at all. She described the natural wonders like the Heart, the sunsets, and the Crystalline Sea in great detail for them, realizing she was providing them with a few moments of fantasy and escape. The edge around Inesia's gaze began to soften the longer Mel talked.

When they all began to yawn, Cope showed her to Salem's room and closed the large hatch behind her. Mel turned the wheel on the door all the way until it gave a satisfying locking sound. It was like the other rooms, only larger. A desk took up one wall with a spindly metal chair. Holographic screens of different sizes hovered over the desk. The bed was just a metal bunk connected to the wall by metal cables, a thin, tattered blanket lay across it. The only surprise was the window. Curved out like a shallow bowl, the transparent material gave her a view of more tunnels, cables, controls, and drains. She guessed this space was originally designed for utility workers.

Claustrophobia tickled the back of her neck. She missed the sky, *any* sky. Turning away from the window, Melina undressed. She needed to take care of her possessions. There weren't new ones she could get in a place like this. Her boots went under the bed next to her folded coat, jeans, and shirt. She climbed on the bed in her camisole, boy shorts, and socks.

Tears threatened as she pulled the skimpy blanket over herself. *I love you, Rhain. I'm coming to find you. Wait for me.*

Thirteen

Nocturne

Seraph turned and admired her willowy, naked body in the mirror. The golden morning light was particularly flattering to her skin tone and hair. Her mind flitted back and forth between vanity and self-doubt. Not for one second could she neglect her appearance. Beauty was the greatest misdirection. Innocence, kindness, and stupidity all carefully gauged, filled her violet eyes. No one would ever suspect her of malice, well no one who mattered anyway, and she didn't associate with people who didn't matter.

Shivers of desire spread over her skin. She would go to the palace today. Her feet would grace the floors that would be hers soon, and she would steal into a dark corner with Haru and remind him why he'd picked her as his mistress.

Don't get careless. Cold control was needed to see the plan all the way through. Half measures would lead to ruin--possibly death. The throne was worth it. Haru was worth it...

She glanced at the naked guard, lounging in her bed and scowled. It was past time for him to leave her room. She didn't remember his name. He was new, and she welcomed him in as she did most of the royal guards who worked security at the villa. Sex was an easy way to hold total control of them. She made them all love her.

Seraph slid her arms into her silk robe and belted it just as her fingertips began to tingle. She lifted her hands and looked closely at them, pursing her lips. The tingling grew stronger.

"Discretion is important, my good sir," she said sweetly.

He frowned and didn't budge.

"Get out," she snapped. "Or I'll never invite you to my bed again."

He threw on his clothes and left. She reached for a bottle on her dressing table and uncorked it. The sweet smell of desert flowers filled the air as she tipped the bottle into her palm. The oil was warm to the touch. Rose gold hieroglyphs burned bright on each fingertip as the oil absorbed and the tingling subsided.

Her heart clenched as she read the message. Angrily she wiped the oil from her skin and stalked down the hall. *Calm down. You don't know what you're walking into. You don't know what state he's in. He might not remember anything.* She schooled her breathing for a moment before cracking the bedroom door open.

He was there, on the bed. Her husband. His sharp eyes cut to her instantly and he sat up.

"How are you feeling, my love?" she asked pleasantly. "You drank too much last night."

Scowling, he rubbed his hand over his chest. "I don't feel well."

"Don't push yourself, Rhain. Take care of your health. Lay back down. It's still quite early in the morning."

Suspicion filled his eyes as he lowered himself back on the pillows. "What's got you in such a good mood?"

She flipped her hair over her shoulder. "I had a wonderful time at the party last night and unlike you, *I* know when to quit drinking."

She backed up and shut the door before he could see her sweat. Her heart was racing, panic licking around her lungs. He seemed the same, but he might be faking it. What was wrong with her curse work? Why was he here? How did he look like himself? Did he have the slightest idea he wasn't really there in bed? Could he tell his physical body was buried elsewhere? He didn't look like a ghost. She'd have to wait and watch him to know more. What did he remember?

If he suspected the truth, she'd have to work to convince him he was wrong, and she was nothing but his doting wife, happy with her station and happy with her marriage.

Seraph gritted her perfect teeth. She'd have to kill him this time. Getting to his body was an even bigger problem than what he might say or remember. She drifted quickly back to her room and began to dress for the day. Nothing was going to change her plans. She had to see Haru as soon as possible. She needed his help getting rid of Rhain for good this time.

Music flooded his mind, a stabbing, pulsing, excruciation of conflicting notes coming from every surface in the room. It flowed inside him, wild, unchecked, chaotic until he wanted to slam his head against the wall. Behind the music was the static. He focused on the white noise, reaching for it, embracing it, gorging on it, until it drowned out the music. He achieved one breath of peace before all the pieces of him that had gone missing came rushing in. Rhain pinched his eyes shut and bit down on his knuckle to keep himself from crying out as it all came back. His identity. His world. His occupation. His status...Seraph...his wife.

At first, it was as if he was waking from a troubled, feverish sleep. Disoriented, but after a moment, fully aware where he was, and who he was. He was just sick. Hungover as Seraph said. Had he been dreaming?

No. His mind begged in a heartbroken hiss. *I remember you, Melina. You weren't a dream...my true wife. The wife of my heart.*

Memories of twenty years splintered into hazy fragments. He struggled to grab them, determined to not forget. Regia. X. Tesla. The wizards. The war. His house. His job...Melina most of all. His love for Melina.

He sat up, feeling the oddity of his body. He wasn't the demonic looking smoke monster now. Rhain flexed his hands close to his face, before pulling his collar open and looking down at his chest. The broken circle was still there, like a whisper of death around his heart, but the darkness was faded now, barely visible.

He'd keep it a secret. He'd tell no one until he sniffed out the person or persons who cursed him and kill them.

The room spun as he got to his feet. How long had he been asleep? He'd spent over twenty years in Regia, but...here in Nocturne, it was as if no time had passed. Only a few days... Perhaps, a month? No, it couldn't have been that long. Seraph would have...he paused. Seraph would have what? Was she the one who cursed him? Surely not. She wouldn't have the ability even if she had the desire. Hiring such a thing would have been an extreme risk. Seraph didn't take risks and she never got her hands dirty.

She didn't love him, but did she really hate him? She always seemed more apathetic than anything. He grimaced, trying to firmly grasp his memories. Their marriage was arranged by the emperor himself. Rhain sighed, remembering how it had come about to begin with...*careful what you wish for.* Too late to heed that advice.

He inhaled fast. The emperor, Koda. Was he all right? Rhain had discovered an assassination was being planned. That was one of the last things he remembered. The party at the palace. How he tried to get Koda to talk to him privately, and it hadn't worked out. The memory went fuzzy. He didn't remember it right.

The morning light burned beautifully in his eyes as he came out of his bedroom. The open air hallways gave him a clear view of the villa's courtyard. The rose-gold sand shifted tint in the light and sang a constant, quiet melody.

I know who I am...and I didn't deserve damnation.

I'm not a monster.

Melina, I wasn't unworthy of you. He closed his fiery hazel eyes and tried to hear her song. There was so much music inside him, but her sound was missing. His heart broke. Lost! Her sound was lost! What would have been his greatest comfort, separated from her, was gone.

How do I get back to you? Despair sank all the way through his strange body. Even if he broke the curse over him, he'd never see her or Regia again. Letting go of her was always a part of the deal, but this was so much worse than he'd imagined. Much too soon. Melina moving on from him was inevitable, but he thought he'd still be able to see her. Stalk her, make sure she was happy, and protect her from the shadows.

I love you...Feel it...It's okay... Her voice, the way she looked when she'd said those things to him. He remembered that even if he'd lost the sound of her soul.

Despair mutated into fear. Was she dead? Was that why he couldn't hear her? It was his fault the curse had infected her. Had it killed her? Had he killed his own wife? Why did he ever touch her? Why did he sell himself such a lie? Why had he been so greedy? Had he taken everything from her?

Melina was dead, and it was his fault.

If that was the truth, she'd never made it to Destiny. Her soul was forever trapped with Tristan.

In his mind, he saw her, in a dark swamp, wrapped in that evil bastard's arms. The image poisoned him through and through, all the way, over and over and over.

He'd never forgive himself.

She thought she locked the door. It opened anyway. Silhouetted in the open hatch, Salem stared at her. He sauntered in and shut the hatch behind him.

"What are you doing?" she demanded.

He didn't answer as he turned the wheel until the gears clicked into place. He tapped a code on the small screen on the wall, and a snake of red light ran around the edge of the door.

"I've locked it now. You're stuck in here with me tonight. The door won't open again unless I open it, so don't get any ideas about trying to kill me in my sleep."

"But…"

He sat on the edge of the bed and unlaced his boots. She scooted away from him until her shoulder hit the cold, metal wall.

"I thought you said I could sleep in here tonight."

"I did… You didn't really expect me to give up my bed for you, did you?"

"But…"

His eyes glinted metallic in the dark. "Believe it or not, but I care for them." He nodded toward the door. "I don't know if you're safe. Until I know, you sleep with me. We can have sex all you like, but you're not getting out until I get some sleep."

She huffed. "I told you, I'm married."

"I couldn't care less."

"Hard pass on sex."

He smirked and shrugged before pulling his shirt over his head. She gasped before she could stop herself. His body was gorgeous. Three small ports illuminated aquamarine on the vertebrae at the base of his spine. Light threads like the ones in Inesia's hair laced up his spine, spreading over his shoulder blades like the branches of a tree.

"You're beautiful." The words whispered out through her parted lips before she could think. *Oh shit. He's going to pounce on me now. He's going to take that as an invitation.*

He glanced at her over his shoulder, one eyebrow raised. Disdain flashed in his eyes. "I've heard that many times before."

What was that in his voice? Regret? Pain? She shook herself. He was messing with her. A person like him didn't show vulnerability unless it was a ruse and certainly not to an almost stranger.

She lay back down. "Stomping my pity button won't get you laid."

Laughing, he stretched out beside her, yanking the blanket from her grip, pulling it over himself. "You haven't disappointed me so far, Melina."

"We're just sleeping here. Don't try to take advantage of me."

"Hey, you give me an advantage, I'm going to take it. Besides, isn't you giving me an advantage just a cowardly way of asking for it without having to say it aloud?"

"You're a bastard."

"Here, will you like me if I give you some of the blanket back?" He held out a corner of the fabric, making huge puppy eyes at her.

She snickered, shaking her head, declining the blanket. "I like you anyway," she admitted, crossing her arms over her chest to keep warm. Chills rushed up her skin. The difference a day could make... She'd never gone through such a drastic change so quickly. Last night she'd been warm, wrapped in Rhain's arms. Now she was cold, beside a beast of a man, in another world.

On his back, eyes closed, an undeniable trace of amusement played around his lips. She stared at his profile, a tug of admiration in her gut. Gradually his face relaxed, and his breathing slowed until she was sure he slept. He obviously wasn't fussed about her in the slightest. He wasn't worried she was a threat. Did she seem that weak to him?

Value. Provide value. How did she persuade him to help her get her memories? Tomorrow she would learn more so she could figure out a way to be helpful.

It was hard to fall asleep next to Salem. How do you relax next to an apex predator anyway? He wasn't going to hurt her, she figured that much. But if she fell asleep and dreamed about Rhain, would she accidentally snuggle up to Salem? She wanted to avoid that more than anything.

Keeping her arms crossed over her chest, she rolled away from him to her side and faced the wall. Sleep...sleep...sleep... the stress and heartbreak of the day reached into her and pulled her down until she fell into shadows and smoke and nightmares.

"Rhain, wait for me," she whispered, waking in the dark.

Clutching at her chest, her heart sobbed and burned with every beat.

"I'm sure he's waiting, baby," Salem whispered behind her. "I would be, if I was him...Thank goodness I'm not. I'm the one who has you."

"You don't have me."

Taking a deep breath, she rolled over. His eyes shone in the dark across the room. Chills lifted on her back as she met his intense gaze. He lounged in the chair, barefooted and bare-chested, idly twisting a short piece of cable around two fingers. What was he doing, staring at her while she slept? Creep. Tension and desire rolled through his aura. She could feel it, hell, she could almost see it.

"Your stomach's been growling in your sleep. Didn't you eat? I ordered Inesia to make sure you had food."

Stay calm. If you're calm, he will be, too. "I declined it."

He smirked. "I see. Felt guilty?"

How could he see right through her so easily? She huffed. "Of course. Food is scarce and I wasn't able to contribute anything today. Inesia glares at me anyway. I didn't feel right about taking any."

"I want you to stay healthy. That's hard enough in this place. Next time, eat."

"Don't act like you care. I'm not your pet."

He chuckled. "You're my prize."

"The hell I am." What did that mean? Did she want to know?

"Were you dreaming about your man? You sounded sad."

"So, what if I was? Are you going to mock me?"

"Relax," he sighed. "We don't need to be adversaries, Melina."

"I don't trust you."

"Of course you don't, you're not stupid...I did some reading about your kind. How often do you need to drink blood?"

"Every few days, unless I've been injured, then I need it to heal."

He stood and walked toward her. "Don't bother Cope or Inesia with that. When you need it, drink from me."

Did he say that out of concern for them, or was it something else? She was afraid to ask.

"I want to know what that's like," he said.

"Huh?"

"I want you to drink my blood now."

"Oh, well...I guess... Do you mind where I bite you?"

He flashed a wicked smile and held his hands open as if to display his body to her. "I'll let you choose."

She didn't want to be that close to him, but she was thirsty and if she drank, her hunger would slacken also. She slid toward the edge of the bed and stood, instantly self-conscious at her scant clothing. Where should she bite him? What was the safest place? Not his hands, goodness knows where they'd been. Not his forearm because she'd have to dip her head down and she wasn't okay with showing him any level of submission. Damn it. His shoulder or his neck...perhaps from behind, then he couldn't grab her. She circled to his back. He turned on her abruptly.

"What do you think this is?" he demanded.

"I'm sorry, I just thought—"

"You said you don't trust me, well same goes here. Stay where I can see you."

"Okay. I can understand that."

"Is this a meal or foreplay? Stop messing around."

She scowled. "Definitely not foreplay."

"Yeah, but now you're thinking about foreplay, aren't you?"

"Shut up, please." She sank her fangs into his neck.

Salem inhaled sharp and fast. "Oh, that's awesome... Harder."

She did pull harder, only to hurry this up, so she could step away from him. Heat was rising on his skin. His blood was an unknown flavor, not that she expected it to taste familiar, but it was good. Really, really good. Guilt flooded her along with his blood. He felt good. He tasted good. She needed to keep her distance from him. He was temptation. She jolted as his hands gripped her ass.

"More. Harder," he demanded.

She choked on the blood in her mouth as he pulled her as close as she could get against him. He was already lowering her on the bed when she got her fangs loose. She pushed him backward.

"Stop it!"

He still came at her. "Come on. You know you want it, too."

"No, hell no." She scrambled off the bed. He followed her.

"I'm not reading you wrong, Melina. Admit you want me."

"Never."

Chuckling, he lunged at her, catching her wrist. She slapped him with her other hand. He pulled her against him, pinning both her arms down. Oh, she wanted to kill him, but he was the only one who could get her future memories. How did she stop this without conflict?

"Let me go. I don't want to fight you."

He shivered, his eyes flashing. "Resist me more, princess."

"I don't want it to be like this between us."

"Liar. This is so much of what you want."

"Stop it! Please!" The word burned her throat. "Please, don't do this. I need you."

"I know, baby. You need me as much as I need you. You seem almost virginal. I'd swear you were if I didn't know better. So clean and so dirty at the same time. I'm sure your husband plunders you as much as possible...oh ho, now what's this? You're blushing." The heat in his eyes surged. "No fuckin' way. Don't tell me..."

"Please, let me go."

Shivers rolled through his body again, and his eyes burned as if there was no person in front of her, just an animal. "Will you beg?" Light flashed on a small blade as he brought it up and held it against the side of her neck. "I've got plans for you. Shall I show you?"

He pushed her against the wall, scraping the blade on her skin, enough to scratch a line.

Backed in a corner...trapped...no escape... Rage ignited. "*You* beg," she snarled.

Her head cracked into his face in a sharp head-butt. He staggered back. She barely had time to blink before he was charging at her. He punched deep into her stomach. So deep, her whole body crumpled in around his fist. Melina had never been hit with so much force. All her training, all her arrogance surrounding her ability shriveled up at that moment.

She thought she was formidable. She thought she was ready to face any adversary.

She wasn't.

Her vision jittered around the edges, and she gasped for air, only vaguely aware she was being restrained. Salem smiled and backed away from her as her senses righted. Her arms were over her head, tied to the wall by a cable. Likewise, her feet were connected to the wall. She pulled and strained against the bonds. Panic flooded into her blood and raced through her body.

"Cool off, baby. We're going to be stuck together for a very long time, so let's get to know each other. You think I just want sex? In truth, I want much, much more than that." He grabbed a small cube off the desk and brought it to her. "Look closely."

The cube projected a holographic screen in front of her face. She blinked a few times, looking at an image of herself sleeping.

"I mapped you as you slept and I've made a plan for alterations. What do you think?" The image changed. She choked on her breath. "Much better like this. A few surgeries, some mods, see what you will be? This is what I want. Once you're like this...oh the things we can do together. You have no idea, but you will."

Her throat was dry as she tried to swallow, looking at the image he'd created of her. Both of her arms were robotic from the shoulders down, ports covered her torso and face, and light lines like the ones on his back ran up her legs.

"No. No. No. No." Her voice was deadly calm like a mother laying down the law to a small child. "Do you understand me? You're not going to modify me. Not ever."

He smiled easily. "Actually, I'm going to modify you right now, and I'm going to have my way with you, too. I hope you have a strong mind, otherwise, I fear you're about to break. I wonder how much pleasure and pain you can take at the same time."

Setting the cube back on the desk, he sauntered to her, a laser in one hand, his knife in the other. Sweat slicked her skin.

"This laser is designed to cut through metal, so it will slice through your flesh fast. You probably won't even feel it, but hold still, I want to make a clean cut. I haven't done that many surgeries before. I don't want to accidentally kill you."

"Why?" Her lungs trembled. "I just want my memories. Please. That's all I want. You don't need to do this to me."

Pressing intimately against her, he kissed her cheek before biting her earlobe. His knife pressed to her neck again. "I can't give you your memories." He whispered in her ear. "I never could. It's impossible. Give up."

Tears blurred her vision as the smell of smoke filled her nose. Burning heat caressed her skin from the laser. The next second it wasn't tears but rage blurring her vision. His eyes filled every bit of her sight, taunting, perverted, sadistic.

Give up?! Not today, motherfucker.

Straining, she slipped free of the bonds that held her without stopping to question how. She threw herself at him with no thought of self-preservation. No care for her own pain, just the pain she would inflict on him. *Die! Die! Die!*

His blade slashed the back of her forearm as she tried to punch him, her blood spraying his torso. Her fangs were on fire. She'd tear his throat out. He moved, but she was faster, jumping over him and onto his back, her arm banded around his throat. He fell backward, slamming her into the floor with the full force of his weight. Her vision blacked. *Am I dying? Can't breathe. Can't breathe. Can't breathe.*

Consciousness glitched, failed... Gliding down a dark hole, Tristan's hands slid around her, his tongue plunging into her mouth. Her left hand scratched down his back erotically. Her right hand clawed at his face. Tristan held her soul, Salem held her body. She was caught in a tug of war.

Let me go!

The air scorched all the way down her lungs, like a flammable gas.

Get up! Move! Now!

She struggled to lift herself up on her elbows, her vision distorted. Hands clenched around her neck, and he hoisted her high into the air. His fingers dug in as she clawed at his hands. Her knee connected to his face, his head snapping back, and he dropped her.

One second to inhale before charging at him again. Side-stepping her, he shoved her from behind as she rushed past him. Crashing over the chair, her face smashed on the floor.

Salem grabbed her by the ankle and dragged her backward. Rage burned through a new level. She rolled to her back and kicked as hard as she could, her foot thrusting viciously into his crotch. He hissed and let go of her, all the color draining from his face. She took advantage of his momentary weakness to fill her lungs again and spit the blood from her mouth before getting to her feet and facing him again.

"Stop now. This is over." His voice was calm.

Stop? I hardly think so.

Her hands lifted and clenched into fists. Through the haze of pain, she could hardly see him, even though he was right in front of her. He deflected her strike, grabbing her forearm as she punched, pulling her arm straight up and back over her shoulder, sweeping her feet out with his foot. She was flat on her back, winded again. Burning, her muscles refused to move. *Air*, her lungs screamed for air as she tried and failed to breathe. Helpless and trying to gasp, Salem bent over her and zip-tied her wrists and feet.

He gazed down at her. "Calm down, Melina. Breathe. I'll be back when you've relaxed a bit."

He unlocked the hatch and left her all alone. What was going on? Straining, her lungs opened again. She struggled only once against her bonds. They were too tight, not like the cables on the walls. What was he going to do now? Rape her, modify her, kill her...all three?

She wasn't finished. He won this round. That was just fuel. She knew what she was up against now. How could she get the upper hand? Humiliation stung hot. She was well trained, but everything she learned from her father...she never had to use it. She'd never faced the type of danger Salem offered.

The hatch swung open, and he strolled in, a glass of water in his hand. Totally composed, he set the glass on the floor next to her. A broad smile spread his face.

"Oh, sugar, don't look at me like that. It really works me up. I don't want to fight anymore. I'm going to cut you loose. I went easy on you and you never had a chance. If you start back up after I free you, I'll put you down fast and hard and you won't like it." His whole demeanor changed as if he was an entirely different person than the one she'd just fought. Jekyll surfaced. She didn't want to face Hyde again.

Taking a calming breath, she painted the background with resolve and readiness. She'd watch him closely.

"I don't understand... You were going to cut my arms off."

He wrinkled his nose. "Eww. That's gross. I wouldn't do that. I was just testing you."

She blew out a breath. "Oh, you suck."

He cut the ties and took a step back. Salem wiped the blood on his mouth and gazed at her with admiration. Sitting up, she grabbed the glass and drank.

"That was gorgeous." His voice was quiet.

"What?"

"I knew you were a savage. I could smell it on your skin, I could see it buried behind your eyes. You've made me happy, you beautiful, crazy bitch."

"You were just trying to get me to fight? All you had to do was ask."

"No. Sparring is all well and good, but I needed to tap into your fear. I had to convince you there was no alternative. I wanted to see you fight for your life, if you would at all. I had to trigger you to see if you had the light. You do."

"The light?"

"It looks like a light to me. When I look into the eyes of someone willing to kill to live. You're a beast, Melina."

"What if I didn't fight back?"

"I'd have been disappointed."

"What the hell is wrong with you?"

"Quite a lot, I'm sure, princess," he chuckled.

"I don't understand you at all. You're insane."

He smirked. "You will understand, eventually. I won't screw with you like that again. Promise. You've shown me what I wanted to see. I won't lie so *extravagantly* anymore."

"But you will lie?"

"Of course. You can trust me to a certain degree. As I said, you're my prize. You're no good to me if you get damaged. I won't hurt you."

"Can you really not give me my memories?"

"Hmm...you'll find out, won't you?"

Sighing, she put her head in her hands. "I think I hate you."

He sat next to her. "That works. So, tell me. Have you killed before?"

"Yeah. Once."

"Who?" he persisted.

She pulled her knees up to her chest. "My life mate. The one person in my world destined to love me the rest of my life."

His eyebrows rose. "Interesting. I thought you were married?"

"I am. Different guy."

Salem barked out a short laugh. "Did you fight the guy you killed?"

"Not really. I kissed him before I stabbed him to death."

"Damn…I like you. You've got potential."

"Potential for what?" she demanded.

"All sorts of things…" His smirk was cheeky. "So, my vicious little virgin, tell me about this guy you're chasing. Your husband. The one who doesn't fulfill his duties to you physically."

Melina closed her eyes for a moment and fought for patience. "Not that it's your business, but it's not his fault…he gives me other things. Amazing things…" She wasn't going to stand for this creep maligning her husband. "We don't care if anyone else understands what we have. He doesn't know where he really came from. He's not Regian. He can hear music in silent things and he can make time echo." Her heart burned. "I don't want to say any more about Rhain right now. Maybe some other time. Tell me something about you. Where did you come from?"

Salem hesitated a moment then he stood and headed to the door. "Get some sleep. I won't bother you again tonight."

Confused and sore, Melina lay back down on the bed and crashed into sleep.

Cope smiled down at her as she shook her awake.

"I knew you and Salem were compatible. Your antics last night woke me up, all that crashing and whatever else you were doing. You look like hell. He really put you through the wringer, huh? Did you enjoy it?"

"Ugh. Enjoy it? Please." She rolled her eyes.

Cope chuckled. "That's not really a denial, you know."

"I don't want to talk about it."

"Okay. Get dressed. The brain-bleached have been active already today. Not sure what's driving them so hard at the moment."

"I can fight." Mel offered.

"Nope. Not today. Salem's orders. He and Inesia are gone. They're fighting. I'm protecting you today."

"Why? Does he think I'm that weak?"

Cope shrugged. "I don't think that's it. He didn't go into detail, he just said I needed to keep you safe and undamaged."

"He's so weird. He says he wants me *undamaged*, but he didn't stop from roughing me up last night."

"Well, whatever he says, he has reasons for everything he does. And he doesn't want us hanging around here today. So, we'll go scouring and see if we can find anything. It's highly unlikely we will, but you'll get to see more of this level, so pay attention. Before we come back, I'll show you where we shower. You look like you need it after whatever Salem did to you last night."

"Thanks."

The idea of a shower was wonderful. Mel dressed quickly and followed Cope out.

Fourteen

I'm not going to settle. Not ever. I'll do what I have to, to achieve my dreams. What could be more pure or admirable than that? The people in my way are the stain. They're the ones keeping me from having what is rightfully mine. I won't feel sorry for punishing them for that. It's justice.

"Where is your head, Seraph?" Haru demanded. "I'm starting to feel rejected."

"I'm sorry." She embraced him and tried to focus on their lovemaking. She needed to keep him happy. "I'm stressed."

"You came out here. Do you want me or not?"

"I love you, Haru. I always want you."

She did her best to prove it, allowing him to do whatever he wanted. They tried to keep their affair secret, but of course, the slaves knew. You didn't bed the emperor's nephew on a regular basis without someone knowing something.

Seraph buried her face in his neck and inhaled. His skin was soft and fragrant. He cared about his beauty the same way she cared for hers. They understood each other. Tears threatened, anger and regret filling her up.

It shouldn't be like this. He said he wanted to marry her. She should be his wife. She would be...

She'd been telling herself that for too long.

If only the emperor hadn't forced her to marry Rhain, just as Haru was about to claim her as his bride, destroying her dream of becoming empress.

The warm breeze swirled into the room and danced over her bare skin as she stared at the ceiling, while Haru caught his breath. The expansive bedroom was plain, the way he liked it. No art, no rugs, nothing added any flare to the bone-colored stone floor and walls. Even the sheets and canopy over the bed were bone-colored. It would have bothered her, but this wasn't going to be her bedroom once she married Haru. They'd kill Rhain, then they'd kill the emperor. Haru would become the new emperor and then he'd marry her.

The emperor's bedroom was where she would sleep. It was her space. Everyone else just had to catch up to her. She was the Empress. The empire would know it, soon. Very soon.

Haru rolled over and gently traced lines on her back with his fingertips.

"So, tell me what's wrong."

She sighed. "Rhain is back."

"What? How could that happen?"

"I don't know how, yet. The curse is holding, sort-of. He seems oblivious, but he might be faking it, shrewd bastard. We need to get to his body and kill him before things get worse."

"We can't kill him another way?"

She shook her head. "I wish there was another way. The apparition of him that showed up this morning will be impervious to harm."

Haru groaned. "After all the trouble to put him in the tomb, now you want me to get him out? I can't just go there and stab him in the heart. I'll have to find a new mercenary or assassin. I killed the guy I paid to put Rhain in the tomb to begin with." He sighed heavily and scratched his head. "Can't you put a different curse on him?"

"I don't think that would work."

"Well, you better keep him in the dark. Distract him. Keep him away from Koda."

"How am I supposed to do that?" she demanded.

He shrugged. "Sex. Pretend you're madly in love with him."

"First of all, it hurts me you could suggest such a thing so flippantly. Second, nothing would make him more suspicious than that. Third, his real body is buried, and the body now occupying my villa is incapable of sex."

He snickered. "Incapable?"

"He's just an apparition. Insubstantial. Solid enough to do damage in a fight, but impervious to harm. He's in stasis. No type of stimulation will have the slightest effect on him."

Haru scowled. "He's the one who's cursed, but we're the ones in danger from him now. Why did you choose that curse to begin with? Why isn't it working? Your skills as a Strexa are severely lacking. I shouldn't have trusted you with this."

Tears came fast, not ugly ones. Pretty, manipulative, tears. "I'm sorry, my lord. Please don't be angry with me. I'll do anything to please you. I love you so much. Give me a chance to fix this. I'll find a way. I promise."

He leaned close and kissed the corner of her mouth. "You better, or you'll never be empress. I don't want any other by my side after I kill Koda. It has to be you, Seraph. Please don't let me down."

She kissed him hard. "I won't. I swear it."

Haru didn't like to linger in bed playing the besotted lover, so she dressed and fixed her hair quickly. A small sigh of relief blew out through her lips as she left his room. He was annoyed and worried about the situation, but he hadn't raised his voice or ended their relationship. He still wanted her.

Her mind flitted off self-conscious anxiety and alighted on smug conceit. Of course, he still wanted her. She was the most beautiful, the most refined daughter of nobility in all of Nocturne. She lifted her head as she sashayed down the empty palace hall, allowing her senses to drink in the atmosphere of her future home.

The floor under her feet should beg her forgiveness for being so plain and unworthy.

"Seraph?"

A small gasp filled her lungs, and she stopped in her tracks, before smiling and turning around to face the emperor, Koda. He stood a ways down the hall, a few servants behind him. She bowed gracefully.

"Is Rhain with you?"

"No, Excellency. He's still not feeling well."

Koda scowled as he strode up to her, his white robes billowing out as he walked. "You've been saying that for a while now. What's wrong with him? I'm going to have my personal physician come to your villa and examine him."

She hid her panic behind a beguiling smile. "He's getting better. He told me so this morning. I'm sure he will be fully recovered by tomorrow." She leaned closer to him and lowered her voice. "He drinks too much, you know, my lord."

"Hmm...be that as it may, do not criticize your husband. It's not an easy job, being the captain of the guard. I ask a lot of him." His attention seemed to wander off her, and he looked back down the way he'd just come. "Tell him I want to see him. If he doesn't show in a few days, I'll send the doctor."

"Thank you, Excellency. You're most kind."

He grunted and turned, striding down the hall and around the corner. Her eyes narrowed. She didn't understand why Koda never responded to her the way other men did. Her charms fizzled in the air as if non-existent with the emperor. He was unmarried and enjoyed women, why did he ignore her?

Seraph tried to shake it off, but it was a defeat, through and through. Perhaps it was out of his loyalty to Rhain. She exhaled and continued to walk down the hall. Whatever the reason, she wasn't ever going to catch that fish, so she'd settled on killing him instead. Haru was the next in line for the throne and he loved her. That was fine. It would all work out fine.

Now she had to go home and spin many intricate lies.

"Here it is. Your own personal spa." Cope spread her arms out theatrically. "The water here is always a little warmer."

After following Cope around all day, mentally mapping the tunnels, keeping her footsteps quiet and her voice at a whisper, Melina was ready for something else. Cope maintained a cool exterior, but her anxiety throughout the day wasn't lost on Melina. She didn't see or hear anything that would indicate danger or they were being followed, but Cope's tension absorbed into her.

Water poured freely from a pipe in the ceiling, through the grated floor. After the day of stress and her fight with Salem last night, she was more than ready to get clean.

"I'm going to walk off a ways. Give you some privacy."

"Thanks," Melina said.

Cope vanished around a corner. Mel stripped down, carefully keeping her clothes away from the splashing. It wasn't as hot as she would have liked, but it didn't freeze her. The pressure of the pelting water massaged her shoulders. She closed her eyes and let her mind drift, longing for home. Her heart clenched, and she gasped. Looking back would crush her. She had to keep her eyes on the path in front of her.

Goosebumps rose on her skin. She squinted into the darkness. Salem's copper eyes shone through the shadows.

"Pervert."

He strode out of the darkness. "Ingrate," he shot back as he leaned against the wall, arms crossed over his chest.

Mel saw no point in trying to cover herself. He'd seen all of her already, and he was still lazily taking in the view. Defiantly, she faced him fully to show him she didn't care, and he hadn't upset her. Appreciation shone through the arrogance of his gaze, but as his eyes roamed over her, the blood drained from his face. He looked the same way he had when he'd found out she was Regian as his eyes locked on her chest. Shock, disbelief, and then greed.

"Music...time echo...I get it now." Salem's voice filled with hunger.

Mel looked down and realized it wasn't her amazing rack that brought the change to his expression and demeanor. It was the broken black circle between her breasts. Hope jolted through her.

"You recognize this mark?"

"I do..." He shook his head. "You truly are my prize. This changes things. I'm starting to get a *real* idea how to use you. Finish up. We have work to do. You are surprisingly undisciplined. I've been following you for a long time today. You had no idea. If I wanted to kill you, I had so many opportunities. My favorite being the one just a moment ago when you took your clothes off."

"I see. Is this a lesson?"

He grunted and gave a curt nod. "I intend to teach you to protect yourself better. Get dressed. I'm sick of looking and not touching."

"Then go away."

He shook his head. "I'm watching over you while you're vulnerable. Hurry up."

Her clothes clung to her wet skin as she dressed, excitement budding in her chest. Salem recognized the mark on her chest. Would he tell her the truth?

"Cope was going to come back for me."

"No, she's not. I got you, princess."

She followed him back to the hatch. Inesia and Cope were already there, playing a game that resembled makeshift, apocalypse chess. The pieces were made of bolts, screws, and bits of random broken stuff.

"All right." Salem clapped his hands together. "We're going to get out of here, and Melina is going to be our ticket. I'm working on a plan, and I want your total commitment on this. Got it?"

Both women raised their eyebrows but nodded. He faced Melina, the same question in his eyes.

She crossed her arms. "Pitch me your scheme and we'll see."

He gestured for her to go to his room. He followed her and shut the door behind him.

"I know a few slave traders who would jump at the opportunity to have you in their stock. If I send out a message detailing your *assets,* I'm confident they will show up and spring us from this hellhole. I've been thinking how to sell you from the moment I found out you were Regian, but since then, what I've learned about you, makes me more than confident in this angle."

"What angle?"

"Part of the deal is the slaver has to take the rest of us along with you."

She frowned. "But that means all of us will be slaves."

"So? I've been a slave on and off many times in my life. If you're strong and calculating, it doesn't have to be a permanent thing and taking a short stint in slavery looks better on my end than this existence."

"What do I get out of this?"

"You get a ride to your husband's world."

Her heart jolted. "What?"

He pointed at her chest. "That's a Nocturne glyph. Your husband gave you that mark, right?"

"Yes."

"Nocturne is a hotbed of activity for the slave trade." He shook his head as if he couldn't believe his good luck. "You are worth so much, a fortune! You're beautiful, sexy, strong, skilled, all that makes you an easy sell, but add on that you're a virgin, Regian, and marked with Nocturne magic...let me just say, your auction will be a blood bath."

She tried to process the picture he painted. "I can't do anything with Nocturne magic, though."

"The people bidding on you don't need to know that...If you play along..."

"What if I don't? You'll use me anyway, right?"

He shrugged. "Of course. But if you trust me, I'll teach you how to navigate the dangers of slave life. We'll make up a history for you that will not only protect you but will give security to me, Inesia, and Cope through the transaction. If you could just--"

"I'll do it," she cut him off. "Since you won't or can't give me my future memories, I'll do whatever I have to, to get to my husband."

"Excellent...I..." His expression shifted, softened. "Thank you."

She smiled. "Like I told you before, I'm in a hurry. What's first?"

He pursed his lips. "I guess we'll see if you really meant what you just said about doing whatever you have to... You look too perfect at the moment. You need some scars. Some random, some specific. Not too many, or it will take down your value. And you need a little modifying. Just a little, so it's believable you arrived here at the same time we did and the poppers added stuff to you, too. The modification I have in mind will also add to your value."

She exhaled and met his gaze without flinching. "I meant what I said. Bring it on."

Possessive sexual heat flashed in his eyes. "You should rest for a bit. I want to start on you tonight." He turned on his heel and breezed through the door.

Scars...modification... she sighed and lay down on the bed. Salem was probably right. She should take the chance to rest. Unconsciously, she began to trace the line of the broken circle on her chest with the pad of her fingertip and closed her eyes.

You're a slave. Get it through your pretty little head. A slave. A woman whispered in her memory. The vision coming back in sharp detail. She could almost smell her mistress' perfume, almost feel the touch of her elegant hands. Until this moment, she'd dismissed and all but forgotten the future memory.

She was on the right path. It was odd to have such a thought. Slavery was the right path for her to get to Rhain?

Her chest tightened as she thought about him, her heart starving in the absence of his voice, emaciated and crazed for his touch. *So be it. Whatever it takes.* She dozed off.

"You're enjoying this, aren't you?" Mel demanded through gritted teeth.

Salem chuckled behind her. "Of course."

"Sadistic bastard."

"Trying to sweet talk me won't make this go any faster, princess. Now shut up. I have to concentrate."

Stripped to the waist, flat on her stomach, her sweaty hands gripped the metal bar at the end of the bed, and she pinched her eyes shut, burying her face in the mattress. The stylus bit into her flesh again. Salem straddled her ass, cutting designs in her back. The stylus cut going in and cauterized going out.

"You heal so fast," he complained. "I have to make a few passes at each line before it seems to want to take."

He'd showed her the scars on his back that he was recreating on hers. It wasn't that they were terribly intricate but according to him, had to be a perfect copy, so their story would hold water. This first set of scars marked her as an inmate of the same prison mines as him.

For the first few minutes, Inesia and Cope watched from across the room, occasionally giving him criticism on his work, like backseat drivers. He threw them out.

"You still haven't explained very much. Why does it matter if anyone believes I was a slave at the same place as you?"

"The Zorcha mines are well known to classify their slaves after thorough tests. No one will question these marks when I've finished."

"What does it say about me?"

"That you're for fighting, not pleasure."

Mel lifted her head. "Huh?"

"Everyone goes into one of those two categories. Forgive me for choosing for you, but if you're marked for sexual use, then your value will go down, and we can't use your virginity as a bonus to raise your price because no one would believe you're untouched. So, once we get to Nocturne, you'll be working on your feet, not off them."

"Oh...thank you. I'd rather be fighting."

"I figured as much. I don't want you passed around like that anyway. I've seen what it does to the spirit. And if I can't have you, I don't anyone else to either...Be very still, now. I'm almost finished on this part."

She grimaced against the pain and the smell of her burning flesh.

"Okay, done with that bit. Now, I'm just adding my signature. Then you can take a little break."

"Why are you adding your signature?"

"I'm infamous among the slave traders," a thick layer of pride filled his tone. "My name marks you as someone I've trained. This will give you instant respect as a badass fighter and ties you to me. So, it protects me a bit, too...Well, I hope it will anyway."

He got up and tossed her shirt on the bed by her head. He didn't turn away when she sat up and pulled it on, openly leering at her instead. She didn't expect any less from him.

"What's next?"

"Tally marks on your arm."

"How many kills I've made pit fighting?" She smirked.

"Exactly."

"How many do you have?"

He rolled his short sleeve up to his shoulder and showed her the scars on his upper arm. Her eyebrows rose unconsciously. Half inch tally marks in neat rows covered his arm from his shoulder to his elbow. She didn't figure she'd bother trying to count them all.

"Wow...okay. You have my respect."

He winked at her and lowered his sleeve. "Those in power like watching fights to the death. I wasn't given an option on participation... These marks are just for the ones while I was in the mines. Keeping track like that isn't the custom in the other places I've been a slave and I didn't care to keep it up."

"Do you remember all the people you've killed?"

His eyes went strange as if he was staring into an abyss. "Every one of them. Even if I didn't know their names, I remember their faces."

Her heart gave a pull. He'd lowered his guard, if only for a moment. She swallowed. "Um...so, how many tally marks are you going to give me?"

"Eighteen. Enough to mark you as deadly but still a bit green. You don't look hard enough to pass as more than that. We don't want you looking hard anyway."

"I would have thought eighteen was a high number if I hadn't seen yours."

He grabbed his desk chair and dragged it over next to the bed, sitting down close enough, his knee touched hers. "Roll up your left sleeve."

She blew out a breath, steeling herself for another round of pain and pulled her sleeve up. He moved quickly, slicing and burning her with the stylus again, racking up her fake kills across her bicep in thin scars. She counted all the way to eighteen in her head.

"You've handled the pain well, so far. Both hands out now. I'm going to add some random battle scars."

He was fast, slicing a few jagged lines over her hands, up her forearms, and one on the side of her neck. He put the stylus down and grabbed her chin, forcing her to look him in the eyes.

"Do you want some of my blood?" he asked. "You need to recuperate before we start your mod surgery."

She eyed him suspiciously. "After the way you acted last time?"

He laughed. "I'll hold still and keep my hands to myself. I can't guarantee I won't get a little turned on, but I won't act on it."

"Such a gentleman."

"Watch your mouth. Don't class me with slime like gentlemen." He gave a fake shudder of revulsion.

"I don't think I need it right now. After the surgery would be better. Can I see it again?"

He sighed. "MUGi, show my little coward the mods again."

The bot rose into the air from where it was resting on the desk and zoomed over to her. It projected a mocked-up image of Mel like an x-ray, highlighting the alterations Salem suggested. She frowned, imagining what it was going to be like when it was done. She would have been too scared to undergo such a thing, had it not been for her mother's arm, and her growing comfort with her own android eye.

MUGi moved the projection onto her skin, showing her what it would look like when it was finished. It was the bot who would perform the surgery based on Salem's design.

"Melina," Salem's voice commanded her attention. "You will be so beautiful. Trust me. I'll take care of you. This is for your protection."

"Okay. Let's do it."

He looked somewhat surprised. "Oh yeah? Just like that, you're going to trust me?"

Mel laughed. "Hardly, but I know becoming a slave is the right thing. I've had a future memory about it."

"I see. If that wasn't the case, I'd seriously question your state of mind." His expression turned stern. "You have to be more guarded and suspicious to a fault once the slavers get here, otherwise no one will believe our story."

"That makes sense. I'll put that in the forefront of my mind. But for now, let's just get this over with before I really do lose my nerve."

"Want me to knock you out first?"

"Please." She pointed sharply at him. "No funny business when I'm unconscious."

"Only a little." He smirked.

She braced herself for him to punch her in the face. Instead, he snapped his fingers, and MUGI zipped behind her. The fast bite of a needle stabbed under her ear before darkness swallowed her whole.

Consciousness came back in a jolt. Mel gasped, instantly covering her android eye with both hands. Her eye opened from deep inside, expanding, contracting, and unlocking as it connected and synchronized with her new enhancements. The light filaments sparked to life around her muscles as the sharp, cold edges, of her new weaponry adhered to her bones. The smell of blood hung thick in the air. Her blood.

"Don't move too much just yet, Melina," Salem said. "Relax. Everything came out perfectly. MUGi is nothing if not precise."

Heavy and sore, she lowered her hands.

"Here, drink." He put his wrist up to her mouth.

She bit down into his flesh, grateful for the blood running down her throat. She could feel it now, the trauma all through her body. Her eyes locked on his. An odd serenity filled his expression, and he swept the hair off her forehead with his other hand.

She swallowed and groaned. His blood was already sparking through her.

"Get some sleep. When you wake, we'll test all your mods."

"I've slept enough. I want to know it all now."

He took a step back. "Well, get up then, if you can."

She didn't try, instead, she began gingerly touching the places she knew had been modified with her fingertips. From her wrist to her elbow, twelve blades, two inches long, shaped like scales, now adhered to her ulna bone, lying flat under her skin.

"Roll your wrist," Salem said.

Her wrist popped in a way it never had as she rolled it and the blades up the back of her arm jumped out through her skin. It didn't hurt and she only bled a tiny bit. She rolled her other wrist making an identical set jump out.

"Just roll your wrists again to make them retract."

Mel moved her arms in a few different ways, contemplating the damage she could do an opponent with these mods. It was all close range, but unless her arms were cut off, she would never truly be disarmed ever again. Not only that, the lowest scales sprang out just over her wrist bone, so if her hands were tied with something like a rope, she'd be able to cut herself out with ease.

"Even if scars surface where the blades come out, you can still explain them away as just different types of tally marks. The longer you can keep the truth to yourself the better."

Rolling her wrists, the blades slid back, lying flat against her bones again. Getting up was awkward. Every joint flared, her skeleton rattled and clicked into a new alignment. Every part of her connected to her grey eye, as if it was her control center.

She padded toward the window to see her reflection since there was no mirror. Bluegreen light lines coiled once around her legs from her ankles to her knees. Her breath fogged the window as she gazed deep into her own eyes. No change she could see there. Overall, she didn't look that different, aside from her new scars and the light filaments on her legs, which flattered the shape of her legs.

Salem explained all the mods beforehand. The surge of strength the light lines added was shocking, as if she could jump a building in a single bound.

Despite the novelty and rush of power, the weight of her heart filled her lungs and eyes. Sorrow was so heavy. She was a real freak now. She would have done more if necessary. A strange and dangerous road lay before her. What was yet to be required caused pangs of terror, but she swallowed it down.

She didn't count the cost of love before she fell. No, she wouldn't take it back. She'd give it all. If that was the price, she'd pay it. Hopefully, there would be happiness on the other end when she was able to finally wash all the blood away.

Salem came up behind her, crowding her. She looked into the reflection of his eyes on the window.

"It's time now. I'm starting a game with you. Life or death."

"What if I don't want to play?" Mel asked.

"Oh, you don't. I know that already. It doesn't matter. Play or die. Those are the only choices."

"What are the rules?"

Salem smirked. "There are none."

He gripped her shoulders and put his mouth next to her ear. She waited for him to say something. Instead, he just breathed against her lobe. He didn't have to say anything. Each time he inhaled and exhaled translated perfectly. She understood he was throwing her off balance for some twisted reason. But he needed her and perhaps it was the stupidest thing she could have ever done, but she decided to trust Salem.

Had the game started?

"You're the devil." It sounded like a compliment instead of an insult.

He smiled. "You'd do well to remember it, princess. From this moment, until we are picked up, I am no longer the loveable guy you've grown sorta used to."

She snorted.

"I'm going to open your eyes and tune your mind."

"Sounds unpleasant."

His lips pressed to her cheek. "Let's begin."

FIFTEEN

The close confines of the hatch created a mutated, supercharged type of intimacy between Melina, Salem, Inesia, and Cope. Their habits, the way they interacted with each other, even the way they breathed, it all became familiar so fast, as though she'd known them her whole life. The small nuances of personality, only comprehended over long and deep intimacy, were now a part of Melina's knowledge of her companions. Laugher, sighs, jokes, frustration, anger, and desire... She knew the facial expressions, body language, and tones of voice. She knew them, just as she was sure Cope, Inesia, and Salem, now knew her.

Sleep, the way she'd experienced it her whole life, was a distant memory after only a week of Salem's game. The soft, pale flesh of her innocence had been stripped naked and tossed into a pit of claws and teeth. It wasn't just Salem, either. Cope and Inesia joined in. They both took the time to meticulously share with her the details of every horror they'd ever endured. The longer she was forced to listen the tighter she pulled into herself, closing her eyes and wrapping her arms around her knees for comfort. Neither Inesia nor Cope showed any emotion while they forced her through the psychological trauma of imagining their individual histories.

Melina's mind twisted along their words. She raged against what she learned at first, attempting to convince herself cruelty to the level they described couldn't possibly exist, and they must be lying... Surely.

Round one of Salem's game left her cringing and heartbroken, with a deep frustration that she was powerless to change events that happened long ago. She wanted to walk into the past and rescue the children. Those children were the adults she now lived with, and there was nothing she could do. Were they trying to teach her to swallow poison? To accept what she couldn't change?

Nightmares plagued her. She woke on a groan, her heart thrashing, and sweat coating her skin. Salem gripped her hand.

"I don't understand what you want from me," she rasped. "What do I do with all this horror you've poured in my mind?"

"You have to know the reality of what you're up against and you have to numb your heart to it."

"I can't... I don't want to. I'll lose what makes me, me, if I can reach a place I don't care about such things."

He gave her hand a soft squeeze. "You have to learn to hold still. Sharpen your eyes to see your next move. If we end up in a place where there are children, or just people weaker than us, how can we help them by reacting rashly and just getting ourselves killed? Accept the fact you will see things that make you burn with rage. Freeze the fire and wait for your time to strike. Otherwise, you won't survive."

A shaky breath sighed out from her lungs, and she nodded. "I'll try... It's so hard to sleep now."

"As a slave, you must not sleep, Melina. Rest your body, doze perhaps, but you cannot sleep. Part of you must always be awake and listening."

I hate this. I hate all of it.

She closed her eyes, trying to hide the horrors in her mind behind a curtain. She let go of Salem's hand and rolled away from him, curling into a ball. Only when she remembered the sensation of being wrapped in Rhain's warm smoke, did she doze off again.

Maybe it was a few hours later or only a few minutes, but when she woke again, the tears she'd been holding so hard finally broke free. The light sliding along the cables on the walls dimly lit the room. The moving lights blurred through her tears. She slithered off the bed, took two steps, and sank to her knees, her hands pressing hard over her heart. It beat as always and yet...under her ribs was a void, aching for the past, cold searching for heat. Every time she blinked, tears broke over the edge and rolled down her cheeks. She didn't wipe them away.

Rhain. Wait for me.

Her lips trembled with the strain of holding her sobs in her throat. Salem woke anyway. She turned her head away from him as he got up from the bed and came toward her. She braced herself, ready for him to mock her.

She could feel his heat on her skin as he sank to his knees beside her.

"Look at me," he ordered in a quiet voice.

She turned her face to him, one hand raised, about to wipe the tears off. He caught her by the wrist.

"Don't," he whispered.

She stared at him, confused, while he gazed at her tears as though mesmerized by art. His breathing grew ragged. She didn't understand, but the intensity of his stare held her still. She blinked again, and a new tear spilled over. He leaned closer, watching it slide down her face.

"So beautiful," he murmured. "It's been a long time for me...I'd forgotten." He lifted his hand close to her face. "May I?"

What? What did he want? To touch her tears?

"Okay," she breathed.

Salem skimmed the pad of his thumb under her eye. He looked closely at the saline clinging to his thumb before pressing it under his own eye, swiping it down what would have been the course the tear flowed down his face, if it were his own. Shivers lifted on his skin, and his eyes rolled back in his head as he moaned.

He shook himself and smiled. "I owe you one."

His hand caught her roughly by the chin, and he brought his face an inch from hers. "So beautiful," he said again. "If you were mine, I'd make you cry every day."

She tried to recoil. He pushed her down on the floor and pinned her hands over her head.

"Get off me!" she shouted, struggling.

He laughed, immune to her attempts to move him, he was so damn strong. It was shocking.

"I owe you. I don't always pay my debts, but I feel like it right now. MUGi!" he called for the droid. The next second MUGi hovered over Salem's shoulder. "Hold her down."

"Stop! What are you doing?"

A rush through her bones locked her down, white light blinding her. The smell of burning flesh filled her nose.

"Okay, let her go, MUGi."

Black spots hung in her vision, but she jumped to her feet and landed a right hook to Salem's face. The same punch would have knocked Maddox on his ass, but Salem only staggered back a step.

"What did you do to me?"

He rotated his jaw before giving her a smile. "Nice punch."

"What did you do?" she demanded again.

"I seared your tear ducts. You'll never cry again."

"The hell?" She was taken aback.

"You can thank me now…" He chuckled as she glared at him. "Or later."

Melina rubbed her eyes and blinked a few times. The black spots faded. Her vision wasn't damaged. "Why?"

"If you don't understand now, you will in the future."

"Is this part of your game?"

"No." The quiet of his voice caught her full attention. "That was a gift, as best as I can give."

Heat lit his eyes again, and his demeanor shifted. Fear and adrenaline tugged in her core. Shapeshifter, she thought. She wasn't confronted by Salem. This person wanted to hurt her. His hands clenched into fists, and his nostrils flared.

Salem's game restarted… Round two.

"You see what I am?"

"Yes," she whispered. "You're my jailer."

"How are you going to survive me?" he demanded as he punched her in the stomach.

The hit sent her to her knees. She wrapped her arms around her torso, trying to breathe, staring at the floor. Her mind raced. This wasn't about fighting or winning. *How are you going to survive me?*

She was the slave and he was the guard… It wasn't about escape. There was none.

She forced herself to stand. He slapped her hard enough to make her ears pop. Then he slapped her again, this time breaking open her cheek. She didn't try to touch it, but the heat of the blood running down her face let her know the damage. He grabbed her chin and snarled into her face.

"Think you're special, you ugly bitch? It makes total sense you're a virgin. Only a blind man would hit that. Tell you what, I'll make you a hood, to cover your hideous face." His snarl turned into a simper. "Oh, poor baby. Did that hurt your feelings? You're not the pouting type, are you? You're a scrapper. Here, I'll let you hit me. I'll just stand here. Go ahead."

Her hands clenched. No. That wasn't the right choice. It was a trap…wasn't it? She looked down and shook her head.

"Appease me. What do I want?" he demanded.

"You want dominance. You want my submission through pain and fear."

"Sort of. What do I hate?"

"Umm…"

He slapped her again. "What do I hate?" he shouted.

"I don't know!"

Her face was on fire where he slapped her. Rage ignited. She saw red and her fangs throbbed. She lashed out, but before she could land a blow to him, he struck her again, and this time her vision darkened. Everything went sideways. He caught her and lowered her to a sitting position on the floor. Shaking her head, she tried to remain lucid.

"I hate beauty. I hate unbroken things." He crouched in front of her.

Her head swam. He cupped her chin, gently this time. She looked into his eyes.

"The moment you lose control, you die." He spoke the words as if reciting scripture. "Don't ever forget that. Promise me."

"I promise."

He sat on his butt and crossed his legs. "I'm going to ease off you for a moment, even though I think it's a mistake." He sighed. "You're going to be an exotic animal in a cage when we get picked up. The guards will smell you out in no time. They'll know you're unusual immediately. That's going to get them salivating. They can't kill you or rape you, but anything else goes...Most guards are hardened monsters, but they used to be people, once. Think about it."

Mel winced as she touched her aching cheek. She engaged her imagination. "They'll beat me."

"Often."

"They'll humiliate me."

"Every day." He nodded.

"I'm special. I'm worth something. They aren't. My presence offends them. My worth stings them, for their lack of worth. They're broken and ugly so they can't stomach someone who isn't...They've given in to the injustice of their lives and let it consume them."

"Very good...so how do you appease them when they begin to beat you?"

"I don't know."

"You better figure it out." He shrugged. "Or don't. You will eventually. When you're living it."

"You're a really screwed up teacher, Salem."

A loud knock sounded on the door.

"Hey!" Cope shouted from the other side. "You two at it again? The day is starting. We're ready and waiting."

"Go on ahead of us," Salem yelled.

"What's happening?" Mel asked.

He pulled his shirt on and sat on the bed to lace up his boots. "Get ready to go. Everyone is helping with your training today."

He walked out of the room and came right back with a clean, wet rag in his hand. She reached for it, but he smacked her hand lightly and pressed the cloth to her face himself. She watched him for a second and then turned her eyes to the floor. He took more care than was necessary, his touch slow and prolonged.

It was possessive.

She glanced at him again and a certainty settled under her ribs. She never had nor would she ever meet someone else like him. Part of her was grateful.

He released her. She dressed for the day, putting everything she owned on her body, so she was as prepared as she could be for whatever Salem was going to put her through. Her anxiety ticked up a notch when he put his gloves on and picked up his makeshift, scrap metal sword by its cloth-wrapped handle.

"Ready?"

She nodded, rolling both her wrists, making the blades up the backs of her arms spring out.

He smirked. "Save it until the right time."

Slightly let down, she rolled her wrists again and followed him through the door and out the main hatch. He walked swiftly, making hardly any sound. What game were they playing now? She didn't know anything. What did she need to focus on in order for him to be satisfied? She tried to walk as quietly as he did. They went far down the tunnels and the floor began to slope upward. Her senses sharpened. They were going to the second level.

As soon as the floor flattened out again, Salem stopped abruptly and held one hand out in a signal for her to stop. He turned his head to the side and held one finger to his lips. She nodded, listening. She heard it half a second before Salem charged into the tunnel before them. They didn't have to run far. She skidded to a halt behind him as he stopped.

Unfair. So unfair.

Her heart and stomach clenched. A second of shock. Another second of denial. A third second to cringe as screaming and rage filled her head. Her hands stung as if her friends had just been ripped from her palms. The smell of blood threatened to choke her. Her eyes focused on the details, imprinting it all on her brain. Images she didn't want now chiseled deep inside her permanently.

Multifaceted, sensory...death was ugly.

Both Cope and Inesia lay broken and butchered on the floor at the feet of the first brain-bleached she'd ever seen. Half of his face and hulking body was modified. Strange light lit his pupils. More like cameras than eyes.

"There you are, Salem. You're too late to save them," the man hissed, holding his blood covered hands up close to his face. "I didn't want to. I'm sorry." His voice was fragmented with glitches of electronic sounds.

"I know, Innis. And I'm sorry I have to kill you, now."

"The rest are coming. All of them. Your time's up. The poppers want her." He pointed at Mel.

"Try and take her then."

Innis stepped over Cope and Inesia, his movements careful. Salem raised his sword. Mel backed up, watching for an opportunity. The tunnel didn't give them any extra space to fight.

"If I die, run back to the hatch and lock yourself in," Salem ordered her.

"I'm sorry," the brain-bleached said again.

"Me too."

Innis' arm extended out in three snaking cables. One wrapped around her leg, another around Salem's arm, and the third was trying to constrict around his neck. She rolled her wrist, her blades jumping out from the back of her arm, slicing through the cable.

The severed end constricted tighter, bleeding burning acid on her skin. She cried out as she charged forward. Salem blocked her, knocking her backward. "Stay out of it," he snarled as he hacked the cable around his arm off with his sword. He tore the cable off before it could burn him the way it had her. Salem turned the end toward Innis and squeezed, spraying him in the face with his own acid.

Innis cried out and covered his face a second before Salem began hacking him to pieces. He died long before Salem was finished with him. His real feelings played out in his strikes. Breathing hard, he turned to her and knelt down, grabbing her leg, and tearing the cable off her. He hissed as acid spilled on his skin when he threw it at the body.

Fury surged in his eyes as he examined the burn on her leg.

"I'm all right. I heal fast."

He sighed and straightened up, offering her his hand. She took it and he pulled her up. She rolled her wrist, the blades retracting. He opened his mouth, about to say something, but changed his mind and turned his back on her.

She moved closer to the bodies. Unfair. It was just so damn unfair. Mel looked into her reflection on Cope's open, glassy eyes. She wouldn't leave her or Inesia there like that.

"What are you doing?" Salem demanded as she picked up Inesia.

Adrenaline and grief made the body feather light in her arms. "I'm taking them home. I don't care what you say."

He raised his brows but then he nodded and hefted Innis over his shoulder. "You do that. I'm going to move him up higher. It won't throw the others off the track very long, but it's better than nothing."

She couldn't stop or slow down until it was done. She couldn't feel it. Not yet. After laying Inesia down on the bed in Cope's room, Mel turned and ran back. She didn't have to worry about getting lost, her feet took her straight back to the scene.

Her heart threatened her with the pain it was holding. *Not yet. Not yet.* Mel looked away from Cope's face as she lifted her. The heat of Cope's blood turned cold as it soaked through Mel's clothes.

"You saved my life. I'm sorry I couldn't return the favor," she whispered as she laid her out beside Inesia.

What have I become? She wondered as she began to take the weapons and jewelry off the bodies. Just two small knives, a machete, and one earing. Salem came back through the main hatch as she was laying it all down outside Cope's room. His eyes reflected the emptiness she felt.

"Should I take their clothes, too?"

He looked past her into the room and shook his head. "No. Too torn. Leave them."

Salem shut the door and leaned against it, closing his eyes. Mel stood beside him, her arm touching his. Neither of them moved for a while. The tears she could no longer cry turned into a wash of bitterness that coated her soul. She pressed her eyelids and then covered her face. It was wrong. The dryness was wrong, it shamed her.

"We have to burn them." Salem straightened up, his demeanor shifting back to normal as if nothing had happened.

"Can it wait, just…just a little longer?"

"No." He turned away from her and opened the door to Cope's room again. "MUGi."

The droid flew into the room and hovered close to Salem's face. "Burn the bodies. Control the flames. Clear up the ashes."

"No! Wait!" She tried to get MUGi's attention. Salem looked furious. "Leave the ashes, at least a little. I want to take them with us when we get out of here."

"Don't be stupid."

"Don't tell me how to grieve!" she shouted.

"This is so disappointing, Melina. Have you learned nothing from your time here?"

"I've learned! But it's just the two of us. So, what if I show how I really feel?"

His nostrils flared and his eyes narrowed but after a second he nodded. "Fine," he said tersely. "Save a small amount of the ashes, MUGi."

Salem closed the door behind the droid as it hovered into Cope's room.

Inesia was dead. Cope was dead. Even though they'd only known each other a short while, they were her friends. Reality twisted a knot into her stomach and her emotions built new layers of pressure inside her. Things she had to keep bottled up and deny their existence. Even as she locked it all in, anger slipped past and rose to the surface. She wished she had been the one to kill Innis, or at least severely injured him.

"Why did you stop me in the tunnel? I could have killed him. Don't you want me to up my fighting game, isn't that the purpose of training me?"

He hung his head and laughed. His response felt so wrong in the moment, he scared her. The second her foot scraped the floor as she tried to step back from him, his head snapped up. He turned and charged at her. She backed up until there was nowhere to go.

"No!" he shouted punching the wall next to her head. "Be strong, skilled, fast, that's good. There will always be someone stronger, faster...You will face them every day. Walk next to them, break your nails beside them as you scratch for an existence. Shatter your hands in their flesh and bones when your owner tells you to."

He was breathing hard, emotion storming in his eyes.

"You're all I have left and I will break your heart over and over and fill the gaps with stone until that is all there is."

So that was it? He had broken her heart. That was his way of surviving? What did she do with the man standing before her? Mel shook her head.

"Then what will be left to love? Why should I search for my husband if there's nothing left of me but stone? Or is that your goal? Are you doing all this just to make me yours?"

All the fire in his gaze died and the color drained from his face. "Maybe I am..." he whispered.

"You're despicable."

"You already knew that, princess. Even though it's true, don't say it. I hate that word."

"What? Despicable?"

"Yes."

A tremble began in her chest. The tension in the space between them ached. What was going on with them? Why did it feel this way?

"Do you... Do you love me?" she whispered.

He flinched. She couldn't believe it, but he actually flinched. Fire flashed back into his gaze, rage surged all around him and he punched the wall again. "I don't know!" he shouted.

"The moment you lose control, you die," she quoted.

He blinked once and then laughed. He took a step back from her, his demeanor relaxing. "Very good... Listen to me. I want you to live, regardless of my reasons, you know I want you alive. So, take my instructions. I don't want to lose you, too." He sat down and put his head in his hands. "We can't leave the hatch. Not for any reason. The poppers will be relentless now. It's too dangerous out there. We just have to wait it out until the slavers get here. It won't be long. A few days perhaps. We can live locked in here that long."

"How will we know when the slavers get here? Won't we have to go to the surface?"

"No. They will come directly to us. If we can just hold up long enough, as soon as they come, we'll be out of here."

Mel crossed her arms and held herself tightly, trying to do as Salem was trying to teach her, to go numb. She watched him. He didn't look very numb to her at the moment. Grief filled the air around them.

"Do me a favor."

"What?" she asked warily.

"Please stop showing me how you feel. It's tempting me to be genuine."

"I'll try harder, but...I'm hurting so much."

He closed his eyes and exhaled as though she'd just made it worse for him.

The door opened and MUGi came flying back out. How could their cremation be over so quickly?

Where their bodies had been, now only two small mounds of ashes remained and a trace of smoke in the air. Mel inhaled deeply, taking her friends into her lungs. With her index finger, she touched first one pile and then the other bringing the ashes to her tongue. The bitter taste saturated deep before she swallowed.

Salem was silent behind her, but she felt the weight of his gaze.

"I need two containers," she said.

"I'll find some later. Come out of there and leave the dead in peace a while."

"But..."

He huffed. "Jeez, you're argumentative today. I've let you have your way, now do what I ask."

She walked past him and went straight to the other room and lay down. Her heart was so heavy, she didn't have the strength to stand any longer.

Mel woke on a jolt, her heart straining. She was alone in Salem's room, light pouring into the darkened space from the open doorway. She grimaced as she got up. Her blood-dried clothes peeled away from her skin like a scab as she moved. The taste of ashes lingered in her mouth.

Walking out of the room, she stopped when she heard his voice. He was talking quietly in Cope's room. Sitting on the floor, he was cutting into his forearm with a small knife. He didn't notice her, or he was just ignoring her.

"I know it's not something I would normally say...but...I'm sorry. I really did try to get us out of here. I was so close," he whispered. "Mel's right, though. We're taking you with us."

Setting his knife down, reaching over to the ashes, he buried his fingers, coating them. He smeared the ashes on his cut forearm. He wiped his hand on his pants before putting his fingers into the other pile of ashes and smearing those into his cuts as well.

His head shot up, pinning her with his gaze. Holding her breath, she waited for him to lash out at her. He blinked and held his arm out to show her. He'd carved their names before rubbing their ashes into his flesh. She nodded approvingly at his choice.

"Are you hungry?"

"I don't know," she admitted.

"All that's left of the food will go bad soon and we can't get anymore."

"Let's eat it all then."

He stood and took her hand. She waited, apprehensively, but all he did was squeeze gently. "Thank you."

"What for?"

"You stood up to me, so you could respect the dead. It…" He looked down, his expression troubled. "It helped me. Somehow, you gave me permission to grieve as well. I don't understand why, but it did. I'm grateful."

He let go and moved past her, opening the metal box where the last of the food was stored. She ate, not looking, smelling, or even tasting the food. She worked hard to go numb as she ate, otherwise she was sure she would have thrown up. The food filled her stomach and calmed her.

"We can't take their ashes, you know?" Salem said when they finished eating. "The slavers will take everything from us, especially things we really want to keep, even if it's worth nothing to them."

Getting to her feet, she strode back into Cope's room. She looked intently at the ashes and sifted through them until she found what she was looking for. Back in the main room, she held the two bone shards out for Salem to see. Each one was about the size of a fingernail.

"If I cut two of my tally marks open and slip these in, I can carry them with me. When I get to the best place, I'll cut them out and bury them."

"I'll help you."

It was fast. He cut open the first and last tally marks on her arm with the same cutter he'd used to make them originally and slipped the bones into her flesh. As her skin pulled back together he cupped her chin in his hand. They gazed at each other, and for the first time it seemed there were no lies in his eyes.

It was there, deep in his gaze...the truth.

She shook her head and looked at the floor. "I can't return your feelings...not the way you want me to."

He dropped his hand. "I never said it, and I won't. I'll never tell you. So, you can't say that. You don't know what I want."

He walked out of the room. She closed her eyes and shook her head again. She shouldn't have said anything. She shouldn't have acknowledged what she saw in his eyes.

They didn't speak again until bedtime.

She could have slept on Inesia's bed. She tried for a while, but it was no good. It was lonely and made it impossible for her to forget the fact her friends were dead long enough for her to relax and fall asleep.

The door stood open to his room. She hesitated in the doorway, struggling with herself and about to go back to the other bed.

"It's okay," he said. "I'm having a hard time falling asleep without you next to me."

She lay down beside him. "I'm sorry for what I said earlier...about your feelings."

"I'm sorry you said it, too. It hurts...but I shouldn't have lowered my guard like that."

"I don't know how to thank you for what you've done for me without violating my conscience."

He smiled. "That admission will do for now."

They were quiet for a few minutes. It wasn't a comfortable silence. Then he laughed darkly and took her hand. She didn't pull away.

"I'm in a strange mood, Melina. I feel the desire to tell you the truth."

"I'll listen."

"I want you for myself. I've worked my whole life to never want anything but having you here...right beside me and I can't reach out and claim you...it's fucking cruel. I didn't know people like you really existed. And...I have to respect the boundary of your marriage," he groaned. "I know you feel something for me, but it can never be... all because someone else found you before I did. It's the cruelest thing I've ever felt and I'm no stranger to cruelty."

"I know I said I'd listen, but please don't say any more. You're breaking my heart and you're tempting me to betray."

He smiled again, somewhat miserably. "Thank you for that admission as well."

"I appreciate your restraint. You have more power over me than I want to admit."

His breath came out in a ragged sigh. "Turn away from me."

She rolled to face the wall. His arm came over her and held her, but he didn't do anything else. Even still, she felt guilty.

"We don't have much time left before the slavers get here. This might be the last time we can speak openly for a while."

She nodded.

"Listen closely. Your spirit is the only thing you own. The real you, don't show it to anyone ever. They'll be looking. There are always eyes probing, learning how to break you. If you let your guard down for even a minute, they'll know how to turn you into a shell.

"Desire is weakness. Never forget that. Your goal...what drives you, you can never show or tell anyone. The trick is to move the pieces of the game with misdirection. Create a fake version of yourself. Fake desires close enough to the real ones, you can move freely toward your goal with no one the wiser. They'll think they know your mark and will try to thwart you, but it won't matter. Get it?"

"Yes. I understand...I will do that...for you. To show you respect."

"I don't deserve respect."

"You're wrong, Salem."

He put his hand over her mouth. "Shh... Don't pile on my misery."

They fell asleep in the terrible regret of what could have been. He was a choice she could have made. No, that was wrong she realized. Loving Salem was a path she turned her back on. She chose Rhain. Every moment, being close to Salem, acknowledging he tempted her, but her heart was already gone. It didn't return to her. She had many feelings for Salem, but Rhain was something she could not give up.

A blast and screeching metal startled Melina awake. Salem's arm tightened over her. "It's okay. Our ride is here."

Smoke and dust billowed through the huge blast hole in the main room of the hatch. Mel pressed her back to the wall as far away from the wreckage as she could be. She looked around Salem's shoulder as he stood protectively in front of her.

A giant size man in a hood came through the hole and stood to the side, crossing his massive arms over his chest. Another man, almost exactly the same size and wearing an identical hood, came through after him. He too took up a bodyguard stance.

Mel's heart filled her throat, her breathing shallow, and sweat slicked her palms. Salem tensed as a woman came through. Her sharp, dark eyes darted around the room before landing on Salem. A half smile lifted her plum colored lips and a slight blush colored her cheeks. She was very tall and thin, with long black hair.

"Edith, what a wonderful surprise." Salem's voice dripped with honey, but Mel could tell he was lying. "Finally killed everyone in your way and took command of Horace's ship?"

"That I did, lover. You don't look pleased to see me. It was obvious from the message you sent out, you were expecting the old perv and not me. I won't be as easy a sell on your stock as he would have been."

"And yet, here you are," Salem countered.

She shrugged. "I've got a few empty cages. Step aside and let me see this prize sow you claim I can sell for a fortune."

He nudged Mel forward.

Edith circled her once, examining. She came closer and pulled her collar open, looking down her shirt at the broken circle. A satisfied expression settled on her face. She backed away and laughed. "Bullshit."

"What's that, Edith?" Salem asked calmly.

"In your message, you claimed she was a virgin. No way have you had such a beauty locked away with you and you didn't defile her."

He shrugged. "She's worth a lot more like this. Scan her, if you don't believe me. Besides, no one has claimed a place in my heart since you."

Edith blushed again and turned her face away. Mel stood still and kept her mouth shut. Edith recovered and lifted her head a little higher, looking him determinedly in the eyes. "I loved you... I know now everything you ever said to me was a lie. You used me to escape...but the past aside, you're right. I can sell her for a very high price."

Edith pulled a gun on him and fired. Salem staggered back against the wall, covering his stomach with both hands, blood gushing out through his fingers. He slid down the wall.

Mel screamed as she ran to him, covering his hands with her own. He coughed, blood running from the side of his mouth.

"Psycho ex-girlfriends ruin everything." He gave her a feeble smile, his voice disjointed. "Remember what I taught you."

"I will. I promise." Dryness burned her eyes. "I can't even cry for you, bastard."

He gripped both of her hands and she pressed her cheek against his. "I'm going to kill her for you," she whispered in his ear.

"You do that..."

His breathing slowed. She turned her face and kissed his lips. When she pulled back, he blinked once, a smirk lifting his mouth.

"Now who's the despicable one, Melina?"

"Me. It's me," she breathed.

"What I felt...I think...it might have been love."

His eyes hollowed out and he breathed his last.

The moment you lose control, you die. She heard his voice in her head as she closed his eyes with her fingertips. She licked the blood from her lips and swallowed. *I'm taking you with me, Salem. I'll never forget you.*

One of the hooded men grabbed her by the arm and pulled her away, forcing her to face Edith. The numbness clicked into place as she looked at her owner, just the way Salem taught her. Her face became a mask. Her eyes showed only what she wanted to be seen.

"No tears?" Edith said. "I guess you were smarter than I was. I was stupid enough to love him." She glanced at his body and then away. "I have my revenge now and a new goldmine. Are you going to play nice, slave?"

"Yes, ma'am. I will play any way you require."

Edith gave a curt nod and marched back through the hole in the wall. One guard in front and the other behind, Mel was led into the slave ship.

Everything was tarnished, gold-colored metal, ceilings, floors and the bars of the slave cages lining the walls. She didn't look at the people behind the bars. She couldn't handle that just yet. Instead, she focused on the ship itself and its strange technology. It felt more mechanical than magical. The floor vibrated hard under her feet as the engines roared to life and the ship lurched forward. The real her, the one buried deep inside, cried hard for Salem. His death brought her sharp awareness of just how deeply he'd touched her heart.

He wanted her to live. She would.

The guard behind her shoved her into a cage and locked it. Edith gazed in at her, critical assessment in her eyes. "What's your name?"

"Melina." She saw no reason to not give her real name.

"I'm going to build some buzz around you before I put you on the auction block...not too much. I don't want other slavers killing me so they can steal you. Exhibition fights will be your whole life while you're with me. Blood and sex. That's how I plan to sell you. Get it?"

"I understand and I will be the perfect asset, just so long as you auction me in Nocturne. That is my only condition. If you try to sell me somewhere other than Nocturne, you will find me damn near worthless."

Edith gave a little chuckle. "We are in accord. I'd be a fool to sell you anywhere else." She pursed her lips. "You need new clothes and a bath. Some food, too I bet. I'll take good care of you."

"Take me to Nocturne, and I'll take good care of you, too."

Until the moment I kill you, spiteful hag.

Edith nodded and walked away. Mel lay down on the floor and closed her eyes, the movement of the ship vibrated her bones.

I'm coming, Rhain.

Sixteen

Nocturne.

"What's this about, Koda?" Rhain asked as he walked beside the emperor.

Disguised in a turban and a veil that draped over the lower half of his face, a mischievous glint lit the side of his eye as he glanced at Rhain. "The auction is starting any moment."

Since Koda was incognito, he'd told Rhain it was okay to be relaxed. They were good friends but usually it was only okay for Rhain to drop formalities when they were alone.

"What auction?"

Koda huffed. "You really should pay better attention to the pulse of the people. Everyone is all tingly over some pit fighter. They say she's as deadly as she is beautiful."

Nocturne's huge orange sun beat down on them as they walked into the amassing crowd, not that Rhain could really feel its heat. This oddity he called a body was as numb as the smoke monster he used to be. Koda's bodyguards sprinkled through the people, plainly dressed so no one would spot them and realize the emperor was nearby.

Rhain groaned. "I can't believe you're making come with you to the seediest part of the city, just so you can play at an auction. You're the emperor. If you want this chick, just order her to the palace, and she's yours."

"Where's the fun in that? I want to win the auction." He twisted his numbered paddle in his hands. "If someone outbids me, good for them."

Rhain shook his head. "Unbelievable."

The auction block was a little ways ahead, but there were so many people already there, they wouldn't get a good look at this woman in any case. "I hate the slave trade. You know this." He sneered at the people around them. "Disgusting. I would never buy and sell a person."

"What are you talking about? You have slaves."

"Slaves are Seraph's thing, not mine. She's probably somewhere in this crowd dying to spend my money."

"Don't you want to see the woman everyone is so excited about? She's got to be seriously hot. Maybe you'll change your mind and bid yourself once you see her."

Rhain closed his eyes and fought for patience. "Not a chance."

A thin, dark-haired woman strode out on the stage and everyone began shouting and waving their auction paddles in the air. She lifted her arms and the people quieted.

"This is it!" the woman shouted. "The auction you've all been waiting for. The auction of a lifetime! You all have seen the fights with your own eyes. You know her skill and amazing speed, not to mention her *curves*..." most of the men in the crowd shouted. "And today, she can be yours!"

The entire crowd waved their hands and paddles as they all shouted excitedly.

"This is crazy!" Koda exclaimed. "I've never seen this many people so hyped over a slave. I wish I would have watched one of the fights."

"This makes me sick," Rhain growled through clenched teeth. "You've got other bodyguards here. Can I leave?"

"Hell, no."

"You all know her pedigree, but I will list it again!" the woman on stage was shouting again. "All these facts have been verified!" She lifted her hands and began to tick off her fingers one by one. "She's a deadly fighter! She's a vampire! She's a virgin! She's been modified in Polyhedron! She's Regian! And amazing...hard to believe even...she's marked with Nocturne magic!"

Cold shock filled Rhain. Did he hear that right? Surely not. His ears were playing tricks on him. It's because he wasn't paying close attention and there was so much noise from the crowd. He strained his ears now.

"No time limit! Highest bidder wins! Here she is, the object of your desire, *Melina!*"

Adrift in the middle of an ocean of movement and noise, suddenly he couldn't hear anything, the people surrounding him turned into a blur as she walked out on the stage. Melina. His wife. She was here! Right in front of him. She was alive and she was here!

He couldn't move or speak, mesmerized as she strode boldly to the center of the stage. She didn't slouch or look at her feet. She didn't tremble with fear or cry. Scantily clad she walked like a model down the runway, flaunting her beauty, working the onlookers. And for a moment, he was owned by her like everyone else in the crowd. His mind blank except for, *I've got to have that.*

Through the chaos, his gaze glued to her, he begged her, *Look at me, Mel. Look at me!*

Koda lifted his paddle and shouted a bid, bringing Rhain back to reality. All the noise flooded his ears again. The auction was in full swing, bidders shouting in quick succession over one another. The price shooting up with each new bid.

"Give me that!" Rhain grabbed the paddle from Koda's hand.

"Hey! I know I said for you to be casual, but you're taking it too far. Give that back. I want her."

"She's mine!" Rhain growled.

"What? I thought you despised the slave trade."

"She's mine!" he said again pushing forward through the crowd.

Rhain was taller and broader than most. People moved aside for him, or he shoved them out of his way as he fought to get closer to the stage. She flirted with the top bidders, flashing seductive smiles from her sexy pose on the stage. Why was she here? Why was she a slave? Why did she smile and wink at those around her as if this was what she wanted? Was she really his Melina? Or was he just having a terrible nightmare?

He pushed all his questions to the background, his mind locked on the only thing that mattered at the moment, winning the auction. He stopped a few rows back from the edge of the stage, not far from the top bidder. He'd kill the guy if it came to it.

Rhain watched and waited. He looked away from Melina so he wouldn't lose his concentration on what was happening. The bidders began to drop off as the price skyrocketed. He waited. Down to the last two. He didn't consider the amount or if he could even pay it. One pulled ahead and the other shook his head, lowering his paddle.

"Is that all? The bid stands at three million," the dark-haired woman shouted to the crowd. "Anyone else?"

Rhain lifted the paddle. "Five million."

Melina turned and looked at him. She smiled as she had to all the others. She didn't recognize him, he realized. But then she blinked and narrowed her eyes, her gaze probing, questioning. He nodded. Her cheeks flushed. She faced him, her breathing labored, eyes on fire. Then she quickly turned away, recovering her swagger.

"Well, now here's someone who understands the lady's worth! Five million." the auctioneer said, gesturing to the other bidder.

He sneered and raised his paddle. "Six million," he shouted.

Rhain caught his eye and the man blanched and recoiled, deadly intent coming through loud and clear. But he wasn't defeated yet. Anger colored his cheeks and it looked as if he was about to dig in.

"Ten million," Rhain said calmly.

The crowd cried out again, riding the tension. The other bidder shook his head and dropped his paddle. The crowd cheered as the auction ended and Rhain was announced the winner. His eyes sought Mel's. She looked as close to bursting as he felt. He shook his head at her. *Not yet. Not here.*

Koda came up behind him. "Well, that was unexpected. Do you even have ten million?"

He shrugged, "If I shift some of my assets around, I can come up with it."

"I'll spot you. Pay me back in a few days."

"Thanks."

"No problem. I'm seriously shocked here, though. What possessed you?" Koda asked.

"I'll explain later, somewhere no one can hear."

Koda raised his eyebrows. "There's more to it than a fit of madness brought on by lust?"

"Much more."

Mel was ushered off the stage, flanked by two massive guards. She glanced at him over her shoulder before she disappeared behind a curtain. The crowd began to disperse and the auctioneer walked up to him.

"Please follow me to my ship, sir, so we can complete the transaction." Her eyes gleamed with satisfied greed.

Koda went with him and paid the slaver. Rhain looked for Melina but didn't see her. He fought to clear his thoughts and calm his emotions.

"Pleasure doing business with you sirs," the slaver said. "Would you prefer to take her with you, or shall I deliver her to your residence? It might not be too safe to just walk her out of here, given her celebrity status."

He saw right through the lie and reached forward, grabbing the woman by the throat. "Nice try. Bring Melina to me now!"

Koda grabbed him by the wrist. "Ease up. I'll have my guards take your winnings to your house. While you come with me back to the palace."

Rhain let go of the woman. "What? No. *I* need to take her home."

"I order you."

"Why?"

"I need someone to watch my back since I'm sending my guards with your woman. And I demand an explanation out of you."

She kept her eyes on the ground as she walked, her mind tripping as hard as her heart. Was the man who bought her really him? Was it Rhain? What did she do if he wasn't? What did she do if he was? Measuring the time was confusing. How long she'd been with Edith, hacking her way through flesh just to get to this point.

Sweat beaded and slid down her skin under the heavy cloak and with her hands tied she couldn't wipe it off her face. The hand on her arm tightened and pulled her to a stop.

"What's going on here?" a man demanded.

Mel didn't look up but gazed at the sandaled feet on the ground in front of her.

"Delivering your master's new slave." The guard let go of her and walked away along with all his buddies. She listened to their retreating steps.

The hood was pulled back off her head. She glanced up into the bald man's pinched face and then looked down again.

"I am the steward," he said in a haughty voice. "I was not informed of your arrival, so until I know what your station is to be, you will be confined. Follow me."

He strode away. She followed him, taking in as much of her surroundings as she could. He led her through a beautiful, stone courtyard. It was a villa, she realized. Pale cream stone buildings, muted mosaics on the ground, and long desert grass, swaying in the hot breeze. They passed through some columns into the shade just as a door opened at the end of the open hallway and a woman came out. The steward halted and bowed. Mel stopped short behind him, gazing intently at the woman, her memory pulsed.

She glanced down the hall, her violet eyes falling sharply on Melina. She hesitated, her willowy frame turned halfway toward them. Then she pivoted and flounced the other way. Mel watched her, a sharp thorny emotion sticking in her brain. Elegant, gorgeous, elite...who was that woman?

The steward straightened up and sighed before continuing forward, leading her through a door and into a laundry room. He clapped his hands and the frail-looking teenager folding linen set her work down.

"Kari, I need you to take care of this new arrival. Get her cleaned up and in proper clothes, then take her to one of the *empty* rooms."

The girl wiped her hand on her brow and nodded. "Yes, sir."

He turned on Melina. "You're not going to cause any trouble, are you?"

Mel smirked. "Not today."

His pinched face contracted in further, but he didn't reply and walked out of the room.

"Don't mind him, he's not as cranky as he seems," The young woman said. "He wouldn't hurt anyone. It's security you have to watch out for. They aren't like the rest of us. They're palace soldiers." She winked and smiled. "I'm just a maid, no more, no less. I keep my head down, you should, too. Call me Kari."

"I'm Melina." She held her tied hands up a little. "I'd love to get out of these, and this cloak. I'm burning up."

"I'm sure you are, miss." Kari untied the rope.

Mel peeled the cloak off her sweaty skin.

"My goodness!" Kari exclaimed, looking at Mel's auction attire. "Where did you come from wearing something like that?"

"The auction block."

"Ah, yes. That explains it. Well, follow me. I'll have you looking like a proper house slave in no time."

"Great," Mel answered with sarcasm. Kari made her feel at ease, but she instantly checked herself. She couldn't lower her guard. Not yet.

The bath was actually a small pool in the middle of the main house, the ceiling opened to the sky directly over the bath. The lukewarm water cooled her core temperature as the sunlight kissed her skin. Sliding all the way under the water, music filled her ears. She surfaced and the music stopped. Intrigued, Mel took a deep breath and sank under the surface again. It wasn't something in the water, it was the water itself that sang. Faint, the sound flowed like a woman humming. Water was maternal, cocooning her in a blanket of peace.

She wanted to loll in the pool and just relax, but she wasn't on vacation, she was a slave. The loose clothes she was given were the same cream color as the stone, and light as breath. A sleeveless tunic, drawstring pants, and plain sandals.

Kari led her to a large, near-empty room and quickly left. The thick wooden door clicked loudly as it closed. She tried the handle. It was locked from the outside. The only light came from a plate-sized window close to the ceiling, too high for her to look out. She sighed and lay down on the only piece of furniture in the room, a hard, narrow bed. It was just another cell. Bigger than her last, and private. No one was staring in at her, at least not that she could tell.

I want my husband! I want my husband! Where is he? Her heart wailed desperately.

So, what happens now? The peace she felt in the water dried up. Apprehension and exhaustion twisted inside her as she waited. She'd made it, so everything was okay now. Everything was okay.

SEVENTEEN

The hinges creaked. Mel jumped to her feet as he came in and closed the door behind him. The surface of her skin buzzed as though she'd been jolted with electricity. Her heart stopped and restarted so fast it choked her. The air was too thin, she could hardly breathe. He was so different...and yet the same. She was still afraid she was mistaken. As if she'd fallen in love with a black and white photograph and now she was face to face with the real person. His skin was a rich tan, not grey. His hair a dark red. The masculine planes of his face were the same, but his eyes no longer glowed like demonic magma. The outer edges of his irises were black, sliding into a bright multifaceted hazel of gold, yellow, orange, and red, all the shades of a real fire.

"Is it you?" Her voice trembled.

"Of course it is, Bunny."

Oh, gosh! His voice! How she'd missed his voice, and it was still the same. She'd made it. She'd found him. All her strength left her. Her back broke as her muscles tore. She sank to the floor on her knees. The tears she could no longer cry built an ocean inside her. She looked up at him. He didn't move. He didn't reach for her. What was wrong? Wasn't he happy to see her? She couldn't stand, why didn't he lift her up? It was him, he remembered her. He called her 'Bunny'. Why didn't he reach for her?

She struggled to speak. "Have you forgotten what we are, Rhain?"

"No."

Then why won't you touch me? She screamed in her head. "Um...You look different."

"So do you," he said.

"I've been through a lot..." She gave a weak laugh and a miserable smile. "Your hair."

He touched the end of one of his long dreadlocks and grimaced. "Yeah...sorry about that."

"I wouldn't have guessed you were a ginger. Don't apologize. I love it...and your eyes...incredible. So this is the real you? What you used to look like?"

He nodded.

"Just how tall are you?"

"Six-eight. Am I not recognizable?"

"You look the same, for the most part. Just not monochrome. It messed with my brain a bit."

His hands shook. "I thought I'd never see you again...I thought you were dead. I couldn't hear you anymore... Why did you come here?"

"I missed you."

"What have you done?"

"It's a really long story."

Finally, he moved forward, reaching down and picking her up. Touch, after so long, shattering the doubts that this was all a dream. She broke to pieces in his arms, able to breathe for the first time in so long. She closed her eyes. He didn't kiss her. He didn't tear her clothes off. Fierce tension rolled up his body. She could feel it. He shook with the effort to restrain himself. Why? She pushed out of his arms and took a step back.

"What's wrong? Why are you treating me like this?" she demanded.

"I'm still cursed. I can hardly feel you. If I let myself go, I'm scared I'll really hurt you."

"I'm not fragile! Don't you love me anymore?"

"I love you, Mel. I love you so much! It's because I love you. I can't contain this inside the confines of my body. If I turn it loose...I can't. It will destroy you. I thought I killed you once. I can't risk..." He looked away. "And things are different here. This isn't Regia. My life hangs by a thread. I'm not free."

She'd been fighting so hard to get to this moment, she never thought she'd have to fight him, too, for what she wanted. Her memory pulsed again and a hot, angry spark flashed in her heart. Her nostrils flared and she bit down on her lips. A question burned in her mouth. She was terrified of the answer, but she had to ask it.

"Who is she? The woman with the violet eyes?"

He sighed. "My wife."

Oh, if only he would have lied. *"I'm your wife!"* she shouted, slapping him in the face. He grabbed her wrist as she lifted her hand to strike him again.

"You are! Yes."

"How could you? You don't know what I've been through just to find you!"

"I don't love Seraph. I never have. I didn't remember her. I didn't even remember who I was. Our marriage was arranged long before I ever met you."

She couldn't see for the rage, unjust as it may have been. "Have you slept with her?"

He scowled. "Of course I have...but not since I've been back. I'm still numb. Even if I could, I wouldn't. She doesn't turn me on. Our marriage was always cold. In any case, she doesn't want me any more than I want her. She has a lover."

"Is she the only one, or are there more?"

He touched her cheek. "There are no more...just you. You're the one I love."

Mel looked at the floor. Her strength sapped, her heart scorched. "Leave me alone."

He sighed and turned away from her. She pinched her eyes shut and held still, listening to the door opening and closing again. Alone, she lay down on the bed, phantom tears drowning her eyes. Nothing was how she imagined it would be.

Unneeded, unwanted, in the way. Did he even still want her in his life? All the blood, her own and those she'd killed…Her scars…was it all in vain? He had status and wealth here. He had a beautiful wife. So, what if she was cold? She looked like a real princess. How could Mel compete with that? And even if it was in the past, she'd had him in a way Mel never had. Jealousy burned so hot in her chest. Just from glancing at her at the end of a hallway, Mel could tell, they were as different as two women could be.

Her last night with Salem came back into her mind. He said it was the cruelest thing he'd ever endured, that she was there with him and he couldn't have her only because someone else had found her first. She understood his feelings now. Someone else had claimed Rhain long before she ever met him. Salem was right…It was fucking cruel.

The door opened again. "No!" Rhain growled, striding back to her. "I won't leave you alone."

He picked her up and, against her will, she clung to him, her arms shaking with the strain to hold him as tight as she could. Angry, jealous, insecure, and yet, still desperate for him. The longing for things to be right between them was stronger. His hands ran over her back as he buried his face in her hair and inhaled. "I love you, Mel." His voice broke. "I thought you were dead, and it was my fault."

His mouth crushed hers, jolting her memory of their first kiss and she knew it was true... He couldn't feel her any more than he ever could.

"Please don't turn away from me now. I'm so dead inside, but if you don't love me anymore, that death will overtake me. I'll have no reason to fight against my curse. I'll just let it have me."

She couldn't answer, she just shook her head and hung on to him, fighting her way through her emotions, so she could see her way clear. For what felt like hours, they didn't move or speak. She didn't trust herself or her feelings. It was a tangle of sorrow and envy inside her. It wasn't fair. Nothing was fair, to him or her. She'd clung so hard to her assumption that once she found him it would all be okay.

Foolish, she realized. But she had to think that way to come as far as she had. Instead of being at the finish line of her trials, a new gauntlet stretched out before her. She promised she'd survive. Time to regroup. New world, new rules, new enemies. She wasn't going to be destroyed by this. Maybe she was 'the other woman', but that was circumstance only. Rhain's heart was *her* throne. Elegant, skinny bitches who tried to cash in on a previous claim to her place would feel the edges of her blades.

Maybe that was unfair of her to think of Rhain's first wife that way but forgiving him was the most she could manage at the moment, if she could really call it forgiveness. She'd have to work on it.

"I'm still yours," she managed. "It's not easy, but I promised to stay. When I married you, remember?"

"Yes. I remember. In my heart and mind, you are my only wife. I swear it."

She sighed, letting go of her grip on her dark emotions.

"Slave wife," she corrected.

"No. You're not, nor could you ever be my slave, Mel."

"So, you've granted me my freedom?"

"Of course… but will you pretend to be my slave for a while, until I can find out who put this curse on me? Will you help me?"

"Well, it's a little annoying, but compared with all the other stuff I've done to get back to you, I guess it's not that bad."

He kissed her hand. "What have you done?"

She gave him the fast and dirty version of her time in Polyhedron up to the point Edith picked her up.

"Show me…please."

She pulled her loose shirt over her head and dropped it on the bed. His eyes flashed with desire. It made her feel so much better. He wanted her, even though he was still numb. Rhain blinked and circled around her, touching her scars gently with his fingertip, pausing on Salem's signature.

"Who was he to you?"

She swallowed. "He was my teacher."

"Did you have feelings for him?"

"He...he had feelings for me." She hesitated. "I never betrayed you. Even when I was tempted to give in, I didn't...I did have feelings for him, but they were nothing like my feelings for you. You have no rival. Salem is dead. I will be forever grateful to him for all he taught me. I wouldn't have made it this far without him."

Rhain sighed. "Then I'll be grateful to him as well. I think I can manage that since I never have to meet the bastard. Otherwise, I'd have killed him for trying to take you from me."

Mel glowed with satisfaction.

He touched the back of her forearms.

"Careful," she warned him with a smile before rolling her wrists.

His eyebrows shot up. "That would be convenient in hand to hand combat."

"It is," she assured him, rolling her wrists again. "I've killed a few in the pits with these."

"Is there anything else?"

She sat on the edge of the bed and pulled her pant legs up to her knees, so he could see the light lines that wrapped around her legs.

"Gorgeous." He knelt in front of her and gripped her calves in his hands. "I want your legs wrapped around me."

She smirked. "Phantom desire again?"

"Must be... Damn, I want to feel you."

"I'm a little concerned what you're going to do to me once we break this curse."

"You should be."

She giggled, her mood lightening. "Oh, there's one last thing...I can't cry anymore. Salem seared my tear ducts... I was pissed at him for that because he didn't tell me what he was going to do or ask if I wanted it. He said it was a gift, but I didn't understand until I became a slave just how big a gift it was."

Rhain looked furious. "How is that a gift?"

"There is a sadistic type, rather common actually in the slave culture, who want nothing more than tears. Nothing turns them on more. Nothing prompts them to cruelty, in all its many forms, more. If you don't cry, they give up sooner with the harassment, humiliation, and beatings. They'll try harder at first, hitting you harder, making you bleed more, thinking you just have a higher tolerance, but then they stop and move on. Those who cry get no reprieve. I saw it, many times on the ship."

His eyes burned, and he gathered her into his arms. "I'm sorry. It's all my fault. Everything you've gone through is my fault. How could you ever forgive me?"

"It was my choice. I would have gone through worse. If it killed me, I was going to find you."

"How can you love me that much? I'm not worth it."

"I do love you that much, so be nice to me."

He chuckled. "Nice? I can do a lot better than that."

She reached for her shirt, but he grabbed her hand and pulled her to her feet. She held still as he traced his finger along the black circle on her chest.

"What did I do to you?" he whispered.

"I don't know...what about yours? What happened when Tesla touched it?"

He pulled his shirt open.

She frowned. "It's so faded. I wouldn't have seen it if I wasn't looking for it. Mine hasn't changed at all."

"I don't know what really happened or why. I woke up in bed as if my whole life in Regia was nothing more than a dream. I knew who I was. I remembered, but either the curse mutated or I'm running out of time. I don't understand why I look normal now but I'm still numb."

"What do you have to do to break the curse?"

"Unfortunately, I have no idea. I need to know who cursed me first. This is not a typical thing. Not many have this kind of power. Only a Strexa could wield this type of magic and Strexas are rare."

"What's a Strexa?"

"For lack of a better term, a witch."

"Whoa, you mean like Maggie?" Mel asked.

He shook his head. "No, Maggie is a *real* witch. She was born a witch. One has to train to be a Strexa. The dark art is actually outlawed, so you can't just go down to the corner and find a teacher offering lessons."

"So, how..." Before she could finish asking her question, Mel's stomach growled loudly.

Rhain smiled and kissed her softly. "Give me a minute. I'll be right back."

Melina waited, but he didn't come right back. He was gone for quite a while. The warm, orange afternoon light coming through the small window darkened into a rich plum, casting shadows through the room. The passing of time in this place made her dizzy. Unlike the ticking of a clock, a steady beat you can count on, this world moved over time like jazz, an unreliable, freeform entity. How much time had passed in Regia while she paced the floor in this bare room?

"I'm sorry. That took longer than I thought it would," Rhain said as he came back.

She rushed into his arms. However long or short his absence had been, it was too long for her taste.

"I had a chat with the main household staff about you and how they are supposed to treat you. Dinner has been laid out for you in the dining room. After you eat, I want to show you around. I told the staff to make themselves scarce, so we can be alone for a while."

"What about *her*?"

"She's not here," he assured her. "She won't be back before the third moon rises. I'm sure you will see her tomorrow, but tonight we are by ourselves."

Everything inside Melina twisted around. It was so wrong, the presence of this other woman. She didn't know how to overcome this. She didn't know how to endure it. He seemed eager as he took her hand and squeezed it gently. Regardless of her internal battle, they were alone at the moment. She didn't want to ruin the time they had with harsh words or arguments.

Mel smiled. "Show me around."

She couldn't help but be impressed by the size and simple luxury of the villa. The muted colors of the stone buildings seemed to absorb the deep red and purple hues of the evening sky. Courtyards and hallways, open to the outside, designed so the warm desert breeze could dance freely through the whole place. He took her to the edge of the property where she could look out over the vast landscape of rose gold sand dunes. Three crescent pink moons glowed faintly on the horizon like islands in a sea of blood and wine. Melina never thought a desert could appeal to her, but this one proved her wrong.

"That's the capital," he said, pointing at a city of muted stone buildings in the distance. "Can you see the palace?"

She nodded. The palace stretched up toward the sky, covered with stairs like a Mayan pyramid. Spires of gold circled the palace like fence posts. A sleek white train slithered around and through the city like a snake, and flat boats hovered in the air, just over the surface of the sand, carrying people to and from.

"What's that?" She pointed at a white pillar beyond the clusters of the city. She squinted. Bands of rose-gold wrapped around the pillar, perfectly spaced all the way from the bottom to the top.

"The Tomb of the Kings. Here, put your hand flat against the sand."

She crouched down and put her palm against the ground.

"Do you feel it?"

"Oh! Yes! It's like a slow...heavy pulse." She put her ear to the sand. Just like a heartbeat, the deep base surged through the ground flowed out, pulled back, flowed out again.

"It's the Tomb that does that. It's not unlike the Heart of Regia. The Tomb is the power...the engine of the world. No one made the Tomb. It existed before anything else here."

"Is it a deity like the Heart?"

"I don't know. I don't think so. Some Nocturnes worship it, but it doesn't communicate with us in any way. It never changes and only royalty are allowed inside."

Melina straightened up again. "It's incredible. The whole city is beautiful."

"I'm there most of the time. My work keeps me close to the Emperor."

She turned and faced him. "Just who are you? What do you do?"

"I'm the captain of the guard."

She snuggled close to his chest. "I married a rich and powerful man and I didn't even know it... And you're a good man, right? You were so worried about learning the truth of who you are. You were sure you deserved to be damned, and you didn't. Did you?"

He lifted her hand to his lips and kissed it softly. "No, I didn't. Come on, I will tell you everything, and I have more to show you, but I think you need to eat first. Your stomach is starting to sound like a crabby troll."

The dining room was designed for company and parties. He pulled out the chair at the end of the table. She sat, a small gourmet feast on the plate in front of her. Rhain didn't eat but sat beside her and waited for her to finish. He must have given orders for her dinner to be made when he left her alone in the other room. What had he said exactly to his staff about her? How many other people lived in the villa? The situation began to needle at her.

"Don't you think it's wrong to have slaves?"

"Most certainly, I do. I think I understand how terrible this must look to you. The fact is the slave trade is something I consider a very personal battle. I'm determined, one day, I'll finally convince the Emperor to do away with it for good. Despite how good of friends we are, he still has all the power, and he doesn't agree with me." He sighed and hung his head. "Seraph had her own slaves when we married. I didn't have any. Being newly married, I looked for an opportunity to deal with the issue in a compassionate way. She adamantly refused to free them. In a fit of tears, she convinced me that she deeply cared for all her slaves, and since she had grown up with them a part of her life, they were more family than anything else. But as time passed, I came to realize nothing was quite as she said, especially when she began to buy new slaves."

His eyes hollowed out, and a haunted look covered his face. Mel put down her fork and reached for his hand.

"I made a decision without consulting Seraph. I granted everyone their freedom and instead offered them all generous compensation for their years of service and new employment. I thought they would stay because I believed they loved Seraph like family, the way she had described. Instead, they all quickly packed up and left as if the devil was chasing them. Only one woman thanked me on her way out. She had been the closest to Seraph, serving as her handmaiden for many years. There was such a mixture of hope and fear in her eyes. It startled and confused me." His haunted look shifted into one of rage. "That was the day I learned my wife's true nature."

"What did she do?" Mel asked.

"I didn't know the truth of what she did until a long time after the fact. She had them all killed. She hired contracts on each and every one of them. Just as they were trying to start new lives, it was all taken away from them. Simply because Seraph considered them her property...her toys. Like a spoiled, possessive child who would rather break what they have instead of sharing it... By the time I learned of it, there was no real evidence left. But she let me know that it was her because soon after she began buying new slaves. I told her I wouldn't stand for it and it was not the way our home would be. That was when she told me, very sweetly and with a smile, 'Remember what happened to the last ones?'"

"Whoa... How did you end up married to that monster to begin with?"

"That's another story... I want you to know that I was only at the auction today because the Emperor had ordered I accompany him. And I only bought you because it was you. None of the slaves in my home are actually slaves. They are employees, with wages, time off, and rights. They are free to leave at any time, unfortunately, the fear of what may happen to them if they do hangs over their heads. I don't want any of them to die, so I treat them as I would want to be treated... I must seem so weak to you."

"You seem trapped to me. Not weak."

He gave her a miserable smile and stood. "You always show me mercy."

Mel pushed her empty plate away and yawned, exhaustion refusing to be put off any longer. He took her hand and led her back out into the courtyard. Glancing up at the sky, Rhain scowled.

"I wanted to show you more, but I'd rather you were settled for the night before Seraph gets home. I can see you're tired." He picked her up and carried her. "This is my room," he said stopping in front of a large wooden door. "I told the staff you're my mistress. No one will question you coming or going. This is your room now, too."

"So, you don't share a room with her?"

"No. Like I said, our marriage is cold. We haven't shared a room since shortly after we were married."

He carried her inside and laid her down on the bed. Her eyelids drooped. Further exploration of this place would have to wait. Still so much to talk about, still so much to learn, and still trapped in the whirlpool of the storm that was her life, as soon as he wrapped his arm around her, she found a moment of peace.

"You don't believe it's your other wife who cursed you?"

"The thought has crossed my mind. I have to be careful though and act ignorant. I don't know how long you've been chasing me, but as far as the time moves here, I've only been awake a few days. Before I was cursed, I stumbled on some information that there was an assassination plot in the works. I didn't know much at all, but I started digging. That was the last thing I remember. So, I've assumed I was cursed because of what I knew."

"That makes sense. And Seraph wouldn't have her hand in that?"

"I can't see how, but I guess anything's possible. And if she is a part of it that puts me in even more danger. The way my body is, how numb I am and the fact I can't be harmed leads me to believe my real body is hidden somewhere. Since I don't know where and the curse maker does, I'm extremely vulnerable."

His words ran together in her mind. He said something that was important. Something she knew something about...what was it? "I'm sorry," she murmured as she yawned. "I'm so tired. I can't think clearly."

"You're alive, you're here, and you still love me. That's all that matters. You've been through too much. Rest a while. I won't leave your side."

In spite of the training Salem had given her, Melina fell into a deep sleep.

Her body was warm beside Rhain, but he couldn't feel it. He touched her and was denied any sensation. Bittersweet. That hadn't changed. Everything was bittersweet for him where it came to her. She'd fought her way across galaxies to find him. *Him*. And in spite of her effort, he still was only her husband in a symbolic way.

Could they win? Was it possible?

Giving up seemed like a good idea when he thought she was dead. But now...

The melody of her whispered to him. The second her lost sound came back, his heart shattered. She was altered and her resonance sang a different set of notes than before, but the main chord was still the same. Even in sleep, or silence, he could hear her love.

A tide of immovable resolve broke over him as he touched her scars. He wouldn't give up now. He'd borrow her courage. No hell, or army, or curse would keep them apart. Her scars were not in vain. He would live again.

His arm tightened over her. He would hold her like this, not as a monster but as a man.

He would live again.

Eighteen

Seraph excused herself from the banquet, exchanging a meaningful look with Haru before she slipped out the side. The eyes of the guards followed her, but they made no sound or any other indication she was of interest. Her heart was racing, but she flounced down the hall at the same speed as she would have if she were aimlessly wandering. It was only when she reached the end of the hall that she glanced back to see if anyone was watching.

Through the carved archway, leading her down the snaking tunnel, master Strexa, Yadira didn't hide, neither did she advertise. Everyone knew the general location of her in the palace, even if they didn't know the exact spot. Feared and shunned, she hardly made appearances at social events. The emperor had his reasons to keep her close. He let her use her power without repercussions even though her practices were illegal.

Seraph respected and despised Yadira. When she was empress, Seraph planned on killing her, as soon as she'd taught her to tap fully into the shadows.

"Come in," Yadira said through the door before Seraph could knock.

Her lungs constricted as she entered, the air hot and heavy with incense. Tingling began in her fingertips as she approached Yadira. Jealousy tugged at her insides. The Strexa sat on her high-backed chair as if it was a throne. Loose, black sheer cloth, wrapped over her hourglass figure, showing all her impressive assets. Gold trinkets laced through her dark dreadlocks caught the candlelight. An overwhelming air of sexuality surrounded her. She closed her eyes as Seraph approached, taking a puff of her gold pipe. Yadira never looked her in the eye. She said it was dangerous for Seraph.

"Smile for me, my pathetic, little disciple. You look worried."

The question of how she could see her with her eyes shut always bugged Seraph, but she smiled as directed. Yadira tsked and set her pipe down before standing up and coming close to Seraph.

"Give me your hands," Yadira ordered.

The rose-gold glyphs on her fingertips burned bright as Yadira grabbed her by the wrists. She looked at them with her closed eyes for a second before dropping her hands. She sneered and then gave a throaty chuckle, backing away from Seraph.

"Your curse work is pathetic. I told you not to cast for revenge. You didn't listen."

"I didn't do it for revenge!" Seraph argued. "It was self-preservation. Rhain was about to find out our plot to kill Koda."

Yadira sighed and sat back down. "You could have just killed your husband, but you wanted him to suffer as undead forever. That was revenge and it will be your downfall. Have you even noticed how your glyphs have changed? Do you even understand what it means?"

"If I did, I wouldn't be here. I need your help."

"There's nothing I can do for you. You're a mediocre witch and you will always be a mediocre witch. I never should have taught you…" Yadira shook her head and sighed again. "I'll tell you one thing since you humbled yourself enough to come here. I don't want to see you again when you leave. Understood? Our relationship is over."

"I understand."

"The curse on your husband is in flux. Check your glyphs every day."

Seraph waited a beat. "That's all you're going to tell me?"

"How about you tell me something first and then I'll tell you something more useful."

"What do you want to know?"

"Rhain is powerful, proven in many battles, respected for his fairness and intellect as a leader. On top of that, he's got the looks and muscles to make most women swoon. I'd bet most of the women in the kingdom would kill to be his wife. Why do you hate him so much?"

"I don't care about his character or his sex appeal. I never did. He stole my dreams. Him and Koda. *I'm nobility* and I was forced to marry a commoner just so the emperor could elevate his favorite subject into a power position. I did nothing to deserve such shame! I love Haru and Haru loves me! I was supposed to be *his* wife. And I will be…Those are my reasons."

Yadira crossed her arms over her large breasts and pursed her lips. "I see. Your husband is strongly against the slave trade is he not?"

"Yes," she spat. "The fool."

"You haven't heard the gossip?"

"What gossip?"

Yadira laughed. "It's all the buzz. Apparently, your husband bought a slave earlier today at an auction."

Seraph frowned. "That can't be. He rants about the auctions."

"This was no regular auction, either. The bidding was so fierce, Rhain only won by offering ten million for the woman… So, as I said, you better check your glyphs every day. Your husband is acting out of character. You better find out why."

She'd get to the bottom of this disturbing news, but for now, she pushed it aside and focused back on what was most important. "I could have learned the gossip from anyone in the palace. You still haven't helped me."

"The sooner you kill him the better. Your time's running out. Your window is shrinking. Now leave and don't knock on my door again unless you've somehow fulfilled your dream and become empress."

Seraph left and retraced her steps back to the banquet, but she didn't sit back down at the table. Haru glanced up at her and she looked pointedly at the exit closest to his room. He nodded once and turned back to the person talking next to him. She went for the exit, still carefully measuring the speed of her walk, down to Haru's room.

In the dark, her stress overtook her as she paced and wrung her hands.

"Don't get careless on me, Seraph." Haru came in a few minutes later.

"Yadira said we're running out of time."

"I know that. Didn't you understand what we talked about last time? I've found an assassin."

"Something's wrong with Rhain. I'm worried he's going to learn it was me, if he doesn't know already. He's not himself. He's done something... odd."

Haru chuckled. "You mean him buying a hot blonde at auction?"

"So, you know about that?"

"Of course. Everyone's talking about it. She must really be something. If she is ten million worth, I'm going to add her to the palace slaves once Rhain is dead."

"No, you won't!" she snapped.

"I'll do as I please. Just because you're my choice for empress, doesn't mean I have to be faithful to you. I'll take what I want when I want, and you'll accept it in silence."

She clamped her lips shut and crossed her arms over her chest. "After all I've suffered, you intend to shame me, too."

He came close and wrapped his arms around her. "Relax. I love you enough to be discreet. And you're looking at this turn of events all wrong. Since you're worried about him catching on, maybe this woman is the distraction we need... Regardless, I've come up with a plan."

"What do you mean?"

"I've arranged for some skirmishes to kick up tomorrow on the border settlements. The guard will be called out to handle it, and the guard can't do that without their captain. This is your chance. He has to disappear. Everyone has to believe he's dead. You've got to curse him again. Make his apparition vanish. I'll send you a message when it's time to play the grieving widow. The timing has to be just right."

Seraph softened. "Clever." She took a deep breath, calming herself. "You've thought of everything. This is why you're going to be a superior emperor. I feel so much better now. Everything will work out fine." She kissed him. "I'll make it all worth your while."

He shoved her down on the bed. "You're staying here tonight."

"But..."

"You're staying." His tone made it clear the discussion was over.

NINETEEN

Frantic pounding woke Melina.

"Master! Are you there?" a man said from the other side of the door. "An urgent message has arrived from the palace. Master?"

"Sorry." Rhain kissed her temple, before moving from her side to open the door.

The light stung her eyes as she looked at the steward, standing stiffly in the doorway. Rhain took the scroll from his hand.

"If you require anything, master, I'm ready," the steward said.

"Thank you, Jonas."

Closing the door, he pulled back the curtains. He unrolled the scroll and read it, leaning on the window frame.

"Is everything all right?"

Rhain sighed. "No. There's been a massacre. The palace guard is being sent to deal with it."

"You have to go?"

"I do...but I can't. I can't leave you here, but I can't take you with me either. I have to keep acting natural."

She came to him, nestling against his broad chest. A smile curving her lips as she thought about what this could mean.

"I'll be fine. What are you worried about?"

"Well." He squirmed a bit. "You'll be here alone with Seraph."

Mel chuckled. "Afraid it might get a bit awkward?"

"Yeah."

"*Please*. After everything I've gone through. Awkward is a walk in the park. And she's the one who's going to feel awkward, not me."

"She looks innocent but she's dangerous. Don't underestimate her."

"I won't. I'm going to see that *she* underestimates *me*. Don't worry. I'm dangerous, too. Do what you need to do and I'll see what I can discover on my own."

"I'm so powerless...I can't lose you again, Mel."

"I've no intention of being lost. Have some faith in me. I'm a badass, pit fighting, organic android."

He kissed her hard on the lips. "I only want to be with you. I don't care about anything else. I wouldn't even care about breaking this curse, except it's in my way, preventing us from being fully together."

"When will I see you again?"

"It's hard to say. I'll be back as soon as I can and not a moment longer. The type of fighting I'm about to deal with usually only takes a few days to neutralize. My men are efficient." The rumble of an engine sounded outside. He frowned. "I think Seraph is home. I guess I'll have to talk to her before I leave. Get back in the bed and pretend to be asleep."

She put her hands on the sides of his face. He leaned down until his forehead touched hers.

"Be careful."

"You, too." He kissed her again just as a knock sounded on the door. "See you soon."

Laying down, she turned away from the door and closed her eyes.

Seraph fought for composure as the small palace sand ship dropped her off in the front of the villa. The situation made her skin crawl. Escorted home in the morning after a party like a whore, in a vehicle used for commoner and servant transport. Haru was punishing her.

Running her fingers through her hair, she straightened her dress before lifting her head and striding through the main entrance. She averted her gaze from the house slaves and turned down the hallway to her bedroom. Rhain blocked her way, arms crossed, and a scowl on his face.

His presence added insult to injury. Why was he still here? He should have received his summons by now. He looked her up and down and then smiled.

"Doing the walk of shame, are we?"

"How dare you speak to me like that?" Her fragile composure crumbled. This was too much after the night of degradation and disrespect Haru put her through. "Hypocrite!" she spat.

He just lifted an eyebrow and smirked. "How so?"

"*How so?* Everyone is whispering behind my back. I know all about it. You bought a woman at auction yesterday. *You!* Who passionately professes to hate the slave trade. So, tell me, husband. Why did you do it? How could anyone be worth the fortune you paid?"

"You want the truth?"

"Yes, I want the truth."

"She's a skilled fighter. I thought she would make a good bodyguard. And she's a beautiful woman. I want her in my bed. That's the main reason."

"That's ridiculous. You aren't even capable--" Gasping at her slip, she clamped her mouth shut.

"I'm sorry, what was that?" he demanded, his demeanor shifting to stern.

If he realized she knew his physical limitations, he'd know she was the one who cursed him. She had to get a hold of herself. "Um... I mean...How are you capable of bringing such shame on our house? Our marriage? I thought appearances meant more to you." She pulled out a quick, pretty pout.

His demeanor relaxed again, and he shrugged. "Our marriage is in name only. Don't pretend otherwise. It's true, I used to care, but that was before you began to step out on me. If I want a dalliance with my slave, that's my right as master of this house. And I must say, she's a much better time on the sheets than you ever were. Now, if you'll excuse me. I have a job to do."

He brushed past her. She stared at his back, outrage, and confusion coursing through her. He couldn't have sex. He was lying. He had to be lying. She rubbed her fingertips, frowning. She needed to check her glyphs. Had the curse changed that much? Surely not. He was definitely lying. She sniffed. The personal jab at her sexuality enraged her. What did a lowlife commoner like him understand? She was a lady. Ladies didn't engage in the bedroom practices of slaves and whores. The way Haru had treated her last night surfaced in her mind and it didn't help her internal argument.

Seraph glanced down the hall at Rhain's closed bedroom door. Was she in there? The slave. She obviously meant something to him... for him to have bought her to begin with. He wasn't acting like himself at all. But maybe this woman was good for her. One more thing she could take away from Rhain before he died. She strode down to his door, grasped the knob, and hesitated.

She sighed and pulled her shoulders back. No reason to be concerned. No reason to be self-conscious. What did she care who Rhain messed with, capable or not? She didn't want him...but still. She shook herself again. The woman behind this door was a slave, worthless, disposable, nothing, and *she* was the future empress.

Quiet sobs came from the other side of the door. It encouraged Seraph to go in.

"Ahem."

The woman started and wiped her face before turning over and facing Seraph. Her eyes rounded and she got out of the bed and down on her hands and knees at Seraph's feet. Well, at least she knew how to grovel.

"Are you the mistress of the house?"

"I am," Seraph answered. "Stand up. Let me get a good look at you."

The slave stood but kept her eyes on the ground. Seraph circled around her once, assessing, picking apart her appearance. The woman was muscular, but she had perfect breasts and a nice flare to her hips. Her figure annoyed Seraph. But the woman was also scarred from fighting...she was far from perfect. Her short, platinum blonde hair hung down over her eyes and was shaved to a fuzz on the sides of her head.

"What's your name?"

"Melina, Mistress."

"Look me in the eyes."

Seraph tried to school her expression as she gazed directly at Melina, but she could feel her resting bitch face take hold and jealousy flare. The slave was beautiful. Sexy lips, strong cheekbones, glowing skin, and brown and grey mismatched eyes that Seraph found more captivating than strange. Was that it? Was it as simple as Rhain said? Were his reasons for buying her honest? She wasn't a race Seraph recognized. Was it because she was exotic?

She moved closer and put her hands on Melina's cheeks. "Why were you crying when I came in?"

She blushed. "I can't say, Mistress."

"Of course you can… Did my husband do something bad to you? He did, didn't he?"

"He…" Melina began to tremble. "He is the master. I can't speak against him."

"Oh, now," Seraph leaned close, dropping her voice to a whisper. "I understand. You can trust me. I'm not on his side. When it is just the two of us, I give you permission to speak as you please."

She fell back to her hands and knees, gripping the hem of Seraph's dress. "Please, I beg you. Let me be your slave instead of his. I can be anything you want. I can be your handmaiden. I can protect you, too. Please claim me! I don't want to have to submit to the master again like last night."

"What did he do to you?"

"Well, he... It was strange."

She knew it! He couldn't have sex, so he'd done something else, something aberrant to this woman.

"What do you mean?"

Melina shuddered. "I can't... Can't say it... He's a disgusting man. Nothing but a brute."

Seraph smirked. Perhaps she wasn't a total loss. Still, she would have to die as soon as Rhain was dead. There was no way she was going to let this woman anywhere near Haru. Especially since he expressed interest in meeting her. Melina was too beautiful. Too sexy. She'd capture Haru's eye.

But for now, she might be very useful.

"I'll make you mine on one condition. You have to be my spy."

"Spy?"

She reached down and cupped Melina's chin, lifting her face up. "Spy on my husband and when I've learned what I need to, I'll grant you your freedom."

"Oh, Mistress! I will do whatever you ask. I promise."

"Good. Now, I've had a long night. I'm going to take a bath. You can wash my back for me."

Rhain sensed eyes on him. All day, as soon as he and his men arrived. Everywhere he went in the small settlement, someone was watching. The fighting they were sent to stop was little more than a weak skirmish and ended as soon as the guard showed up. Unfortunately, a few innocents were killed, caught in the crossfire as they were going about their business in the open market. It wasn't the massacre described in his summons. Why was his information so wrong? And now he was being followed by a complete amateur at stealth.

It was a setup. How stupid did his enemy think he was? He was being pushed around the game board. That was just fine with him. He acted natural. It was time to scour the town, taking eyewitness accounts of this fraud.

He looked up at the sky. It was midday.

Hmm…how were his wives getting along?

The ground began to pull at him as if gravity had just intensified. He didn't feel numb now. The breeze blew through him. Holding his hands up close to his face, they vanished before his eyes.

TWENTY

"You're the most beautiful woman I've ever seen, Mistress."

"Your skin is perfect."

"I love your hair."

"I've never seen eyes like yours. They're stunning."

On and on it went. Those were only a few of the gushing compliments Melina said to Seraph as she washed her back, lotioned her feet, laid out her clothes, plaited her hair and cut her food into tiny pieces. Seraph had complained to Mel over and over how tired she was because she didn't get much sleep last night. She began to act antsy, looking out the window at the sky, and picking at her fingers in a strange way. Finally, she said she was going to take a nap and sent Melina from her room.

Mel closed the bedroom door after Seraph was tucked in like a child. She walked to the edge of the property and looked out toward the capital, smiling to herself. *Thank you, Salem.*

Nothing Seraph said or did had fooled her for one second. Takes a bitch to know a bitch. Seraph played little miss innocent as though it was her favorite game and Mel could see why most would believe her performance.

There might be more players. Assassination of the emperor probably took more than one spoiled little princess, and maybe that was something apart from the revenge Seraph wanted against Rhain and the curse on him. Maybe the two things were unrelated, but Seraph had spent the night at the palace and she was tired and needed a bath. Didn't take a genius.

Regardless, Mel knew without a doubt she'd been playing man-hating besties all day with a black widow.

The broken circle on her chest pulsed once, a surge of heat running around the edge. She couldn't breathe. The mark turned hard as bone, power vibrating deep inside the curve. The ground rolled under her feet, and she went down on her knees. It was changing, growing stronger.

"Miss? Are you all right?" the young maid, Kari, came up beside her.

"I think so," Melina panted as the sensation turned dull.

The girl offered her hand. Mel took it as she got to her feet.

"Thanks. I'm okay."

"I'm glad. I was looking for you. I wanted to say sorry if I didn't treat you properly yesterday when you arrived. I didn't realize who you were...your relationship to the master."

"I have been treated very well, thank you. I'm not above you, Kari. I'm a slave."

The girl frowned and looked as if she was going to argue, but she didn't. "Is the mistress asleep?"

"Yes."

"Be careful around her, miss. She uses the shadow arts."

"How do you know?"

"I've seen the glyphs...on her fingers. They don't always show. She tries to hide them. I don't know how they work, but I know they mean she's a Strexa."

"I'm not surprised. Thanks for the tip... By the way, what did Rhain say when he told you about me?"

"He said the staff was to treat you the same way we treat him." Kari blushed. "He said, you were the most...no, the *only* precious thing in the world to him."

Her lips curved. "Only precious thing, huh?" Mel continued to gaze at the city in the distance, and she was struck with an idea. "How long do you think Seraph will sleep?"

"Probably until dusk. She's been going more frequently to the palace, especially at the fall of night."

"I have some business, there..." She pointed at the outskirts of the city where Edith's ship hung low over the sand. "It won't take me long, but I need a ride and a sword. Can you help me with that?"

An excited light lit the maid's eyes. "You want *me* to drive you?"

"Why not?"

"Oh, I can do this! I'll get you a sword and pull our fastest ship around the front gate. Meet me there. I'll keep the engines quiet."

Mel chuckled as Kari took off. She walked to the front entrance just as the ship pulled up. The hovercraft only had two seats and a sword rested in the passenger side. She smirked as she climbed in. It looked like she'd made an ally in Kari.

The vehicle zipped over the sand dunes to the capital. Not that she had another experience to reference, but it seemed to Mel, Kari was a maniac driver. She laughed at bursts of speed and shouted at other drivers when they got too close. They approached Edith's ship. Mel instructed her to pull up close to the side of the hull.

"Okay, Kari, you're the getaway driver. I'll be in and out. Keep the engines running."

"Yes, miss." Her hands tightened on the steering wheel, the excited light in her eyes flashing brighter.

The unfamiliar sword felt good in her hand. She swung it once. No problem. Climbing the spindly stairs up to the ship's back door, she knocked on the metal hull. The guard who used to beat her first thing in the mornings opened the door. She stabbed him through the heart before he could say hello.

A second guard barreled down the row of cages toward her, his massive footfalls shaking the ship. His sword swung over her head as she ducked. So easy. He was so slow. Her sword sliced through his torso, tapping the edge of his spine. Blood flooded the floor under his body where he fell.

"Melina."

"Hey, Melina, get us out of here."

She held a finger up to her lips to silence the caged slaves.

"I won't leave you. Just keep quiet for a minute."

They nodded and shut up.

Mel crept forward to Edith's closed door, hoping to catch her off guard. The bitch always carried a firearm.

The hinges creaked. Edith glanced over her shoulder from where she sat at her desk. Rolling to the floor, the slaver dodged Mel's sword, losing only a chunk of hair. Pulling her gun, she shot at Mel's knee, missing by a breath. Mel kicked the gun out of her hand and stabbed her through the stomach, pinning her to the floor.

Coughing blood, grabbing at the blade, Edith struggled to pull it loose. Mel yanked it out and put her foot down on the wound.

"Why?" Edith rasped. "I was good to you."

"You're a worthless, bottom feeder, who trades people's lives, and forces friends to fight to the death in the pits. What goes around, you know. Right before he died, I told Salem I'd kill you. You were wrong about me, Edith. I did love him."

"Not as much as I did," she gurgled, her eyes clouding over.

"That's fine. Now you can go to hell with him."

Mel took the keys to the cages, all the money from her auction, and the weapons from the cabinet. Opening the locks, she handed each person something to arm themselves with and enough money to be comfortable for a lifetime. They stood around, gazing dumbfounded at the loot in their hands.

"Get out of here while you have the chance. Start over."

None of them needed telling twice. Whispering their thanks, the ex-slaves scattered.

Alone in the ship, Mel exhaled, regret pressing under her ribs. Salem, Cope, and Inesia should have been there. The four of them, celebrating the victory and hard-earned victory together. Missing them throbbed like an open wound.

Stepping over the dead guards, she left the ship, wishing she could set it on fire. Slamming the back door, she jumped down and climbed up beside Kari, diligently standing by.

"Let's go."

White-knuckled, Kari nodded in quick jerks and turned the ship around. They sped out of the capital to the villa. "Those people who left the ship...what did you do?"

"Paid a debt. Probably best if you don't know the details."

"Yes, miss."

Kari put the engines on quiet as they pulled up at the villa and parked the vehicle in a garage.

"I like this sword. Would anyone notice if I kept it a while?"

"I doubt it, miss. There are many other swords."

Coming through a servant entrance, Mel contemplated where she wanted to hide the sword. They walked into the courtyard... and the shit hit the fan.

"How dare you?!" Seraph blocked their way, two large security guards standing behind her. "Slaves like you two are good for nothing but bleeding out." Her eyes fell on the sword in Melina's hand. "Drop that."

Her grip tightened as she gauged the moment. Not yet. She couldn't act yet. She had to wait for Rhain to come back. Mel dropped the sword.

"Beat them," Seraph ordered.

The men behind her moved forward. Mel grabbed Kari by the arm and pulled her behind her.

"Kari did nothing wrong. Beat me if you want but leave her out of this."

"Wait!" The steward came running out.

"What do you mean, Jonas? How dare you interfere with my orders?"

Jonas bowed to her. "Forgive me Mistress, but the master gave the staff orders as well. Orders about how we are to treat the new arrival, Melina." He stood between them and the guards waiting to beat her and Kari. Arguing erupted between Jonas and security.

"Silence!" Seraph's voice was shrill. "Jonas, explain this."

"Well, Mistress, the master said we were to treat her the same way we treat him. He spoke in very strong language about how important she is. He said she was precious to him."

Seraph narrowed her pretty eyes. She crossed her arms and paced for a few seconds. "I was unaware of his instructions. Very well. Beat Kari then, for her poor judgment, and lock Melina up."

"But, Mistress--"

"Quiet, Jonas! I'll not harm her. Kari, however, doesn't have the same level of protection as the master's whore. Any disputes over my orders will be between my husband and myself when he returns. Now obey me or I shall cast you all out."

Mel watched Seraph turn on her heel and flounce back to her room and slam the door. Everyone turned their eyes on her, hesitating. Even the security guards looked unsure. They all were in a sticky position and she realized they were looking to her to tell them what to do, based on what Rhain had said. It wasn't fair to them.

"Do what she says, but use a light hand on Kari... I'm sorry, Kari. It's my fault. If I can, I'll make it up to you. Everything is going to change soon. Keep your heads down and obey Seraph until it does."

She didn't look back, remembering what Salem taught her. Go numb. Wait for the right moment to strike. She'd been able to do this, even though it went against her nature. However, as soon as Kari began to cry out in pain, Mel felt each blow in her own chest. She continued to walk forward, not seeing where she was going until the door shut behind her. She was locked in the same bare room as before with nothing to do but watch the light change outside the small window.

Kari continued to cry out. The sound of the lash on her small body echoed in Melina's ears. They weren't going easy on her. Finally, finally, everything went quiet.

I will break your heart over and over and fill the gaps with stone until that is all there is. Salem's words came back to her as she touched her aching chest. Was she stone? Would it hurt this much if she was?

Time, so freeform in this place, mocked her as it passed, refusing to be measured. It seemed to take a whole day for the warm peach color of the sky to darken purple.

A quiet knock sounded on the door before it opened. Mel grabbed Kari as she limped into the room and helped her to the bed. Someone had cleaned her up, but her eyes were swollen into slits, and it looked like the bones of her cheek were broken on one side. She held her arm close to her body.

"I thought they broke my arm." Kari's voice was weak. "It was just dislocated. Jonas popped it back."

"I'm so sorry. I wish they would have just taken it out on me."

"I've been beaten before, it's just been a long time. I haven't been abused since I came here. That's why we all love the master. He gave us our freedom." Kari swallowed, her breathing labored.

"Don't talk. Just rest."

She shook her head. "I want you to know…We can leave, but the rumors keep us here. I was scared. When you showed up and the master told us you were important…I had hope. It's silly. I'm just a silly little girl to still have dreams, but I can't seem to help myself." She coughed, a thin line of blood running from the side of her mouth.

Just how injured was she? Was she bleeding internally?

"Don't you get it?" Kari rasped. "The master said we were to treat you the same way we treat him. He gave you the authority. All of us, the whole staff, we are yours. You don't have to pretend or obey."

Turning away from the girl, Melina paced. What was she to do? Kari's words made her burn. She touched the wall, the music of the stone flowing into her fingertips, up her arm, and deep into her mind. She looked back at the injured teen and gasped, her thoughts snapping in a different direction.

Kari was her responsibility. She would protect her. She'd cut off the hand of anyone who tried to hurt her again and make them eat it.

Tracing lines on the stone, Melina wrote the word, *mine*. It was *her* damn wall. It was *her* house. *She* was Rhain's wife. Not his slave. Not his whore. His wife.

"Kari?"

"Yes, miss?"

"White sarcophagi on stilts. Milk under a glass floor. Sound familiar?" Melina asked.

"The Tomb of the Kings, miss. I've never seen it with my own eyes, but I've heard stories."

Absentmindedly, she ran her fingertips over and over on the broken circle. It was the answer. It always was.

A bell rang out, echoing through the whole villa. It sounded over and over.

"It's an alarm," Kari struggled to sit. "Everyone is being summoned. Something has happened. We have to go. I left the door unlocked. We can get out."

"You should stay here. Lay back down. I'll come back for you."

The bell continued to sound as she made her way to the courtyard. The rest of the staff was there along with the security guards, and Seraph was in the center, tears running down her cheeks, a piece of parchment clutched in her hand. She held the parchment up.

"I've just received word...the master is dead. He died in a terrible fight in one of the border towns. The house will begin mourning for Rhain." She broke down in sobs and turned away from everyone, walking back to her room.

The ground ripped out from under her feet. Dead? Rhain was dead? Her mind raced, her heart filling her throat. He wasn't dead. She'd know if he was.

The moment you lose control, you die. Maybe this was that moment.

"Bullshit!" Mel shouted.

Everyone gasped. Seraph was the last to turn and look at her.

"Lock this woman up!" she ordered.

"Lock yourself up. You have no authority over me. I'm Rhain's wife. This is *my* house."

"Wife?" she laughed. "That's amusing, slave. I don't think you know the meaning of the word. And even if he had married you in secret, or something like that... He's dead."

"Not yet, he's not."

She waved the piece of parchment in the air. "I have an official notice from the palace. He's dead."

Mel shook her head, cold clarity of what she had to do clicking into place in her mind. "Not yet, witch."

Everyone watching seemed frozen. Mel moved closer. Fear widened Seraph's eyes.

"Stop!" She held her hands out, glyphs burned on her fingertips. "You're right. I am a Strexa."

Everyone froze. Melina advanced.

"Stop!" Seraph screeched. "Wait! I hold Rhain's life in my hands. Rethink your course if you want to save him. I hold all the power here. I can kill him with one thought."

"Hmm...no, I don't think you can."

Seraph's eyes darted around. "You! Security! Stop her!"

Four men surrounded her. Three of them drew their swords and the other came up behind her, pinning her arms. She smiled as she rolled her wrists. The guard screamed and jerked his hands free, losing two fingers on her blades as he did. She dropped to the ground as the others came at her, accidentally stabbing each other when their target vanished. She kicked out at the feet of the last one standing. He fell on his back. She sliced his throat, sweeping the back of her arm over his neck. Taking the sword from his dead hand, she killed the two others.

She faced her real enemy again.

"Why don't you understand?! You love Rhain right? That's why you're threatening me?" Seraph backed up.

"I do love him. Yes."

"If you take one more step, I will kill him. I swear. I'll curse him to death."

"If you could, you would have done it already."

"It will happen any minute anyway."

"In the Tomb of the Kings?"

Seraph looked winded.

Mel smiled. "That's right. I know where he is. You might be a Strexa, but I can see the future."

"Even if you kill me, you can't save him. If the assassin is unsuccessful, the curse I put on him can only be broken by me."

Smirking, Mel pulled the front of her shirt down. "You mean this curse? Dumb bitch. You've been looking at the wrong target all along. *I* carry the curse and *I'll* be the one to break it."

The color drained from Seraph's flushed cheeks. "It's not possible...Wait! If you spare me, I'll take you with me. I'm going to be empress. I can give you anything you want."

Mel scoffed. "Bluebloods like you can never understand ghetto like me."

Seraph held both her hands up in defense. In one smooth sweep of the sword, Melina cut off Seraph's hands at the wrists. Her screaming filled the whole villa as she fell back, holding her stumps close to her body.

"Oh, do shut up and die with some grace, will you?"

Grabbing her foot, Mel pulled Seraph's leg straight, slicing her femoral artery. Her cries faded.

Mel faced the onlookers, brandishing her sword.

"Anyone else wanna go?"

Everyone shook their heads and backed farther away. She tore a strip off Seraph's bloodied dress before picking up her severed hands and wrapping them in the fabric, slinging it like a pack over her shoulder. The glyphs still burned bright. It wasn't over.

"I need a ride to the Tomb of the Kings."

"Come with me." Jonas turned and ran. "I'll take you."

Come on. Come on. Come on. Faster. She chanted in her head as they sped over the dunes to the capital. They were going as fast as the ship would take them. Adrenaline roped her muscles and gnawed her bones.

She had to get there before the assassin did.

Inside her head, the pulse of the Tomb throbbed.

TWENTY ONE

From the shadows, Mel crept toward the entrance of the Tomb. Strange frequencies buzzed her senses the closer she got. Jonas followed quietly behind her. He adamantly refused to let her go alone. Two armed guards blocked the open entrance. A wall of sand fell like a solid curtain just inside the doorway. Jonas grabbed her wrist as she lifted her sword.

"Don't kill them. I'll draw them away."

"Fine. Hurry," she whispered.

A shadow caught her eye, and she pulled Jonas back. The shadow slunk around the side and jumped behind the guards. Mel charged forward. The assassin dropped the guards and went through the fall of sand before she reached the stairs.

She raced up the stairs, through the curtain. Her heart exploded in a fire. The gold sand sparkled in her vision, stripping and twisting her senses. Her grey eye surged wide open from inside. She knew this place as if she had actually stood right there many times before. Static filled her ears. There was nothing beyond the static, it rendered her completely deaf.

Liquid, the color of milk, lapped at the underside of the glass floor. She was inside a vast hall. The walls and ceilings were white, sleek, seamless. Her body was heavy in the overbearing dry heat of the space.

Smooth, white sarcophagi lined the room in three perfect rows, each one propped high into the air on stilts. The stilts came straight out of the bottoms of the sarcophagi tapering down from the top into stiletto points on the glass floor. They towered over her. She walked beneath them, in between the stilts. Each one had the same symbol on the bottom, a black circle.

She shook her head. The static burrowed into her brain attempting to silence her thoughts. Borderline painful, like a budding headache, not yet blossomed. She sighed, wishing she could sleep, it was so warm. There was something she needed here... What could that possibly be? Where the hell was she anyway?

A dark figure walked beside her, like a companion. He looked at her, his face was covered. *Hello. Do you know where we are?* She wanted to ask but couldn't speak. He reached out to her, gripping her shoulder. *Am I dreaming?*

A sudden pressure just over her navel. She gasped as the pressure buzzed as though charged with electricity. The dark figure darted away. Intense heat and then cold filled her body. Mel pulled her hand away from her stomach. Blood covered her skin and dripped from her fingers. Head spinning, she sank to the floor, gazing up at the sarcophagus towering above her.

Broken clock... Broken circle...Rhain.

She was right beneath him.

Wake up! Wake up!

Stars exploded in her eye. Her hearing came back. Damnit! What was that? She got up, a pool of blood slicking the glass floor under her. The dark figure moved in the distance, slinking through the stilts, looking up at the symbols on the bottoms.

"Hey, asshole! Over here!" she shouted.

He looked around and moved with caution toward her.

"You're not my target," he said.

"Didn't stop you from stabbing me."

He shrugged. "I didn't want you in my way, but I have no reason to kill you."

She took his measure. Clad in black, his face half covered with a scarf. He was thin, and he sounded young.

"I'll give you one chance. You've got no dog in this fight, you're just a hired hand."

"So?"

She brandished her sword at him. "It's not personal for you... It is for me. Even if you cut off my arms and legs, I will kill you. If all I have left is my teeth, I will eat you alive."

He blinked, and his eyebrows came down in a frown. He glanced up at the sarcophagus above them. "That's the one I'm looking for. That's my target."

"That's my husband." She advanced. "Last chance. You're not matching your skill to mine. It's your skill against my burning heart."

His eyes widened, and he backed up. "I recognize you, from the pit fights." He lifted his hands. "This was supposed to be a fast easy job. No one said anything about you. I'm outta here. I was paid in advance anyway."

She watched him, her sword still raised. He went back through the sand fall.

Alone, her breathing grew shallow as cold spread from her open wound up through her torso. She didn't have much time. She dropped her sword.

Hieroglyphs were carved on the stilt in front of her. She unwrapped Seraph's hands. The glyphs on her fingertips matched the ones on the stilt, just not the same order. Carefully checking, she touched the glyphs on the stilt in the order they burned on the hands. Each one clicked as she touched it. The stilts cracked open all the way up like the vertebrae of a spine and began to collapse in on itself. The sarcophagus lowered to the floor. The broken circle marked the lid as well. She traced her finger over it, connecting the ends of the circle with a line of blood. The seal on the lid broke, and smoke wheezed out like an exhale. Screaming in pain, gushing blood as she strained, Melina pushed off the lid.

"Rhain!"

He didn't move. Arms crossed over his heart, eyes closed as though asleep. She climbed on top of him.

"Please. Wake up. I'm here."

This was where her future memory stopped. She hadn't seen beyond this moment. What did she do?

She grabbed his hands and moved them, laying on him, pressing her chest against his. His lips didn't move as she kissed him. She growled.

"I've had enough of this!" she shouted. "You're going to kiss me back, Rhain! You're going to feel it!"

Her fangs sank deep and hard into the side of his neck. Blood pulsed into her mouth. It wasn't smoke or spirit, but warm, living blood. She closed her eyes. *Please. Please.*

The mark on her chest throbbed once, hardened, and fell off like a scab. Startled, she pulled her fangs back as his hands wrapped around her.

Heat and static... Wrapped in a blanket of distortion. Rhain drifted up to the surface, as though rising through water. A million needles stabbed him and threaded his soul back in his body. Jolted awake, sensation rammed through his extremities. He flexed his hands against her. *Melina.*

Her voice. Her scent. Her skin. He felt her for the first time as he opened his eyes.

Am I truly seeing this? Is this real?

The nerve-endings in his fingertips buzzed. He touched her cheek.

"There you are," she whispered.

"Melina?"

"Yes. It's me."

"I thought I disappeared."

"For a moment, you did. I'm pissed at you about it, too."

"I'm sorry. I won't do it again...Mel? *Melina!*"

Her eyes hollowed out, her skin going pale. Warmth spread over his chest.

"You're bleeding!"

"You finally noticed. Think waking you up was easy?" She chuckled but her voice was weak.

He lifted her in his arms as he stood. "How bad is it?"

"Well, it's not good. He was a professional."

Carefully he laid her flat on the glass floor. Heavy, urgent footfalls echoed through the tomb, drawing his attention away from Mel. Straightening, he faced his enemy. The knife flying through the air at his head was too late, barely.

He lifted his hand and tapped time with his finger as it flowed past. His fingernail dragged the current, slowing it down. The knife stopped and held still in mid-air an inch from his eye. He smiled and grabbed the knife, striding toward Haru.

Haru couldn't move, caught in the time echo.

"I had a feeling." Rhain tsked and stabbed Haru in the throat.

It felt good to use his power again. Time rippled and rushed forward as he tapped it again.

Haru fell, gurgling and clawing at the knife.

"Too slow, Haru."

Rhain ran back to Mel and picked her up. She was unconscious, her body light and cold in his arms.

Twenty two

A warm breeze breathed over her skin as she opened her eyes. A creamy canopy rolled in the air over her. Light and soft and warm, the fabric against her skin kissed her nerve endings. The bed under her was so comfortable she could have sworn she was floating.

"Rhain!" She bolted upright.

A soft chuckle came from the corner of the room. She looked at the man who watched her serenely. His skin was a warm brown, a few shades darker than Rhain's, and his black eyes danced with an amused light. Tidy black dreadlocks fell over his shoulders from under a gold brocade turban.

"I haven't been here but a few minutes. I swear. My physician informed me you would be waking soon. You may breathe easy, Melina. There is nothing to fear."

He seemed familiar.

"Who are you?"

"Oh, forgive me." He came close and sat on the edge of the bed, taking her hand and bringing it to his lips. "I am Koda. Emperor of Nocturne."

"Where's Rhain?"

"Waiting for you. Rather impatiently. He was getting on my nerves, so, I sent him away."

"What? You sent him away?"

He laughed. "Not that far away. I know it's really overreaching and inappropriate, but I wanted to be the one here when you woke."

"Why?"

"Will you take a walk with me?"

She didn't see she had much choice refusing the emperor. "All right."

He stood and offered her his hand. She took it, and he helped her to her feet. It was then she noticed her clothes. Lightweight and cream-colored like the canopy of the bed, the hem of the dress caressed the tops of her bare feet. Designs embroidered in rose gold thread, the color of the sand, stretched up from the hem to her knees.

Opening the door, he led her out. They walked unhurriedly down long hallways. He really was just taking a leisurely stroll. Her desperation made it hard to match his relaxed pace.

"Learning about you has been most interesting," he said. "I owe you a great debt. If it weren't for you, I would have lost one of my best friends and possibly even my own life."

"I'm glad it worked out...I'm a bit anxious to begin having my own happiness, sire."

"I know. I know." He chuckled. "I'll let you see him soon. Just give me a few more moments...I hope you will be happy here in Nocturne. You are a noble lady with a position of power. I look forward to seeing what someone like you will do with that power."

"Are you asking me to not take Rhain away?"

He stopped walking. "I will not tie you or him here. You are free to do as you will. Emperor or not, I must pay my debts, too. I have given him complete freedom. In turn, he has freed everyone who used to work in his household. They no longer have anything to fear, and they all decided to stay. I know you will take care of that trust. You understand their position better than anyone."

"Sire, if I may be so bold, would you be willing to reconsider the slave practices of your kingdom?"

He sighed. "Yes. Rhain's constant criticism through the years has worn me down. And since I owe you so much, I promise to look at it with fresh eyes and a more open heart. On this issue, I will listen better."

"Thank you." She bowed to him with respect. "Please, may I see him now?"

Koda chuckled again and led her outside. A flat barge sand ship pulled up close to the palace steps.

"The pilot will take you to Rhain. There is no hurry for your return. Take your time."

Hands braced on the ship's railing, wind sliding through her hair and billowing her dress, Mel sped over the desert. All traces of civilization fell behind with nothing but the evening horizon ahead. Was this land her home now?

In the distance, a tower sprang up, adrift in the ocean of sand.

One door stood at the very bottom, but the ship brought her to the ledge at the top of the flat roof. The ledge circled the whole tower. Sand covered the roof. She stepped off the ship, and it turned and flew away. She watched it go for a minute, her heart in her throat.

She turned around. Stone pillars framed the pergola in front of her. Sand fell endlessly between the pillars like a waterfall. She took a deep breath, nerves buzzing in her stomach, goosebumps rising on her skin.

She was the bride. Her groom was waiting...

Melina walked through the sandfall.

He was looking away, bare-footed and bare-chested on a blanket on top of the deep, shimmering sand. They were alone on a beach in the sky.

Rhain looked at her over his shoulder. He turned, his eyes burning a gorgeous fire as they swept over her. A wall of uncertainty held them apart. His hands trembled, and tears glistened in his eyes. Her pulse sped up, her eyes stinging with the tears she was incapable of crying.

"What are you waiting for?" she demanded.

"Some semblance of self-control."

She moved forward. "Forget it. I'm ready to die."

"Die?"

"I was taught, the moment you lose control, you die."

He smiled. "Let's die together."

His hand caressed her cheek, sliding through her hair, curving the back of her neck. He pulled her forward, his lips taking hers. This was the first kiss. The first *real* kiss. The stone around her heart shattered and fell away. Her heart beat again as it was meant to, soft, warm, alive, and in love.

The world tilted and began to spin.

He took her straight down to the bed of sand under their feet. He ran his hands over her, his eyes unfathomable.

"I can feel you," he whispered. "I feel everything."

He covered her, possessed her. Their souls, held in check, waiting so long, finally broke free.

This is life, she thought as they both sparked and blazed in an exultation of physical love.

He took her virginity in a slow and powerful rite of dominance and possession.

Finally, I have you. Husband.

What had only been breath and spirit was now flesh. She lit up and began to fly. He smiled mischievously down at her. Lifting his hand, time halted. He held her there, making her climax echo over and over. Overwhelmed and trapped in pleasure until she wanted to beg him to release her.

He pulled the time back and let it flow again.

"I love you." His eyes clouded, and he let himself go.

The night spread its plum hue through the sky above them. They lay quietly together for a long time after. He couldn't seem to stop touching her as if the novelty of touch had him addicted. Fingers sweeping over and up her arms, his hands on her hips, his lips on her back, he couldn't stop.

"I'm never letting you go," he whispered.

"I'll kill you if you do."

He snuggled her close. "Let's stay here a long time."

"Hmm...yes. A very, very long time."

TWENTY THREE

A single candle flickered its warm glow over the list Maddox was checking. Erin had gone home ahead of him and Journey was putting most of the orphans to bed. *Most*. Alora was sitting on the floor, her little back resting against his shin. He'd learned to always check for her before sliding his chair out. She often crawled around under his desk.

Maddox had many anchors in his life, events, memories, and people. The little girl leaning against him was one of those anchors. She was the first kid he met when he came here, and she always gravitated to him. Surprising him with her intellect and making him laugh when she tried to talk like an adult. Half of his brain was on finishing the day's work, the other half listened in case the tyke began chirping out her musings. She was uncharacteristically quiet tonight. Maybe she could feel his anxiety. It was more than that really. His palms were sweaty, and his heart was in his throat. An hour had passed with him holding the words in his mouth, afraid to speak.

Alora's back trembled, and she sniffed. She was crying.

"What's wrong, sweetheart?"

She stood and faced him, her cheeks flushed, tears filling her eyes, and she clenched her fists as if she planned to punch him. "I'm so mad at you!"

"Why?" Maddox was totally taken aback. The five-year-old never lost her temper or even sassed him.

"All my friends are gone! You're good at finding parents for kids, but you can't find any for me! Why doesn't anyone want me? Why can't you find me a mommy and daddy? Why?! What's wrong with me?"

Maddox tried to swallow the lump in his throat. He didn't realize it had hurt her, being the one left. She was so bright, of course, she noticed. Damnit. It broke his heart she was hurting. The truth was many people wanted to adopt Alora, but none of them were good enough for her, in his estimation. He'd started the adoption process for her with more than a few qualified, loving couples, only to find some fault at the last minute.

It had been a shock to him when he had to face the real reason why.

Facing those huge brown eyes, now swimming with tears, it was time to confess. His heart raced.

Maddox gently wiped her tears away. "There's nothing wrong with you--"

"Then why?!" She cut him off, sobbing. "I want a dad of my own! I want a mom, too. But I really want a dad! Someone who will carry me on his shoulders. How come you can't find me one?"

"I have, Alora. I've found you one."

She sniffed, her eyes rounding. He gripped her tiny shoulders in his hands.

"It's just...he's young, and scared. He doesn't trust himself to be good enough for you... But he loves you so much. He knows how smart and kind you are. Your strength impressed him from the first. He's giving you the right to say no. You can decide if you'd rather have someone else."

She wiped her nose with her hand and turned her back to him, her shoulders still shaking.

"I stopped a bunch of people from adopting you, Alora. I'm sorry...I just... I couldn't let anyone else have you."

She spun around, the sadness clearing from her eyes, replaced by hope and disbelief as she began to understand what he was trying to say. She wrapped her arms around his neck. "For true?" It was the way she always asked for answers. "Is it you? You and Erin? Is it?"

Choked with his own tears he held her tight. "Yes. For true. It's me and Erin. We love you, Alora. What do you say? Will you be our daughter?"

She nodded and giggled. "Can we go home now?"

He laughed, and she wiped the tears off his cheek. "Yes, we can go home. Erin is there, getting your room ready. I told her to wait until you made up your mind, but she said she knew what she was doing."

Alora nodded seriously. "You shouldn't ever doubt Mommy, you know? She knows her stuff."

"You're right."

He lifted her up on his shoulders and touched the medallion on his wrist, opening a portal home. They landed in the garden, and he set her down. She glanced around the lush garden. Warm welcoming light shone from every window of the house. He waited for her to jump about or exclaim some excitement at having been adopted into such wealth. Instead, she just smiled and gave him a thumbs up before putting her little hand in his.

Erin came out on the porch followed by Forest, Syrus, and Erin's father, Nathan. Alora looked up at Maddox, uncertainty in her wide eyes. He squeezed her hand.

"You didn't think it was just me and Erin, did you?" he teased. "You get grandparents out of this deal, too."

Color rose in her cheeks, and she squealed. "Grandparents!" She bounced up and down. "I get grandparents!"

Despite how short her legs, Alora ran surprisingly fast to the house and up the stairs to the porch, welcomed into her new family with warm hugs. Maddox watched from where he stood, terrified at what he and Erin had done and, at the same time, certain of his footing and inexplicably happy.

The road before him was the best damn road he'd ever contemplated walking.

Mel came to love the odd movement of time during their honeymoon. The tower had everything they needed. Food, water, a bedroom inside, extra clothes-- they weren't too interested in those, but they were there. Weeks passed.

She woke up alone in the bedroom one night.

"Rhain?"

He didn't answer. She threw on her clothes and climbed the stairs to the roof. He was inside the pergola, his arms crossed, a frown on his brow. He looked up and gathered her into his arms.

"What's wrong?" she asked.

"I'm haunted."

"What?"

"We have to go back to Regia."

"We don't have to do anything. We have no way to get back anyway," she said. "You have so much here. Power, wealth, respect. I can't ask you to give that up."

He braced his hands on her shoulders and shook his head. "You didn't leave me to my fate, and I will not leave you to yours. You're still tied to Tristan. We have to go back."

"Oh..." She'd all but forgotten. When she died, she would be trapped with Tristan forever. "How though? How do we get back?"

"It sounds like you could use a little help," a bright voice said loudly behind them, making them jump.

They turned to see Tesla and X standing there, smiling.

"Hey!" Mel exclaimed, running to hug Tesla.

X smirked at Rhain. "What's up with your looks, bro? Creepy."

They embraced like brothers, laughing and slapping each other on the back.

"Everyone's waiting for you two. You've been gone for far too long." Tesla said.

"How did you know? How did you show up at just the moment we were discussing going back?" Mel asked.

"I'll let your mother explain that. Ready?"

Mel looked at Rhain. He nodded and took her hand.

Tesla hit the air with the flat of her hand, opening a portal. They landed in the Everpath and followed Tesla and X down the endless grey hallway to the door to Regia.

It was midday. Regia's pale sun shone in the clear sky. Their feet hit the ground in Tesla and X's garden right in the middle of a party. A party in their honor. All the people they loved most were there.

It took a few minutes for Melina's senses to readjust. It was like a dream.

She looked around, her eyes locking with Maddox's. He had a little girl on his hip. He said something to her and set her down. They ran at each other, practically knocking the wind from their lungs as they collided.

"M! Oh my gosh! It's so good to see you!"

"Mel! Please don't do that again! I missed you and I was worried sick!"

Erin came up behind her and hugged her too, sandwiching her between them.

"We have a daughter," Erin said.

"I haven't been gone *that* long have I?"

"You've been gone two years. We adopted her...Alora, come here, sweetheart."

The little girl Maddox had been holding came over, looking up at Mel with wide, brown eyes. Mel crouched down and held her hand out. "Nice to meet you, Alora."

"Nice to meet you, too," she chirped politely back.

"I look forward to us becoming good friends."

The little tyke glanced up confusedly at Maddox and then back at Mel. "But I thought you were my aunt."

"Oh..."

"We told her all about you," Erin said.

The girl wrapped her little arms around Mel's neck, making her heart swell. "Whoa, I've got to compete with Tesla to be your coolest aunt...that's a tall order. I'm not going to let her win, though."

"Come over to our house really soon, Mel. We have so much catching up to do." Maddox lifted his daughter up on his shoulders. Fatherhood suited him. "There are a few other people wanting your attention and they trump me."

"As if," Melina chuckled. "Who could that possibly be?"

Smiling, he pointed over her shoulder. She turned around, her parents right in front of her. She collapsed into dry sobs as she clung to them. Everything and everyone seemed to fade away. She cried phantom tears until her eyes felt like they would rip open.

She waved at Rhain to come over. "I have to introduce you to my husband. Please be nice."

"We know who he is," Netriet said.

Merick shook Rhain's hand. "You've gone through quite the transformation."

"I owe my life to your daughter. I swear to always cherish her."

"We know you will." Netriet gave Rhain a tight hug. "Welcome to the family."

"Mom..." Mel pulled her mom away from everyone. "What happened? Did you and Dad search for me?"

"No."

"Why? Why did Tesla know exactly when to show up?"

Netriet smiled and lifted her android arm, flexing her black fingers. "I've had this thing a long time, you know. You're not the only one with future memories."

Mel's mouth fell open.

"I knew where you were and that you would live through it. I knew you would come home. I stopped everyone from trying to hunt you down."

The party continued into the evening, and Mel realized that nothing had changed. Not really. Her family and friends were the same, even if their lives had moved forward. As the crowd began to thin, Sophie arrived.

"Hey!" Mel hugged her. "This is my husband, Rhain."

He smiled down at her. "I sort of met you once or twice in the past."

Sophie chuckled and shook her head. "If I didn't know the story from Netriet, I never would have believed it. I'm sorry If I wasn't friendlier in the past. You used to scare the hell out of me... Eli was sorry he couldn't make it. It's too far for him." Sophie moved closer to Mel. "Two things," she whispered. "First, your husband is smoking hot, nice work there. Second, when you're ready to find Destiny, talk to Eli. He'll tell you where to go."

Late that night, after everyone left, Melina and Rhain stared up at the aquamarine moon from the back porch of their house, in the same place they'd been when they decided to commit their lives to one another. He looked different. Physically, he felt different. But he was still the same man as he had been back then. The same man she fell in love with. It was hard to wrap her brain around all they had been through since the last time they stood right there.

"Why are you not tired?" he asked.

"Well...I...I'm scared."

He gathered her close. She laid her cheek against his chest, listening to his heartbeat. She smiled to herself. His pulse was like the time in Nocturne, slipstream.

"I've been clawing my way up a mountain, and I'm about to reach the summit. What if I can't make it? What if I can't talk to Destiny at all? No one ever has. What if I talk to her, but she refuses?"

"If she refuses, I'll lock you in a time echo with me for all eternity, so you will never die."

She sighed and tried to let go of her fear and questions. They would do her no good. She'd marched into the unknown before, and she could do it again.

"Let's go to bed, Rhain. I want you. Make me echo now."

He picked her up and carried her inside. After he stripped her clothes off, she reached for the sunset stone she left on the bedside table and put it around her neck. His gorgeous, fiery eyes flashed as he touched it where it hung between her breasts.

"You are my everything, Melina."

Her strength and spirit were renewed with his love.

It will always be like this, she thought before she fell asleep.

In the morning, she would face Destiny.

Twenty four

As the dawn broke, Melina drank Rhain's blood while he held her against him. She dressed in a plain black shirt, jeans, and combat boots. She chose a sword from the few weapons in the house and strapped it around her waist.

"I'm ready to go."

Tesla and X waited for them in the garden, ready to send them off.

"Come back safe," Tesla said.

"Good luck," X added.

Tesla opened a portal for them to the Wood. Rhain took her hand and they went through it together.

Sophie greeted them and introduced them to Eli, the handsome, blond Dryad historian.

"This might seem a little jarring, but I think it's the best way," Eli said to Mel as he placed his hands on the top of her head. "Close your eyes." He closed his eyes, too and exhaled. "*Pheeren lea mer. Pheeren lea lus'mure*," he whispered.

She gasped as the history filled her head. The whole, horrible story. Every detail down to the location of the entrance. She stumbled sideways. Rhain caught her.

"You okay?"

"Yes. I'm fine." She looked at Eli. "That *was* jarring, and heartbreaking, but amazing, also. To see what you've seen."

"That's all I know," Eli said.

"Thank you."

"You're welcome." His tone and demeanor were sober. "Good luck to you. I hope we meet again."

"Me too." She took Rhain's hand again. "Let's go. It's not far."

No one would come here. No one just passing by would bother cutting through this blight. The ground, the plants, even the air was dead. All the color of Regia's nature was missing here. A dry husk long decayed after a painful death of bitter poison. Every limb she cut through disintegrated and blew away like ashes. Then she saw it...

A hole in the ground, black and twisted like the mouth of a corpse. Too driven to be afraid, too raw to hesitate, Melina walked forward, her steps steady, just like her pulse. The negative energy protecting the entrance pushed against her skin and shimmered a bruised, dingy yellow.

She stopped at the edge of the hole and looked down.

Strange light as bruised and dingy as the energy she passed through slid over the dirt and rocks, deep underground. Grey flecks danced on the air and uneven sounds like dead wood groaning and snapping.

This was it. She turned, gazing into Rhain's eyes. He seemed perfectly at ease.

"I'll wait for you here."

"You're not worried?"

He smiled and shook his head, touching her face. "You can do anything, Melina. Hold your head high."

His calm admonition soothed her nerves. She moved away from him, took a deep breath, and jumped into the pit. Her ankles burned as she landed. Cobblestones crumbled like dry sand under her feet. Alert, she turned in a slow circle. The light moved, the ashes in the air moved, everything else was still. The ruin of a cathedral loomed before her at the end of the cobblestone path. The broken walls, covered in dead vines and a layer of ashes, gave an air of ages of agony. All that should have been beautiful about this place was stripped away, denied.

She approached, slow, steady.

Two statues crouched in the courtyard, flanking the entrance to the cathedral. The polished black stones of their eyes glinted, and they growled a warning from their broken jaws. There was something lupus about them. She liked canines. Instead of a show of power, she put her hand out and touched the left one on the head. It whimpered once before its head crumbled to ash. She pulled her hand back, but it was too late. The other one howled in sorrow.

"You might as well kill the other one, too," a deep voice said from inside the cathedral. "Would be mean to leave it by itself, you know."

"I'm sorry," Mel whispered to the remaining statue. "It was an accident."

It whimpered like the other one had and bowed its stone head to her. Grimacing, she touched it, and it too broke apart. Melina sighed and wiped her ash-covered hands on her pants and walked into the ruin.

Wondrous nightmare.

The tree smiled at her with all its mouths. He was just as Eli had described. Darksong's trunk and limbs were twisted and scorched black. The first dryad…what must have been so beautiful once was now appalling and crippled. She stepped to the side and looked past him.

Melina gasped. There she was, at the far end of the great ruin…*Destiny*.

Tall and extremely thin, her skin was deep blue and purple, swirling with galaxies and nebulas. Her hair hung almost to the floor, perfectly straight, the color of moonlight. She was turned away, her hands up, moving over a black haze. The haze was like deep space with tiny pinpricks of light. Her elongated fingers snagged a light and drew it out like spider silk, threading it to another light on the other side of the haze.

Frozen in awe, Melina realized she was witnessing the creation of a soul bridge. Strangers, being tied together forever as destined life mates. Awe gave way to anger. This was why she was here.

Melina took a step forward.

"Not so fast," Darksong said. "Not so fast, not so fast, not so fast," his many mouths repeated in a sensual whisper. "Tea and conversation first, young lady."

"Tea?"

The tree's limbs moved up and down as though he shrugged. "Perhaps not tea. Blood. *Your* blood to be precise. No one can see Destiny without first giving me their blood. Not too much. Just a taste."

Melina crossed her arms. "I'm not falling for that. And I will get past. If I have to cut you down, so be it."

All his mouths laughed, echoing. She wanted to cover her ears, to block out the disjointed, insane resonance. It was painful. His laugh exposed the distortion of his mind. His psyche was as diseased as his body.

"Do you know why I came here?" she asked.

"No idea whatsoever. Do you mean you came here on purpose?"

"Yes. I have a bone to pick with *her*." She pointed at Destiny.

"Oh, you're feisty...and crazy, but rules are rules...even if I made them up. I need blood to allow you to pass."

"Fine. I'll give you one drop." She backed up, realizing she was within his reach if he wanted to grab her with his branches.

"Where are you going?!" His voice rose to a panic.

"Nowhere, I just need a little more personal space."

"Come back, please." He reached for her as she continued to back away.

"Here you go."

Mel sliced her fingertip on one of her fangs and held her hand out, touching the very tip of his reaching branch. Her blood dropped on the wood. He pulled it back and licked it with his largest mouth.

"Oh..." he moaned. "You're her...I've been waiting. I know you. You fill my dreams, Melina. I didn't think you'd make it. But you're broken now. Broken so good. So wide open. You may pass. I won't try to kill you until you try to leave. I promise."

"Thank you." She pitied him more than any creature she'd ever seen.

Blowing out a breath, she walked around his huge trunk.

This was it.

Destiny didn't stop what she was doing or make any sign she noticed Melina's presence. She stopped just behind her and waited. No response.

"You know who I am?"

"Of course," Destiny said, continuing her picking and threading.

"Remove the curse you put on me."

Destiny turned, facing Mel with the terrible abyss of her featureless face. "Curse?" she hissed. Her voice vibrated with the depth of deep space, so beautiful, and unmistakably angry.

"What else could you call Tristan? I did nothing to deserve that! Untie our souls."

Destiny clasped her long fingers together and moved closer to Mel. "Deserve..." her voice caressed the word. "What you deserve? You're not equipped to know the answer to that question."

She circled all the way around Melina. Warning and danger undulated through the air like heat waves.

"I want what I've fought and killed for. You are the last thing in my way. Who are you to decide what's best for me? What right do you have to twist the hearts of people, forcing them to love without choice?"

"Oh, of course. That would be how you 'd see it."

Destiny's sharp hand clamped over Melina's mouth. Cold, so deep, so intense, as though she'd never be warm again, froze her in place. The only thing colder was her fear.

"So young, and yet convinced you know everything. I am doing what I was designed to do. It was my purpose from the start. Where were you when the world was born? Did you witness the Heart tear its own child from the ground and begin to burn from the agony of betrayal? What pain have you known? A small loss, that's all. A bit of inconvenience. What sins have stained your hands? What guilt do you carry? I was the Heart's second child. I am that old... How will you answer me?"

Destiny pulled her hand away from Melina's mouth.

"I think I will cover my own mouth now," Melina said, embarrassed. "Forgive me."

"I forgive you. Of course. I understand, believe me, I do. For it is I who chose you. Come closer and I will explain."

She placed her arm around Mel's shoulders and pulled her close to the black haze.

"These are the souls I am allowed to touch. Every living Regian is represented here, like stars in the sky. I can see the amalgamation of each and every person. When a soul catches my attention and affection I begin to look for that one other soul to tie it to. Its perfect counterpart. Some souls have no one to fill that role. They might find love on their own, but it will not be the same. This is not a talent or skill. It is my design, what I was created to do. I don't make mistakes."

431

The tears she couldn't cry pressed deep inside Melina's eyes. "So, Tristan really was who I..."

"No, child. He wasn't."

"He wasn't?"

"I don't make mistakes." She repeated. "But I did make a choice for you...a choice I have never made for anyone else. Look." Destiny pointed at a constellation at the very edge of the haze. It wasn't like the other stars. It was brighter, wider, and more colorful. "That's Rhain...He's my favorite, in this expanse of souls. But I can't touch him, no matter how desperately I want to, he's beyond me. He's not Regian. I can't tie him to another, and even if I could, for many years, I couldn't find his equal."

Mel stared at the supernova that was Rhain, momentarily mesmerized.

"Then you were born, Melina, and I loved you. I knew you were the one, but you weren't ready because you were still intact."

"Intact?"

"See here, this is you," Destiny pointed to a sparkling burst of diamond light close to Rhain. "You didn't use to look like this. You used to be dark and small. But I could see deeper. I knew you were agate. Only when broken would your true beauty and nature be revealed. Tristan was my hammer. Do you see?"

"You tried to fashion me to be Rhain's counterpart?"

"As I said, he's my favorite. I wanted to find someone worthy of him. You love him, don't you? Your orbit tells me you do."

"I love him. Is my love of my own free will?"

"Nothing else, child. I put you two close together. You and Rhain did the rest. It was as I hoped. If I could tie you together, I would. And yet you are tied...you have tied yourselves with a thread I am not allowed to touch."

"But what about my tie to Tristan?"

Even though she had no face, Mel felt the warmth of a smile from Destiny. "You are finally here. At the moment you've fought so hard for. So, ask me."

"Will you cut the thread?"

Destiny waved her hand over the haze, exposing the strings of light between stars. She traced the line from Mel down to another star...to Tristan. She grabbed Mel's hand, forcing her fingers to curl in, except her index finger. "Do it with me."

Destiny's finger wrapped like a snake around Melina's. Hands entwined, they cut through the string in one fluid move. The second it severed, Mel felt a tug under her ribs, a pain breaking free. Destiny cupped her face.

"Thank you. Go now. My work is never-ending."

"But..." she looked around the horrible space, her heart heavy. "Is there no end for you? And Darksong? Will forgiveness ever be granted?"

"Forgiveness is not the erasure of consequences. We have been forgiven. Our time here will end. I'm not bound, but I couldn't leave my brother. It's my fault he suffers as he does. So I will continue with my work and wait for Darksong to die. Our suffering will end, and this sacred place will be restored to its original, exquisite beauty." She turned back to the haze, picking at the stars again. "Perhaps it will happen in your lifetime...Go now, child. Live a good life."

"I changed my mind," Darksong said as she walked past him. "I'll not harm you as you go."

"Thanks. I didn't want to fight you. Goodbye."

"Goodbye...goodbye...goodbye..." his many mouths whispered. "I hope I will dream of you again, Melina."

She smiled. "I think I'll dream of you as well. You and Destiny."

Looking up through the hole, Rhain was there, reaching down for her. She jumped and caught his hand. He pulled her up and into his arms.

"It's done. It's done," she sobbed without tears. "My connection to Tristan is destroyed."

He carried her out through the blighted area back into clean light and air. She clung around his neck.

"I can't believe it's all over."

He kissed her deeply. "Some things are over, and others are only beginning."

He set her down, and they looked out through the trees. In the distance, they could see the Crystalline Sea. The late afternoon sun, snagging on the sharp waves. It was a beautiful view. They sat down and waited for the evening. The deep jeweled colors of sunset pulled like brushstrokes over the sky.

Melina touched the scars on her arm, remembering a promise.

"I have the bones of my friends in my arm. I promised to take them to a beautiful place and bury them. It's beautiful here, but now I feel guilty because I have Cope and Inesia but not Salem."

"Do they hurt you? The bones?"

She shook her head. "No."

"Don't cut them out. Let them be a part of you."

Smiling, she leaned her head on his shoulder. "I like that."

For a few moments, she ran her fingers up and down on the scars on her arm. She rolled her wrists, her blades jumping out. "I'm quite the freak." She chuckled, rolling her wrists again. "I'm sorry. I've changed so much since you first met me. My body. My eyes."

His hands framed her face. "You dazzle me, Melina. I love everything about you. Don't ever doubt that. And I love these eyes the most."

"Why?"

"They are the only eyes that ever really saw me."

"We can go back to Nocturne. If you want. I don't mind. I like it there."

He smiled. "Why don't we live in both worlds? Have a home here and there?"

"Really?"

He shrugged. "Why not?"

"The idea appeals."

He gathered her against him again. "I don't want to go back for a while, though...at least not until our first child is born."

Startled, she pulled back from him, her mouth gaping. He chuckled and put his finger under her chin, forcing her mouth closed.

"Don't look at me like that," he said. "I'm not in a hurry. It can be a long time from now, but I like the idea of us making a family. I want a child with you... What do you think?"

She relaxed and stared back at the sea. "Hmm...that idea appeals, too."

EPILOGUE

Sitting on her porch swing, watching the sunset, Forest relaxed after the day's work, with a cold glass of lemonade in her hand. Sitting beside her, legs straight out, Alora clutched her own glass of lemonade, tracing happy faces in the condensation with her fingertip.

Forest glanced at the girl from the side of her eye and pushed the swing into motion with the ball of her foot. This little wild shoot rooted into their family, not through blood, but by choice...by love.

"What do you want to be when you grow up?" she asked.

Alora chewed the inside of her cheek for a moment. "I want to be Hailemarris. Just like you."

"Hmm..." She clinked her glass to her granddaughter's in a toast. "Well now, there's an idea."

Forest gazed at the sky and smiled at the future.

TENAYA JAYNE

THE END

FORSAKEN

ABOUT THE AUTHOR

Reading my bio, huh?
Real life sucks. I bet you feel like that sometimes,
maybe even right now. That's why I write fantasy. I
need to escape depression, bitterness, bills,
illness...I could go on, but you get it. In the pages of
fiction, I can slay the dragons, triumph over the bad
guys, be immortal, and never struggle with love
handles. For a short time, I can let it all go, and be
everything I can't be in real life. Maybe you're
hurting right now. Maybe you're in the waiting
room of the hospital, or just stuck in traffic. I've
brought a portal. Come with me...Let's ditch this
crappy popsicle stand and go somewhere great,
where we can forget all this, at least for a while.

That's why I write. I'm not an author, I'm an escape
artist.

If you want to come play with me, visit
www.tenayajayne.com